D1304910

Against a DARKENING SKY

Lauren B. Davis

FIRST EDITION

Against a Darkening Sky © 2015 by Lauren B. Davis
Cover artwork © 2015 by Erik Mohr
Interior design © 2015 by Jared Shapiro

All Rights Reserved.

The stories featured herein are works of fiction. Any people, events and locales that figure in the narrative, all names, places, incidents, and characters are the products of the author's imagination or are used fictitiously. Any resemblance to current events or locales, or to living persons, is entirely coincidental.

Distributed in Canada by
Publishers Group Canada
76 Stafford Street, Unit 300
Toronto, Ontario
M6J 2S1 Canada
Toll Free: 800-747-8147
e-mail: info@pgcbooks.ca

Distributed in the U.S. by
Diamond Comic Distributors, Inc.
10150 York Road, Suite 300
Hunt Valley, MD 21030
Phone: (443) 318-8500
e-mail: books@diamondbookdistributors.com

Library and Archives Canada Cataloguing in Publication

Davis, Lauren B., 1955-, author
     Against a darkening sky / Lauren B. Davis.

Issued in print and electronic formats.

ISBN 978-1-77148-318-6 (pbk.).--ISBN 978-1-77148-319-3 (ebook)

     I. Title.

PS8557.A8384A53 2015b   C813'.6   C2015-900099-8
                                                C2015-900100-5

CHIZINE PUBLICATIONS
Toronto, Canada
www.chizinepub.com
info@chizinepub.com

A **free** eBook edition is available
with the purchase of this print book.

CLEARLY PRINT YOUR NAME ABOVE IN UPPER CASE

Instructions to claim your free eBook edition:
1. Download the BitLit app for Android or iOS
2. Write your name in **UPPER CASE** on the line
3. Use the BitLit app to submit a photo
4. Download your eBook to any device

Canada Council   Conseil des Arts
for the Arts   du Canada

We acknowledge the support of the Canada Council for the Arts which last year invested $20.1 million in writing and publishing throughout Canada.

ONTARIO ARTS COUNCIL
CONSEIL DES ARTS DE L'ONTARIO
an Ontario government agency
un organisme du gouvernement de l'Ontario

Published with the generous assistance of the Ontario Arts Council.

Printed in Canada

PRAISE FOR
LAUREN B. DAVIS

THE STUBBORN SEASON

"A gleaming debut . . . This is a wonderful novel . . . every character is sincerely drawn; these sentences just gleam. *The Stubborn Season* is one of those rare novels I look forward to reading again."
—*The Toronto Star*

"*The Stubborn Season* is precise, polished . . . bind[s] the attention through the excellence of its sharp, precise prose, generously laced with authentic history. Davis's astute psychological observations render the two main characters insistently real . . . Davis refuses to succumb to the predictable . . . *The Stubborn Season* raises the bar for first novels."
—*The Montreal Gazette*

"Lauren B. Davis's *The Stubborn Season* ranges through a wide land-scape of history and intimacy, thwarted private dreams and public oppression . . . a skillful weaving of emotion and event . . . poignant and well-crafted. [*The Stubborn Season* is] an epiphanic hourglass for the harsh dust that trickled through one of the worst of times."
—*The Globe and Mail*

"Lauren Davis's debut novel, *The Stubborn Season*, is as close as you'd want to get to the Depression without being there . . . meticulous research informs everything . . . The writing is clean, direct, and efficient. . . . Remarkably, in spite of such dire circumstances, Davis makes us believe that the following generation can come through the Depression with little damage, still trusting and resourceful, and stronger for having lived through this grim, stubborn season."
—*Quill & Quire*

"*The Stubborn Season* has the sting of authenticity. The writing is sharp as glass, the sorrow felt and the release on end, redemptive."

—**Barry Callaghan**, author of *Barrelhouse Kings*
and *Hogg, the Seven Last Words*

THE RADIANT CITY

"With extraordinary compassion, insight, and intelligence, Davis illuminates the human aftershocks of senseless violence and in that cold light, somehow, astonishingly, rekindles hope."

—**Merilyn Simonds**, author of *The Convict Lover*
and *The Holding*

"Superb . . . [*The Radiant City*] is engrossing and convincing . . . packed with smells and sounds and street argot, the minutiae and contradictions of Paris life. Davis's question here is how can human beings look into a heart of darkness . . . and crawl back to the light again?"

—*Quill & Quire* STARRED REVIEW

"*The Radiant City* shines. [T]his thoughtful, complex, meditative, at times brilliant novel [is] about the harm we suffer and the comforts we are drawn to when the worst has happened and the world goes on."

—*The Globe and Mail*

"It's difficult to put the book down. . . . *The Radiant City* reveals what's beyond the splendour of a setting or the calm expression on a face. This is smooth, engaging writing that doesn't flinch from the rawness that for so many people is life. 'Light is neutral and indifferent.' We can't afford to be. Perhaps that's the most important revelation of all."

—*Books in Canada*

"... a starkly realistic story of friendship, courage and the effects of violence on the human spirit. Davis's taut, unadorned narrative breathes life into the characters . . . poignant . . . this novel will resonate in the minds of many readers."

—*The Winnipeg Free Press*

Our Daily Bread

"Chilling and emotionally authentic."
—**Jane Ciabattari**, past President of the National Book Critics Circle

"... a powerful, harrowing, and deeply unsettling work. It's the sort of novel that keeps you reading even as your skin crawls and your blood pressure mounts . . . *Our Daily Bread* proceeds like a noose tightening . . . a stark, beautiful, sad and frankly terrifying novel. *Our Daily Bread* is finely crafted, with careful attention to characterization, style and pacing. It succeeds on every level. . . ."

—**Robert J. Wiersema**, *Quill & Quire*

"Thrilling . . . unflinching . . . unforgettable. It's difficult to write about the beauty of Davis's storytelling . . . suffice it to say she seeks to unfold consciousness, including the reader's. Davis makes us care about her characters . . . imaginatively transformed by exquisite prose."

—**Jean Randich**, Truthdig.com

"I'll never forget this book, the stunning power of the descriptions, the attention to detail, the riveting plot, the fully-realized characters—this is storytelling at its very best."

—**Duff Brenna**, author of *The Book of Mamie*
and *The Holy Book of the Beard*

"*Our Daily Bread* is a compelling narrative set in a closely observed, sometimes dark, but ultimately life-enhancing landscape. Lauren B. Davis's vivid prose and empathetically developed characters will remain in the reader's mind long after the final chapter has been read."

—**Jane Urquhart**, prize-winning author of *Away* and *The Stone Carvers*

THE EMPTY ROOM

"Unflinching and unsentimental, *The Empty Room* charts a day from hell in the life of Colleen Kerrigan, alone, nearly 50, and spiralling into yet another alcoholic binge. It is a credit to the brilliance and humanity of novelist Lauren B. Davis that, even in this nightmare, we find utter truth, wicked humour and just enough hope to keep on reading."

—**Lawrence Hill**, author of *The Book of Negroes*

"This is a raw, exciting book—alcoholism from deep inside the jaws of death and denial. To call it 'honest' is a disservice: it is scalding."

—**Bharati Mukherjee**, author of *Desirable Daughters* and *Miss New India*

"In *The Empty Room*, Lauren B. Davis has given us an honest, brave account of self-destruction, one that harrowingly reminds us that recovery from the abyss of alcoholism is never easy, but eloquently hints at what is possible when the self-deception and denial end."

—**Linden MacIntyre**, author of *The Bishop's Man* and *Why Men Lie*

"*The Empty Room* is a tour de force. Brave and beautifully written. It's riveting, compelling, vivid, and hard to put down."

—**Shelagh Rogers**, Host of CBC Radio's *The Next Chapter*

"Davis brilliantly tackles alcoholism. . . . A serious, sorrowful book, *The Empty Room* is a masterful portrayal of an addiction."

—*Telegraph Journal – HERE Magazine*

As always, this is to Ron. You're my candle in the window.

Against a DARKENING SKY

Prologue

The girl held the freckled hand for hours, long past the moment it first began to grow cold. She sat on a stool next to the bed with a sheepskin wrapped around her shoulders, yet still she shivered, for nothing but embers remained of the fire in the clay pit. The bodies of her aunts, uncles, cousins, and neighbours lay scattered about the hamlet, some still in their beds, some on the floor of their houses, some waiting on the burial ground. Those who died early, her father and brothers and sister among them, rested in peace beneath the earth. A terrible silence squatted, troll-like, over the village. The dogs harried the corpses until the girl threw stones at them, and then they disappeared to the hills. The two shepherd boys had either run off or died, and the sheep had wandered away. Even the few remaining chickens refrained from squawking. When she had gone down to the river to get water yesterday, the cries of a pair of early-nesting ravens startled her, but now they, too, were silent. Her swollen eyes felt sand-filled. With her free hand, she touched her neck, her armpit, her groin. Nothing.

Her mother's mouth had fallen open, the skin sagging and mottled, the eyes halfclosed. Her hair, once the colour of autumn barley in the sunlight, lay flat and tangled, and a small brown spider tiptoed through the lank strands. Soon her flame-bright mother would not look like her mother at all. The girl had tried to lure death to her by sitting very still, but death would not come. She could not change the web of wyrd.

The girl closed her eyes and tried to let go of her mother's hand, but the fingers had stiffened. The rigid claw would not budge, and with her heart pounding in her ears, she used force. The stool tipped and the girl thumped on the floorboards. There were more tears then.

She crawled to her bed and imagined her sister's soft scent in the straw-stuffed linen mattress. She rolled over, covered herself with a fur, and stared at the whitewashed wall. The restless dead swirled through the air, hopping from rafter to rafter, their fingers at the shutters, their wails on the wind, their chill breath on her cheek. She thought how easy, how comforting, it would be to go mad. She wondered if she could open herself to it and willed her muscles to relax, her mind to slacken. Like a great ragged owl, despair swooped down, spreading tattered wings. She shrieked, shielded her head with her arms, and curled into a weeping ball until she fell into a sort of sleep. Or, she assumed she slept, for there stood her mother, at the end of the bed, wearing a yellow tunic held at the shoulders with garnet brooches. The girl tried to rise and rush into her mother's arms, but she could not move. Arms, legs, hands, fingers, head—all pinned by a cruel enchantment. She wanted to call out, but her voice was tight in her mouth. Her mother held out her hands—pale, freckled, and callused. Her hair lay unbraided on her shoulders, shining like sunlight. Surely she'd come to take her daughter to the hall of the gods. And yet it appeared her mother could come no closer than the end of the bed, though her grey eyes pleaded. It took everything the girl had to move even a finger. Not enough. Trapped as an ant in amber. Her mother's lips moved, silently, and still the girl heard her.

The dead cannot stay with the living. The living cannot come with the dead. Child, you must walk . . .

The bed tilted, the earth slipped, and the girl slid into darkness.

Under the boy's grip the oar was slippery with sea-water and his hands were cramped claws in the icy wind. Frequently he wiped his hands on his thighs to keep his grip sure. His skin had cracked and flecks of blood spotted his spray-soaked tunic. The salt stung like a thousand wasps, not only in the blisters on his hands but in the still-seeping lash welts on his back. His legs quivered and ached from bracing against the roll and pitch.

The coracle's hazel ribs creaked and muttered, protesting the weight of water, but the little boat was strong and flexible. The boy sat on the transom bar, steering with his oar. Above him the sail strained and bulged against the wind. When he set out yesterday at dawn the sea had been calm, but now the waves were steeper and came faster . . . he knew he might well drown here. If so, then it would be God's plan. His father had tried to beat his obsession out of him to no avail and now the grey wall of water rose before him, terrifying as his father's rage. He closed his eyes. The boat teetered, hesitated, trembled at the crest of a wave, and then his stomach was in his mouth as he rushed down toward the unknown depths.

The prayer was constant on his lips. *Lord Jesus, the power of the storm is thine, the power of the sea is thine. If it be thy will, see me to the harbour of thy love.*

All his dreams had been of the wide sky and open sea. All his dreams ended with the angel of the one true God appearing before him—white and gold, with fire round her head and birds hovering above her, beckoning him, a smile on her rosy lips. Her wings were like sails of finest linen, held in a gentle wind. The placid waves lapped at her fine-boned feet. No matter how his father bullied, no matter how his mother cried, despairing of his sanity, he could not refuse the angel's call. Over many months, in secret moments stolen from his time minding sheep, he built the boat, and set sail without saying goodbye.

The boy opened his eyes. On the far horizon, under a glowering steelish sky, was a glimmer of gold, and in the glimmer a dark spot. Land then. Ioua. The holy island. It must be. His heart leaped, even as another wave rose before him and blotted out the vision. The boat skewed at the wrong angle. In horror, the boy watched as a wave the size of the chieftain's hall loomed overhead, frothing at the lip, and then crashed down. Something cracked, tore, split . . . There was no chance to scream, no chance to howl a prayer. All was black and icy. Rough forces pulled at him. His hands reached for nothing.

The world was gone and below was above and above below. So this was how it would end: the angel calling him to his death. His chest burned, but this wet world was cold and dark and silent. He could drift here, slide into her arms and sleep. As though he would open his mouth and breathe . . .

Part
ONE

Chapter
ONE

Earth and sky press up against one another here, as though battling for dominion. On this particular day, all afternoon the clouds have weighed down, draping across the hills like a wet cloak, the grasses on the plateau dancing to the tune of the wind's lyre with wild abandon. Now it's late in the evening and the villagers are asleep, for the nights are short this time of year and there's much work in the fields. The weather shifts. The sky roils greenish black, shot with blinding gold. Several men stand around the lord's living quarters. Lord Caelin paces back and forth on the muddy ground, drinking wine from a goatskin, glancing angrily at the door of a hut from behind which come the cries of a woman in childbirth.

Inside the hut the air is thick with sweat, mugwort, and juniper smoke. The lamps randomly sputter tallow. Wilona, a girl of some sixteen winters, crouches in the shadows, with her back against a tapestry, waiting for instructions. Her long fingers worry the wool of her brown tunic. Freckles spatter her skin; her eyes are the shade of the palest river stones, and her braided hair the colour of a ginger cat. She stops picking at her tunic, chews her thumbnail, and watches her guardian, Touilt.

Firelight skitters across Touilt's face as she stands by the labouring woman's bed. She smiles, the teeth in her mouth sharp. She doesn't smile often, preferring to cultivate a severe demeanour, and the expression is not now entirely convincing. Her face is craggy, her thin brown hair grey-streaked, her dark brows a forbidding line over her deep-set eyes, which are the colour of wet bark. A fierce intelligence lies behind those eyes, and under their scrutiny more than one strong man has been reduced to admitting a lie. From her belt hang tweezers, a comb, and a loom weight marked with a spiral, sign of a *seithkona*—a spell woman. Touilt has been the village seithkona for many years, since the night a band of raiding Picts killed her husband and three sons. The power of the gods struck her that night and she wandered for a long moon up in the high hills, letting the visions ride her. In return for taking her husband and sons, the gods granted her the gift of prophecy. When she returned to Ad Gefrin, she knew the language of the runes.

"Be brave, little mother, be brave," Touilt whispers to the moaning woman.

Lady Elfhild, loosely wrapped in a linen gown, squats on the straw strewn over the feather-filled mattress. She clenches fists, jaw, neck. The gods hold Elfhild like a flame in a fragile lamp, in a thin place between worlds. Somewhere, the gods are riddling and tossing the dice of fate. If Wilona listens, she can hear them clatter in the gaming cup. The straw is damp with sweat and carries an acrid tang. A sudden gust of wind rattles the door and riffles the wall hangings.

Touilt gestures with an outstretched arm that Wilona should bring her blue cloak and the wolf hide lying on a nearby table. When Touilt dons the garments, Wilona shakes her head to displace the glamour—the illusion—that Touilt, with the pelt's snout over her forehead and its paws on her shoulders, is more wolf than woman. Wilona retreats to her place in the corner. Touilt spits into her palms, rolls a stone rune back and forth between them, lifts the feather mattress and places the blessed rune beneath the writhing woman.

It is Elfhild's second child. The first lived less than a morning, and the birth was hard. Wilona prays. Lady Elfhild's thighs cramp and Wilona watches the pain run in an icy silver slice up to her abdomen, her spine. Like a slithering blade it twists between her legs. Wilona winces.

"The child will kill me! Sif, wife of Thunor, I invoke thee, let this child come. Let me live." Elfhild twists and turns and her eyes focus on something in the corner. "What is that? Some beast!"

"I see nothing. What do you see?" Touilt makes signs in the air with her fingers—the hammer of Thunor, the protective rune *algiz*. "Tell me," she says to Elfhild.

Wilona looks into the dark corner. Something hunkers there, more a dark space in the shape of a beast than a beast itself. Can't Touilt smell its dank, marshy scent? Wilona pushes back into the wall. The spirit shudders, takes more solid form—large, long-necked, great-winged.

Elfhild moans. "I see it. Not Sif. Not her. Sif's swan. She's saying something . . . she calls for a sacrifice!"

"Then pledge it, and trust the goddess."

Elfhild groans as another contraction overtakes her, and Touilt whispers in her ear to seize the bird's neck and grip him, ride the beast of pain. Touilt runs her hands over Elfhild's heaving belly. The mother-to-be collapses on the mattress and pants like a dog.

"Come, Wilona. Make yourself useful. Clean this, and fetch fresh straw. Now."

The straw is wilted and soiled with sweat, shit, and blood. Wilona makes sure not to wrinkle her nose as she gathers the worst of it and packs it, warm and sticky, into a large bucket.

"Go on, fresh straw, fresh straw." Touilt pushes her with urgency, but not violence, toward the door.

Outside, the fresh air carries the metallic scent of the oncoming storm. A large raindrop splatters in the mud at Wilona's feet and then two more on her face. Caelin and his companions huddle under the eaves near the side of the birthing-house. Their eyes follow her. Lord Caelin's face is dark as the roiling sky, and he is just as dangerously unpredictable.

Wilona empties the bucket into the midden pile, wipes her hands on the rag tucked into her belt, and scampers to a nearby byre. Inside, a cow near her own birthing time shows the whites of her eyes. The shed flashes blue and an instant later thunder cracks. Wilona jumps. The rain is as loud as a waterfall. Something scurries near the grain bin. Rats, she thinks and, looping the bucket over her arm, grabs an armful of straw. A figure steps out from the shadows. "Dunstan! You gave me a start!"

He's that sort of boy, always popping up where and when one doesn't expect him. His wide mouth and large ears dominate his thin face; his dun hair is tied back with a leather thong. His mother, upon the death of his father, and perhaps perceiving her oldest son ill-suited to battle, apprenticed him to Alwyn the woodworker, who despairs of him, and more than once has punished his lack of attention by sending him to the fields for a fortnight. "What are you doing here? Have you been demoted to cowherd again?"

The boy's grin is contagious, even at a moment like this. "No, that's not it," he says. "Although she's a lovely cow, isn't she?" He gestures with his chin. "How goes it in there? It's been a long time."

"Difficult. I have to get back."

A frown settles on Dunstan's face and looks unnatural on his usually cheerful features. "Wilona, wait . . . there's talk."

"What kind of talk?" She continues to fill her arms with straw.

"Caelin's worried. He's very fond of his wife." Dunstan reaches out and touches her arm. "It might go badly if Lady Elfhild or this child dies."

" I wish Lord Caelin would go inside the hall and drink like other men."

"He's had enough to drink. More than enough."

"He's drunk?"

Dunstan nods. "Roaring."

Wilona has only seen Caelin drunk on a handful of occasions. The last time, at Yule, he broke a slave's arm for spilling ale on his tunic. The time before that, he'd broken a hound's neck for growling at him. "The goddess will protect us. We're in her care."

Wilona says goodbye to Dunstan, ducks past Caelin and his men, and returns to the birth-chamber, where Elfhild is on all fours, her mouth open, her tangled hair stuck to her shoulders. The lady is clammy with sweat and trembling. Her eyes are not closed but rather are fixed on some midpoint in the air, her breathing shallow and ragged. Touilt mutters something beneath her breath, takes a pouch from inside her tunic, and pinches out some seeds. Wilona counts with her—thirteen. A stool next to the birthing bed is covered with objects now: a blade, herbs in leather pouches, carved sticks with various kinds of animal fur attached, bones of different sorts. Touilt chooses a thread and a small square of clean linen and ties the seeds inside.

Wilona scuttles forward with fresh straw, scatters it, tries to pat it into some sort of comfort, and then retreats to the corner shadows. Thunor claps his hands again and sends a lightning bolt across the sky. The look on Lady Elfhild's face—agony like a red haze—makes Wilona's stomach sour. She hugs her knees.

"No," Touilt says, gesturing. "Come here." She makes Elfhild lie down and the lady moans and thrashes, her hair dragging and pulling. A breast escapes from the loosely wrapped cloak, the veins blue. Touilt presses the linen patch containing the thirteen coriander seeds into Wilona's palm and forces her hand high on Elfhild's left thigh. "Hold that there. Hold it no matter how she flails. Hold it!" The seithkona pours a goblet of red wine and, with her hand behind Elfhild's head, tilts it to her lips. "Drink."

Too weary to disobey, Elfhild drinks. When she is done, Touilt puts the goblet on the stool and picks up a middling-sized twig, the tip charcoal-blackened. She draws runes on her palms. *Berkano. Inguz. Laguz. Eihwaz.* She chants the names. Her eyes meet Wilona's. This, too, is part of the teaching. She begins to hum and mutter, calling in the *disir*, the spirits who guard women during childbirth. Beneath Wilona's hands, slivers of thread-like silver seem to writhe. Her breath is short and ragged. It's as though she's linked to the struggle below her palm, becoming part of it. She pulls away, wanting to remove her hand, but the runes bind her there, near the opening of life. It is as though arms other than hers—vaporous yet unyielding—press down, pinning her palms to Elfhild's thigh. Heat rises from the woman's skin. Wilona swallows her cries. They taste like blood.

A gust of metal-scented wind. At the open door stands Caelin, dripping rainwater from his darkened hair and beard. His bulk fills the doorway. The eyes are probing, used to making quick decisions, and impatience twists his lip. His entire face is skewed with worry masked as fury, and Wilona again notices the two long battle scars on his left cheek. He reeks of ale.

"It's too long!" he thunders, shaking the wet hair from his face. "Why does it take so long?"

"So long?" says Touilt. "What do you know of time, you who are easy in and easy out? Your contribution may have taken only a moment, but you leave us with a longer chore than your swift pleasure merits, I suspect."

Caelin's hand is round Touilt's throat and he has her pinned against a timber, the back of her head thudding loudly on the wood, before she has a chance even to cry out. Touilt's rune-hallowed palms are open, held at her sides, for she dares not fight him. She grimaces and chokes, the cords in her neck standing out. Caelin's face is so close to hers his spittle sprays her. "You wolf-bitch! You dare?"

Touilt's voice is a harsh whisper. "Forgive me. I mean no disrespect. I only meant to lighten my lord's mood." She coughs and her hands twitch, but she does not touch him. "Stupid," she gasps.

"If you cannot persuade the gods to save them, I'll see you burned. You can argue with them from the shadows of Hel!"

"Husband!" Elfhild raises her hand. "I beg you. I need her."

Caelin drops his hand. "You are warned, seithkona."

The mark on Touilt's neck is livid. Sour fear squirts into Wilona's stomach. Shadows flutter in the corners of the room.

The seithkona bows her head. "She will not die, my lord. I swear by Frige, Woden's beloved wife." She glances at him. "I'll call you for the breath."

Caelin stomps out, slamming the door behind him so hard the walls shake. The wavering shadows in the corners go still.

"Forgive my husband," says Elfhild.

Touilt rubs her throat and surprises Wilona when she makes a dry little sound meant to be a chuckle. "Men are fools," she says to Elfhild, patting her on the shoulder, "and softer when in love than women. We endure birth and watch as our men run off seeking death at every opportunity. But men bluster and demand and lay down rules, as though the gods were slaves to be bullied."

Softer? Wilona cannot see much softness in Caelin, and while she understands his fear for his wife and child may be the root of his violence, she marvels Touilt can be so calm in the face of it. Wilona knows if things go badly, she'll be placed as kindling on Touilt's pyre. A seithkona might be honoured by a seat close to the fire in the lord's hall, but only the gods lived beyond reach of his axe.

Touilt turns to her. "You're doing well." Only then does Wilona realize she still holds the charm against the lady's thigh. "Keep your wits, girl."

Touilt hums, as though Caelin had never been there, and sings the charms. She places her palms along Elfhild's belly. She chants the old, sacred words. *"May the holy ones thee help, Frige and Freo and favouring gods, from sorrow now."* She reaches between Elfhild's legs again and feels. Her eyes meet Wilona's. Touilt winks and the girl nods. Touilt whispers in Elfhild's ear, "The time is come, little mother, the time is come." She gestures to Wilona. "Move away, child." With her free hand, Touilt pulls open the thongs of the leather pouch tied to the girdle of her tunic. Her fingers root around inside. Then, finding what she wants, she grunts. In her palm lies a polished river stone with runes carved upon it. She holds the stone against her own breast and then crawls behind Elfhild, holding her upright as she squats. Elfhild moans and grunts and blood spills onto the straw. The baby's head is halfway out. Touilt passes the stone over the straining woman's throat and breasts and stomach, intoning a sacred song. Elfhild's teeth grind with effort.

"One more, one more, that's it. Push!"

Elfhild screams—a short, sharp cry—and from between her legs, the baby falls onto the waiting linen. With a great shiver, Elfhild's head falls back against Touilt's shoulder. Touilt carefully arranges the mother and untangles herself to view the child. The bloody, mucus-covered form lies steaming in the chill air. A girl, quiet yet, still not quite of this world, the blue birth-cord pulsing. Touilt picks up the slippery baby and uses her finger to clear the airway. She rubs the child vigorously, as she would a pup or a calf. As though awaiting the birth, the storm passes. Thunor's hammer pounds the distant hills, and his great lightning spear slashes far-off skies. The baby is still. Unnaturally still. For a moment, all creation waits, some tilted toward life, some to death . . . and then . . . and then . . . a hearty howl enters the chorus of the world.

"Oh, a fine child, yes. A scrappy little wight." Touilt puts the baby on Elfhild's breast.

"She's beautiful, isn't she?" Elfhild runs her fingers over the child's head and neck and belly and legs and toes, holding her fingers one by one. She looks at Touilt. "Do you think he'll be disappointed?"

"A daughter's a great blessing, and there's time for many sons yet. Wilona, tell the father to come."

Wilona opens the door, and Caelin, seeing her, knows, and pushes past. He smiles at last, picks up the child and looks in her face for a moment, then puts his mouth over hers and breathes into her the life of her ancestors and the kin-clan. In nine days the child will be named.

Caelin takes Touilt's hands in his, placing a gold shield-knot brooch in her palms. "I'm in your debt, Touilt." It is an apology of sorts.

"You and I are both, as always, in the debt of the gods," says Touilt. "Sif's swan was here tonight. Your wife has promised a sacrifice."

Caelin nods. "As is only right. We'll feast in her honour. And make offerings, Touilt. The next must be a son."

When Lady Elfhild and the child are settled and safe in the care of servants, Touilt and Wilona prepare to leave. At the door, Margawn, Caelin's doorkeeper, meets them. Next to him stands his enormous grey wolfhound, Bana, his tail beating a calm tattoo on the door frame. Wilona scratches behind the dog's ear. Margawn is a muscled slab of a man, well-suited to his task. Wilona thinks of him as a golden bear, and suspects that beneath the somewhat serious exterior is a man of some kindness, for more than once she's seen him stop a larger child from bullying a smaller one. The other warriors egg on such conflict, seeing it as the making of a future warrior. Now the expression on his face, more uncomfortable than formidable, nearly sets Wilona to laughing. Men are so unsettled by women's labours.

He says, "The hour's late, Lady. May I send an escort to see you safely to your home?"

"No need, friend," says Touilt, "although it's a kind offer. I have no fear of the night."

Margawn nods his shaggy head. "Will you at least humour me by taking a lantern—to guard against disrespectful stones in the path?"

Touilt smiles and takes it. "Your thoughtfulness does you honour."

From inside the chamber comes the baby's thin cry. Bana's ears prick up and he cocks his head. The muscles in Margawn's jaw work.

"All is well," whispers Wilona as she passes him and he nods.

The storm has cleared and blue-white stars float high above in the indigo sky, revealing King Edwin's massive, richly carved hall, temple, and living quarters on the grassy plateau between the village and the sacred mountain. King Edwin visits Ad Gefrin every year during slaughter-month, when the people from across the estate bring their tithe of cattle and sheep to fill the pens. As well as maintaining a battle-ready army, it is Lord Caelin's duty to keep the royal enclosure ready for the comfort of the king and his court whenever it pleases him to visit.

The women walk through the darkened snickets, past the workshops and the weaving house, the tavern and the ovens and the marsh pond. They nod to the keeper of the stockade gate, and he wishes them a good night and a blessing on them for bringing Lady Elfhild safely through this night. Light from a waning gibbous moon shines between the buildings. The people of the village are deep in slumber; neither the hens in their triangular coops nor the geese in their pens raise their heads from under their wings as the women pass. Here and there, through chinks in a door, the red-orange glow of a fire twinkles from a hearth. The seithkona is deep in thought, her brows drawn together, her lips pursed, and Wilona walks slightly behind her, loathe to intrude. From the forest edge an owl hoots.

An ancient yew tree, its limbs twisted and gnarled, is a benevolent giant standing guard over Touilt's dwelling. Prayer offerings flutter from the lower branches—pieces of brightly dyed cloth, red and green, some more faded than others. Nearby is the sacred well. On a post, carved with Eostre's likeness and the hare and egg that were her symbols, a drinking bowl hangs by a chain. As they approach the small, whitewashed hut, with a wolf head and the symbol for peace carved on the lintel, Elba, the sow, faithful as a waiting hound, snuffles through the willow hurdles of her pen.

"Good pig," says Touilt absently, and lifts the door latch.

"Hello, Elba." Wilona offers the pig a dried apple she has tucked in her tunic. The sow takes it delicately from her fingers and shakes her head in pleasure. She lets Wilona scratch behind her ears and then huffs contentedly down in the earth.

Wilona finds Touilt inside with the wolf pelt around her shoulders, huddled over the fire, a stick in her hand, stirring the ashes. In the middle of the dry wooden floor a stone hearth boasts an iron chain from which hangs the cooking pot. Wilona has a bed of her own—wooden, the mattress stuffed with straw—and fine pelts to keep her warm. Next to her bed, on a small shelf, she keeps the antler comb she believes belonged to her mother. Dried herbs festoon the rafters, and clay jars of various unguents and roots and powders line shelves above a rough table. Smoke, thyme, yeast, roasted meat, lavender, and the perfume of grasses and river weeds scent the air. Touilt's large wooden chest, hinged and decorated with iron, stands by her bed. Inside it are Touilt's sacred things: her blue cloak, her cat-skin brodekins, certain special runes, her wolf pelt, and a staff with a knob on the top, set with brass and precious stones.

"Come here," Touilt says.

Wilona squats next to the older woman. She has drawn symbols in the cinders and spread the still-glowing embers in a half-circle.

"Look into the embers."

Wilona does as she's told. Touilt begins to hum. The air in the room thickens, and a thin wisp of smoke trails from a chunk of half-charred wood. Touilt rattles the stones in her pouch and continues humming. Tiny bluish flames tremble and ripple in the embers. Something touches Wilona's neck. Something wet and blunt. She is startled but keeps her eyes on the fire, even as they water and burn. She senses the fluttering of silent wings, feels the wet-knuckle prod at the back of her neck again. Warm. And then it's gone, but the embers have fused into something darker, ragged. Touilt's voice rises and she parts her lips, turning the humming into a long note from the back of her throat. Wilona watches the red-hearted embers and curl of smoke. Something sharp and yet feathered. Her hair seems to lift, as though with the movement of passing wings. Desolation washes over her, a sense of being lost, alone. A beak, it looks like, in the smoke, talons and a clean, sweet smell, like on the moors on a star-bright night. A flutter! With a crackle and puff, whatever was there vanishes and only the lifeless grey coals remain. The desolation evaporates, and she is left merely exhausted.

Touilt asks, "What did you see?"

"A bird, I think."

"You think, or you know?"

"A bird. A dark bird. Sharp-taloned, large. An owl. Yes, an owl."

Touilt sighs and stands up, her hands on her creaking knees. She opens the chest, flipping the iron clasp with a clank, and takes off her cape and pelt. "I thought so. I felt it. You have a strong spirit." She faces Wilona. "Stir the fire into life. This room needs light."

Wilona blows on the embers until a flame licks upward. "I felt something poke at me, Lady. Not a bird."

Touilt chuckles. "My wolf is a curious beast."

Wilona shivers. "What does the owl mean?" She adds more sticks to the flames, and then larger pieces of wood.

Touilt moves behind a woven screen to use the night jar. When she reappears, she doesn't answer Wilona's question right away but removes her outer tunic and shoes and climbs into bed. "Owl is a creature of the night. Does that frighten you?"

The room is brighter now, and quite cheerful.

"No. I don't think it does. I smelled the moors. And a sweet night." *Fearful? No. But what about that great loneliness?*

Touilt grunts. "Owl is a spirit of wisdom and prophecy. You already have knowing beyond your years. Another sign of Owl. The moors, you say?"

"It seemed that way."

"Perhaps it took you there, when you wandered," Touilt says, and then falls silent.

When you wandered. Wilona remembers the moment, five winters ago, when she stumbled out of the moors upon some shepherds tending sheep on the hillside, the only one of her people to survive the sickness that claimed her kin. She was half-mad and could not say her age or even how long she'd wandered. She was little more than a bundle of stick-thin limbs, sunken, pale-grey eyes, dressed in tatters, with a carved antler comb clutched in her hand. Had Touilt not interceded it's almost certain Lord Caelin and his priest, Ricbert, would have hanged her in sacrifice to Woden, so she wouldn't bring to Ad Gefrin whatever wrath the All-Father, Lord of the Dead, had wrought upon her people.

"I see the mark of the gods upon her," the seithkona had declared. "The gods whisper to me. We will name her Wilona."

"Take her if you will, Touilt," said Lord Caelin, "but know you're responsible for the luck she brings. It'll be on your head if the dark folk come to us because of her."

Now, Touilt says, "The owl is a mysterious bird. You'll be able to see the truth beneath a lying tongue. You're gifted with sight into the dark, that's true, but it's a lonely gift. People will shy away from you. You will be alone, but that's what a seithkona's life is and you must accept it, for it has chosen you. You understand?"

Wilona is torn. She always is when Touilt talks this way. She craves the mysteries, craves the power and the knowledge, the sense of being used by the gods. But she fears it. Would she have the strength to stand before Lord Caelin as Touilt did, secure in the gods' protection? She doubts it, but she can't say such a thing. She shouldn't even think it. "I understand. I think."

"Don't think. Do!" The fire has settled down and seems like a friendly, living thing. Touilt's voice softens. "But don't let yourself slide into darkness and bitterness. That's your danger, particular to you. Believe me, all gifts come at a price."

Chapter
TWO

Egan kneels on a rocky crag near the sea outside the earthen rampart and outer ditch that encircle the monastery. He faces east to the rising sun, and as the first light struggles to pierce the heavy fog he prays. At this pre-dawn hour, when there is almost no wind, the world seems poised in anticipation. Egan is ginger-haired and thin, with large hands and feet and knobby knees beneath his cassock. His lips move. His knuckles are white. His brow furrows. His teeth clench. There is so much he doesn't understand. He thought when he followed the angel and she led him here to the holy island that all would be well, that the journey for his soul's home would be over, but even here he doesn't fit in. He took his vows two years after arriving and yet is still treated by most of the community as a leper.

The other monks whisper about him. They say he's mad. They say his vision is unholy, possibly the work of the Adversary. If not mad, they say, then duplicitous. Only yesterday he was milking one of the cows, sitting on a little stool in the barn. He overheard Brother Donnan say, "He shows up here, professing to have been led by an angel of the Lord? More like his people ran him out as Our Lord Christ ran the possessed swine into the sea." And then Brother Niall, a recent novice, said, "Maybe we should all invent visions of the Lord so the abbot might look as favourably on us." "And his facility for languages," said Brother Donnan, "it's not natural. It strikes me not so much as a gift as . . . well . . ." He said something

Egan couldn't catch. When he realized he was straining to hear, he blushed. If it was a sin to speak ill of others, it was no less a sin to eavesdrop.

Egan chooses to believe they didn't know he was there. Surely if they did they wouldn't purposefully speak so cruelly. He must try harder to be liked, not to stand apart so much. Even after all these seasons, they speak of him this way and turn the new brothers against him. Being the cause of disunity makes his heart cramp.

Since long before the day the fishermen first brought him to Ioua Insula, the idea that God had a plan for him lived like a live coal in his chest. He doesn't remember the creatures of the sea, the seals and dolphins the fishermen swore kept him afloat and nudged him toward their boat, but he's heard the tale often enough that the details are as embedded in his imagination as his own memories—the limpid, watery eyes and soft prodding muzzles of three seals, the sleek pair of dolphins. The seals lifted him when he began to slip below the surface. The dolphins circled him as he clung to a spar from his ruined craft. They chattered, the fishermen said, as though speaking, calling out for him not to lose heart. When he had been safely hauled into the fishing boat, semi-conscious and vomiting water over the fish and ropes, the seals and dolphins swam away, the dolphins east, the seals west, uttering cries of praise, perhaps, or farewell, and disappeared like dreams. The fishermen crossed themselves and made to shore as quickly as they could, for surely this strange boy, found so far from land, guarded by Christ's own creatures, must be sent to the brothers on the holy island.

All Egan remembers clearly is being below the water, his coracle wrecked by a great wave; he was convinced he had proven himself unworthy of his vision's angel. He had been so sure all would be well when Abbot Ségéne agreed to take him in, to let him take the vows first of novice, then of brother. However, since the moment the wave destroyed his boat, inexplicably, heartbreakingly, the visions stopped. Perhaps there is no more need for visions; perhaps, his arriving where he is meant to be, the angel's work is done. But, if this is where God means him to be, why is he so disliked?

There was a time, not long after he arrived, when he had hoped his fellow monks would be true brothers to him, that they would be a family and he would belong here as he never did at home. At first he took their distance to be kindness, giving him the space and time necessary to heal and to accustom himself to life at the monastery. How wrong he'd been. They envy him. It is a terrible thing to accuse them of, but Egan can't help but see the dark emotion in their faces as they walk past him, refusing to weed the same patch in the garden in which he works, pulling their cassocks away from his in chapel. What they say is that they don't trust him and that he's not sincere, but he knows differently: It's envy. They wish they, too, had had a vision.

He squinches his eyes tighter, willing away these uncharitable thoughts. He wishes he was as simple as they say, so simple he had no idea of their resentment and suspicion. He might, he thinks, have just as well stayed home, for he was a pariah there and is one here. He opens his eyes and along the horizon shines the red-gold promise of day. The fog shifts and a shaft of sunlight blazes across the water. The dawn chorus begins as seabirds wheel and cry. The pain in his heart lessens as the sense that God is alive and Christ close by engulfs him. *Christ with me, Christ in me, Christ before me, Christ behind me* . . . He places his grief at the feet of Christ, asking, as he always does, that Christ make use of him.

Later, he approaches his *amanchara,* his soul-friend and confessor, Father Bresal, as he walks the beach collecting seaweed in a basket on his back.

"May I carry that for you, Father?"

"Brother Egan, you gave me a start!" The old monk arches his back and rubs his arthritic hands together. His tonsured head is liver-spotted and peeling from the years of battering sun and wind.

Egan eases the basket from the old man's shoulders and transfers it to his own. "This is too much for you. You should let the younger monks do this."

"The pain in my back reminds me of the pain Our Lord suffered carrying his cross." He smiles, revealing his few remaining teeth. "I cannot mind that."

For some time they walk the beach together, sun warm on their skin, salt taste on their tongues. The basket slowly fills. They will use the seaweed to feed the cattle, to fertilize the vegetable plots, and to eat themselves. Food is not plentiful here, but they never go hungry.

"Do you need to confess, my son?" asks Father Bresal.

"I have been uncharitable in my thoughts."

Father Bresal sighs. "Again?"

"It is a weakness."

"What troubles you?"

"The same trouble. It's me, I know that, but what to do about it evades me."

Father Bresal stoops and picks up a white shell. He turns it over and reveals a little crab inside. He walks to the edge of the sea and gently places the creature in the water. "Some things wander into areas that don't suit them. Like that little fellow. The gulls would have pecked him out of that thin shell in a moment."

Egan stops and shifts the straps on his shoulders. He looks out to sea, not wanting to meet Father Bresal's gaze. "Are you saying I'm in the wrong place? That I don't belong?"

"I didn't say that. I'm saying you could use a thicker shell." He reaches up and places his gnarled hand on Egan's shoulder. "We've talked about this. You're so very . . . fervent, my son. Which is a good thing, of course it is. Your heart is pure, there is no doubt in my mind of that. But you must temper your enthusiasm. It unsettles others. If you want to be seen as an equal, you might try acting like one."

Father Bresal has never spoken to him so bluntly. It's as though his confessor has rapped his knuckles. "How can you say that? All I do is try not to offend, and help and pray for them . . ."

"But must you be the *least* offensive, the *most* helpful?" Father Bresal chuckles. "Living in community is challenging, my son, but always being shown up as not quite good enough by a stranger who arrives on the backs of dolphins and spouts off about visions of angels makes it near impossible."

Egan steps back. "You cannot be suggesting I deny my vision, deny my angel?"

"No, but perhaps you needn't wrap yourself up in your piety quite so tightly." Father Bresal puts his hands on either side of Egan's face. "Listen to me. You are a good boy. You are, I believe, touched by God, but that's not an easy thing to be. It frightens people, and frightened people do not behave well."

"I'll try harder, Father."

Father Bresal chuckles. "You might do well not to try at all. All this struggle, all this strain. One might think you don't trust God to do what must be done without your help."

Egan's hands rise in front of him, as though to push away the horror of such a thought. "No, no. It isn't that. I only mistrust myself, my worthiness."

"And is not being more unworthy than most a sort of hubris?" Father Bresal turns to face the sea. "Look, Brother Egan, look at the waves. Some larger, some smaller, some rolling, some spraying, all part of the great body of water, each playing their part without worry. You can almost hear them laughing as they reach the shore. Be like the waves, Brother. Be just a little merry. Rejoice and simply do your part."

With that, Father Bresal raises his hand in blessing and turns to walk back to the compound. Egan understands he shouldn't follow. He wants to ask his confessor how he can rejoice when his visions have abandoned him. It's as though he died out there in the water and all that remains is a damaged husk. The image of his mother returns: she throws up her hands in frustration at finding him in tear-filled prayers, kneeling on the rocky outcropping on the cliffs. "Why can't you be like your brothers, Egan?" she'd cried. "Get into mischief as the other boys do. You'll draw the Devil to you with all this piety." He still feels the sting of her palm against his cheek. "Worship the Lord by minding the sheep, for if you lose another it's your father you'll answer to."

He had tried. Truly he had. As he tries now. But it's never enough.

Or the right thing. Or what's required. Still, there had been peace among the sheep and the cattle. The beasts don't find him strange or worrying. He learned his Latin, learned the dialects of the Scotus and the Picts and the other peoples of the region. He now spends his days toiling in the scriptorium, but perhaps one day he might be allowed to tend the sheep and cattle as he had done at home. He watches the waves roll and shimmer and play. Perhaps he is simply not suited to the company of men.

The shutters on the south-facing windows are thrown open, and the light in the scriptorium is bright and soft with the scent of sun-warmed grasses and stone. Twelve desks with steeply angled writing boards stand around the perimeter of the room and at each one a monk sits. A large table takes up the centre of the room and on it lie a number of parchment sheets, wax tablets, quills made from geese and swan feathers, pots of charcoal, copperas, vermilion, egg whites, and other tools for writing and illuminating manuscripts. The only sound is the scratching of quills, the song of skylarks as they fly past the window, and the twittering of goldfinches.

Egan has just finished marking the parchment with the back of his knife, scoring the skins to ensure the lines of text are straight. It has taken considerable pressure to impress the lines through all eight leaves. Using a short, sharp knife, he trims the sides of a goose quill to form a nib and then makes a slit up the middle and a square cut across the point. He will have to sharpen the quill sixty times or more before the day's work is finished.

He transcribes the biography of Columba from a master sheet held to the top of the writing board with a wooden clamp. He works slowly, trying to move his wrist just so, gracefully, so the letters are pleasing and easy to read, although they look more like the scratch-ings of a chicken than the elegant writing of the other monks. A spot of reddish-brown ink globs onto the page and he catches his breath, using a piece of linen to blot it. It's not too bad, not ruined. With his knife he scratches away the top layer of parchment, and the offending ink. He tries again.

A calico cat, one of many mousers in the monastery, jumps up on the table beside the angled board, and Brother Egan gasps as it nearly upsets a pot of ink, but it manages to tiptoe around the danger. It settles in a ray of sun and begins to purr.

"What a sweet lady you are," says Egan, for all calico cats are female. His heart returns to its normal rhythm. He scratches her under the chin. She rolls onto her back, twisting into an arc. Egan strokes her belly and feels the thrum of her purr under his hand, her delicate rib cage vibrating.

Someone clears his throat. Brother Donnan, at the desk in front of Egan, glares over his shoulder. Egan pulls his hand away from the cat, dips his head, and returns to his work.

He is not supposed to draw illuminations. He is only to copy the text. He doesn't have the talent for the more artistic endeavours. And yet. The cat is so beautiful. It speaks of calm and trust. He returns to his work, the nib scratching . . . *Sing praise to the Lord, you saints of His, and give thanks at the remembrance of His holy name.* He looks again at the cat, perfect simply as she is. This, too, is a kind of praise. Perhaps if he drew just a small cat right there, next to the holy word, just as the cat sleeps next to the holy word as he writes it . . . Might not some distressed soul, looking for serenity, find comfort in such an image?

He makes a mark on the page, in the margin, the sweep of the cat's back, curved like a little shell. The tail comes round to her face, trusting, placid, at peace. The little cat opens an eye and looks at him, as though checking on his progress. He chuckles.

"Brother Egan!"

Someone slaps him on the back of his head. He starts and the cat jumps away so quickly it's as though she was never there. He's jerked his arm and left a great swath of ink across the page. He begins to blot it, turns to the voice. "Father Kenric, forgive me—"

Father Kenric is a short man with a wide girth and a ruddy face. He has the voice of a much larger man, and now every monk in the scriptorium turns to see what the fuss is about. "What have I told you time and time again? You are not satisfied doing the ordinary work, I see. You fancy yourself above such things. Well, you are not above such things. You are disobedient, Brother Egan. What was it last time? Dogs playing bagpipes. Foxes wearing robes." Father Kenric's mouth and brows are pulled down in an expression of grave disappointment. "I have been telling the abbot you are not suited to this work. Do *you* think you are suited to it?"

"I think you're wiser than I am, Father."

"You need humbling, Brother Egan."

"I'm sure you're right, Father."

"Perhaps you'll find your way among the sheep."

And so Egan once again has his duties changed. He has spent time in the kitchens and in the gardens, has repaired the fishing boats and nets. Each time he fails. He spills the soup, daydreams in the fields, and tears the nets. Now he has returned to the task of his boyhood.

But lambs, like Brother Egan, have a way of getting into trouble.

It takes him a long time to find the lamb, and when he finally spots her it is well past Prime and the sun has risen. Egan has missed the service, but he cannot leave the lamb in such distress. It has tumbled from the cliff and is wedged between rocks. The little one's mother shakes her head and paces with nervous, dancing feet, by the drop-off. Egan is afraid she, too, will fall. The other sheep stand in a watchful mass some feet away, their eyes following him. Do sheep pray? he wonders, and then fears this is blasphemy.

He lies on his stomach, with his head and shoulders beyond the stone lip. The lamb's eyes roll back and periodically it struggles, trying to rise, although it seems its leg is caught in a crevice, possibly broken. He tells it to be calm, that he will find a way to rescue it. He would leave to get help, but every time he turns away, the crying of the lamb is so pitiful and it struggles so much more intensely, that he dare not abandon it.

He stretches out, straining, but it's no use. If he's to rescue the lamb, he will have to climb down. The wind has come up and whips his scapular and habit around his legs. He will have to remove his garments to reach the lamb. The long sleeves alone, even turned back to the elbow and tied with thong, will impede his movements. He strips off his outer garments and piles them on the ground with his shoes on top, keeping only the long linen undergarment. He rubs his palms to dry them, lies on his belly and begins inching backwards over the ledge, his toes searching for purchase and finding a little nook. The wind makes his eyes water and the lamb bleats. His linen undergarment catches on a rock and tears. He tests his weight on his foothold, then moves his hands lower on the cliff face. His feet are cramping and bleeding now. He imagines falling through space, flailing, crashing into the rocks and water below, the lamb somer-saulting after him. Grope, seek, panic, find, rest. Grope, seek, panic, find . . . And then, at last, his foot meets the ledge where the lamb waits. Praise God.

He can just kneel down and place his palm on the lamb's head. It feels fragile as an eggshell. The lamb bleats but doesn't struggle. Egan doesn't dare look down, for the drop would make him dizzy. Below, the waves crash and foam on the rocks. He closes his eyes and, when he opens them again, makes sure to focus on the wall and his own feet and the lamb. As he works the lamb's leg free from the crevice, he suddenly realizes how foolish he's been. He will need both hands if he is to carry the lamb to safety. How will he hold it, when it will probably buck and thrash? He stops and considers. There is only one thing to do. He strips off his undergarment and ties it into a sling. The lamb's leg, Egan is relieved to see, is not broken. And now, he prays, climb with me, Lord Christ.

Placed in the sling, the little animal becomes quite calm and rests in the small of Egan's back. He finds the climb easier going up but cries out as a fingernail rips. He presses on. A curious gull wheels past him and screeches. Nearly at the lip now, his heart thuds, but he feels gloriously alive. A wind gust pushes the gull away over the water and then something flaps overhead, nearly blinds him, and—*whoosh*—disappears. He presses his face to the rocks, but over his shoulder he catches a glimpse of his habit and scapular sailing on the air. He closes his eyes and knocks his forehead on the rock. He is an idiot.

But he is an idiot who has reached the top of the cliff. He bends his right leg as his foot finds the final hold. He pushes up and strains, grunting, before landing on his stomach in the grass. A single shoe rests before him. There is no sign of the other. He turns and looks into the water. There, far below, are his clothes. For a second the habit takes on the shape of a man before disappearing beneath the crashing waves. He frees the lamb and watches it gambol off to be with its mother, legs kicking with joy, tail wagging.

He sits down on the grass and thanks God. Soon he will have to walk back to the monastery wearing only his undergarment and a single shoe. *Lord*, he prays, *if it is not too much to ask, walk with me when I face the abbot.*

Chapter THREE

Margawn summons the guests to the naming ceremony with a blast from his goat-horn trumpet. Wilona feels as though a sharp-clawed mouse is running about in her stomach. She lifts the hem of her new linen underdress as she climbs the steps to the great hall. Inside the many-timbered building, the blaze in the centre of the long firepit is welcoming and its flickering makes the figures on the tapestries adorning the walls—the horses and spear-carrying men, the boars and wolves of the hunt scenes—seem to come alive. To the right, six swans roast on a great iron spit over a lesser fire. To the left, three suckling pigs drip fat into the embers below from a similar spit. The smell is rich and wild. Bondswomen in rough-cloth tunics, their hair hidden by scarves, tend cooking pots. Drinking cups line the trestles and those at the high table are made of shimmering green glass.

The guests are awaiting the lord and lady, the rushes strewn on the floorboards rustling beneath their feet. The door opens and Ricbert, the Druid high priest, enters. His beard is grey as granite against his white robes, a wreath of oak leaves adorns his tonsured head, and in his gnarled hand he carries a sceptre made of hazel and topped with silver. His face is a mass of lines and hollows, and his brows float like moth wings above his watery blue eyes. With a measured and solemn gait he takes his place in front of Caelin's chair. All eyes return to the anteroom door, and within moments, Caelin steps through. For the occasion he wears a diadem adorned with a small but cunningly carved figure of the horned god. His beard has been braided. His sword is richly inlaid with silver and gold, and red embroidery ornaments his robe. He stands with his chest thrust out, his chin raised and his thumbs tucked in his belt.

"Welcome. It is a time for rejoicing and gift-giving. Ricbert, your place is here by me. Lady Touilt, who brought the child safely into the world, take the seat across from me, in the brightest light of the fire."

"I am honoured."

Wilona stands behind Touilt's chair. She thinks how like Lord Caelin it is to threaten death one moment and bestow reward the next. At his command, one by one, all the men are seated, the seasoned warriors at long trestle tables to Caelin's left and right, the younger men on either side of Touilt's table. The ladies gather near the anteroom door, ready to assume their duties. When the hall quiets, Lady Elfhild appears, carrying the baby. Her plum tunic sets off her blue eyes, and under the thin circlet at her brow, her golden hair, braided on either side of her face, lends her skin a luminous glow. Gold bands adorn her arms, gold clasps rest on her shoulders, amber and glass beads encircle her neck, and from her girdle hang keys and tweezers, a spindle whorl and comb. She smiles at the baby, and then lifts her face to the people.

"Lady Touilt, approach and guard the child while we drink the first cup," she says.

Touilt takes the child from Elfhild and clucks to quiet it. Elfhild gestures to a servant to bring the great mead-filled bull's horn, bound with bronze and dappled with blue glass and garnets. She holds the cup out to her husband. "Take this cup, my noble lord, sharer of treasure, gold-friend of men, be cheerful toward your friends, and to the babe newly born." Caelin drinks and returns the horn to his lady, who faces the gathering and says, "I greet you, who are in kinship with Caelin, and I offer you all to drink for our friendship, in tribute to our daughter. Lord Ricbert, priest, counsellor and friend, will you drink first?"

"You honour me." Ricbert kneels before Elfhild and takes the horn.

"Drink deep of our friendship, Lord Ricbert," says Lady Elfhild. "Let us be well."

He drinks, perhaps a tad too long, and hands the horn back to Elfhild.

"Rise, Ricbert, and let the naming feast begin."

With this the hall erupts in table pounding and calls of good will. The baby, startled, begins to cry, and the warriors laugh and remark on the strength of the little one's lungs.

"And now, ladies, pass the horn, so we might toast the gods and goddesses for their blessing and protection," says Elfhild.

Touilt motions for Wilona to join the serving women. They toast first to the gods and then to each other's health. Cries of "Be hale!" echo through the hall. Then Ricbert stands and moves before Lord Caelin's and Lady Elfhild's chairs.

"May the gods be with you," he says, and his voice fills the hall.

"And also with you," say the guests.

"Today we welcome the child of Lord Caelin and Lady Elfhild into the family and the tribe. I call upon them to come forward, and to Lady Touilt also, who will bring the child."

Wilona's heart dances on the inside of her wrist and she feels dizzy. It's as if she isn't inside her own skin but inside Elfhild's, feeling the effects of the wine she, and not Wilona, drank. Elfhild rises, steadies herself on Caelin's arm, and although she smiles serenely, Wilona knows she's nervous. A strange energy floats like marsh gas throughout the hall. In the previous nine days and nights, had Lady Elfhild found anything wrong with the child it would have been her duty to inform her husband and accept his decision whether or not to leave the child exposed in the forest, where she would be spirited away by elves or die from starvation, the elements, or the beasts. Happily the child is perfect, but still, a great deal depends on this moment. People shift on their stools, shuffle their feet. The fire crackles and pops. Wilona senses unnamed things watching, waiting for a misstep, and she laces her fingers together tightly. Caelin and Elfhild step down with Touilt following, the baby cooing in her arms.

When they stand before the priest, Touilt unwraps the child, who kicks her legs at the sudden chill. Touilt traces a rune on the child's belly, kisses her forehead, and places her, naked, on the rush-strewn floor before Caelin. The baby whimpers. Elfhild clasps her hands so tightly the knuckles whiten. Wilona's own fingers prickle with desire to pick up the tiny creature, as vulnerable to the spirits in the room as a young hare is to hawks.

"Caelin, lord of this hall," says Ricbert, "will you recognize this child as your own?"

"I will," says Caelin.

"Then claim her."

Caelin plucks the baby from the floor. Colour brightens Elfhild's face. Wilona realizes she's been clenching her fists; red crescents are imprinted on her palms. The world is a sharp and jagged place, and to be included in the embrace of family means everything. Touilt passes the soft wool blanket to Caelin and helps him settle the child.

Ricbert's smile is wide. "Bring the babe forward, father. Yes, just there. Lady Touilt, will you hold the sacred water for this child, and thereby bond yourself to her?"

"I will." Touilt takes a silver bowl from one of the servants.

"Excellent. The time is come, then, Caelin. Tell us the child's name."

Caelin looks down at his daughter and then across the great fire into the faces of the assembled guests. "This name was chosen for her not by me but by the goddess Sif, wife of Thonor. The goddess revealed herself to my lady wife as she laboured, and on her instructions we sacrifice tonight." The hall hums with approval.

"Hail the goddess!" "Blessing of the goddess on the child!" the men cry.

Caelin turns back to Ricbert. "The child's name is Swanhwid."

Ricbert dips his fingers into the bowl of water Touilt holds. He makes the sign of Thunors hammer over the child and sprinkles her with water.

"Welcome to this house, to this family, to this world, Swanhwid, all blessing be upon you." From around his neck he produces a silver hammer amulet, tied to a leather thong, and places it around the baby's throat. "May *Mjölner* protect you. May your aim be true, and may your heart's desire always return to you."

Touilt brings her face close and whispers so only the parents and the baby hear her words. She tucks something inside the folds of Swanhwid's blanket and then raises her head, and her eyes lock

Account <....3026>

with Lady Elfhild's. The shimmering air around Touilt grows more restless still, until Wilona sees figures twitching and writhing about her head and shoulders. Elfhild gasps, as though she, too, sees the strange apparitions. Touilt steps back beside Elfhild and Caelin and faces the priest.

Ricbert smiles. "And so, Swanhwid is welcomed here. Let us all, then, celebrate her arrival. Let the feast begin!"

Three days later the sky is so thick with forget-me-not blue, Wilona imagines she could scoop it out and smear it on her skin. Touilt has sent her into the wood to gather fuel. She walks the path past the yew tree to the sacred well, where she stops to dip her fingers, make the sign of Thunor's hammer on her breast, and say a prayer.

"And what business are you about this day?" says a voice behind her.

It's Dunstan, whom she hasn't seen since the naming ceremony. She's about to admonish him for sneaking up on her, however when she sees him, her smile fades. An angry, puffy slash is visible on his cheek. "What's happened? Are you badly hurt?"

"No. It's all right." He chews the inside of his mouth. "Really, it is. My fault."

"What could you have done to deserve such a lashing?"

Dunstan shrugs. "Alwyn says I'm clumsy. Perhaps he's right. I break things, you know."

"Alwyn did that to you?"

"Not Alwyn. He wouldn't hurt a fly. Lord Caelin, I'm afraid."

"What have you done to anger him?"

"I took him a new chest Alwyn carved. A beautiful piece of work, all dragons and geese. I turned a bit quickly, didn't see a Frankish goblet, blue glass. The chest knocked it. Well, I knocked it. Smashed. And it was a gift from King Edwin, apparently. What does it matter, Wilona? It's his right."

Wilona touches his arm. "I am sorry, Dunstan." She sneaks another look at his face. She will ask Touilt for yarrow salve to heal his wounds. Wishing to cheer him, she says, "I'm off to gather kindling. Come with me; the day's so fine."

"I can't. Alwyn's set me a task—on top of six bowls I must make for Lord Caelin's table, I owe six brace of hares for Caelin's pot as a sort of reimbursement. I set snares two days ago and checked last night, but they were empty. I daren't come back empty-handed tonight. I'll walk you as far as I can, though."

They set off across the small pen where Wilona led the sheep that morning. At their approach the sheep bounce away, kicking their legs out behind them.

"Silly things!" Dunstan laughs. "I found a ewe with her head caught in the hurdles the other day, and when I went to free her, well, I was afraid she'd tear her head off trying to get away! I had to flatten her ears to push her through." As he laughs, he grabs his face. "Ouch! Oh, I mustn't!" And that sets him off again. When he calms down he asks, "What did you think of the naming ceremony? Quite grand, wasn't it?"

Wilona recalls the platters heaped with slices of dark and fragrant meat, the generous cook-pots from which the servants produced sauces made from apples and honey, as well as vegetable stews seasoned with garlic, rosemary, and bay. Bread, still warm, broke apart in the hands, releasing steam and the scent of yeast. Rich cheeses, some creamy, some hard, dotted the tables. Laughter and goodwill filled the hall. The bard sang songs of sweet merriment. "Oh, yes," she says to Dunstan. "It was a splendid feast."

"Ricbert was certainly in his glory in those fine white robes and that oak leaf wreath on his head."

"Don't forget the sceptre! He wielded it like a sword." Wilona grins, although the truth was she found Ricbert, the high priest, intimidating. "He does have a deep voice, doesn't he? It can't help but make an impression."

Dunstan nudges Wilona. "You made an impression of your own, you know. But you're not angry with me, are you? For what I said to Godfred?"

Wilona blushes. While she was serving drink to the men, one of them, so young he was still more willow than oak, put his arm around Wilona's waist and told her she was pretty and he hoped to see her later. His breath stank of a rotten tooth. She twisted out of his grasp while he laughed, and he would have reached for her again, but Dunstan, three men down the trestle, leaned forward and said, "By Thunor Godfred, it's a brave man who'll woo the seithkona's apprentice and risk her wrath." Instantly, the air around them chilled, and Godfred went pale and asked her forgiveness. He muttered how he'd been away, fostered with the headman at Thirlings, a village to the east. "I didn't know," he said. For the rest of the night the men had been courteous but didn't tease her as they did the other serving girls.

Wilona has thought a lot about it since. It was the first time she'd been openly referred to as the seithkona's apprentice and not merely her servant. Seithkona, claimed first by Touilt, and then Eostre. Touilt had dreamed of Eostre carrying Wilona inside an egg, and she said that, along with the fact Wilona had appeared out of the moors on the new moon after the spring equinox, confirmed that she belonged to the goddess of spring and of beginnings—one for whom no marriage is permitted. Touilt had been married, of course, but had been widowed before the goddess claimed her. Being the seithkona's apprentice is more than Wilona, as an orphan without family protection, might have hoped for, and she should be grateful. One day, like Touilt, she'll become the seithkona of Ad Gefrin and spend her days apart, in the little hut by the holy well. Such a life may water the seeds of loneliness, but it also offers position and respect. Sometimes, though, she can't help but wish she was like any other girl, able to invite the attentions of a boy, to live anonymously, beyond the sphere of Lord Caelin's interest. But it does no good to wish.

"I'm not angry with you, Dunstan. Everyone serves the gods, and it's they who decide what becomes of us. It's no insult to speak of it. Nor, I hope, will it insult you if I speak the name . . ."—she bats her eyes and simpers—". . . of the lovely Roswitha!"

Roswitha, one of the goose-girls, is as plump and sweet as an apple. How Dunstan had scowled at the naming feast when Roswitha allowed herself to be dragged to the knee of a young warrior, and how he'd blushed when Roswitha noticed, disentangled herself, and winked at him. He blushes the same way now. "Aha! I knew I was right!" Wilona claps her hands.

"You see too much. Must be Touilt's training."

"I'd have to be blind not to see how you feel about her! Come on, no pouting! She likes you, too. I can see. *Everyone* can see!"

"Do you think so? Really?" And so he is restored to good humour.

As they enter the forest Dunstan says, "We must part ways here. Be careful, Wilona."

"I've no fear of the woods! If I had my way, I'd live alone in the forest." The words surprise her as much as him. She reaches in the pouch tied to her belt and pulls out a linen-wrapped packet. She unfolds it, revealing a lump of cheese, a heel of bread, and a handful of cherries. "Something tells me you weren't fed today."

Dunstan hesitates only for a moment and then breaks a piece off the bread and takes a few cherries. "You are my heart-friend, Wilona. I'm grateful," he says, with uncharacteristic seriousness.

"You're as silly as the sheep, Dunstan!"

She is deeper in the woods and alone now. The breeze plays through the leaves and the ground is spongy with moss and ferns and smells of rich loam. The work of bending and lifting and carrying the twigs and branches warms her, and Wilona ties her shawl around her waist. Then, all at once, an odd chill sweeps over her and the flesh on her arms turns to goose pimples. She squints up to see if a cloud is passing, but there's only blue sky between the tree-tops. The back of her throat tingles strangely, and for a moment she's dizzy, which she puts down to looking up too quickly. As she lowers her eyes, she notices something at the foot of a nearby oak—feathers and pellets, droppings, and bits of bone. An owl must have a nest above. Her heart thumps. There, caught in a piece of bark, lies a long feather, striped black and beige and brown. She plucks it from the bark and places it in the pouch at her waist, with words of thanks. She bows her head, waiting for the presence.

A robin in the oak tree nearby shrieks, startling her. A red squirrel inches along a bough toward a nest, no doubt heavy with blue eggs. The squawking robin dives at the squirrel and then another robin appears. The harried squirrel dashes down the oak trunk and races into the middle of the grove, its tail high in the air. Wilona drops the wood, claps her hands, and yells. The flash of red fur scurries across the clearing, zigzagging to avoid the beaks and claws, races up another tree and, disappearing into a hole, chatters indignantly. Wilona stands at the base of the tree. The robins hop from limb to limb, chirping with triumph, and then fly back to guard their unborn babies. Wilona laughs, and as she does, the back of her throat tingles again.

The red squirrel has ventured out of his hole but this time takes a path away from the nest, across a small clearing. Just then, from nowhere, a great dark rush swoops earthward. Before she understands what she's seeing, a hawk carries away the now-limp squirrel. Poor squirrel, thinks Wilona. It was only doing what squirrels do. What plan can the gods possibly have for the small things of the world? she wonders. What are we meant to learn from the pitiless way of beasts? She swallows some unexpected tears, and when she does, the tingle in the back of her throat grows hot, as though there is a dry spot there, cracked and torn. She swallows again. It hurts.

She presses her now-icy fingertips to either side of her neck. The skin is feverish and too tight, lumpish, and swollen under her ears. She battles a wave of fatigue as she rushes to gather up enough twigs and branches to fill her bundle. The day is no longer full of summer's soft promise, the wood no longer safe. Sharp pains shoot up her legs, as though she's walking on needles. Her heart hammers. She doesn't think she's been elf-shot, but then again, she has no iron on her. She is vulnerable. The oaks and beech trees, a moment ago benevolent companions, now seem like long-fingered demons. She drops her burden and wants to run but is too weak. She sets her eyes on the forest's edge, wills her heart to go there, and prays her feet will follow.

The path leading to Touilt's dwelling seems miles too long, and a sweat breaks out on Wilona's brow. Each step is a bargain with her legs. She pictures herself sitting against the sun-warmed wall. She concentrates on that. It occurs to her that perhaps her people call again from beyond the veil of death, and perhaps this time she will go to them. Everything is too intense. The soft cooing of wood pigeons is like shrieking falcons; the spicy smell of the maiden pinks growing by the path makes her stomach heave; the sunlight is like needles in her eyes.

It seems like hours before she stumbles to the holy well. She bends to drink, her throat dry as straw. Her legs crumple. The ground beneath her, and the moss-covered stone on which she rests her head, feel as soft as duck down.

Someone nudges her. Dunstan is standing above her, a brace of hare over his shoulder, his brow furrowed . She wants to tell him she's just very tired and will be all right soon, but her tongue is thick, and the words spin in her head like lazy hawks.

"Don't move. I'll get Lady Touilt."

Wilona is about to tell him something, but then she can't remember what, and the world begins to look far away. The yew tree dances. Elba stands on her hind legs and hops up and down. Voices somewhere are saying things, but nothing makes sense. Harp music rises from the well, and at first the air smells of strawberries and honey, then of mugwort and burdock. She is in her bed. A great weight upon her chest makes it difficult to breathe. Voices grow louder, and some scream. Shadows twitch and fly all around, forming into dark shapes that cause her to cry out; although she's not sure she's making any sound at all. Wormy fingers slither on her brow. She wants to swat and smash them, but when she tries her arms are like stone. Red flames flicker all around her bed and scratching talons probe, search . . . and she is falling, slipping, sliding . . .

Chapter
FOUR

After Prime, Egan returns to his cell for the daily period of scripture reading and meditation, to find Father Bresal waiting for him.

"I have come from the abbot, Brother Egan. We have things to discuss."

Egan's heart flutters, sure he's about to be sent back to Eire, or sent on the next trade boat for whatever port the traders set. Since the day he rescued the lamb and appeared near-naked in the eating hall, things have not gone well. There was laughter, of course, and pointing and jokes at his expense. This was to be expected. He knows the ludicrous sight he made and doesn't begrudge his brothers their fun. But Abbot Ségéne was anything but amused. Cloth was valuable, even the rough cloth of Egan's habit, and many hours went into its weaving. He had been called to the abbot's chambers and made to give an account of himself. When he finished the abbot asked what penance he thought he ought to perform for the sin of waste. Egan left the choice up to the abbot, and so his rations were cut in half for a moon, he spent two nights in prostration and prayer before the holy cross, and another kneeling on the cold chapel stones. He hadn't protested, and added a fourth night, for he was ashamed of his desire to tell the abbot he thought the life of the lamb worth more than his scapular. The abbot knew best. He had all the lambs of the monastery under his care, human and animal both. What did Egan know?

And now, he hangs his head. "Am I to be defrocked then?"

"Defrocked? Of course not. You've done nothing so terrible as that." He scratches his head. "On the contrary, the abbot and I have been concerned about you. We know you're not happy."

"That's not true, Father. Everything that's holy is here; all my life I dreamed—"

"Yes, I know about your dreams, Brother Egan, but let's not start all that again. You don't quite fit in; there's no point in denying it, is there?"

Egan tucks his hands into the sleeves of his habit, so his confessor can't see how tightly they're clenched . He's correct; there's no point.

Father Bresal claps his hands on his knees. "Look, my son, this is not a punishment; we want you to understand that. This is a great honour. The abbot and I have been praying and asking for guidance. You're an unusual young man and you don't understand your gifts. You want to spend all your time with the sheep, off by yourself, which is all well and good, but it's not the best use of your talents, and not making use of one's talents is tantamount to ingratitude." He stands and puts his arm around Egan. "Come on, let's walk and talk, shall we? I'm to take you to the abbot."

The day is mild and full of birdsong. The rest of the monastery is quiet; the monks are at study. The only people moving about are at the far end of the compound, in the guest house, where travellers are offered shelter. They are traders from the Pictish lands who arrived several days before. It seems an odd time for an audience with the abbot, Egan thinks. In the distance the sea is shining. Beyond that lie Eire and Egan's family, and he prays for acceptance.

They walk in silence for some moments, past the barn where grain is stored, past the garden in which medicinal herbs grow, and then Father Bresal says, "I wonder if you know how very blessed you are? And I don't mean in your visions, although of course these, too, are great blessings, but rather in your skill with languages, and with words generally. Reading came almost unnaturally easy for you, as did Latin, and then the dialects you've learned. How many are there now?"

This puzzles Egan. Learning languages doesn't seem so very difficult. It's just a matter of hearing the music of the words and then understanding which particular sound refers to which particular thing. Just as he heard the ewe's crying for her lost lamb and understood at once—from the timbre of the bleat—that something was terribly wrong. The lamb was in danger, not just lost, so the mother had cried in a completely different way. If she had spoken words she could not have been clearer. And words are so much easier to understand, even if they're different words; at least they're in the human tongue.

"I'm not sure," he says. "Five or six, I suppose."

"Precisely. It's a gift, Brother Egan. One which must be put to good use in the service of Our Lord Christ." He glances at the young monk. "We've talked a great deal, since you came here, of the effect you have on the other monks. No, no, don't speak. There's no need to speak; I'm not chiding you. It's more I who should apologize to you, I think."

Egan's eyebrows shoot up. "Never, Father. You've been nothing but kind and your advice is invaluable!"

"The fact is there's something about you. Something unusual. You are unaware, I know, of the . . . well . . . I don't quite know what to call it . . . but something emanates from you. A sort of intensity. See, the look on your face this very moment tells me you have no idea. But it's there, nonetheless. I had thought that perhaps humility and time would tamp it down so you might become, more easily, a brother among brothers, content in the simple life we live here."

"But Father, I am content. I strive only to be of service to Our Lord."

"Of course. But I fear we've all been mistaken as to what that service may be. The Lord has plans for you, my son, and He has revealed them to Abbot Ségéne." He pats Egan's shoulder. "It's good news. Great news."

They arrive at the abbot's wattle-and-post hut, near his lodging, where he receives visitors and conducts the daily business of the monastery. The door is open. Inside, the abbot, a robust man with a great tangled beard, sits behind a rough-hewn table, writing on a parchment. Hearing them, he raises his face and smiles. Abbot Ségéne is not a man who smiles often, and certainly not at Brother Egan. It seems like the smile of a man who has solved a problem, and Egan, evidently the problem in question, is not reassured.

"Ah, you're here, Father Bresal. Good. Come in, and Brother Egan as well." He puts his quill down and folds his hands as they approach. "Have you told Brother Egan God's plan?"

"I thought that best left to you, Abbot."

"Yes. Good." He leans forward and peers at Egan. "The Lord is working wonders in the world. We live in momentous times. His word spreads throughout the land and a great opportunity has presented itself, by God's will."

"Praise God," says Brother Egan.

"Indeed. Praise God," repeats Abbot Ségéne. "Some years ago, as I'm sure you know, Pope Gregory sent Bishop Paulinus to Kent from Rome, to convert the pagans. He's done wonderful work there and has recently accompanied Princess Ethelburga to Northumbria to marry King Edwin. Her brother and guardian, King Eadbald, permitted the marriage with the stipulation she remain Christian and King Edwin, thank God, agreed. Events have transpired in which the hand of God is evident—a thwarted assassination attempt against the king on the very night Queen Ethelburga gave birth to a child. The details do not matter so much, except to say the king has permitted his daughter to be baptized!" He claps his hands and Egan jumps. "Imagine, Brother, the glory of God. Should King Edwin accept Christ, it is entirely possible he will begin to sow the seeds of peace at last, instead of always thinking about the glory of battle, and these ghastly wars will end. Great changes are afoot."

"God is great," says Egan.

"And you, my son, will be part of the great changes."

"I will, Father?"

"Bishop Paulinus has sent word he needs someone who can translate for him, someone who knows the dialects and ways of the people. Yes, I see from your expression you have guessed it. The Lord has directed that you shall be the very person, Brother Egan. I am sending you to the court of King Edwin at Bebbanburgh."

The floor seems to roll under Egan's feet, and he raises his hands as though to steady himself on a pitching deck. "When am I to leave?"

The abbot comes around the table and stands before Egan. "Go back to your cell with your confessor, Brother. Pray and prepare yourself. You will leave today with the traders' boat. They will take you to the mainland and from there you will travel overland. The journey will be long, but not too long, and your skill with languages will serve you well. You'll learn even more than you know now as you travel, and by the time you arrive in Bebbanburgh you'll have much to offer the bishop. You will make us proud. Now, kneel, Brother, and I will bless you."

The sun is high over Egan's hut when he turns to Father Bresal and says, "I'm ready."

"Are you?"

"I am." He has a light pack on his back, containing a wooden bowl and spoon, some extra linens for his feet for when his wear through, and a small psalter, a gift from the abbot himself.

Father Bresal rubs his arthritic knees and rises from his stool. His joints pop. "Well then, the abbot will be pleased."

Egan goes pale. "Did he think I wouldn't obey?"

"Obedience and submission are not the only thing God requires, Brother."

"I'm ashamed if I gave the impression I was unwilling . . ."

"You think of your shame too much," says Father Bresal, as though reading his mind. "That, too, is still thinking of yourself, isn't it? Better to set your thoughts entirely on God."

"You're right, of course. I'm unworthy."

"And there you go again!" Father Bresal smiles, a little sadly. "The passion of youth, no doubt. I almost remember it. Never mind. But try to pack a little joy in your bundle, won't you?"

Egan frowns. This new life he's apparently to lead, this new path he's to follow, has come upon him so abruptly he hardly knows what to think, what to do, how to behave. All he feels is that he's being cast out. That he's failed somehow. Father Bresal is right, though. What about joy? He does not consider himself joyless. He sees so much beauty in God's world. Has his determination to serve God's purpose been confused with dourness? "I will, along with a pinch of, well, humour, if I can find some, yes?"

Father Bresal claps him on the shoulder. "A grand idea. But remember, you have the thing most necessary for the work you're called to. You have kindness. Others have tried, and no doubt will try again, to bring the pagans to Christ through force. That's never the way. Our Saviour Jesus Christ brings us love and gathers us gently, as a shepherd gathers his sheep." He smiles, which causes Egan to blush hotly. "You may need a reminder now and then to walk the path of moderation, to be gentle with yourself, but there will never be a need to remind you to be kind, and I know that's why our abbot has singled you out for this honour. God blessed you when you floundered in the sea, blessed you and kept you. He'll never leave you companionless." The old monk drops his hand from Egan's shoulder. "Now, come along. The boat leaves on the tide. Imagine what you'll learn with Paulinus! And in the king of Northumbria's court! I won't lie to you. I suffer from the sin of envy, just a little. Just a very little, but there it is."

Egan would gladly change places with Father Bresal, but of course that is not an option. And so both of them must deal with their envy.

Chapter
FIVE

Wilona fancies she can see through her closed eyelids. There is Touilt. Touilt's face, however, does not look like her own—her eyes are strangely yellow and her jaw snoutish. Her teeth are sharp and the smell of the deep-earth den is all around her. Something in Wilona's mouth tastes of roots and bitterness. She gags, but a hand covers her lips, forcing her to swallow. Smoke burns her eyes, and in the wafting, bluish haze, grey imps and spirits hover and squirm. It's as though slivers of ice have been worked between her skin and muscle, sharp and freezing to the bone. Hands float near her, and she knows they are her mother's hands, but they never get close enough to save her. Her mother wants to tell her something, to bring her somewhere. A great tree towers in the muddled shadows, with roots twisted and intricate and deep into the ground. Her mother is not her mother then but a great owl, the colour of storm clouds, and swoops above her. Yet, the owl cannot be her mother, for it is not a female owl. She thinks of it as *him*. The owl folds his wings around her, moulds itself to the curve of her shoulder, the length of her arm. She is lifted up, rushing along a beaten path, sweeping the tops of trees, and then she plunges down, down into the heart of a great oak, slip-flying along one of the great roots, down, down, into the earth itself; she flies down the tree root, as though the dirt and roots are air, twisting, turning, falling . . . And then everything is black, but safely so. The heart nest, she thinks. I am in the heart nest. Soft and dark and hidden away from danger, and she can sleep here, while the moor-scented owl watches, sleep until the end of time if she so desires, and she does; she craves it so . . .

A woodpecker is drumming against a tree. Something metal clatters. Rough burlap lines her mouth; her tongue is thick. Her eyelashes stick together.

"So, you grace us with your presence."

Something tickles unpleasantly on her neck. She raises her hand to brush it away and finds it is her hair, greasy and damp. Wilona opens one eye and then the other. Touilt is sitting on a low stool by the fire, stirring a pot.

"I'm relieved." Touilt stands over her now, feeling her forehead. "Cool. Good." She turns, steps outside, talks to someone. Wilona drifts off again.

When she opens her eyes next, Touilt is holding a cup. She places an arm behind Wilona. "Come on, then, little one. Drink a bit of this."

Suddenly, Wilona is thirstier than she's ever been. She grabs the cup. Her tongue reaches for moisture. Broth. Sweet with onions, rich with beef marrow.

"Greedy! Not so quick. You'll be sick."

The cup disappears and Wilona groans, too weak to do more.

Touilt laughs. "You'll live. But you did give me a scare, and Dunstan, too, I'll warrant—his poor face." She winks. "It's much better now."

The shadows under her eyes, and the lines around her mouth, are proof Touilt has been worried. Touilt hands her back the cup and Wilona sips, although it's hard not to gulp. The warm, rich brew hits her stomach and it cramps. "How long?" Her voice croaks.

"This is the fourth morning."

"Are others ill?"

Touilt shakes her head. "Only you. It came to you alone." She wipes Wilona's face and neck with damp linen. "We're lucky in that. Rumour spread that your dark luck might have finally caught up with you."

For a moment Wilona fears she'll vomit. "Lord Caelin?"

"Ricbert persuaded him to wait, before . . . well, it's no matter now." She takes Wilona's chin in her palm. "Sleep. I'll return later. We've much to talk about."

"You're sure? Lord Caelin—"

"We have nothing to fear. He's had a boy watching us. I've told him to go back and tell Lord Caelin you're returned to us."

Wilona studies her guardian's face but detects no dissemblance. She's safe. What Touilt might have to discuss with her is puzzling, but Wilona's far too tired to think about it. She's permitted to drink a bit more of the broth, and she barely swallows before she feels the gentle slide leading to sleep. *Raedwyn*. The word echoes along beside her as she glides into a dreamless land.

When she wakes, the room is bright and sounds drift in through the open window—a hammer ringing in the forge, the twitters of wagtails, the fluting *too-eet* of a redstart, the wind's hush through the leaves. Wilona is weak, but a strange itch spreads through her. She remembers seeing a pair of fat and stubby fox cubs walking along a low rock wall at the edge of a meadow last spring. They rubbed their still-blunt muzzles against tree trunks, gambolled and jumped and tussled, and generally seemed to have more joy inside them than could be confined in their limbs. Wilona feels like that. She wants to run somewhere, and her toes twitch.

She's alive, and grateful for it. She's also ravenous. She thinks it odd, this vigour, but fears that questioning it will chase it away. She wiggles her toes and shakes her legs under the coverlet. Everything in the room seems clearer, brighter—the stool in the corner, the shutters thrown back from the window, the stone lamp, the ivy-and-garland-patterned hangings on the wall, the reeds on the floor, the ant crawling there. All things are distinct, pure unto themselves. The threads in the hanging cloth stand out so clearly it's as though each one has a name of its own. The glint of mica in the lamp glistens like a precious jewel, and the cracks in the wood of the stool are like ravines in a great dry landscape. Even the spider, waiting patiently in a web in the corner, vibrates with life. A loaf of bread and a bowl of wild strawberries, along with a jug of water, sit on the stool next to her mattress. She reaches for them greedily and, as she does so, the odour of her own body wafts out from under the bedclothes. It's almost enough to put her off her food—almost. The bread is warm, and when the crust breaks beneath her fingers, the yeasty aroma sends water rushing to her mouth. The bread tastes like life itself. The water is cool and sweet. She wants to laugh out loud. Surely, nothing in the world is better than fresh bread and clear water. And then she stuffs a handful of red berries in her mouth, where they explode—sparkling, acidic, and sweet.

A sound, a chuckle, and there is Touilt in the doorway, a half-smile on her lips. Her face is softer than the last time Wilona saw her, although some shadows remain beneath her dark eyes. Her head is bare, and her hair, streaked with grey, falls loosely about her face. Wilona swallows the bread. It seems drier than it had a moment before. It's not right she should be in bed when her mistress stands. She makes a motion to rise.

"Stay." Touilt holds her palm up. "You're ill yet. Another day or two of rest, I think." She pulls a stool close to the bed and sits, her eyes boring into Wilona. "How do you feel?"

"I'm well."

Touilt arches an eyebrow.

"Better, Lady. Grateful for your care."

"As you should be. It was dangerous."

Wilona doesn't know what to say to that, so she says, "Thank you."

"You were away from us." Touilt doesn't blink as often as most people, and under her stare Wilona makes an effort not to fidget. "I have questions. Pay attention." Wilona nods. "What were you doing right before the fever came upon you?"

"I was in the forest, gathering kindling."

Touilt leans her elbows on her knees and the necklace of wolf-teeth around her neck rattles. "Where in the forest? Be specific."

Wilona tries to remember. Where was she? The forest is a sacred world unto itself, and within it are places more sacred yet—the place in the river where the great rocks sit like sleeping giants; the mirror-still pool; the elder tree where the Old Mother lives, her head covered in tiny, creamy flowers; the ash tree near the clearing. "Near the stand of oaks, to the west."

"And what did you notice there?"

As Wilona concentrates, an undeniable sense of presence returns. Not frightening. A whiff of heather and the night moors. Owl scent. The scent triggers memory. "Birds in a tree. A squirrel. The birds chased him to protect their eggs. And then a hawk." It seems childish, this small forest drama.

"What about the hawk?"

"It killed the squirrel. It was so fast. I . . ."

"Go on."

"It's silly, but I felt the squirrel was badly tricked somehow. He was just going on . . . and then the hawk came. It didn't seem fair."

Touilt nods, as though she has said the right thing. "And the illness came upon you then?"

"Yes, right after." The strange energy she felt upon waking drains, as though she is reliving the moment in the forest. "It frightened me. I was alone."

"Were you?" Touilt fingers the wolf teeth, rubbing a large incisor.

Wilona's not so certain then. She had feared elves, and elf-shot. The trees had seemed malevolent. "Perhaps not. But what was there frightened me."

"I'm not surprised."

Touilt's eyes never leave Wilona's face. All the exuberance Wilona felt earlier is gone. The things in the room are just things, ordinary and functional. The little spider has disappeared. She wants only to curl up, away from Touilt's eyes. She cannot hold her gaze and starts knotting a loose thread in the coverlet. Her greasy hair clings to her neck and she longs for a knife to cut it all off with.

At last, Touilt saves her. "You're a most unusual girl, Wilona. I suspected as much when I first saw you."

Wilona shivers. "I don't think so. You're wise, Lady, but I'm just a girl."

"See, you know some truths, even now. I am wise, wiser than you." She smiles. "And do you not wish to be more than just a girl? Have you no better sense of your fate, here, in my house, as my apprentice?"

Hope is dangerous but, then again, so is being without allies, protectors. "I'm grateful for all I have, Lady. I owe my life to your generosity."

Touilt snorts. "I loathe fawning. Don't argue with me. And do *not* try to hide from me."

Wilona raises her eyes and her lower lip quivers.

"Wilona, didn't you notice something else in the wood?"

She closes her eyes and thinks hard. Something flickers at the edge of her mind, like a half-forgotten vision. She relaxes, tries not to frighten it away. Feathers. Bits of bone. "There was a tree, an oak, with droppings and scraps at the base."

"An owl tree," Touilt says. "I thought so."

The memory returns in a rush, and with it, a flare of wild excitement, a longing for the tree-root ride. "Oh, the owl! I dreamed of him."

"Yes," Touilt says, "but it was no dream."

Touilt is right. Whatever happened does not feel like a dream. It's more than that—something bigger, meatier. Wilona tells Touilt of the flying descent upon the tree root to the owl's cave-like nest. Touilt's eyes widen and she makes complicated symbols with her fingers in the air.

Touilt leans back and folds her arms. "From this it's clear—your *fetch,* your soul-self, your true nature—has come to you in the form of the owl. He is both you and not you; he is the part of you that lives after death. He is your guide, your wisdom, and your power. Did your fetch reveal his name?"

Raedwyn. The word that echoed as she fell asleep. *Raedwyn.*

"He did, Lady."

Touilt nods, and then stands. "And so you are twice claimed. Once for the goddess, Eostre, once for your fetch, the owl. You progress more quickly than most do. I was older when the wolf came for me. It bodes well. And your owl protected you, child."

Touilt frowns, bites her lip, and drops her eyes. She considers the floor for several minutes, and Wilona senses there's more she wishes to say, and so she waits. As the minutes pass, her uneasiness grows.

"How should I put it?" Touilt looks at her. "Not all who are chosen survive the testing. You've been tested twice. The spirits rode you when you wandered the moors. They rode you again in this illness. Strong magic. Powerful danger. Lord Caelin will be pleased. You'll prove useful."

Wilona grips the blanket over her chest, to keep her fingers from trembling. "And is it over now?"

Touilt shrugs. "Who knows what the gods have in store? We must ensure you carry iron with you at all times. I've placed some in the pouch around your neck."

Wilona reaches for her neck and finds there a new leather thong with a small pouch attached. "Thank you, Touilt."

"There's something in the pouch you were carrying at your waist when we found you; it is not mine to touch."

The feather. "Yes."

"Place it with the iron. No evil will pass it. Do not remove it. For now, rest. Tomorrow will bring what it brings, and take us where it will take us." She removes a small vial from her apron pocket and pours a little of the contents into a cup of water. "Drink this."

It smells like the barn floor, but Wilona does as she's told, and after she drinks, Touilt leaves her. Wilona lies still for a while, wishing she could bathe, and then she imagines the tree root against her chest, feathers under her fingers, and the slip-slide down . . . *Raedwyn*.

Chapter SIX

Egan wakes up in the dark. Each dawn is a miracle, a reminder of God's first act of creation. It amazes him anyone would miss it, and yet, here in the great fortress Bebbanburgh, the royal court is not much disposed to pre-dawn prayer. Egan shakes his head.

Bishop Paulinus, Queen Ethelburga's confessor, sleeps in a tapestry-laden chamber next to her quarters. Paulinus arrived in Northumbria from Kent convinced the king would quickly convert, and is displeased he still refuses to deny the old gods. Last year, Edwin promised to convert if Paulinus's prayers for King Edwin's victory against the West Saxons were answered. Even after defeating his enemies, he did not fulfill his promise. Pope Boniface V himself has sent letters, urging his conversion, but still . . . Egan prays for the king to see the wonder of Christ's message, and the queen is tireless in her efforts.

While Egan's prayers for the king have not been answered, others have been. He's been allowed to move to this small wooden hut just outside the fortress's southern wall, near where the shepherds keep the flock on the plateau sloping up from the sea. Bishop Paulinus had at first insisted Egan sleep in an antechamber near his own quarters, so he might be available whenever necessary, but apparently he had kept the Father from his sleep, and thus, after several weeks, was granted permission to remove himself. Now, Egan sighs, rises from his pallet, lights a candle, and washes his hands and face in a stone basin of cold water he placed by the bed the night before. Something tickles his skin and he realizes a beetle has crawled into the basin. He coaxes the drowning creature onto his finger and sets it outside the doorway. "Be safe, brother beetle."

He straps on his sandals and heads to the shore. To reach the sea he must walk round the long, high fortress wall to the gate near the narrow harbour. The path is adequately wide, but men have been swept off the edge in the devilishly high winds of winter, and even now Egan must be cautious. When the tide crashes against the cliff walls he prays, standing before his hut, occasionally joined by indifferent sheep, but this morning the weather is calm enough.

As he reaches the gate he coughs, so as not to startle the doorkeepers. They are not accustomed to anyone approaching at this hour, even though Egan comes here whenever tides permit. Still, it's prudent to alert them of his presence. He greets the huge, black-bearded twins standing guard and they nod silently in return.

He descends the slippery rock steps. The air smells clean, and salty, and slightly overripe from the seaweed festooning the beach. In the near-dark, he puts his life in Christ's hands, offering each step into the unknown as a confirmation of his faith. This time of day is the most blessed but also the hardest. Without the distraction of work and the bustle within the fortress walls, Egan is ragged with longing for the simple life of the monastery. The rejection he suffered there seems but a distant memory in the face of all the complexities of the royal court. The stretch of sand before him is pocked with lugworm castings. His eyes rise to the sweet plumish-rose ribbon of light on the horizon. The sun is still nothing but a pearlescent promise.

To his left, in the distance, he can just make out the tidal island known as Medcaut. He has been told there is another island, just a tiny one, near it. He closes his eyes and imagines a small hut, with a door facing the rising sun. He would sing songs to the seals and whales. He would have a patch of garden. Protected by the wall of tides, he would be alone with God's miracle, free to give himself completely. His heart feels as though it bleeds into his belly.

He kneels on a rock, picks up several small stones, and sets them beneath his knees. He must drive out desire. He grinds his knees into the stones and clenches his teeth against the pain shooting up into his thighs, his loins. God is everywhere—in the great-spanned bird, the seal in the cove, the raven, the red deer, the lamb, the hound, the otter, the hooded crows. God is in the grasses and the sandy beach, in every rocky crag and cloud and star, in every iris and orchid, in every patch of hogweed and lowly bracken. An eye-shatteringly bright bump appears on the horizon, and as it does, the world, in that suspended moment, once again turns toward life and light, away from death and darkness. Terns wheel overhead; a flock of gulls appears as if by magic and squawk just offshore, probably over a shoal of herring. The air fills—kittiwakes, eiders, razorbills, and guillemots. On the sea's surface shapes materialize. Smooth round heads. The seals have appeared.

Egan raises his arms.

A short time later, he ascends the steps and already the sun warms his back. The bang and clatter of the metal workers who ply their trade just inside the fortress near the gate, along with their good-natured shouts, reach him and he thinks perhaps today he will offer his services there, if Paulinus has no need of him. The smithies are rough men, but patient, and since he asks no pay and doesn't complain no matter what's asked of him, his hands are welcome. In truth, his services as translator do not seem to be much needed here, since Edwin, and most of the court, speak Latin fluently.

Hourly, he tries hard to accept this mission to the royal court, but with the stench of decadence, the perfume of politics so thick in his nostrils, it's difficult. He supposes it's to be expected that even good souls might be seduced by the gold and the velvet, the soft beds, the ale and wine, the fine jewels and furs and rich food. Bishop Paulinus confuses him. That he is pious and devout is beyond a doubt, but his apparent attachment to gold crosses and fine linen robes, to scented oils and a diet that includes meat shocks Egan. He wants to believe the elder priest behaves this way so as not to offend his hosts, but it does seem in contradiction with the simple life Christ exemplified.

"Brother Egan!"

He is startled out of his thoughts and looks to see who's calling. It's one of the young slaves who serve Paulinus, and he looks decidedly unhappy.

"I've been looking everywhere for you!"

"Except, of course, where I was, and since I am now where you are, it's worked out well enough," says Egan, trying not to laugh at the indignant expression on the boy's face.

"Lord Paulinus says you are to come *at once*. And that was long enough ago that I'm bound to be beaten for it." The boy pulls at Egan's tunic.

"All right, lad, I am coming and I'm sure the good father wouldn't beat you."

The boy rolls his eyes.

A few minutes later, Brother Egan is standing in front of the bishop's quarters, sweating in spite of the chill wind, and he can't help but wonder if Father Bresal would still envy him. With a small prayer, he steps over the threshold and is surprised to find Paulinus pacing. The man is tall and he stoops slightly, as though to disguise himself as a man more like other men. He strikes Egan as a kind of predatory wading bird, picking his feet up slightly higher than necessary, as though afraid he might trip on something; bobbing his head with each step, as though looking for a plump frog to skewer on his beakish nose.

"You wanted me, Father?"

Paulinus claps his hands as he swings round to Egan. His eyes gleam. "Great tidings, Brother Egan! Everything is about to change, praise God! Yes, yes, the tide is turning! By the grace of God, King Edwin is ready!"

"Excellent news! What's happened?"

Paulinus tells Egan how, years earlier, when King Edwin was in exile in Kent, he dreamed of a stranger who told him power would be his when, in the future, someone laid a hand on his head. "This morning I recalled that dream to him and laid my hand on his head. He could not deny it was the prophecy fulfilled. He will convert."

"But how did you know about the dream?"

Paulinus chuckles. "It was revealed to me by our Lord, of course. What other way could there possibly be?"

Brother Egan falls to his knees. "Praise God!"

"Get up, you fool! We've work to do."

Chapter SEVEN

The day is as mild and fragrant as udder-warmed milk. Wilona, her skin stained russet-gold by long hours out of doors, is nimble as a sheep as she steps lightly along the worn path running by the edge of the grassy riverbank. On one shoulder she carries a basket filled with herbs and flowers; on the other a creel, inside which two bright trout rest on a bed of leaves. The light dapples through the trees, shining on the amber-coloured water. Here, in what she considers *her* place, great rocks have piled up in the bend, with a flat slab in the downriver spot, a sheltered and perfect seat for a moment's rest. Behind her, more moss-covered boulders sit on a slope, half-buried in earth, forming a fair-sized cave. She first ventured inside one day when she was caught in a thunderstorm, and found it snug and surprisingly dry. She nodded off and dreamed of Raedwyn, the owl, and when she woke she felt the place was meant for her.

Now, she puts her baskets down and lies on her stomach, trailing her fingers in the cool water. She adjusts the pouch hanging between her breasts. The tiny iron hammer Touilt gave her after her soul-sickness is still there, as is the owl feather. Behind the cave, the earth rises into the thick woodland, full of damp, twisted, moss-furred oaks, and to the meadow beyond. Past these stand the yew tree, the sacred well, and Touilt's hut. Wilona daydreams, recalling the sacred rites of Eostre's spring festival, when the new fires were lit, and the cattle driven through it to purify them. Girls and women danced and wove their garlands about the trunk of the stripped Yule tree. Touilt, as seithkona, oversaw the ritual alongside Ricbert. Lord Caelin and Lady Elfhild sat beneath a bower festooned with spring flowers. Wilona was permitted to join the other girls, weaving her blue ribbon in with the rest, their hair unbraided, their bare feet muddy. Twice as she twirled round, she caught Lord Caelin staring at her, with a strange, fierce expression on his face. The first time she thought she must have been mistaken. The second time his eyes clamped on her like hands. She missed a step and nearly stumbled. When she came round again he was talking to Lady Elfhild and she dared not look after that.

When the dances finished Lord Caelin thanked the girls for their efforts, patting some on the head, pinching others on the cheek. He stood before Wilona and smiled in a way she found confusing, and then passed on without saying a word. He led the men and older women to the hall, where a roasted ox waited and ale flowed. The girls, with Touilt leading them, made their way to the river, to bathe and pray for rain. No men were permitted to watch the girls in the water, of course. And when the last of the prayers were said, Touilt left them as well, but Wilona, with Touilt's permission, stayed.

She set off with some of the other young female servants and slaves who were not expected to marry. Each found their own path through the woods, and soon giggles echoed off the trees. Wilona went to the riverbank, by a lightning-struck, hollowed-out oak, the cleft deep enough to fit three. The spring forest's clean, rising-sap scent was like a veil around her, and she waited for the gods to reveal what they might. It was Godfred who found her. He'd grown even taller since the naming ceremony, when he'd dared to put his arm about her waist. He was one of Lord Caelin's bodyguards now, and the muscles in his shoulders were bunched from hours of practice with sword, shield, and spear. His hair flowed down his back, and two braids framed his face. His beard was soft. His thighs were strong. His breath no longer stank of a rotten tooth; it was sweet as clover. He took her again by the waist and whispered that he had scoured the woods hoping to find her, only her. Her heart felt like a trapped sparrow beneath her breast and she shivered. He pressed her back to the oak and himself upon her, his cock a staff against her. Warm honey flowed to her belly. She opened her arms, and together they lay back on the pine needles. She opened her thighs, and after the first piercing pain, let him teach her what pleasure might be. When she returned to the hut, Touilt did not ask where she had been, or with whom, but the next morning she reminded her which herbs were useful should a woman not wish to conceive.

Now, remembering Godfred's tongue on her nipple, his hands on her buttocks, the sensation of his belly pressed up against hers, Wilona smiles and blushes, her knuckle rising involuntarily to her mouth. She giggles, pushes herself to her feet, dusts off her patched tunic and re-shoulders the baskets. She walks along the worn path; the shadows tell her it's mid-afternoon. On the margin of the woodland Wilona bends and runs her hand over the grassy mat of hare's-foot clover. She snips some and places it in the basket. It will make a good tea for Touilt, who's suffered with a stomach ailment the past week.

She crosses the meadow, and as she nears the well and the yew, she sees someone in the front of the house. Roswitha, Dunstan's wife. The two were married the past Yule, for Alwyn, the woodworker to whom Dunstan was apprenticed, died fighting with King Edwin against the West-Saxons the previous Weed-Month, and so Dunstan now has a trade to support a family. The wound Dunstan earned during the same war has irreparably weakened his spear arm and made him no good for fighting, but Wilona thinks this isn't such a bad thing. She knows, though, that the loss of honour stings him. He'll never rise in Caelin's favour now. Roswitha says she'd rather have a live husband than a dead hero. At the handfasting Wilona had offered her blessings and truly meant them. Roswitha had put her arms around her and called her sister. Wilona rolled that word around in her mouth for days. It had a pretty taste. "Good day, Roswitha," she says now.

Roswitha stands, her hands on her knees. She rises slowly and then arches her back. Although she's only four months pregnant, she affects the aches and pains of a woman further along. Wilona hides her smile.

"I brought news, and some honey for Touilt." She inclines her head toward the dwelling. "She was asleep when I arrived and I didn't want to disturb her, but I think she's awake now."

Wilona nods and says she'll check on Touilt. "She'll want to hear your news."

Inside the dwelling the air is close and the light dim. It smells stale, although Wilona changed the bedding just the week before. Touilt's used the bucket, a sign she's feeling poorly indeed, not to have made the effort even to leave the house for a trip to the netty. Only one window is open. Flies drone lazily around the waste bucket and over an uncovered jug of milk. Touilt sits on the edge of her bed, pushing her hair under a scarf. She twitches, scratches, and then cracks something between her thumbnails. "Bloody fleas. Are they never sated?"

"How are you feeling?"

"Much better. A case of tainted milk perhaps." Touilt never admits to anything except bad food as the root of any illness she suffers, for she thinks to do otherwise would be to bring into question her powers as a healer.

Wilona sets her baskets on the table. "I have trout, if you think it might tempt you."

"I might be able to eat a little." She smiles. "Or perhaps a little more than that."

"Roswitha's here. She says there's news."

"News? I've heard nothing of news." Scowling, Touilt wraps a shawl around her shoulders, her movements slow and deliberate.

Wilona sees nothing to be gained in pointing out that the definition of *news* is that you haven't heard it yet. She knows it both rankles and alarms the seithkona to consider her spirits have not sent advance warning.

Touilt stands and takes up her staff. She steps to the door and opens it. Wilona follows Touilt into the yard.

"Are you well, Lady Touilt?" says Roswitha.

"Wilona tells me you have news."

Roswitha nods. "A messenger from King Edwin." Her eyes sparkle with delight at being the bearer of royal tidings.

Wilona's stomach jumps. "Is it war again?"

"No, not war, but the king's coming. His entire court, the new queen, Ethelburga from Kent, and the baby, the queen's confessor, Biship Paulinus, they're all coming. We're to prepare with haste."

"So soon?"

"With the new moon in three weeks' time."

"He's coming early for the tax?" Touilt sits on the bench set in the sun. "Why now and not during Blood-Month? It's a hardship to hand over animals before the harvest slaughter."

"I don't think he's coming for tribute alone," says Roswitha.

Touilt sniffs. "With kings it's always either war or tribute."

"Ricbert's all flustered. The king's ordered an amphitheatre built in the Roman fashion, next to the temple."

"What can it mean?" Wilona picks up a basket of beans and begins shelling them, happy to have something to do with her fingers, for the news fills the air with restlessness.

"Edwin's always had Roman pretensions," says Touilt. "Trooping about the countryside with a standard-bearer before him. He caught the Roman disease when he was in exile in Rendlesham with King Raedwald ten years back. Marriage to Ethelburga was meant to bring peace with Kent, where they also drop a knee to Rome. Queen Ethelburga's priest, the follower of the White Christ, is Roman, is he not?"

Roswitha glances over her shoulder and fiddles with the belt at her thickening waist. "We must respect the king, Lady Touilt, even you. Edwin's an honourable king who's brought security and wealth to Northumbria. The countryside's safer now. You can travel to Bebbanburgh without fear of brigands."

Wilona runs her thumb along a bean pod and splits it. The beans are withered and she tosses them on the ground for the chickens. "And he's put gold and bronze drinking bowls at all the wells, I've heard," she says. "The traders say no one will steal them out of love of Edwin."

"Or fear of Edwin," Touilt says. "Can a man, even a king, claim the right to water? I thought Frige was goddess of the water."

Roswitha ignores this. "There's no word about what the

amphitheatre's for. I think Ricbert fears the king wants to replace him, and rumour has it he said as much to Lord Caelin, although what he might have done to offend the king he doesn't know."

Wilona considers the possibility of a new priest. Ricbert is a proud and prickly man, jealous of his position next to Caelin, but she's fond of him nonetheless. He's always been friendly to her and respectful of Touilt, asking about her health, sending his servant with small pots of thyme-infused honey, or a hen or hare, or a basket of plums or quince. "You say Paulinus, this Christ-priest from Rome, is coming with the king?" Wilona asks.

"He goes where the queen goes," Roswitha replies.

Touilt and Wilona glance at each other.

"Well, I must get back." Roswitha rubs her belly. "My husband will be wanting supper, and there's the patch to be weeded yet." She embraces Touilt and Wilona. "It'll be a busy time, so much to do, and as you say, Lady Touilt, out of season. The king cannot catch us unprepared."

"Surely not," says Touilt. "Kings and their court eat triple their own weight."

Later that evening, Touilt and Wilona lie in their beds, talking.

"I've paid this new religion little mind," Wilona says. "What do you know about it?" She props herself up on one elbow, and moves the stone oil lamp to the floor so it doesn't block her view of Touilt's face.

The air in the hut is sticky and Touilt leans back on a pile of furs, with only a light linen over her. "Christ is said to be the son of a god who lives in the sky—a god who cannot come to Middangeard himself but must send his messenger to impregnate a girl. Imagine. They worship a god who can't even do *that* himself. Do you know why we call him the White Christ? It's because he's a coward, a son with no honour. Aethelfrith the Fierce killed a thousand of his monks before the battle of Legaceaster. They wouldn't fight, or so I've heard. Let themselves be slaughtered like sheep, weaponless. Where's the honour in that? Where's the power of their god? This Christ let himself be hung upon a criminal-tree, but not of his own volition, like Woden when he climbed the holy tree as a sacrifice to gain knowledge. They say Christ was ordered there by the Roman chief and hung alongside thieves." Touilt shudders and draws her wrap tighter. "His followers have been in these lands for longer than my memory tells, but they've been few. What could Thunor have to fear from this milky shade? Still, these priests of his are aligned with Rome, and King Edwin is nothing if not ambitious." She rubs her eyes. "I must think, Wilona. I must think." And with that she turns to the wall.

The next afternoon, Wilona and Touilt are working in the field, filling their baskets with white carrots, cabbages, peas, onions, and beans. They bend and pluck and dig with their trowels and short-handled rakes, twisting frequently to ease their muscles, the earth working under their nails and into the creases of their palms. Now and again, Touilt closes her eyes and tilts her head this way and that, as if listening. The distant sound of hammers on wood comes from the great plain where the king's compound stands; the men are constructing the new amphitheatre. At last, Touilt stands and points to the great hill. Under a grey blanket of cloud, the ancient, long-deserted fort is no longer visible.

"Good," she says. "Looks like a nice pelting rain. That'll keep everyone away from our door." She picks up her basket. "Come along. It's time."

Wilona follows her across the field. In the pen attached to the house, the chickens squawk and flap. In a somewhat pushy squabble, they rush into their coop. Elba snuffles. Wilona tosses her a few white carrots and pats her, the bristles on the sow's back rough against her palm. "Good Elba. You'll be wallowing in some lovely mud soon." The air has a greenish, milky quality and Wilona wonders if it's a trick of the light only or something more. The door of the hut is open and Touilt calls for her to hurry in and close up.

While Wilona secures the door latch, Touilt uses one of the keys tied to her belt to open her chest, the lid creaking in protest. She pulls out her cushion of hen feathers, and the one she gave to Wilona the year before, shortly after her soul-sickness, when she also gave the girl a fine blue-wool cloak. Touilt hands the garment to Wilona now and reaches for her own cloak. In silence both women put them on. Wilona's is adorned at the throat by a bronze clasp in the shape of two owls; a pair of wolves' heads decorates the closing of Touilt's. The hoods are lined with cat fur, as are the brodekins they slip on their feet. The soft cloth's feel on Wilona's shoulders and neck, against the swell of her hip, is so luxurious she cannot help but smile. Touilt clears her throat and Wilona blushes. Touilt wraps her wolf pelt about her shoulders, the animal's head atop her own. Then the seithkona picks up her staff with rune stones on the knob and retrieves her drum and the tipper from her chest.

In the far corner of the room, behind a hanging, a ladder leads to a secret, sacred area, a platform high off the ground. All around this alcove the walls are blue, the colour of deep ice, and painted in the centre is the great tree Yggdrasil, surrounded by runes and drawings of wolves, bears, ravens, geese, and salmon.

When they've climbed this ladder before, Wilona carried up a low bench for Touilt to sit on, so Wilona sat lower, but now Touilt waves her hand, indicating it's not to be so today. Wilona's heart thumps. Touilt slowly nods, the faintest upturn to her lips. Today, Wilona ceases to be an apprentice; she shall henceforth be a partner. Now that the long-anticipated moment is here, she feels clumsy and inept. What if she fumbles or says the wrong words? Touilt watches her calmly. If Wilona doubts her abilities, she must trust in Touilt's.

Wilona's throat is tight. All the long hours of study—the names, uses, and habitat of medicinal plants; the sacred stories of the gods and heroes; the endless nights spent honing her skills at visualizing the spirit forms of wind, earth, water, and fire, that she might work with the elemental beings; learning the runes and their applications; memorizing the charms and rituals and songs—whirl like bright moths in her mind. She closes her eyes and listens to the rain hitting the thatch. For an instant she sees the faces of a woman and man, her mother and father. She almost cries out, but they are gone. She opens her eyes and feels not only the binding of all she has learned but also the support of her ancestors. They have watched over her and are proud.

Touilt climbs the ladder. She hands Wilona the drum and tipper, and Wilona follows. Touilt sits down with her back against the drawing of the great tree Yggdrasil, and it seems as if she's growing out of the tree itself, or perhaps the tree grows out of her. Touilt points and Wilona puts her cushion down, her hands trembling only slightly, and sits facing Touilt. The seithkona brings out the rune stones while Wilona lights the lamp. The drumming begins, and the singing . . . the air grows still . . . all things fall away . . . the women sing together, focusing their intention on the lamp's flame. Before long Wilona feels the owl's presence—the soft sweep of Raedwyn's wings behind her, lifting her, taking her along the root of the great tree down to the place where future and past and present combine, where things are shown as they are, without the distracting garments of Middangeard . . . slip-slide, sloping ride, swift and sure, wind and feather, wild and pure . . .

The light is dazzling, no colour at all, so bright it isn't even white. She wants to turn away, but the light is all around. She begins to make out shapes—a hill, a great stone—and in the distance women are wailing, their grief rending the light, so that the ordinary dullness of day seeps in. Blood oozes from a stone. Tree roots wither, black and rotten . . .

. . . More noise. Terrible cracking and the ring of metal against wood. A mist lifts and on the other side a circle of men wield axes. The ground shudders and ripples. The men with axes attack the oaks. Each stroke cuts deeper into the tree-flesh and the limbs quiver, the moss shakes, wood chips fly like scraps of skin.

. . . Wilona smells salt, and although she's never seen the sea, she recognizes the rolling rush of noise as breakers crashing against rocks. She's in a great hall in a high place. Birds roost in the rafters at either end, away from the hearth-fire's smoke. Women stand in small groups near the wall, flagons of ale at hand. Men sit at long benches forming a U-shape around the hearth, with a raised dais before them, at which sits King Edwin on his throne. His cloak sparkles with precious stones, and

a golden buckle graces his belt. His long, light-brown hair falls straight across his shoulders and his forehead is wide over a pale knot of brow. The whites of his deep-set eyes are visible all round the mousey irises, as though he's holding his eyes open, trying to see everything at once, convinced perhaps that things are being hidden from him. They are not eyes Wilona wants turned on her. A scraggly beard, which doesn't cover the hollows beneath his cheekbones, frame his thin lips. Coifi, the king's Druid priest, stands near the king and addresses a strange man—also a priest in white robes, a tall man with a slight stoop, tonsured oddly, with a ring of black hair all round and a shaved crown, a beardless face, and a narrow, aquiline nose. This man is calm, while Coifi's agitation is palpable—his arms raised over his head, spittle flying from his lips . . . no words, just the sound of wind and waves . . .

. . . Something thumps and cracks, rhythmically. Caelin with an enormous axe, chopping at the roots of a great white tree. He stops, turns, sniffs the air like a hound. Wilona knows he's looking for her, and then he fixes on her and comes toward her, leering, dragging the red-stained axe . . .

. . . From behind her, Raedwyn shrieks, piercing as a dagger. It rattles her heart-cage, as if she's been struck by the great talons . . . trying to knock her from the oncoming rush of slaughtering riders, from Lord Caelin's hungry axe . . .

The drum beat slows now and the singing quiets. Raedwyn's scent, like the heather-strewn moors, dissipates; his presence recedes. Slowly, Wilona returns to herself, her feet dead stones from sitting so long. She unfolds her legs and rubs her ankles to bring the blood back. She winces. The pain is like needles. The night is thick around them and the lamp has burned low. She wonders how many hours have passed. To judge from the silence, the rain has stopped. Her head feels as though elves are hammering on it with sharp stones, right behind her eyes, and she's faintly nauseated. Her hands tremble. What did the vision mean? At first she feels only a dreadful menace, as when she wakes in the middle of the night from black dreams of dead bodies and a woman's clawing hands, as still she does sometimes. Then, slowly, the images return to her: the oak grove, the axe, the hall, and the king—the strange cold light, yes, that too. Caelin. The axe. The tree. She frowns and bites her lip. She breathes deeply and looks at Touilt.

After a few more minutes, Touilt opens her eyes. "Help me, Wilona. My limbs don't obey as they once did."

Wilona rises, not without some stiffness herself, and helps the older woman. It takes a while to get Touilt on her feet. The seith-kona's pulse races beneath Wilona's fingers and her skin is clammy. "Come, we'll get you to your bed before we talk."

It's not easy to manoeuvre the ladder, and once Touilt almost falls. At last they have the sacred objects back in their locked chest and Touilt's in bed, piled high with blankets. In spite of the warm night it's a while before her teeth stop rattling. She sips an infusion Wilona has brewed.

"Are you in pain?" Wilona sits on a stool beside the bed.

"No more than usual after riding the wolf."

"The tea will ease it. Shall we wait, then, to talk?"

Touilt lowers her cup. "We must talk now. But first, tend to the fire."

Wilona takes a prickly bough from a basket near the storage area. Soon the sharp, clean scent of juniper fills the hut, the smoke wafting to the rafters. Outside, a fox yaps in the wood and an owl hoots. Two white moths flit near the flames and at last succeed in immolating themselves with a sharp hiss.

"Tell me what you saw," says Touilt.

Wilona recalls the vision as best she can. ". . . and I was filled with a nightmare feeling. I saw Lord Caelin with an axe, striking the roots of Yggdrasil." She shudders. "Have I misread the signs?"

Touilt presses her thumbs into the hollows above her eyes, near her nose. "No. You didn't misread them." Touilt looks up and folds her arms across her chest, rocking slightly. "In your vision, did Caelin see you?"

Wilona's mouth is lined with dust. "Yes. He came toward me when my owl called me back." She pulls at a broken piece of fingernail and it rips too close to the quick. She brushes the blood away with her finger.

Touilt grunts and a shadow passes over her face. "We'll talk no more tonight. I must be still. Tomorrow there are charms to make."

The older woman is silent after that, although Wilona doesn't think she's sleeping. Wilona's mind keeps circling back to the expression on Lord Caelin's face as he came for her. Just then, lying there in the dark, Wilona does not want to be a seithkona. She does not want dreams and premonitions, does not want obligations to the gods. It's ungrateful not to want to repay the gods. They have given her many gifts. She could well have died out on the moors, or she might have died at Caelin's hand when she arrived here, or become a slave in the hall, subject to the whim and desire of every man. Roswitha pops into her mind, ripe with pregnancy, in love with Dunstan, a simple girl with a simple life. The green worm of envy burrows into her breast. No life is without danger, and life is precarious for everyone, but to go through a single day without the never-ending prodding of the spirits, their demands, their enigmatic omens . . . Like a child, she wants to cry out, "It isn't fair!" She runs her hands across her abdomen as a cramp twists inside her. Tomorrow she'll have her moon-time. She lets the heat of her palms warm her skin. Touilt must still be in pain; she's restless, moving so the hay in the mattress rustles, and now and again she groans softly. Wilona prays to Eostre that Touilt might be granted rest.

The king and his court will be here soon. She must trust the gods. She pillows her head on her bent arm and tries to breathe slowly, but every few minutes her eyes open and she finds herself staring into the hearth-embers.

The next morning, Wilona wakes to find Touilt has already cleaned the hearth and built a fresh fire of apple wood.

"You should have woken me up," says Wilona, wiping the sleep from her eyes.

"I don't sleep much these days and you needed the rest. Now, go and find a rowan tree in fruit. I know it's early, but the tree by the meadow's edge is in full sun and should be ready. We need red fruit. Find a branch that leans toward the south, shake it, and gather four berries. Bring them to me, along with four leaves."

Wilona runs to use the netty and then splashes water on her face and hands at the well, uttering a prayer, for it would not do to gather medicine unclean. She finds the tree and when she returns Touilt takes the berries. She casts one into the flames, along with one of its leaves, saying, "Goodness is mine, just like this tree, beware the flames I cast at thee." Then she takes the second berry, and a leaf, saying, "Knowledge is mine, as of this tree; beware the flames I cast at thee." And with the third, "Strength is mine, just like this tree; beware the flames I cast at thee." She then takes several strands of hair that were wrapped in a little cloth inside her pouch and puts them, with the fourth leaf and fruit, into an iron pot. She roasts them over the fire until they're dry and black, the hair sizzled away to nothing.

"Lord Caelin's hair?" Wilona asks.

"One never knows when one shall need such things," says Touilt, staring at the pot. "I keep my eyes open. Found these the night Elfhild gave birth."

When the berry and leaf are cooled, Touilt wraps them in a red cloth and, with Wilona's help, buries it near their threshold. "This should protect the house and us from whatever evil has sickened Caelin. We shall trust the spirits. I'd place a charm near him, but it's too dangerous."

Touilt does not need to elaborate. A charge of witchcraft could mean death.

Chapter EIGHT

Servants and slaves run back and forth, scattering the chickens and geese. The air is full of dust and shouting and the smell of manure. Servants seat the ladies of the court in carts lined with bolsters and shaded with brightly coloured awnings so they will be neither jostled nor overly warm on this fine day. Other carts are packed high with things the court cannot, apparently, live without: glassware and silver platters, fine clothing and tapestries, pillows stuffed with eider feathers, flagons of wine, and sweetmeats. The king's companions are already on their horses, and the beasts stamp and toss their heads. The craftsmen usually in charge of this section of the fortress—carpenters, metal workers, masons, and weavers—keep to the doorways of their workshops, well out of the way of flashing hooves and irritable noblemen. Egan, having already packed his meagre possessions, does the same.

Little Hild, the king's ward and great-niece, waves at him from her seat beside her mother, Breguswyth. Her father, Hereric, one of Edwin's chief nobles, was poisoned by Cerdic of Elmet, a rival king, with whom Hereric had taken refuge while Edwin was in exile. The first thing Edwin did when he regained his throne was to invade Elmet. He blood-eagled Cerdic himself, cutting the man's lungs out of his back and laying them on his shoulders like bloody wings.

Recalling the story, Egan shudders, crosses himself, and shakes the image out of his head. The unpredictable storms and horrors of war, so far outside the laws of Christ, frighten him. He smiles and waves back at the freckled, pug-nosed little imp. Hers is a spirit of unbridled enthusiasm and she is always off somewhere at a gallop. It's no wonder she's excited. Bishop Paulinus baptized Hild and her mother earlier in the year, and Hild has taken to Christianity with a vibrant devotion. The child bounces up and down in the cart. Her mother utters a sharp word and Hild sits and smooths her tunic. Egan smiles. It will be hard to mould Hild to the life of a peace-weaver princess. He wonders if she might one day hear the call and devote herself to monastic life. The Lord Christ would make good use of such a bright flame.

He rubs his temples. The day is barely begun and already he has a headache. From Bebbanburgh to Ad Gefrin is not far. If he was permitted to go alone, Egan could travel it in less than half a day, instead of the two days it will surely take with all this pomp and foolishness. He had, in fact, begged the bishop to let him go alone, but he'd timed his request badly.

Egan had found the bishop playing nine-men-morris with Coifi, the king's Druid priest, recently converted to Christianity. The board was set on the table between them, the fire danced merrily, and a young man sat on a stool by the hearth, playing softly on a lyre. Paulinus rose and glowered at Egan, telling him there had better be a good reason for the interruption. Coifi, a stout badger of a man whose nose was at that moment even redder than usual, refilled his glass of wine, ignoring Egan completely.

"Your lordship," Egan stammered, "Might I not go ahead and meet the people of Ad Gefrin? I speak their language, and perhaps I could set the groundwork for you and the king, opening hearts and allaying any fears a large deputation might invoke?"

Bishop Paulinus looked down his great beak of a nose. "Are you saying, Brother, that a bishop of Christ would frighten the people?"

"Certainly not, your lordship. It's just with all the court—"

"Ah, then perhaps you're implying the king's subjects don't love him and will not welcome him with open arms?"

Coifi at last seemed to take an interest in the conversation. He put the glass down and chuckled. "Insolence!"

"No, no, of course not," said Egan. "King Edwin is the most beloved of kings and deservedly so—"

"Then clearly, you're saying you're better suited to deliver the good news of Christ's message than either of us?"

Egan thought he might faint. "Forgive me."

The bishop, looming above Egan like a stork over a minnow, was silent for the longest time. Egan's legs were flimsy as boiled cabbage leaves.

"Paulinus, we've a game to finish here," said Coifi.

"Get out," said the bishop. "And pray to God that you might understand your place in the world, Brother Egan."

Egan backed out. Obedience. This is, he told himself, a lesson in obedience. As he shut the door, Paulinus said, presumably to Coifi, "That sanctimonious cur. I can't bear him around me much longer." As Egan slunk away, Coifi said something he couldn't quite catch, but he thought he heard the name "James."

For a while, Egan feared he might be left behind entirely, but now, at last, the procession is ready to depart for Ad Gefrin and he's among the company. Paulinus and Coifi ride identical grey stallions, their bridles adorned with silver and their manes braided with ribbon. Earlier in the day, a stable boy informed Egan he was to be given a roan mare to ride. Egan had declined, and the boy tried insisting, but Egan was politely firm.

Even now, watching the bishop and the newly converted priest on such fine horses, Egan struggles not to let his distaste show. The procession moves beyond the gate, and Egan falls in step with the cooks, servants, and slaves.

Chapter
NINE

As the new moon approaches, the village is in a frenzy of preparation. The king's feasting hall has been swept from top to bottom, spiders and mice banished, hangings beaten, paint refreshed, wicks trimmed, mattresses re-stuffed, bedding aired, furs and pillows set out for the comfort of the king. The thatch has been repaired, the exteriors whitewashed, the tapestries hung, and the lamps filled with oil. The king will bring tents with him, but Caelin and Elfhild are expected to provide comforts fit for the royal household, including servants and grooms for the horses. Feeding and caring for the royal mounts is a heavy burden. Livestock have been rounded up into the great enclosure and animals slaughtered before their time—pigs and cattle, hens and geese.

The new amphitheatre, constructed to the specifications of the king's builder, is impressive, if plain. There's been no time for decorative flourishes. It stands behind the royal quarters and temple buildings, where during Blood-Month Ricbert sacrifices garlanded cattle, horses, swine, and sometimes wild goats to the gods. A totem pole stands there, guarding the nearby graves of the village's recently dead, just as an ancient one guards the old graveyard at the end of the great enclosure. The amphitheatre is the shape of a large wedge, with stepped platforms rising from the ground in a semicircle, the first of which seats ten men, the next fifteen, and so on, until, on the topmost bench, thirty good-sized men may sit side by side. In front of the lowest step is a half-moon dais with a high wall all around and a canopy above so that whoever sits upon the chair will be protected from inclement weather.

There is great speculation about the king's speech, and why it was so important the amphitheatre be built just so. Wilona walks around it and tries to determine what its placement signifies. She's watched the royal builder checking the line from the great mountain, through the ancient burial place and the king's hall in one direction, to the temple of the gods and the cemetery in the other. Whoever sits in that chair will face east, the mountain behind him, as though the light of the dawning sun and the new day is before him, while the weight of the past backs him. She runs her hands over the oak beams and smooth-planed planks but discerns nothing more than warm wood. She walks to the dais and nods to one of Lord Caelin's companions, who stands guard.

"Forgive me, Lady, but you're not permitted here." He is roughly her age. His eyes look over her head, past her. He's scratched a pimple on his cheek and inflamed it.

"And why shouldn't I draw near a vacant seat? I don't wish to desecrate the place that will soon cradle the royal buttocks. I only wish to admire the craftsmanship."

"It's not permitted." He shifts a bit from side to side. No one likes to deny a seithkona what she wants, even a young one; it may bring bad fortune.

"May I simply stand beside you then . . . What's your name? Garth, isn't it?"

"It is, Lady Wilona."

"Well, you see, we're old friends already. May I just stand near you and observe this wondrous, forbidden object?"

He glances left and right. "Be quick then."

"As a summer storm."

The chair, like the amphitheatre, is oak, with a high curved back and broad armrests carved with Woden's sun wheel. Good. And there, in the middle of the chair back is the hammer of Thunor. Wait—or is it? She squints. No, it is not. It's been inverted; a cross, not a hammer, the sign of the criminal tree Touilt told her about, on which the Christian god died. She peers at the armrests. No, not quite sun wheel, either, not quite Woden's symbol of life and death, because there at the uppermost spoke is a strange symbol, a loop within the circle, an arc turned sideways, like the crook on a shepherd's staff. She turns back and faces the rising seats. The temple is hidden, completely. Not even the totem post guarding the dead is visible.

"You have to go now," says the guard. "Quick."

"With pleasure." Her voice is surly. "My thanks, Garth." He doesn't answer. Then she sees Lord Caelin and Cena, one of his closest companions, striding across the field directly toward her. Caelin's face is a black cloud.

"*You*, girl!"

She freezes like a hare and drops her head, remembering Caelin's hand around Touilt's neck. Her own throat constricts. His boots sound on the planks. She glances up in time to see him backhand young Garth.

"Did I not say no one is allowed here?" Garth mumbles something. "You're not worthy of my trust. Go to the pigsties. Send someone else."

Garth runs, and Caelin takes two steps toward her. It's all she can do not to scramble backwards. She doesn't dare raise her eyes.

"What are you doing here?"

"It wasn't Garth's fault, my lord, I was only curious—"

"Not his fault? Why? Did you put some charm upon him?" Caelin cracks his knuckles. It sounds like snapping bones.

"No, Lord. I saw no harm—"

He steps closer, so close his beard hangs in her face. She smells his yeasty breath. "Since the first day you came here, I sensed something unwholesome in you, girl. I let Touilt keep you because she's been of value to us and, with no slave of her own, I thought you might be useful. But you hold yourself too high, too high by far. I saw you at the spring rites. You flaunt yourself."

Wilona's mouth opens and, in surprise, she meets Caelin's gaze. How could he think she acts immodestly? That look she saw on his face at the spring rites—she knows it now. Hunger, as a falcon gazes at a mouse, but more personal. His eyes spark with it. Anger. Those cracking knuckles. The desire to break bones. But *why*? Why does she anger him?

"Oh, I saw you." He takes a strand of her hair between his thumb and forefinger and rubs it, then quickly tugs it hard, making her head snap back. "I think you put what Touilt teaches you to your own dark purposes. I can put an end to that. I can put an end to *you*, if I choose."

"I'm your humble servant, Lord, nothing more." Her voice is a ragged whisper.

Cena clears his throat. "There are other options, my lord."

"Indeed. Perhaps she might serve us better in the hall, much better."

With a *whoosh* she senses the flash of wing and feather above her and behind. Raedwyn. Understanding flows through her in an instant. Apart from Touilt, whose years protect her from the desires of men, Wilona is the only unmarried woman in the village who is truly beyond Caelin's reach, and for some reason he has developed a fixation with her. She cannot imagine why, not with all the pretty girls in the village, all the slaves and serving women to choose from. But he is lord, and accustomed to getting anything he wants, whenever he wants. Pride then, at least as much as passion. An image comes to her of a grass snake she had seen near the riverbed, with a weasel nearby. It played dead, flipping onto its back, its mouth open, staying limp and seemingly lifeless even when the weasel pawed at it. The weasel soon lost interest and wandered away, and the snake quickly returned to life. She'll be the snake.

"My lord," she says, smiling as sweetly as she can, given the cramping fear in her belly, "I'll gladly serve you wherever and however you desire. I only ask you allow me to serve the gods as well. You are beloved of the gods, as your good fortune evidences. Let me continue to make offerings and prayers on your behalf, as Lady Touilt instructs me." She scratches her head, as though fleas are bothering her. Let him think she's no challenge. She imagines Raedwyn circling his head, cooling Caelin's ardour with his wings.

Caelin looks at her for a moment and then sharply, painfully taps her three times in the middle of her forehead with his finger. "Mind yourself, little stranger. I've my eye on you."

"I'm honoured, my lord, and will make an offering for the success of the king's visit."

Caelin has already turned away, toward the new guard running across the field. "Don't defy me, if you value your life."

Cena leans toward her and says, softly, "Good advice that, my young friend. Perhaps it's time to take a protector."

"The goddess protects me," she says, "as does my lord."

Cena chuckles, and although Wilona wants to run as fast as she can, she knows she mustn't let Caelin know he's frightened her. She is seithkona. If she's worthy of that title, she must trust the gods. She walks away with her back straight.

Chapter
TEN

Halfway to Ad Gefrin, Egan walks at the back of the procession with the servants and gamesmen, the lesser guards and craftsmen. There is a noisy, celebratory air to the group, and tumblers and musicians entertain the noblemen and women at the head of the line. The pace has lagged slightly and Egan has a clearer view of the bishop now. Next to his lordship rides a young monk, the newest member of his retinue. His back is straight as a sword, his hand rests on his thigh with the nonchalant ease of one accustomed to horseback. His eyes are blue and merry, his fine pale hair tonsured in the Roman fashion, and his robes are of dyed wool. His cheeks are wind-blushed. His white teeth flash when he smiles.

It's a glorious day and enormous white clouds rise overhead like towers in the robin's egg sky. Hawks wheel in the high drafts. Purple heather carpets the hills and the breeze is heady with honey. Egan tries to concentrate on the light, which glows so brightly here, reminding him of God's glory and putting his own insignificant concerns into perspective. Still, his eyes repeatedly drift to the bishop and the young monk. Paulinus seems at ease with his new companion, in a way he has never been with Egan. Even now they're sharing some joke and throwing back their heads, laughing. A small thorn pricks Egan's heart. He used to laugh with Father Bresal like that, watching the otter kits frolic and play, watching the gulls squabbling over some tidbit, watching the lambs gambol. He cannot recall Paulinus ever even smiling at him. From the first moment they met, the bishop regarded the Irish monk with distaste. Unlike the monk now at Paulinus's side, Egan lacks the gift of elegant manners. Father Bresal said his coming here was a great opportunity, and that he would bring much honour to the community. But what plan can God possibly have for him here in this role to which he is so clearly unsuited?

A middle-aged woman leading a donkey laden with baskets full of clanking cooking pots draws next to him. Her cheeks are stained with a network of red veins and a wen mars her forehead. Egan recognizes her as Ida, a woman with an ear for gossip.

"Blessings on you, Sister Ida."

"And on you, Brother. It's a grand day for a mucking about in the hills and would be grander still if they'd let us stop for a bite to eat, I'm thinking."

"Indeed, but we'll be in Ad Gefrin shortly."

"Aye. And then there'll be no end of palaver before we see a morsel of bread. Fine for them." She jabs her chin toward the front of the procession.

"Might I ask . . . do you happen to know who that is riding with Bishop Paulinus?"

"You don't know?" The gleam in her eye tells Egan that now she has more gossip to spread. The monk from Ioua Insula has no knowledge . . .

"It was such a busy time, getting ready for the journey."

"Right enough. Well . . ." She leans in. "That's Brother James from Eoforwic, come at the express call of the bishop himself, I'm told."

Eoforwic, where there are plans to build a fine cathedral. The king and his retinue will, after leaving Ad Gefrin, travel through the kingdom teaching the people of Christ's message and baptizing them. The journey will end at the king's seat in Eoforwic. For the first time, Egan wonders if he might be permitted to go back to the monastery, rather than accompany them. *If it be Your will, my Lord.* "Ah, I see," he says.

"I'll bet you do," says Ida.

Brother Egan has the uncomfortable feeling that, once again, he knows nothing at all.

Chapter
ELEVEN

AD GEFRIN

Strangers mill everywhere and pitch tents past the royal buildings. Stalls are hastily erected and craftsmen and women barter their wares—iron tools and fine textiles, beads of amber and of glass, drinking cups bound with silver, wine from distant lands, brooches, strange smelling spices. Others have set up booths offering ale, bread, and cheese. There is even a man trading slaves.

The squabbling, raucous voices, speaking several languages—the tongue of the northern tribes, the dialects from the south—the lowing of the beasts, the banging of hammers and *screeing* of saws and pole lathes, in short, all the general hubbub of a village swollen far past its normal numbers, combine to grate against Wilona's already exposed nerves. The wildflowers on the plain have been trampled underfoot. The smell from the midden heaps, which some have obviously chosen to use as a netty, mingles with the smell of the frightened livestock. Her dark mood must show, for a woman gestures to her, offering some pretty baubles, but when Wilona glances her way she falls immediately silent and drops her eyes.

She tries to decide if she should tell Touilt about her exchange with Lord Caelin. She needs the older woman's protection more than ever now, but Touilt warned her against going to the amphitheatre. She may punish her for being too bold. If she could come back to Touilt with some useful information, it might lessen her disapproval. She makes a decision then and heads across the plain, toward the temple buildings, hoping to find Lord Ricbert. He is, after all, the one who interceded for her when Caelin nearly lost patience during her soul-sickness, and he has a great deal to lose if the king puts a new priest in his place. He might prove a useful ally.

As she nears his dwelling, the high priest, his hair thin as dandelion tufts on the breeze, shuffles round the side of the building, his arms full of kindling. She runs to him.

"Lord Ricbert, where's your servant? Let me help you." She reaches to take the bundle and he hands it over without protest.

The old man can be hard and bitter as an old hazelnut shell, but Wilona feels affection in spite, or perhaps even because, of his gruff ways. He has little patience for fools, and holds the world at bay with a sharp eye. She thinks of it as a talent.

"You're a kind girl. Set it inside near the fire if you will." He sits on a bench by the wall and closes his eyes. "You'd think that at my age carrying wood would no longer be required, wouldn't you?"

"Where's Aloc, then?"

"I sent him to cut reeds for the thatch. There's yet another hole." He snorts. "A single servant. And I'm Caelin's priest."

She carries the kindling inside and comes back, slapping splinters off her palms. "Lord Ricbert, may I speak candidly?"

He pats the seat next to him. "Sit. Unburden yourself." He tilts his face away so she might speak her mind freely, without his gaze upon her.

"Do you know why the king visits us?"

"Because it pleases him to do so."

"What do you make of *that*?" She juts her chin in the direction of the amphitheatre, which blocks their view of the royal hall.

"Quite the structure."

"You once had a view of the royal hall, but this new amphitheatre comes between you and the king."

Ricbert inhales deeply. "So it has." It doesn't sound as though he's surprised.

"What does Woden tell you?" she asks.

Ricbert chuckles softly. "What makes you think old Slouch Hat tells me anything?"

Wilona's head snaps round. The old priest's expression is slightly amused, his eyes crinkling, but there's sorrow in his countenance as well.

"But he must speak to you. You're the priest."

"So I am. And yet." He bends down and picks up a small pebble, tosses it into the grass, where it falls silently. "And yet."

"Forgive me if I'm impudent, but surely I misunderstand you. You cannot mean that Woden . . . that he doesn't . . . You are faithful . . ."

"Wilona, listen to me. Just now I'm very tired, for the faithful service I give the gods demands more energy than this old body has today. In short, you've caught me at a moment when I'm not inclined to dissemble. And so, since it seems important to you, I shall, this once, speak without a veil on my words, for I haven't the strength to hold up even the flimsiest of cloths. Ask me again tomorrow and I'll deny it. Is that clear? So. You want to know what Woden, the Ancient Father of Men, tells me about the future, what guidance he gives me. I tell you this: I've spent my whole life in His service, and never, not once, have I heard His voice, nor have I felt His hand upon me. My whole life, do you understand? Why have I neither heard a word nor felt His touch? Because there is nothing to hear, nothing to feel. If ever He lived, He lives no more." He closes his eyes and recites from the ancient poem of prophesy, "*Brothers will fight and kill each other, sisters' children will defile kinship. It is harsh in the world, whoredom rife—an axe age, a sword age—shields are riven—a wind age, a wolf age—before the world goes headlong.*" He opens his eyes. "Ragnarok, Wilona, the Twilight of the Gods. Surely we've lived through it, or are in the midst of it, or are entering into it. What does it matter, when Woden's silent as the icy depths of Hel."

She feels as though all the air has rushed out of her lungs. *How can he believe such things?* And then, there in the back of his eyes, simmering on a low flame, Wilona senses an old loneliness, an old soul-grief, both the burning and the cold embers. Shadows flit about him. He frightens her, yet her instinct is to soothe him, to tell him he's wrong, the world is not dying, the gods are still powerful.

"The power of the gods is all around us, Lord. Look to the sky, the wind, the earth, the beasts, the spirits of the woods—"

"Don't presume to lecture me on the sacred, Wilona."

"No. I didn't mean . . . forgive me."

His eyes flash beneath the bushy white brows. "You think power comes from unseen forces?" He raises an eyebrow and then chuckles. "You look like an otter kit caught in a trap. Don't worry, I'm not going to eat you. You don't have a subtle mind. I'd hoped for better."

On the inside of her wrist her heartbeat flutters like the wing of a panicked moth.

He presses his bloodless lips together. "There's no power other than what we forge for ourselves. There's no charm except for intellect and cunning."

"You deny the power of wyrd?" She makes the sign of Thunor.

"Fate and time, fate and time. All nonsense. Utter nonsense." His voice is a little louder, a little more strident than Wilona expects, almost as though he's protesting so strongly in order to cover up some other emotion—fear, disappointment? "I put my faith in a strong alliance, in a debt owed, a favour recalled." He shakes his head. "Wilona, you should not put your faith in the gods so strongly. Be a willow, not an oak. Bend. Don't break. Beware of unshakeable faith, especially if it puts you in the path of a powerful man's displeasure."

Wilona's face burns. "Why is Lord Caelin so displeased with me?"

"Lucky for you, Caelin's eye rarely settles on anything very long, but be careful, Wilona, you don't cause it to linger by any sign of defiance. That has a way of intensifying passion." He looks at her thoughtfully. "It would be better if you had another friend. Remember, be a willow, Wilona."

She wants to ask more, but Aloc appears along the path, a basket full of reeds on his back. "I've taken too much of your time, Lord." She stands and brushes off her tunic. "I'm grateful for your counsel and in your debt."

"There's no debt, since I'm sure my counsel is seed spread on fallow ground. Still, my conscience is clear. I tried." Ricbert stands as well and rubs his knees. "Good day to you, Wilona, and give my regards to your mistress." With that he disappears into the dark temple.

Wilona's head spins and her heart drags as she makes her way through the throng toward the village. She sidesteps a flock of sheep driven by a young boy with the high topknot and small bones of the northern people. The sheep bleat and protest the stick at their back.

She doesn't know what to think. Even Ricbert's noticed Caelin's antagonism toward her, if it can be called that. But that's not nearly as distressing as Ricbert's apparent lack of faith. If Ricbert had exposed his private parts to her, she could not have been more shocked. Surely he's merely exhausted and worried, and has convinced himself of the worst so, should he be disappointed yet again, the pain won't be so great. To devote your entire life to the gods and receive nothing in return? Unthinkable. Either Ricbert has angered the gods in some way, so that they've removed their favour, or he's lying. But what would be the point? Does he want to shake her own faith in order to undermine her power? If so, he's wasting his time. No one can take her experience from her. She has felt what she has felt, heard what she has heard, seen what she has seen. She has Raedwyn. He comes to her. That's a fact. She's ridden the visions. This, too, is a fact.

But as Ricbert spoke it didn't seem as though he was trying to weaken her. Wilona senses no lies in him, and as someone with owl-sight, she trusts her intuition. No, if he's lying, it's not for her sake. He appeared, if anything, petulant, disappointed, and hurt, as though he wanted to punish the gods for their silence. Or perhaps he's afraid of what the king is bringing with him. This seems the most plausible. If he's to be replaced, if he's to be cast out, then it makes some perverse sense that he's tried to convince himself there's nothing to lose. She chews her lip. It's alarming to see a man with power and position be so frightened that, like a child, he'd sulk and pout and turn away from a beloved object for fear it will be snatched away by another.

"Wilona! Wilona!" Dunstan comes toward her, carrying a stack of wooden trays.

"Be hale, Dunstan. You look happy, but forgive me; I'm not in the mood for chatter."

"What? Grumpy as an old bear on such a fine day, with all of Northumbria come to see the king and feast? Need a tonic, do you? Perhaps a purgative?" He winks. "Well, you're in luck. I know a woman makes such remedies . . ."

"Truly, I've no patience for joking."

Dunstan, his wild hair floating in the breeze, and one of his socks drooping over his shoes, turns serious. "So I see. What's the trouble?" He puts the trays on the ground, kneels, and looks up at her while tucking his stocking into a leg-binding.

It won't do to talk about Lord Ricbert, or Lord Caelin. Although she's hollow and confused, she can't drag Dunstan into a conflict with Caelin—he's not strong enough to be an ally—and Ricbert's words were meant for her ears only. "I'm worried, Dunstan. Why is the king coming out of season? What's this strange thing he's built? I hear it's in the Roman fashion. Doesn't it seem our king is over-fond of all things Roman?"

"Hush, Wilona." His eyes dart to the people near them, but he keeps a pleasant smile on his face. In a low tone he says, "Will you never learn to practise discretion?" And then, more loudly, "Yes, we're greatly honoured to have the king visit us."

They walk along the path near the great enclosure where Lord Caelin's companions are rounding up the livestock into pens for slaughter. Everyone who's travelled from the vast corners of the estate, and beyond, has brought tribute with them, grain, precious metal, or livestock. The number of mouths to feed is staggering.

"If the king comes again in Blood-Month and asks for his annual tithe, we'll have a hungry winter," says Wilona. The path is steep and she steps sideways to keep her footing.

"Is this what's bothering you?"

"That, and certain rumours on the wind."

"Why pay attention to gossip? The world's full of things to fret about, and most never come to pass."

It is quieter in the village, especially since most of the men and women are either in the workshops, in the fields, or up at the compound with the rest. Wilona can breathe deeply here, away from the tumult. "I can't help it, Dunstan. I fear the demands of the king."

"It's our duty to serve our lord. Northumbria's a great nation now. Who else but Edwin could have brought together the two kingdoms of Deira and Bernicia?"

"Kingdoms don't stay stitched together though, do they?" She pats his arm. "You are loyal."

Dunstan chuckles. "And yet somehow that doesn't sound like a compliment."

"I don't deny the kingdom's well ruled, for the moment. And King Edwin is deserving of our fealty and tribute, but I don't like this talk of new religion." They take the hard-packed path to Touilt's hut, the great yew tree a beacon, the sound of the river audible now that the wind has shifted.

"It's only the chatter of gossips."

"I'm not persuaded."

"Then I suppose you must worry." He shrugs. "And I must leave you to it. I have to get these trays to Caelin's cooks and have already taken too long. I'm sorry you're unsettled." He gestures at the roof. "Your thatch is wearing thin on the north side. Why don't I fix that?" Dunstan likes easily fixable problems.

Two days later, Wilona is sitting on the bench in the yard, plucking a hen. Touilt is inside, grinding dried herbs for her potions. Wilona thinks she'll have to mix more daub in the next few weeks and patch the chinks. She rubs her back against the wall, scratching a flea bite. She must change the bedding as well, and make sure the lavender and tansy are fresh to keep the little monsters at bay.

When Wilona told Touilt what had passed between her and Lord Caelin, the seithkona had gone dead still for a moment and then her hand had flashed out and caught Wilona across the jaw. She still bears the bruise. It wasn't the first time Touilt had struck her, and Wilona took it as a sign of how serious the matter is. Later that day, Touilt came to her with an amulet carved on one side with water flowing around a rock, and on the other certain words in the old tongue. She told Wilona to wear it next to her skin, to tell no one, and to be sure she does nothing to draw Caelin's attention.

"You must be as a wisp of smoke in the corner, invisible, of no consequence."

Now, a noise catches Wilona's attention. A young boy lollops down the path. He's one of Maccus the bone-worker's brood, whose names she never can keep straight. This one is eight or nine perhaps, small-boned like his mother but with his father's broad nose and mouth. He skids and his feet go out from under him, his palms slipping along the dirt and pebbles behind him, but he bounces up, laughing. It can only mean one thing. She shades her eyes and stares into the east toward a telltale dust cloud. Touilt appears in the doorway, blinking in the bright light. Wilona points at the approaching boy.

"And so," Touilt says, brushing the dust from her palm. "The king has arrived."

The boy slides to a halt in front of the women, his arms wheeling, his chest heaving. He bends over and puts his hands on his knees, his mouth open. "The king," he pants.

It would be unkind to deprive him of his moment and so Touilt and Wilona wait, their faces feigning curiosity.

"The king," he starts again, straightening. "Ladies." He bows, remembering his manners at last. "Lord Caelin and Lady Elfhild send me to announce the coming of the king and his court. As honoured seeresses and healers, beloved of the lord and lady, you are invited to the greeting ceremony, which will take place at the approach to the royal compound."

"Tell Lord Caelin and Lady Elfhild they honour us and we will, of course, attend," Touilt says. "You've done your duty well, boy."

The child's face breaks into a wide grin, and he turns to dash off, but then stops, shakes his head, and blushing, bows to them. "You're gracious, ladies. Now, by your leave."

"Off you go," says Wilona, frowning, so that he doesn't see her mirth.

He scrambles up the path, feet kicking pebbles.

Lord Caelin. "Perhaps I shouldn't go," says Wilona.

"You'll displease Caelin more with your absence. It's not wise to refuse an invitation from one's lord. Put your faith in the gods,

Wilona. Come, it's too warm for the cape, but I'll wear the blue tunic and you'll draw a bind-rune on my forehead."

Wilona arranges a single braid down Touilt's back and two along-side her face, then sets small bronze amulets and two tufts of fur from the tail of a wolf into the hair. She helps her into the blue tunic and the wolf-figure shoulder clasps. Around her guardian's neck she places a silver necklace with Eostre's symbol on it—a full moon disc, and half-moons on either side. The necklace is heavy but Touilt carries her head high. Wilona picks up a charcoal stick to draw the bind-rune on Touilt's forehead and as she does, she sees again the terrible devastation of her vision, hears the screeching of the owl and the crack of the axe against the sacred oaks.

"Come, girl, take that look off your face," says Touilt. "None of us can see into the wyrd. Isn't that what this signifies? She holds up the little loom weight with the carved spiral hanging from her belt. "A circle without beginning or end, moving ever inwards, living and dying and living again, just as the sun dies each day and is born again each morning, just as the moon swells with light and then dwindles to darkness? The Norns don't weave as we do, back and forth, back and forth; they weave in and out and back and forth and round and round, through all time and space, in patterns not even they can discern. What's the point of anything but acceptance and faith?"

"Then why bother? Why ride the vision-drum? Why climb the dream-tree?" Wilona thinks of Ricbert.

"There's no harm in asking the spirits for guidance, so we might serve more faithfully, so we might ease the suffering of others." Touilt waves her hand. "I can't argue these matters now."

Wilona draws the bind-rune, combining *uruz* and *ansuz* on Touilt's forehead so she'll carry wisdom and strength with her. And then, at last, she puts on her own blue tunic and the owl clasps, and settles the pouch with the feather and iron hammer between her breasts, next to the amulet Touilt gave her to ward off unwanted attention. She fastens a band around her forehead, with *ansuz* and *raidho* woven into the cloth, for true vision and for journeys. It describes her as someone who has visions, who travels between worlds, and hints of the death that's also part of her story.

When they're done, Touilt takes up her staff. She taps it on the ground and mutters words under her breath as though to activate the power in the wood and bronze. "I am ready," she says.

Elba snuffles against the fence as they pass. "Guard the house, Elba," says Wilona. "We can't take you to meet the king, now can we?" Elba sticks her nose through the willow-hurdle and grunts.

Part
TWO

Chapter TWELVE

When Touilt and Wilona arrive at the outskirts of the royal enclosure, the stalls and makeshift shelters are mostly vacant. The two women make their way through the mud and muck, the ground underfoot slippery with rotten vegetables and other detritus, left by people who won't stay long and don't care about the mess they leave behind. Between the booths and lean-tos a large ragtag group, smelling of ale and cattle and unwashed flesh, jostle and elbow one another. Dogs run here and there, barking madly, dodging kicks. Wilona doesn't know how she'll force these strangers aside.

"Make way!" Touilt shouts, in a voice that would make a warrior flinch. "Make way!"

Wilona joins in. "Make way for the Lady Touilt, seithkona to Lord Caelin. Make way!"

A woman turns around, looking as though she is about to say something less than courteous, but when she sees Touilt and Wilona, their clothes and the rune-signs, she balks. "Beg pardon." She thumps the man in front of her on the back with a hand from which two fingers are missing. "I'd move aside, I were you."

Others turn to see what the fuss is about and, just as quickly, turn back, shoving and stumbling to get out of the way, as someone pushes through the crowd in front of them. Then Margawn appears, the shaggy beast of a doorkeeper, his head above everyone else's. Lovely Margawn, thinks Wilona, beautiful Margawn, who looks just like a grumpy, golden bear. His hound is with him, snapping, growling deeply.

"Stand aside, you rabble. Stand aside or I'll push you aside, and if I push you, you'll tumble 'til you reach the River Glen!"

A path clears. "Ladies, my apologies no one came to escort you. The dishonour lies with me. I should have thought. There's been," he scowls at the crowd, "some confusion and considerable details . . ."

"You owe us no apologies, Margawn," says Touilt.

And so, thanks to Margawn and his hound, the seithkona passes through the sea of bodies. They step into a clearing where Caelin's companions stand with their backs to the crowd. The lord's and lady's chairs have been placed beneath a canopy. Cuthen the bard, Ricbert, and Caelin's closest companions, Alfrith and Cena, stand behind the chairs. Margawn guides Touilt and Wilona to stand with the rest.

Even in the shade of the canopy, the air is too warm. Beads of perspiration stand out on Touilt's lip and her brow is damp, smearing the runes. Wilona pats her face gently with her sleeve and discreetly gestures to Margawn. "My lady feels a little faint. Can a stool be found?"

He nods and returns moments later with a seat. At first Touilt does not wish to take it but, in the end, agrees to rest, at least until the king arrives.

Lord Caelin and Lady Elfhild appear, followed by servants, and little Swanhwid in the arms of her young nurse. The poor girl looks about ready to vomit with nerves, thinks Wilona, and prays she doesn't drop the baby. Wilona stands behind Touilt's chair, imagining herself as nothing more than a wisp of smoke. She has nothing to worry about for the moment; Caelin is occupied with his men, shouting orders and generally fussing and stomping about.

A horn sounds across the plain and all eyes turn to the east.

The standard-bearer, riding a grey horse, carries the Roman-style banner topped by a winged globe. Behind him, the king sits on a jet-black horse, its hooves kicking up clods of earth. He holds the reins loosely in one hand, as though his will alone controls the creature. The gold brooches on his cloak sparkle and glint. His boots gleam; his cape is of the deepest amethyst, trimmed with marten fur. Wilona thinks he must be as hot as a cooking stone. His chest, shoulders, wrists, even the horse's saddle and bridle, all flash with gold. His face has the always-angry look Wilona remembers, the look that makes her feel like a small frog before a sharp-sighted snake. If King Edwin considers this a joyful visit, it doesn't show. She can't help but wonder what makes the king so furious with all the world. He looks above the crowd, even above Lord Caelin, as if his sights are fixed on the next place he seeks to conquer.

Behind the king, his companions ride black horses too, their bridles and saddles trimmed with silver. They are enormous men who dwarf the king, oaks to his birch. Wilona tries to recall the names of the companions she recognizes—Edwin's sons are there, Osfrith and Eadfrith, by Edwin's first wife, Cwenburga. Wilona thinks again how they must take after their mother, for they are black-haired and pale-eyed, as many Mercians are. Still, they have their father's haughty bearing. A ginger-haired warrior she remembers as Indulf, but the names of the others are lost.

A great cheer goes up from the impatient crowd. "Hail to King Edwin!" "All honour to King Edwin!" "The blessings of Woden be upon him!" The king nods absently, in the way of men accustomed to having their approach met with celebration. She joins in.

A brightly painted canopied wagon comes into view, pulled by two white oxen. In it reclines Queen Ethelburga, her hair thick golden ropes, her face square and serious. Her tunic is a deep purple, trimmed with fur, and the buckles holding her cloak sparkle with jewels. She holds a baby. Riding on a grey horse alongside the wagon is the man whom Wilona saw in her vision. He wears the white robes he did in her dream; has the same black, strangely tonsured hair and beardless face, the same narrow nose; and even though he's on a horse, she can see he's tall. His waist is belted with rope, and other than a gold cross, he wears no adornment. He must be the Roman Christian. No priest of Woden is allowed to carry arms or ride a war-steed.

Then Wilona's mouth falls open. There, astride a horse, bold as any chieftain, is Coifi, King Edwin's priest. A murmur runs through the crowd. Wilona's eyes meet Touilt's. The seithkona's brow is smooth, but from the flash of her eyes and the purposeful set of her smile, it's clear she, too, is deeply shocked.

And then comes the rest of the king's retinue: noblemen and women of the court, the men on horseback, the women in wagons. Behind them, troop servants and supply bearers, royal administrators and tax collectors, musicians, hunters, the men who repair the saddles and bridles, the weapons and the wheels. Cooks and seamstresses, nursemaids and waiting-women. Either the king intends to be in Ad Gefrin for some time, or else this is the first of many stops on a long journey.

People throw flowers at the horses' feet. The companions toss glass beads, bits of amber, and coins. When the king nears, Lord Caelin and Lady Elfhild step forward. The king's great horse stops, shies, paws the ground ten feet from the lord and lady, but they do not flinch. The king makes a noise in his throat and the horse quiets.

"I welcome you with all honour, King Edwin, to the house that is already yours."

"Is all well, Caelin?"

"Under your protection and your bounty, Lord, we prosper."

"I'm glad to hear it. I trust my coming has not discomfited your people."

Wilona wonders if he truly cannot see the upheaval all around him. And then it occurs to her that this may very well be the way the entire world looks to kings, since when would they ever come upon a place unannounced, unheralded? Mind you, Edwin lived as a fugitive and exile for many years. He should know better.

"We are, as always, at your pleasure. Your quarters are ready and the amphitheatre has been constructed to your specifications. You bring honour, joy, and comfort to your people, my king."

Edwin smiles for the first time. "I bring you more than that." He scans the crowd. "But it can wait. For now, I would settle my lady and my court. You and I shall talk before the feast. Come to my quarters and," he stretches his neck, "there—Ricbert, are you well?"

"I am, my king."

"Caelin, bring Ricbert with you."

"As you wish, my liege."

"Tonight the companions will gather at the feast and I'll give instructions for tomorrow."

With this, King Edwin and his retinue lead their horses and wagons around the canopy and disappear into the compound, the servants rushing ahead of them. Apart from the trampled flowers, they leave only muddy tracks and horse dung. The people shuffle about, unclear if it's really all over, and then the companions wave their arms and tell them to go about their business. Some grumble.

Caelin steps up. "You'll have meat to roast this night, and ale."

They are pleased at this and disperse, but Wilona notes the frown on Caelin's face. At last, she's not the only one worried. She wonders what he thought of the mounted priests; she wonders what Ricbert thought. A snort erupts from Touilt and she sweeps past Wilona. The king had not greeted her nor invited her to the evening's gathering. There's no doubt about what the seithkona thinks. It's as though a cloud of black gnats circles her.

———◆———

Egan stands in the doorway of his tent and considers the nearby temple. It's well carved, heavily thatched, with solid timbers, and will, Christ willing, make a fine church. Egan has a good feeling about Ad Gefrin, with the sacred hill, the sparkle of river-water, the land's placid roll. The evidence of God's utterance is all around. When he first arrived he removed his shoes because he wanted to feel the earth on his feet. Now, he prays he'll have a chance to speak with Ricbert. At the greeting ceremony the pagan priest seemed kindly. Coifi says Ricbert will be an easy conquest, that he's ambitious and will quickly pledge fealty to whichever hand extends the most gold. Egan chews his lip. That may be Coifi's sole motivation but, God willing, not Ricbert's. Prior to his conversion, Coifi had said, "No one has applied himself more diligently to the worship of our gods than I; and yet there are many who received greater favours, who were more prosperous and preferred above me. If the old gods were good for anything, they'd favour me, who's served them with greater zeal." Egan had winced at that.

There's still some time before the *witan*, the assembly, is to begin, and surely Ricbert will leave the temple soon and make his way to the king's hall. Egan doesn't want to presume to call upon him formally—doing so would only bring on the bishop's wrath—but he might just step alongside him as he walks. During the journey from Ioua Insula to Bebbanburgh, God provided the opportunity to convert many pagans. What a wonder it is to be present at the moment when they recognize the light of Christ's love within them. Egan holds the wooden cross to his chest now. If Ricbert converts, Egan thinks he'll make a wonderful shepherd for the lambs of Ad Gefrin.

"Brother Egan. Bishop Paulinus requests your presence." So concentrated is he on the temple doorway that the voice startles him. He turns to see a servant from the royal household. "You are to follow me," the man says.

"I've prayed on the matter and decided how we're to proceed, you and I," says Paulinus. He is sitting on a backless chair fashioned from what look like two arches, the bottom one forming the base, the sides of the upper providing armrests. He dips a slice of plum into a small bowl of honey on the table before him, pops it in his mouth, and chews slowly. Tapestries adorn the walls and candlelight flickers. Fresh rushes on the floor release a sweet scent.

Egan stands with his hands clasped in his sleeves, his eyes on his feet. They are dirty. "I am ever at your lordship's service."

Brother James is sitting on a cushion-strewn couch, and Egan has the impression he might have been sleeping there a few moments ago, for the handsome face is slightly puffy. When Egan greets him, he raises a languid hand.

"We are all at God's service, Brother Egan," says Paulinus. "But God has singled you out for special work." He holds up a finger as Egan begins to protest. "All the stories we've heard about how you were plucked from a stormy sea by a whale—"

Egan thinks it imprudent to mention it wasn't a whale but seals and dolphins. Still, he cannot help but wonder if the mistake isn't deliberately made. There's mockery in the bishop's tone.

"—so very Jonah-like—it's obvious you're not like the rest of us, my son."

"I don't understand, my lord."

"No, of course not. That's due to your humility, I'm sure. But never mind. The point is: When we leave here, we'll be travelling, as you know, to Eoforwic. We'll be there for a time, I suspect, for there's much work to do establishing the cathedral on the spot where King Edwin was baptized."

"It will be to the glory of God, my lord."

"Indeed. You, of course, already have vast knowledge of the ways of these people, being one of them yourself."

"I was born in Eire—"

Paulinus silences him with a wave of his hand. "But Brother James hasn't had the experience you have and is eager to attend the *witan*. In short, your services as translator will not be required tonight. Coifi will assist me, and this is, after all, a meeting of warriors and noblemen. And you are . . ." His voice trails off.

". . . but a humble monk, your lordship."

Paulinus smiles. "Exactly. Brother James will see to my needs. Better you save yourself for working with the people of Ad Gefrin directly. As you'll see, I have plans for you."

———— ◆ ————

Through the night, Touilt sits by the hearth, casting the runes, stirring the ashes, and gazing into the embers. When Wilona offers her a cup of broth she flicks it away without a word, and after that the younger woman sits on her bed, knees up to her chin, trying not to doze off. For a while, in the darkest hours past midnight, an owl hoots from a branch in the yew, softly, almost timidly. In the firelight, Touilt's face glows, by turns wild and sorrowful. Once, when Wilona nods off, she's startled awake by a wolf's howl, but doesn't hear it again and decides she must have dreamt it.

Dunstan appears on the path just after dawn, as the women are at the well, finishing their prayers to Eostre, their faces shining with the holy water. Birdsong fills the trees as the long, rosy tendrils of light lure the world into wakefulness. The women are drawn and tired, and from the set of Touilt's mouth, it's evident the pain in her belly bothers her.

"Have you heard?" says Dunstan. "Did anyone come yet to tell you?"

"If you have something to say, spit it out." Touilt's scowl stops Dunstan in his tracks.

"I see no one did. I thought Caelin . . . well, I wasn't sure . . ."

"And now you are."

"I don't mean . . . I just thought . . . to see what you think of it all . . ."

"By Woden's ravens, Dunstan, I will slap you!" Touilt stomps past him into the hut.

"I think you'd better come in and tell us. She's had a difficult night," Wilona whispers.

"Maybe I shouldn't have come."

"You're here now."

Wilona closes the door behind her as they step inside. Touilt sits on a stool near the fire, her eyes flashing. Smoke hovers near the ceiling.

"You think I need anyone to keep me abreast of what's important to the gods?" Touilt's voice is sharp as needles. "The spirits beat you to it, boy. The White Christ has taken hold of Edwin. Am I wrong?"

From the expression on Dunstan's face, it's obvious Touilt's spirits have spoken the truth.

Chapter THIRTEEN

The next day is almost as fine as the one before, and the amphitheatre is filled. The women, in the first three rows, sit tall and straight with their hands folded in their laps. They're unaccustomed to being idle, but they've been instructed to pay full attention, and thus their distaffs, niddy-noddies, and sewing kits have been left behind, and their children are in the care of neighbours or relatives waiting their turn. Paulinus stands, stoop-shouldered, under the canopy, addressing the crowd in a strong voice.

Wilona has declined a seat, although it surprised her when Ricbert offered to give up his so she might sit. She waved him away and stood her ground at the edge of the theatre, where her attendance won't be confused with acceptance. She tried to stay away, but in the end, curiosity won out, and she tells herself it's best to know everything one can about an adversary. Touilt disapproved of her coming, but didn't forbid her. Touilt knows her own absence will displease Lord Caelin, but to attend would mean she considered conversion possible. "If anyone asks, tell them I'm indisposed," she said. "Tell them I ate a bad eel."

Wilona takes note of the translator standing near Paulinus. He is thin as a willow switch, but his hands look strong, and there are muscles around the curve of his shoulders and in his neck. No feeble court-rat, this one. His mouth is wide and he smiles often, a little too often, perhaps. But his eyes intrigue her. They are a remarkable shade of green, even from this distance, bright as a spring leaf. It's hard to turn away from them, but this could be trickery. The Folk, after all, are known to have such eyes. Regardless, in his simple robe of undyed wool and his wooden cross, he makes a poor figure next to Paulinus. As the canopy moves in the breeze, sun glints off Paulinus's gold cross.

Although she doesn't wish to admit it, the elf-eyed one is a good speaker and understands his audience. She's sure Paulinus doesn't have the gift of storytelling, but the plain-robed monk does. She sees it in Paulinus's face: the ideas may be his, but he has no sense of poetry.

"Beloved people, we come to reveal secrets of great worth, full of life-giving wonders, and to invite you to enter under the protection of the Almighty and Merciful God, who never scorns or rejects those who approach with humble hearts. How beloved you are, that the highest chieftain in Rome, Pope Gregory the Great, sent his companions and me," here he gestures to Paulinus to make the reference clear, "across the land and sea and land again, a great journey, so you might receive the good news.

"This is how it came to pass: One day some merchants, recently arrived in Rome, displayed their wares in the marketplace. In the crowd the high chieftain himself, Gregory the Great, saw some boys for sale. They had fair complexions, fine-cut features, and beautiful hair." A murmur goes through the audience. They don't like to think of themselves for sale in a market. Paulinus bows his head, and the elfish one holds up his hand and continues.

"Much taken by their beauty, he enquired what part of the world they came from. He was told they came from the island of Britain, where all have this appearance." The people are quiet, pleased to be called beautiful.

Wilona fingers the warm and comforting rune stone she has placed in her pocket.

"The chieftain asked if they were Christians and, learning they were ignorant of Christ's message, said, 'Alas! How sad such graceful features conceal minds void of God's grace! What is the name of this race?' 'They are called Angles,' he was told. 'That is appropriate,' he said, 'for they have angelic faces, and it is right that they should become joint-heirs with the angels in heaven.'" The crowd chuckles at the pun, and then sounds of approval fill the air, for as pleasant as it is to be told one is beautiful, it is more pleasing still to be told it's one's right to inherit great treasure.

Wilona sees what's happening. A clever mix of flattery and glittering promises. The people, fickle as bees, will be seduced. She tsks and, as she does, realizes people have begun to take notice of her. Touilt was right to stay away.

As she rounds the edge of the amphitheatre, she nearly runs into Margawn and his hound. Margawn's size is always somewhat overwhelming. He looks down at her, frowning. His eyebrows are the colour of otter pelts, darker than the golden blond hair curling unbraided about his face.

"I hadn't thought to see you here today, Wilona."

"Shouldn't I be here?" She scratches Bana behind the ears, and he leans against her leg, heavy as a pony.

"That dog takes to you. He doesn't take to many." Margawn smiles, his teeth surprisingly white behind the trimmed beard. "I didn't think there'd be anything of interest to you."

"I have a curious nature."

"But you're not staying?"

"I'm not staying." The dog is sitting on her foot now, wanting her to keep scratching. She pulls her foot free. "If your dog will let me leave."

Margawn chuckles. "Get off, Bana. Get off. I think I've heard enough as well. Will you permit me to escort you?"

Wilona blinks. Margawn has escorted her and Touilt home from the hall occasionally but has never suggested such a thing in daylight. She looks at him, opening herself to an inquiry that cannot be spoken. A certain tension flickers round him. "If you've no other pressing duties, my lord."

As they pass among the wattle and daub buildings of the village proper, people waiting their turn for a seat in the amphitheatre pop their heads out of windows and doorways. Wilona wonders what the village gossip is, what people think of this new god, but it wouldn't be fitting for a seithkona to ask when she claims to receive messages from the spirits. She lets her mind open to the energies around her. There is no open hostility, but she senses the distance Touilt has warned her about time and again. *Our place is near the holy spaces, guarding and watching the borders, the doorways between worlds. The people are not entirely comfortable with us.*

A small girl, holding a wooden doll, runs through the snicket, her mother chasing after her, laughing. Maccus, the bone-worker, sits on a bench talking to his daughter, Aylild, who holds her own child in her arms. Again, Wilona wonders what it would be like to share her bed with a man every night, to wake up to the laughter of children, to sit by the fire in the evening, watching the light play across the faces of her loved ones. What would it be like to spend her days in the laughter and gossip of the weaving house with the other women, known and knowing, claimed not by the gods but by her friends and neighbours? Tonight she and Touilt will sit again by a lonely fire, sleep at the edge of the village, now without even the comfort of knowing their purpose is valued. She will drink from a solitary cup, eat from a solitary bowl.

Margawn clears his throat, and Wilona shakes off the sticky tendrils of self-doubt. Borders, doorways between worlds. Perhaps it is impossible to ever really be alone anyway, not if one lives in the company of the spirits and the dead.

When they arrive at Wilona and Touilt's hut, Elba is lying in front of the door, her tiny eyes closed, her mouth open, showing her short tusks in a sort of smile. Bana's hackles rise and Margawn makes a low noise in his throat to calm him.

"I see you have a guard pig," says Margawn. "Some people use geese."

"I expect she serves as well. Thank you for your escort. I'm in your debt."

"You and Touilt should have been included in the hall last night."

Wilona's eyebrows fly up. She has never heard Margawn criticize any of Caelin's decisions. "I agree. It was a great insult to Touilt, and she won't forget it."

"There was a lot of talk. Most of it none of my business."

"Can it be we agree on this issue of gods?"

He drops his head, purses his lips, and then looks up at her from beneath a furrowed brow. "I'm Lord Caelin's man. I have my oath to honour."

"So do I."

"And is your first oath also to Lord Caelin?"

She searches his face. It could be he was sent to test her and Touilt's loyalty. "I've never forsaken an oath."

He looks at the ground, shifts his balance from one tree-trunk leg to the other. She finds herself hoping Touilt will not come through the door.

At last he looks up again. "You need a friend, Wilona."

Sensing he has more to say, she waits. He tucks his thumbs in his belt and looks down for a moment before meeting her eyes again. Blood tints his cheeks.

"I would be honoured to be that friend."

Wilona's heart pulses in her throat and, at the same time, she is in danger of giggling. How soft his lips look, under that sweep of moustache. It would be fatal to laugh at such a proud and powerful man and it would carry a meaning she does not intend. Besides, an entirely different feeling, all warmth and longing, blossoms in her belly. And yet there they are, giggles, bubbling like an overheated soup in her chest. She bites the inside of her mouth, hard, and continues to do so until the urge disappears. It's impossible to know what to say. An hour with Godfred during the spring rain festival is the sum of her sexual experience. As seithkona, she's not forbidden sexual contact, but the gods' claims take precedence, and she may never marry. But here, now, this man stands before her, looking more uncomfortable by the second. Oh, how theoretical her mind gets, when the practical is right in front of her! Then, too, there is Lord Caelin's wrath to consider. Margawn is taking a great risk.

"Lord Caelin—" She falters.

"My lord is a man of strong . . . appetites . . . but an honourable man, faultless in this way." Margawn squints, and pauses before continuing. "During the battle against Cwichelm of Wessex I had the opportunity to do Lord Caelin a service, one which left a debt of honour."

Several things occur to her simultaneously: it's known Caelin has his eye on her; Margawn saved Caelin's life; and how serious this is, if Margawn would choose to ask for the right to approach her as the settling of an honour-debt. "You've spoken with Lord Caelin?"

"Yes."

"And?"

"As I said, he's a man of honour."

"You're presumptuous, aren't you?"

"If my friendship is unwelcome, you've only to say so."

She sees she's offended him but can't seem to stop. "So why not ask for a parcel of land? Or a fine horse?"

"The debt's worth more than land or livestock."

There's no clever answer for this, and the flattery sends blood to her face. "The honour would be mine," she says, surprising herself, and then, recovering, "and I do hope our friendship will . . . deepen. However I have my duties, to Lady Touilt, to the goddess, as you have yours to Lord Caelin." She drops her eyes before raising them again. "We must trust to the gods for the proper time, I think, and the proper place."

The bold words scald her mouth and throat, making them as dry as heated wool. Margawn holds her eyes and there's no fear of any laughter now; it's far more likely she'll either vomit or faint. His eyes, she thinks, are the colour of the tawny river. She never noticed that before.

He smiles, a little, at last, and the lines in his brow soften. "It is well, then." He taps Bana on the head, turns on his heel, and, the hound at his side, strides up the path, the muscles of his long legs showing through the lacings on his trousers. She watches him, baffled, fearing she said the wrong thing. Is this the way lovers behave? He disappears over the hill. She sits on the step next to Elba and, feeling decidedly woozy, lays her head on the pig's belly. They stay like that for some time, Wilona listening to the heartbeat of a pig, wondering what it would be like to lay her head on Margawn's chest.

When she opens the door and steps over Elba, she finds Touilt wrapped in her blue cloak, gazing into a bowl of dark water. Whatever spell she has woven is broken by Wilona's entrance, and she agitates the water's surface with her finger before looking up. When she does, her eyes hold anger, sorrow, and fear.

Wilona's thoughts of Margawn scatter. "What do you see?"

"Very little, which is the worst of it," says Touilt.

The next day, Touilt is up early, and she is firm. Wilona is to go to the river and check the eel-bucks. Wilona protests, but Touilt will not have it; they must be seen going about their business as usual. To huddle in the doorway, waiting, gives away their power. Trust the gods, she says, over and over, trust the gods. And so, with the warmth of the morning sun on her face, Wilona sets off down the pebble-strewn path to the water's edge, turns right, and follows the river until she comes to the place where she set the traps. She's taken Elba with her, and the pig roots happily in the undergrowth, grunting when she finds something she likes. Wilona hauls up the willow eel-buck and can tell by the flapping and struggle inside she has a catch. She unlatches the lid and looks. Sure enough, a lovely eel, not too big, writhing furiously.

She says a prayer of thanks to the nixie who lives by the willow, who Touilt saw once, a beautiful, water-pale woman wearing a green cape, with sharp green teeth. Nixies were often treacherous, and some credited this one with the drowning of two little boys three springs ago, but Wilona never feels the presence of evil here. Still, the nixie might merely be satisfied by the annual gift of a young lamb or piglet, and if more than one of Elba's offspring have been offered to her, it's a worthwhile sacrifice.

Knowing how long an eel can live out of water, and not relishing having it flop about in the creel all the way home, she quickly kills it and cleans it, tossing the skin and entrails to Elba, who slurps and gobbles with gusto. Wilona rinses the eel thoroughly in river water, making sure every bit of slime and grit is gone, and all that remains is the firm flesh. She thinks how good it will be, stewed with garlic, onion, and parsley. Wilona cuts it into several pieces and wraps them in large green leaves before settling them in the creel. She spies some crowfoot and picks a bunch; she will make a salve for blisters. She wonders: Will these new Christians have the same respect for the old charms? She chuffs. Of course they will. The ways of a lifetime can't be overturned in an instant like some wobbly stool.

Away from the burbling waters, she spots wood avens in the shelter of an ash tree. Such a useful plant, good for diseases of the chest, for pains and stitches in the side, it dissolves bruises and, if the roots are boiled in wine and drunk, stops the spitting of blood. She heads toward it. It's pleasant in the wood, with the gentle river beside her as a laughing companion. She thinks all will be well. The people of Ad Gefrin know the gods of this place too intimately to abandon them. Elba has stretched out in a soft hollow beneath an oak. Wilona looks up and realizes how high the sun is in the sky.

"Come on, lazy one, we've left Touilt alone too long." Wilona finally picks up a stick to prod the pig with and Elba, grunting protest, gets to her feet.

Now and again the pig stops to root in the earth, and Wilona sings a song about a prince lured into the woods by a beautiful elf, never to be seen again. Then she stops. Elba has halted, nosing the air. What is that sound? At first she thinks it's a trick of the river babble, and then wonders if hunters are in the wood; but no skilled hunter would make such noise. She adjusts the creel's leather strap across her chest and tucks her dagger into the herb basket. She removes her belt and fashions a leash for Elba, fearing the pig will run off into the forest in fright. Wilona moves off the trail, picking her way through the underbrush, following the swelling voices. Her heart begins to beat erratically, and she tenses as any wild thing in the wood will when confronted with an unusual phenomenon. The noise is coming from the direction of Touilt's dwelling.

Wilona has a sudden image of a mob, festooned in crosses, crying out oaths to the White Christ, searching for her and Touilt. Her stomach clenches. She's heard tales of Christians killing the priests of Woden and Thunor. Is it possible the people, realizing she and Touilt will not become priestesses to the new god, now seek to kill them? She shouldn't have left Touilt alone.

She follows the noise. Some laughter, yes, and many voices, but it doesn't have the raucous excitement, the ferocity, of a hunt. She creeps closer, able now to see flashes of brightly coloured cloth. She slinks through the trees, ties Elba to a river birch, and puts the baskets in the branches where the pig cannot get at them.

Wilona goes from boulder to tree trunk to boulder, craning, stretching. Whoever they are, they're not moving nearer, yet neither are they moving away. She spots a good-sized ash with low branches and dashes to it, her sides heaving. She waits to catch her breath, her back against the tree. When she's calmed, she grabs a branch, hikes up her tunic, and climbs hand over hand, her feet straining for purchase, grateful for the deep fissures in the tree's aged bark. At last she's high enough to view the happenings below.

A line of people snakes from the river's shallow bank to the water's edge. Men and women, children and the aged. She sees faces she knows—Farman the tanner and his wife, Sunild; Osgar the black-smith and his family; women who have sought out Touilt, looking for tinctures and teas—Begila, Wynflaed, and Saewara. Those closest to the water are quieter, even the children, who shuffle nervously, without their usual boisterous ways. Her eyes follow the line. A young Christian monk stands at the riverbank, and in the water a little way from shore are Coifi, Paulinus, and Paulinus's elfish interpreter. Ricbert, too, stands on the bank, his hands at his chest with palms together. A woman Wilona doesn't know stands before Paulinus and, with a quick movement, Coifi takes hold of her and throws her backwards into the water.

Wilona only just stops herself from crying out. Mass drowning? What madness is this? Her mind explodes, searching for some charm or song to break the spell, but then Coifi hauls the woman up. She is wide-eyed, braids dripping, her wet tunic clinging to her body, show-ing every curve and fold, her hands covering her nose and mouth. The priest makes the sign of the cross over her, says something, smiles, and turns her over to the interpreter, who helps her to the bank where other women wait with dry blankets.

So, this must be the Christian rite of baptism. Symbol, no doubt, of dying and being reborn, as was their Jesus. Good thing they've chosen water and not fire, Wilona thinks, and that they don't demand followers be hung on the criminal tree like their god. Why have they

come this way, though? Why not on any of the shorter paths leading from the village to the river? Of course, it's deliberate. They're
flaunting the new god in front of Touilt to show her powerlessness,
parading past the sacred well, the great yew. Wilona's heart sinks.
She should never have left Touilt alone, left the well and the tree
untended. Her vision flashes before her—the felling of the sacred
trees! But the great yew tree is waving gently in the breeze, still
standing. She wants to yell and hoot. Kings come and kings go.
Woden has protected the tree.

She smiles, careless now of who might see her. Let them think she's
a daughter of the horned one. She studies the faces of the people
coming to the water and those leaving, dripping and exhausted. How
many of them truly believe in this new god and his promises? How
many just want to please the king and curry favour? How many are
merely caught up in the drama of the moment? Those swept along
by fine speeches and dreams of new glory, not to mention promises of peace and comfort, doubtless will slip back to the old ways
at their first disappointment. Without a strong hand to hold them
to the new faith, it will amount to little. Here and there, the set of
someone's lips or a frown reveals there's no belief at all, not even a
temporary one, only a fear of going against the wishes of the king.

Then she sees Margawn. Her heart clenches, her breath catches,
and her belly warms infuriatingly. The sun shines on his golden hair
and his face is an unreadable stone. Bana rolls in the grass at his
feet. Now and again, Margawn glances across the fields, scanning
the trees. Is he being a good soldier, or is he, perhaps, searching for
her? His arms are folded against his chest and he speaks to no one.
Margawn will guard his truth, but he has to follow orders, and who
knows what order the king, and Caelin in turn, will expect him to
carry out concerning Touilt and her?

A child runs along the line, with Dunstan close behind. He sweeps
the boy up into his arms and tosses him, shrieking with laughter,
into the sky. It's his little nephew, Deneheard's boy. When the child
quiets, Dunstan returns to his place next to Roswitha and some of
the other villagers—Baldred the woodcutter and his family, and
Aelfric the potter. Dunstan holds his nephew in one arm and puts

the other around his wife, who gazes up at him in open adoration. She reaches up and brushes his unruly hair from his face, tucking it behind his ear.

Wilona's heart flinches. How simple it would be to have nothing more to worry about than food and shelter, and not to feel the presence of restless, displeased spirits, not to be prodded by them at every turn. The tree at her back seems to shiver and shake, as though some great beast stands below, rocking the trunk, and for a moment she fears it may reject her, toss her to the ground far below as punishment for her blasphemy. Soft, silent wings brush her cheek, but she senses talons as well.

She presses her hand to the pouch at her chest and waits until the tree stills. Her eyes remain on Dunstan's face. He looks upon the closing gap between his family and the waterlogged priests with an expression not unlike hunger. In fact, she's surprised to see he's trembling with longing. *He believes!* Can it be? She fixes her eyes on his face and sends everything she has along a silver line of power from her to him. He raises his eyes to the heavens, and closes them. He prays to this strange new sky god. He *prays*.

Wilona wants out of the tree. She wants to be back on solid ground where she doesn't have to see such things. This Christ is taking hold, not merely because of politics and power, but through some strange magic of his own. There's no other explanation for it. Dunstan's no fool, nor can he be bought with cheap promises. She sees it in his face. His heart is taken. He believes.

She clambers down the tree and, with every branch she grasps, her resolve hardens. Let them go, then. Let them all go. She needs none of them. Until this very moment she might have harboured some hope that when the king's party left, the world would return to sanity, but she sees now how unlikely that is. If whatever the Christians are offering is enough to lure an honourable man like Dunstan, the new faith will spread. She snaps off small branches, hoping she will wake the gods of the wood and they will do something—fire or flood or ravaging winds. Surely they cannot expect her and Touilt to guard the old ways alone.

She jumps the last few feet to the ground and sets off running through the wood, something wild and savage rising up in her. She fantasizes Touilt will wrap herself in her wolf pelt, pin her wolf clasps to her blue cloak, take up her staff and cat-skin gloves, and parade up and down the line of converts. Perhaps she's doing that even now.

She comes upon Elba and throws herself around the pig's neck; the coarse bristles prickle her cheek and she smells earth and decaying vegetables. Perhaps the animal senses Wilona's distress, or perhaps she's frightened, but whatever the cause, after a moment's squirming she permits this intimacy. At last Wilona wipes her eyes, unties Elba from the tree, and takes up her baskets. She brushes a bit of bark from her tunic. She shakes her head and sets her shoulders back, her spine straight. She considers keeping the lead on Elba, but she doesn't want people to see her dragging a pig along—or being dragged by one. Let them say, "How calm she is, how untroubled. Look how the seithkona stands tall in her belief and does not waiver."

Wilona says, "You must be a good girl, Elba, and stay with me."

Luckily, Elba seems interested in getting back to her familiar surroundings. They come to the boundary of the wood and the grassland sloping to the river. Wilona gathers her strength. She closes her eyes and breathes deeply. *Come, Raedwyn, come.* She sings his sacred song, and draws the rune of *eihwaz*, the yew tree, on her palms, her chest, her forehead, for protection. She feels him, and her heart strengthens, for she's not alone.

She and the sow step into the open and, for a few moments, no one notices them, and then one woman does, and she nudges the man next to her. Others follow their gaze and soon the entire line is looking at her, or trying not to.

Chapter FOURTEEN

A ripple runs through the crowd as people look to the east. Egan searches for the source of the distraction. A pig steps from the edge of the wood, and behind the pig a young woman. She is tall and carries herself with a straight spine and a determined thrust of her chin. Her uncovered and unbraided copper hair, adorned with feathers and somewhat tangled, curls over her shoulders. A mark on her forehead . . . blue . . . a rune, mark of a seithkona. This must then be the one called Wilona, the orphan who came from a dead village over the moors who is said to be touched by the gods. He sees pride in her, perhaps coupled with self-consciousness. Look at the set of her mouth, the lips pressed together. She is struggling. His heart goes out to her. He wants to tell her there's nothing here to be afraid of, and without realizing, he makes a move to step out of the river toward her.

"Brother Egan, stay where you are," says Coifi. "We have work to do here."

He apologizes and returns to the task at hand, but he can't help watching her from the corner of his eye. Wilona walks along the line of villagers, her gaze resolutely ahead, catching no one's eye. A man steps into the river, and the ritual begins again. She seems to be making an effort to walk neither too slowly nor too fast. She lifts her feet a little higher than normal, too, as though afraid of tripping. Egan admires her carriage, her resolve.

Another man, this one with a belly like a boulder and a complexion the shade of turned liver, breaks into a snaggle-toothed grin and he waves at the woman. She smiles back. How it lightens her face! A radiant smile. A group of men Egan doesn't think come from the village snicker and whisper jokes, jabbing their thumbs in the seithkona's direction. Wilona neither flinches nor flushes, and soon their snickers die away.

Good girl, thinks Egan.

A splash and spray of water and Egan reaches for the next Christian, a boy of no more than seven or eight winters, so small he barely weighs anything. Wilona nears one of the king's companions and Lord Caelin's doorkeeper, the one who always has the pony-sized dog with him. Both are enormous honey-haired men. The doorkeeper's arms are folded over his chest and he bends his neck to the right and left, as though to ease the muscles. Or perhaps not. Perhaps he's trying to draw the seithkona's eye. He's successful; for a moment the two are locked on each other. The doorkeeper's lips move, continuing his conversation with another man, but his eyes are arrows. She is passing by him now, and either she'll break their gaze, or she'll have to turn her head. She nods with a tiny motion. His eyes do not waver, and she moves on.

"Brother Egan!" Paulinus's voice is crisp with irritation. "That woman is not your concern. Your concern is the sheep entering Christ's fold."

------ ◆ ------

Wilona struggles to deepen her breath, which she's horrified to admit became dangerously shallow when she passed Margawn. *In and out, in and out. Calm, calm.* Elba trots a little quicker now, unsure of the crowds. Wilona taps her rump with the herb basket. "Go on, now. Home!"

Soon she'll be at the well and the tree. How sheepish Dunstan looks. She focuses on him as she draws near. Sheepish or not, his face glows, and Roswitha's too. It's as though some brighter sun shines on them. There's no denying they've been struck with something from this new god. Were it anyone else, she'd want to rub a little mud on that glow.

"Are you well, Wilona?" Dunstan calls.

"I'm well, as you seem to be."

"We'll call on you and Touilt later, if we may," Roswitha says.

"Perhaps tomorrow. I've work to do today."

Roswitha nods and looks a little hurt. Her eyes catch Dunstan's, as though she wishes he'd do or say something, but Wilona moves past them, her eyes on Elba's bouncing hindquarters. Once beyond the well, the awkwardness she felt lessens, and her muscles move with more of their natural liquidity. *Where is Touilt?* Wilona doesn't want to turn and look behind her, for more damp new Christians follow her as they return to the village. She supposes they'll troop past this way all day, excited as new brides. She vows to stay in the vegetable garden behind the house where she can ignore them. *Where is Touilt?*

Just then Touilt rounds the corner of the hut, a scarf tied round her head, with a basket full of chard and cabbage. She waves and smiles to Wilona as though nothing whatsoever is wrong, and it isn't until Wilona secures Elba in her pen and follows Touilt into the dwelling that she's close enough to sense the fury sparking from her.

"Tell me!" Wilona cries.

Touilt rinses the leafy greens in a bucket of water. "Tell you what?"

"Did they harm you? Say anything to you?"

"Who?"

"Touilt!"

Touilt keeps tearing the leaves into pieces and tosses them into the pot simmering in the fire. "I pay no attention to ants passing before my door. I don't even see them."

"We can't just ignore what's happening! We can't."

Touilt stops what she's doing and hangs her head. "But I will do that for today, while it's possible, Wilona, as should you. In a very short while, I fear there will be great changes, and we can do nothing to stop it." She looks up and her eyes sparkle with tears. "Let's be easy for a few hours yet."

———— ◆ ————

Later, when the final convert of the day is baptized, Coifi rushes to report their accomplishments to the king. Paulinus, James, and Egan trudge up the hill to their quarters. Their sandalled feet are muddy and their robes wet and heavy.

"I shall want a good cup of wine and a dry robe as soon as possible," says the bishop. "Still, we've had a good start. At this rate we should be done in a few weeks. Word will spread. I'm pleased."

"As well you should be, my lordship," says James. "The Lord has blessed you with a silver tongue. Who could resist the eloquence of your teaching?"

"The words are God's, Brother; I am but a humble conduit."

"Ah, but it's a reflection of my lordship's pure soul," says the blond monk.

They reach the great yew tree, and the holy well beyond which lies the seithkona's hut. A thin trail of smoke rises from the vent in the thatch, and the pig is in the sty, but there is no sign of the women.

Bishop Paulinus turns to Egan. "You were mesmerized today by the sight of that woman. It doesn't bode well for the state of your soul, my son."

Egan starts. "I'm distressed if I gave the impression of any impropriety. I don't know which woman you refer to, in truth, Lordship, there were so many," he stammers, trying to cover his discomfort.

"Not the women in the river, Brother. No one would accuse you of lechery!"

James chuckles and rubs his nose to hide it.

The twitch of mirth on Paulinus's mouth evaporates in a flash. "I meant the young witch."

"Witch? The holy woman? The one who walked from the forest this afternoon? I don't believe she and the other are witches, are they? They're handmaids to the old gods, yes, but there are no charges of sorcery." He thinks it best not to remind the bishop that Brother Coifi, until recently, also served the old gods.

"The issue isn't whether they're witches or not. The issue is your interest."

"I only sensed her discomfort. It touched me, Bishop. We must seem threatening to her and her guardian. Perhaps you would let me give them instruction."

"They were invited to the teachings and refused, from my information. Am I wrong, Brother James?"

"I'm told the old one spit on the ground at the mention of Christ's name," says James. "God forgive her."

Paulinus tsk-tsks. "You see? You cannot coddle such blasphemy, Brother. It must be dealt with firmly and decisively."

"I've found—"

A sharp wave of Paulinus's hand cuts him off. "I'm not interested in your findings, Brother, only your obedience. I fear your faith isn't muscular enough to do what must be done."

Egan wants very much to know just what that might be, but they've reached the edge of the village and Paulinus dismisses him. He's left standing on the pathway, watching the two men saunter away. He looks at the hut, isolated by the yew tree. The door opens and the young seithkona comes out, carrying a pail. She catches sight of him and stops. He smiles and raises his hand. He feels he's wronged her somehow, feels there's something he should do or say, but he's all hollow inside, just a cave of foggy uselessness. "Greetings, Sister," he calls at last, praying she'll offer him a way to approach her.

The hatred in her glare, the ice streaming from those chill grey eyes strikes him like a wind-slap. Without a word she turns on her heel and disappears once more into the hut, slamming the door behind her.

"May Christ bless and protect you," says Egan, his heart a lump of clay in his chest. He turns and walks away from the village. He cannot bear the thought of the crowds and feasting in the royal compound. He'll spend the night standing in river water, purifying himself.

Chapter
FIFTEEN

A.D. 627, *Holy-Month, Ad Gefrin*

People file past their door every second day. One day Paulinus preaches from the amphitheatre, the next he leads converts to the river. A few come on the teaching days, but Ricbert and Egan baptize these smaller groups of five or six or seven. Busy days or slow days, Wilona and Touilt recognize almost no one among the new converts. Some of the faces wear that same hopeful glow Wilona first noticed on Dunstan, but others look merely curious, nervous. One elderly cripple, who had to be carried down on a bench, looked somewhat stunned. Certainly, thought Wilona, he's more in need of a good poultice than a dunking in the river.

The effort of pretending the converts are invisible proves to be too much for Touilt. After the third night, as they sit eating their stew, she says it's as if every Christian is a cut to her skin. She won't hide, but she can't stand to be gawked at. Thus, once they've noted the pattern, Touilt and Wilona take advantage of it. On baptismal days, if the weather's fine, they tend the garden or move the loom to the back of the house, any task that shields them from prying eyes. Touilt stands in her doorway, spinning, only in the early morning and evening, when Paulinus, Coifi, Ricbert, and the two younger monks come and go. She wants them to see her.

"I suspect it annoys them," she says, although they typically nod to her solemnly, as careful to be polite as she. She wants them to know she's staying and they don't frighten her. She wants them to understand the gods still have a place here, where the fox bids goodnight to the hare, in the liminal space between the village and the wild wood. She wants them to see the wolf head over the lintel, and the freshly carved runes.

At night, Touilt seeks guidance in bowls of dark water, in the pattern in the hearth-embers, and in the cast of the runes, but the messages are obscure. This worries the women, who fear the Christians are working spells to impede the spirits. They carefully, secretly, place charms and amulets along the path and by the river-bank, but every day there are more Christians. At night, Touilt and Wilona fall into bed exhausted.

The elf-eyed monk is particularly vexing. He hangs back from the other men, smiling and blushing. Wilona decides he must be half-cracked. She's followed him to the river at night and watched him stand in the water for hours, hands outstretched to the night sky. What she sees unsettles her. The animals—the badger and the mink and the deer—come to drink and seem unafraid. Animals are often spies for the gods, she tells herself.

There's a terrible sense of anticipation in the air, and the spirits fly about the rafters at night and crackle the thatch. Someone— Wilona suspects Dunstan and Roswitha—has been leaving baskets of bread and meat for her and Touilt. Three times she's heard something in the night that she assumes is an animal, but in the morning, there, hanging from the yew bow, is a basket of food. And it's welcome. Since hunting is men's craft and the crowds have scared off the small game near the river, the women have no meat. Touilt doesn't want to kill the chickens until she must. Eel and the occasional trout, porridge, and turnips are fine as far as they go, but hare and venison give strength. Dunstan and Roswitha are good friends, Touilt says, even if they're Christians.

It is a grey day; the low sky drizzles chilly rain. There is no mistaking the turn of season, no resisting autumn's charms or the snap of winter's hungry jaws close behind. Touilt works inside, storing dried herbs in jars and clean cloth packets. They must be ready to prescribe if anyone should come to ask, although since the upheaval, no one has. This worries them both, since it's their livelihood. The weeks have passed as though under a sort of caul. No one is speaking to them, so they get no news. In one swift slash of the cross, they've been excised. Touilt's face as she bends over the herbs says it all; she has the bitter air of a woman betrayed.

Wilona's belt is nearly worn through and she sits in the doorway weaving a new one on small wooden tablets. She jumps whenever Touilt slams something. Wilona fights the urge to run away entirely, to find a new place where the old gods are still honoured. Surely it is only a matter of time before Lord Caelin sends word they are no longer required at Ad Gefrin, or worse. It's tempting to be angry with the gods. She frowns and tries to concentrate on her work.

She hears a noise and looks up, ready to go inside if Christians are about. But no, it's Dunstan. Seeing him is like having a heavy, wet cloth removed from her shoulders. How she's missed him. He lopes down the path, the hood of his cloak over his head to protect him from the drizzle, and a loaf of bread tucked under his arm.

"Touilt, Dunstan is here." She gathers up her weaving. "I see our provider chooses daylight to come calling this time."

"And when else would I come calling?"

"Fine. A kind gesture performed in anonymity doubles its worth."

"What?"

"No matter. It's good to see you. Roswitha's well? And the child coming?"

"Everything's fine. I have news along with the bread."

"Well, come inside. The season's turning, although Weed-Month is barely over." She pats him on the shoulder, as though to confirm he's really there. She wants to keep touching him, and chides herself. There's no dignity in behaving like an eager hound.

Touilt greets Dunstan with more reserve. "Sit. Let me get us a slice of Roswitha's wonderful bread. I have honey, as it happens, also from a friend," she winks at him, "which will be a fine treat for us."

He hands her the bread, only slightly damp, and bends to pluck a bramble from his trousers. "You shouldn't waste your food on me."

"Waste?" says Wilona, laughing, "No need for that much humility! And not after your generosity."

"It's only a trifle."

"Not this, you goose! The food you've been leaving."

He blinks at her.

"The baskets. With the food, the bread, the meat . . ." She shrugs, her hands wide.

Dunstan pulls his head back on his neck, giving him the look of a startled turtle. "I can't take credit for the kindness of another. Should have thought of it myself, but honestly, we don't have that much. I did bring this bread, though."

Wilona looks at Touilt, who shakes her head.

"But if not you, then who?"

"You have more friends than you think."

"So it seems," says Touilt. "A mystery to be solved, but for now, eat with us."

Dunstan's good manners will not allow him to have more than the smallest slice of bread and the thinnest smear of honey. Touilt natters on about the crops and the weather. In Dunstan's presence the older woman's face is lighter, the furrows between her brow not quite so deep. He accepts a mug of apple cider, and sits on a stool by the open door.

"The king's announced he's moving the court to Catreht."

Wilona's heart leaps.

"Well," says Touilt, "the people will miss all the feasting."

"Yes. The music and the stories have been good. The king's bard's a wonder." Neither woman replies, and so he says, "You'd be most welcome."

"Would we? I wonder." Touilt nibbles a piece of bread.

"I heard Lady Elfhild ask about you."

"She's a good woman. I'll serve her as I always have."

Wilona tests the temperature of the milk in the pot she's stirring. She adds a small piece of salted kid's stomach. "And what about our honoured guests?" she says, watching the milk slowly separate into curds and whey. "Are they tearing down the tents? Moving along as well?"

"Some of them, but others are arriving. Edwin sent messengers throughout the land, apparently, telling the chieftains when to bring their people, so they're not all here at once. Paulinus is to stay until the new moon, and then travel on to meet the king." He blows a lock of hair from his eyes. "How are you getting along then?"

"We're managing." Touilt smiles at him gently.

"Winter will be hard this year, I think. The trees have been full of woodpeckers and there've been a lot of fogs this moon."

Wilona nods. There have been a lot of fogs, particularly in the past week, with mist creeping up from the ground in the morning like the souls of the restless, searching dead. "Last night the mists twirled round the house so thick I thought something was on fire. I couldn't see so far as the yew," she says. "And the cobwebs are unusually dense."

Dunstan looks across the meadows. "Don't you feel too alone sometimes, here?"

"And where else would we be?" Stone has replaced the previous gentleness in Touilt's voice.

Dunstan's expression is serious. "I'm your friend. Always have been, isn't that so?"

"You've certainly made a habit of visiting over the years," says Touilt.

"Then trust me when I say it's better to shelter under the chieftain's roof than to set yourself apart."

"The gods choose where I make my home, boy."

"Can't you consider the possibility your gods take more than they give?"

Touilt gasps at his audacity but, if he hears, he doesn't let it stop him.

"Can't you consider," he continues, "what it means to place yourself outside Caelin's protection?"

"Is the only way to keep my lord's favour to hang myself up on a criminal tree?" Touilt slaps the table. "Have you come at his command, like a dog to bark a warning?"

Dunstan chews his lip. "No, no, of course not. But you might consider being a little less . . . well . . . stubborn." He sounds like a mardy child. "They're good people, the priests. You should talk to Brother Egan."

"Who is this Egan?"

"Paulinus's interpreter."

"The one with the elf-eyes?" Wilona asks.

"He comes from Eire and was brought by angels to Ioua Insula, a community of great teaching and kindness. He rode to shore on the back of whales."

"Did he?" says Touilt. "Did he really?"

"He's a very humble man. He wears only the simplest cloth, eats no meat—I like him." Dunstan pulls at a ragged thumbnail.

Touilt throws the wooden pestle she's holding across the room. It clatters against the wall near Dunstan's head. He doesn't flinch. If she'd wanted to hit him, she would have. "We've a choice here, Dunstan. We can either talk about this, or you can continue to be the friend you claim to be."

"I've handled this badly. I've been rude. Forgive me."

"You have a generous heart," says Touilt, but her voice is as sour as the milk.

Wilona takes the pot off the fire and pours the thickening cheese into a basket placed over a pail to drain out the whey. Dunstan takes a wooden flute from his pocket and perfects it with the tip of his knife. Touilt drops rosehips into a clay jar and covers them with liquid honey. Wilona watches Dunstan out of the corner of her eye. He may be a husband and will soon be a father, he may have been to war and wounded, but he's still a petulant boy with his lower lip stuck out. The corner of her mouth twitches in a small smile. It's a good thing he had no ambition to be the king's man, for he has no subtlety; his face reveals everything.

"So we're still friends?" he says at last.

"I don't understand you or Roswitha, Dunstan." Touilt holds her hand up to stop him from speaking. "No, do me the courtesy. I'll not debate you. But we must be clear. There can be no talk of our converting, and in return I'll not share my thoughts with you on what a great fool I think you are."

"Oh, will you not?" He grins now, the old playful Dunstan again.

"I, too," Wilona says, "would like to go on, as much as possible, as before." She will not tell him of the knife-twist in her heart at seeing the wooden cross around his neck.

"I say this only because Roswitha and I are frightened for you. You've chosen a hard path. The priests are clear. There are to be no more runes, no more visions, no more altars to the gods. Everything's being rededicated. Coifi threw his spear over Ricbert's altar and did so with Ricbert's blessing."

"So, it has come to that." Touilt's eyes gaze into some middle distance. "So soon."

Wilona's skin prickles. Why don't the gods act? Why don't they cast out these interlopers? It's a disloyal thought that shames her. "Not even a king has the power to banish my visions," she says. "They're gifts from the gods. If people are that fickle, how faithful can they ever have been? The gods reward loyalty."

"Well said, Wilona." Touilt sits down, as though she's suddenly tired. "Enough, Dunstan. You came to tell us the king was departing, yes? And to warn us. I'm grateful. Is there more?"

"Only that Brother Egan will stay on as our new priest when Paulinus leaves. The care of our souls is to be in his hands."

Wilona blinks, and then feels something very much like a laugh rise up in her. "Oh, let me be sure I understand. This monk, Egan, is to be the new priest? Not Ricbert?"

Dunstan's lip curls. "Ricbert's to be his assistant and learn from him, but apparently Brother Egan will be the chief priest."

Wilona claps her hands and laughs. "Oh, poor Ricbert! For all his ambition, to be underling to that elf-eyed Egan! Oh, poor man!" She covers her mouth with her hands but is unable to stifle her laughter, and after a moment, even Touilt chuckles.

Chapter SIXTEEN

Egan argued against it, and then begged. He was given a hard penance for his impudence and, in the end, it made no difference. Bishop Paulinus wants it done now, on the eve of his departure. He said he would be neglecting his duty if he permitted the women to continue as before. "I won't leave the worm in the apple," he said. "It disturbs Lord Caelin's faith to have these women defy him." But both Paulinus and Lord Caelin declined to join them. When Egan asked to be excused as well, saying it might taint any future hope he had of converting the women, the bishop said he needed toughening, and Christ required strong arms as well as hearts.

It is just before dawn. They are six: Ricbert, Coifi, Egan, and three of the king's men, who are the size of stallions. Egan thinks this show of force is both unnecessary and unwise but has been told to keep his opinions to himself and learn by the example of his superiors. His stomach is queasy, and he's sweating. He holds their single torch in one hand but must keep changing hands to wipe his slippery palms on his tunic. They are huge shapes in the pre-dawn shadows; Ricbert, tall and gaunt; Coifi, muscular, heavily bearded, carrying a large bronze cross atop a highly polished staff before him as though to ward off evil spirits.

One of the king's men kicks the door open. It slams against the wall and the upper hinge snaps. The three warriors and Coifi rush forward. Ricbert and Brother Egan lag back and exchange a quick glance. Ricbert's face is grim, and in the torchlight the pallor shows.

The women have no time to even throw a shawl around their shoulders. In their still-sleepy shock they scramble toward each other while the men kick aside the stools and table. Wind gusts through the door and scatters ashes from the near-dead fire.

The elder seithkona, her hair in grey straggly braids, her eyes full of crackling torchlight, stands with her legs wide beneath her sleeping tunic and her arms held out, fingers spread. "You have no right! There is no honour in you, to treat women and hand-maidens of the gods this way. You dare? Have you no respect?" She makes the sign of the hammer. "By whose authority do you commit this violence?"

Coifi steps toward Touilt. "We are here by order of the king and your Lord Caelin. You dare to challenge the king's men?" He raises his hand.

Wilona lunges at him, but one of the guardsmen sweeps her aside and sends her tumbling to the floor. Her head cracks on the end of the bed. Egan cries out and hastily places the torch in a wall bracket. He takes a step toward the younger seithkona. Her eyes are glassy. The man who struck her points a spear at her, his face impassive.

Coifi pushes Egan aside with a curse. "Stand back! Do not touch her. I forbid it!"

"But—"

"If you interfere I'll have her pinned to the wall."

Coifi approaches Touilt. Wilona scrambles to her feet, winces, and grabs her head. Egan prays, *Protect all here, Lord Christ. Protect all here.*

Ricbert reaches for the warrior's spear and pushes it aside. "There is no need for that. She's only a girl." He gestures to Wilona as she stands. "Stay back, or you'll find yourself on the floor again."

Egan silently thanks Christ for Ricbert, while horror at his own weakness swamps him. Wilona glares at Ricbert and then at Egan. He tries to communicate he will not harm her, that he is no enemy.

Touilt will not step back, and now she and Coifi are nearly nose to nose. "Why would the king send his men against two women, who are, as ever, his loyal servants?" she says.

Coifi peers into Touilt's face as though looking for a sign. "You were invited to hear the good news of Christ, woman, and yet you refused."

"An invitation can only be called such if one has the right to refuse, is that not so?"

"You refuse the gift of great worth so generously offered you by your king?"

"Good King Edwin himself took his time deciding; may his servants not do the same?"

Coifi's mouth softens, almost forming a smile. The king's men, resolute and grim, stand by the doorway, axes in their belts. "Is it time you need? That seems unlikely, since you shunned the teaching and kept to your hovel, mocking the holy ones as they passed your door. Still, if it's time you need, I'm a patient man, and Christ the Eternal will leave no lamb lost who seeks to be found. Let us sit down now and you shall hear the words of the hero Jesus. You shall receive the gift here and now, for if you're receptive to the message of Christ, we'll not leave your hospitality until you're satisfied. Will you hear the teaching?"

Touilt's eyes are steady. "We've already heard your words. They've drifted to our house on the lips of our friends and neighbours." She looks down for a moment, then plucks a shawl from the foot of her bed and wraps it around her shoulders. She raises her chin as she turns back to Coifi. "We remain unmoved."

Brother Egan cannot help but be impressed. The woman has such strength, such courage, such faith. Why can't Coifi see that with patience and love such a heart cannot fail to turn to the true God? Wilona touches the back of her skull, and her fingers come away bloody. Her face shows no fear, and Egan sees that although it is misguided, her faith is strong and pure. Oh, Coifi, he thinks, you're making grave errors here. These women will die if they must, and we'll make them martyrs.

Wilona points at Coifi with her bloody finger. "You think if violence doesn't work, you can trick the seithkona with clever words?"

"Friends, be reasonable!" says Ricbert. "We've come to include you in this new and wondrous world, not to harm you."

Wilona cacles, sharp and scoffing. "With splintered wood and blood instead of flower garlands and roasted pig? How inviting! We depend not on your invitations, *friends,* but on the protection of the gods!"

"It doesn't appear your gods are here." Coifi glances at Ricbert and his eyes tell Ricbert, too, to be careful. "Where's the power of Woden now? Where's Thunor's hammer?"

The smirk on his face makes the hairs on Egan's neck stand. Her eyes on the bullish priest, Touilt chants a spell in words Egan does not understand. The air shimmers and shifts. Wilona makes rune-signs with her blood-stained fingers while Coifi makes the sign of the cross.

"You don't behave like a person with an open heart, seithkona. You and your girl—"

"Wilona is seithkona, as I am, priest, and it would serve you well to treat us with the respect due our position."

One of the guards laughs out loud, and Coifi says, "Make no mistake, the magic of Christ Jesus is stronger than anything you can imagine. Woden and Thunor are no match for the power of the Christian God."

"The gods perform what wonders they wish, at a time of their pleasing, and no one escapes their wrath. You should know that, Coifi. Has some enchantment erased your learning?"

Coifi is the one to laugh now. "I see there's no reason to think time will change your mind or sharpen your wits, woman." He turns to the guardsmen. "Proceed."

Their hands go to their axes. Egan's stomach plummets to his knees, and he reaches out to the bedpost so as not to fall.

Wilona cries out, "Eostre, save us! Woden save us!"

The men step toward the tapestry dividing the room. In an instant, Touilt is before them, her hands up. Wilona rushes to her side but is blocked by a guard. He holds her arms from behind, pinning them easily with one hand.

"Release me!" she shrieks.

Egan regains his senses and tries to step between the axes and Touilt, but Ricbert gestures for him to stay where he is and puts his hand on the guard's arm. "Gentle, man. There's no need . . . Wilona, stop. Touilt, let it be, let it be. It's done already." The lines on his face are deep as knife cuts. He seems to have aged a dozen years since he stepped through the door.

"I forbid you to take another step!" Touilt's voice is imperious. For a moment she appears more wolf than woman—her mouth a snarl, her teeth bared, her hair wild as fur, her eyes feral. The men freeze, for they know the power of a seithkona's curse. And then Coifi strikes her with the back of his hand. Her head snaps round with an audible crack and she falls. He raises the staff with the heavy cross on the end, as though to club her. The guard holding Wilona loosens his grip, perhaps in shock. She breaks free and leaps to Touilt. She covers the older woman's body with her own.

"Leave her! I'll curse you all! Leave her!"

Before he knows what he's doing, Egan kneels beside the fallen women, facing Coifi, ready to take a death blow. "Remember Christ's love, my brother. Think of Christ's love!"

"My lord," Ricbert says, "you've done your duty. Do no more."

"Get on with it then," Coifi snaps.

Touilt stirs and her hands reach up. Blood smears her teeth. "Stop them," she whispers.

In Touilt's eyes there is rage, and even fear, but also something else, a deeper grief. It transfers, all of a moment, to Egan. He opens his mouth, searching for words. The woman breaks her gaze and looks upon her ward, who now, at last, begins to cry.

"They're killing the gods," she whispers, and the women embrace.

Egan stands, his throat constricted. There's no victory here, only a terrible wrong that may never be righted, save by God's almighty plan. These women love their gods as he loves Christ. He can only leave them to their mourning and pray for them to receive, by grace, knowledge of the One God. Shame burrows in him like an egg-laying blowfly.

The guards rip the hanging from the ceiling, exposing the vision platform, the great tree, and drawings of wolves and bears, ravens, geese, salmon, and the great owl. Wilona whirls around and stands before the platform, eyes closed, head back. She calls out something . . . Egan blinks. There, above her head is . . . what? Something. She opens her eyes. Egan is not the only one to see some change in the air, for he senses their fear, even Coifi, whose knuckles are white on the dark wood of the cross-staff.

"You may not do this thing," she says. "You do not *wish* to do this thing."

The guards shuffle their enormous feet and adjust the grip on their axes. Ricbert steps back.

Coifi turns on them. "What are you waiting for, you cowards! You have your orders. Destroy it!" Spittle flies from his lips. He grabs a spear from the nearest guard and hurls it over the vision platform. It sticks deeply into the wall, in the heart of Yggdrasil, the shaft quivering. For a second it seems as if everyone in the room is waiting to see if Thunor will crack the place in two, or if Eostre or the horned god will send the forces of the wild wood to rip and destroy these violators. "Do it!" shrieks Coifi.

The spell is broken, and one guard reaches for Touilt and tosses her aside. She lands near the hearth with a thud and a gasp as the wind is knocked out of her. Another guard reaches for Wilona, while the third destroys the ladder to the platform with one blow. Wilona claws at her tormentor's eyes and is rewarded with two blows to the head that leave her senseless. To his eternal shame, Egan simply stands there, frozen with confusion.

It's over in moments, the platform in splinters, the tapestry shredded. Coifi steps outside and returns with a bucket of whitewash, which he hurls at the wall, defacing the sacred symbols. Then they turn to Touilt's trunk. One of them snaps the lock with his dagger and the other slices through her wolf pelt, then the blue cloaks, and her cat-skin gloves. They punch through the drum and stomp on the wolf and owl clasps. Finally, Coifi slashes at their pots and jars of ointments and herbs and powdered roots.

Egan cannot bear to watch. He steps outside into the morning light. That the day is breaking with such golden splendour feels all wrong.

And then, with the same suddenness with which they came, the men are leaving. Ricbert hesitates and Coifi shoves him through the door. At the threshold, Coifi turns and says, "You were given chances, Touilt. The decision was yours. And now you have another one. Remember that the door to Christ's hall is always open to you."

Touilt spits on his tunic, and the saliva is streaked with blood. He laughs. "Be grateful we didn't burn you out." They don't bother to shut the door behind them.

Coifi shoves Egan and he stumbles up the path. "Wretch. Fool. Paulinus is glad to be rid of you. But if we return and find the village has slipped back to the old ways, it'll be your hide stretched on the door of the king's hall!"

———◆———

The rest of the day is eerily silent, as though by destroying the vision platform the Christians have also banished the birds and the wind, and the distant sound of the babbling brook. Fog rolls in from the sacred mountain, first consuming the royal compound, and then the village, and then the women's hut, the well, and the yew. Wilona wonders if Woden's handmaid is dragging her mist across the land as punishment for the blasphemy. Part of her hopes so.

Touilt lies on her bed, her back to the room, her eyes shut, and will not be roused. "Leave me," she growls when Wilona approaches. At first, Wilona tries to gather the herbs, to sweep the floor, to return the unbroken furniture to its place, but Touilt threatens to strike her if she doesn't stop. And so she sits and watches the shadows move across the room, as fog curls under the shutters.

At last, she slips outside. Either Touilt doesn't hear her or is beyond caring. The fog is so thick she can barely see her feet, and if she didn't know the path so well, she might be lost. She throws herself beside the holy well. On a wooden block, not very large, perhaps the length of her forearm, a carving is affixed to the dipper post with iron bands. Even Wilona must admit it's beautifully painted. A woman, in a blue robe, stands under a brightly shining sun. Her skin is white, with a tint of rose. Under her feet rests a crescent moon, and on her head a crown of twelve stars. On the top is inscribed "*Sancta Maria, Mater Dei*," markings which mean nothing to Wilona. It's puzzling, for it might almost be a portrait of Eostre. A little pallid, perhaps. But why is she surrounded by symbols of the air only—the moon, the sun, the stars? Why is she so removed from earth, from fecundity, from life?

No, Eostre would not be pleased. This can only be Mary, the Christian virgin-mother, untouched by life, removed from blood and pleasure. She's covered in light, standing with her foot crushing the moon, the night. It is enough to make Wilona laugh. How can you deny the forces of the night? How can you desire to crush the wisdom residing with the creatures of the dark, who make up one half of life? Putting them under a virgin's foot will not banish them.

A little trail of ants marches along the stones at the base—efficient as these Christians, one after the other on their errand, doing exactly as they're told. A perfect new god for the king. A single god for a single king, one who—what was it Paulinus said from the amphitheatre?—urges his people to turn the other cheek and repay violence with forgiveness. Hypocrites! The only cheeks turned that morning were hers and Touilt's, stinging from blows. They know how to turn a riddle, these Christians. A meek king. A virgin mother. A god who dies and does not die.

She wants to saw the new goddess off the post and fling it into Elba's slop heap but doesn't dare. She must be smart; she must be patient; she must trust the gods. Does the goddess live here still? She dips her fingers in the water and brings it to her lips, longing for the sweet kiss of holiness. Still there—no trace of Christian poison detectable. She bows her head and prays, begging for strength and forgiveness. She washes her face in the holy water, and her fingers touch swelling flesh. It's hard to see out of her left eye. Her lip is puffy and ragged, and her cheek feels as though shards of glass are buried below the skin.

As she turns to go back inside, she finds the chickens pecking and scratching, but there's no sign of Elba. Inside, Touilt sits staring at the floor.

"The gate's open. Elba's gone," Wilona says. Touilt coughs deeply and clutches her side. Her face, too, is distended, bluish purple, red and black. Blood cakes her nostrils. "Are you badly injured?"

"A rib perhaps. Cracked, I think, not broken." Touilt points at the ruined blue cloak. "Cut it into strips and bind me. It might protect more than my bones." It's hard to think the bitter sound she makes is laughter. "And bring water; we'll wash away their taint."

Chapter
SEVENTEEN

In the morning Touilt's face is a mass of bruises. She hands Wilona a piece of stale bread dipped in buttermilk. "I'm going to leave you on your own for a few days."

"What? Why? I don't want to be alone."

"Can't help that. I need guidance." Touilt chews thoughtfully, slowly, and pats her jaw gently, as though to ease the hurt. "I never thought Caelin would treat me like this, or that Elfhild would permit it. Dangerous pride." Her brow furrows and she speaks more to herself than to Wilona. "I thought I was special. That may be why the spirits have been distant lately. I don't know, but perhaps they've retreated. I dreamed last night I was on the sacred mountain. The spirits are calling me to their high place. I feel it."

"Let me come with you."

"I doubt they'll return. Not yet. You're safe."

"You can't mean to climb the mountain alone?"

"That's exactly what I mean. I'm called. But your place, for now, is here. Someone needs to make it clear we won't be intimidated, nor will we abandon the holy tree and the well, even if they've nailed a virgin to the post. Besides, you need to clean up this mess." She means it as a sort of joke.

"You haven't been well, Touilt."

"I'll be with my spirits. One cannot ask for more."

"I can't let you go off alone. I can't stay here alone." Wilona throws her hands up. "I can't!"

"You can and you will. You'll do as you're told."

"But Touilt!"

"But nothing. If you say more about my being too old or too frail, I'll slap you!"

Wilona had been considering saying something exactly like that, although perhaps not so bluntly. She bites her tongue. She won't admit she's as worried about her own safety as Touilt's.

Touilt huffs and continues. "I'll skirt the village so they don't see me. If I leave by mid-morning I'll reach the summit in time to make a snug camp among the ruins and be ready by nightfall. You'll see my fire, no doubt, if you look hard enough."

"And if bad weather moves in?"

"Then Thunor will speak to me all the more clearly." She holds up her hand. "There's nothing else to be said." Touilt smiles. "Besides, you need to cultivate closer relations with spirits of your own, I think."

Wilona nods. While Touilt's on the holy mountain with the spirits, she'll fast and pray as well. Still, she's never spent a night alone in the hut, and she anticipates an anxious night. "Fine. If that's your will, so be it. Being alone will be good for me. I'm sure it will."

"If you call living with the spirits 'alone' you're not the seithkona I taught you to be."

"I didn't mean that."

"I hope not. We've some decisions to make, Wilona, and I can't make them without guidance from the gods. I don't know if we're meant to stay here."

"We might leave?"

"We might. If the gods call us to retreat into the wild places with them, then that's what I'll do. But if you wish to stay, to eat and sleep in Caelin's hall, and bow your knee to the new god, I'll not stop you. You're not my slave."

Wilona's mind splits—one part thrilled at the idea of moving deeper into the world of the spirits, but the other part snagged on the desire—there is no other word for it—she feels for Margawn. Where is he? Where is his protection? At the same moment desire flares, resentment sparks. He vowed his friendship. What's his vow worth, if it's so easily forsaken? *Margawn's mouth, soft, the teeth shining . . .* but bow to the new god? Abandon Touilt? Impossible. "I go where you go. You're the mother of my heart." She bites her lip, forgetting, and winces as it splits open anew.

"What, girl? Out with it."

"Winter's coming at a gallop. And if we go we won't be here to share in the slaughter, so food will be scarce. And there's shelter to consider. The season won't soften because we're homeless."

"That's why I'm going today. The sooner I discern the gods' wishes, the better." Touilt looks at the ruined pots and jars. "While I'm gone, salvage what you can. If we stay, there's enough to treat what I expect will be diminished demand." Her lip curls.

Before the sun climbs much higher in the sky, Touilt is standing with a pack on her back and her staff in her hand. She embraces Wilona. "All shall be well, little one. Our wyrd is in the hands of the Norns."

As they turn to open the door, there's a noise on the other side. Something heavy, pushing against the door. Wilona grabs Touilt's hand, her skin prickling, the hairs on her arms rising, preparing to fight if they must. Some snuffles, a loud squeal. Touilt and Wilona look at each other and burst out laughing, which causes them considerable pain, but they can't stop. They lift the door and, as soon as there's enough space, Elba scrambles inside, her tail and snout held high, emitting squeals of delight. She trots to a clear spot on the floor and plops down, her sides heaving.

"Oh, Elba! Where have you been, you niddering pig?" says Wilona.

"I take this as a good sign," says Touilt. "A very good sign indeed."

It's dark now, with the sound of wind in the thatch and rain on the shutters. Elba is snoring on the floor, and Wilona, having placed a hide-rug next to her, leans against her. The sow quite likes, it seems, to feel the comfort of Wilona's body next to hers. Perhaps to her, Wilona is just another of her kind. To Wilona, having another living creature nearby, even a pig, is solace.

Wilona had spent the day setting things to rights. She repaired the table—it wobbles, but will do—and salvaged one of the stools. The beds are fine, although the trunks are beyond repair. The hut looks better, but the scar where the vision platform stood is hideous. She thinks she caught sight of Touilt's fire on the mountain before the rain moved in, just a tiny speck of reddish orange against a darkening sky. She tells herself Touilt is safe with her spirits. Wilona is bone-weary. She means to pray, to call in the spirits, and she will, in just a few minutes, after a short rest. She watches the fire, the orange and red and blue, sprites and dark elves and fingers and faces. Her eyelids droop. She drifts into a dream of the high moors, a gathering fog . . .

Then she starts, bolting upright. Elba, too, jerks and swings her head around to the door.

Tap tap. Tap tap.

Wilona pulls the dagger from her belt. She crouches, ready to spring. If it's Caelin, come to—she cannot even think it—she'll kill him if she has to and take the consequences.

"Wilona?"

Margawn. Her hands fall to her sides, although her breathing remains harsh. If she ignores him, he'll go away.

"Wilona, open the door."

If she opens the door she won't easily be able to close it to him again. Her fingers tingle, wanting to let him in, but at the same time, it's the last thing she wants to do.

"Open the door, Wilona."

She walks over. "Help me. The upper hinge is broken."

The door is suddenly as light as mist, and just like that, there he stands, his mass filling her sight. There's ale on his breath, and the smell of smoke and roast meat on his clothes. Rain has left dark stains on his shoulders, and his hood flaps as the wind reaches its cold fingers round him. Bana sits beside him, jaws open, almost smiling. Margawn hesitates, and shock registers in his eyes when he sees the damage to her face.

"Will you let me in?" His eyes flicker to the dagger in Wilona's hand, and he regards her as he might a rabid terrier. "I come as a friend."

"The king's gone then? Caelin's granted you permission?" She doesn't step aside. She wants him to feel her anger, although she also wants him to think he's displeased her only in terms of honour, and not because she longed for him. He vowed his friendship and then disappeared. That wasn't friendship. That wasn't honour. The wind lifts her hair, and even with his bulk before her, sheltering her, cold wet drops sting her cheeks. Touilt flashes in her mind. *Let her be warm and dry somewhere.* Margawn's eyes are steady. They haven't even begun, she thinks, and already they're sparring for the upper hand. Bana stands and shakes, sending water flying.

"Will you let me in?" he says again.

The dog cocks his head and whimpers. It's almost humorous, the way the dog's and man's expressions match.

If this moment passes there will be no other. If Margawn goes away now, he won't return, and they'll nod at each other when their paths cross, and keep every courtesy, and that will be that. Something splinters in her, something as brittle and sharp as river ice, and cracks spread through her. She steps aside. Elba sniffs the air, nervous at the scent of the hound.

"You already have company I see."

Wilona turns her back and walks past the fire. "Come in."

He ducks to avoid hitting his head on the lintel.

"Bana! Sit!"

The dog obeys instantly, still wagging his tail.

"The dog must sense you on the pig," says Margawn, chuckling. "He was slashed by a boar once, protecting me during a hunt. He's a brave fighter but tends not to like pigs."

Wilona is less concerned with pigs and dogs than the state of her face, her uncombed hair, and the sweat of the day's toil on her body. She hides the dirt under her nails by clasping her hands in front of her. "I wasn't expecting you," she says.

"Yes, you were."

"Oh, it's late to call, don't you think?"

His hand moves, as though to touch Wilona's battered face, but he resists and tucks his thumb in his belt. He takes in the condition of the hut. "I see they spared no effort to make their point." He whistles through his teeth and Bana's head snaps toward him. Margawn points at a spot on the floor near the door. The dog scuttles there, as though it's always been his place, and heaves an enormous sigh. Margawn sets his sack down and rights the door. He points to a piece of broken ladder-rung. "Hand me that, will you? It'll serve as a shim until I can fix it."

"A pretty gesture. But again, too late," says Wilona.

"I'd have come sooner if I could. It was out of my control."

"Always the loyal companion." She hands him the rung and he wedges it between the door and the wall.

"There. Now no one can open it unless you remove that first." He faces the door for a moment as though gathering his thoughts. Then he turns around, his expression serious. "You wrong me, and you give my position with Lord Caelin too much credit. I didn't know."

"And if you'd known, would you have defied your lord for our sake? Would you have placed your sword between us and our tormentors?"

"You ask me if I would break my vow of loyalty."

Wilona snorts. "There's no need to answer."

"I'd have spoken for you!"

She waves her hand. "I thought you already had. I'm a debt cleared, wasn't that it?"

"Where's Lady Touilt?"

Wilona stiffens. "She's out using the netty."

"No, she's not. A boy saw her on the path this morning."

"She came back."

Margawn runs his hand over his jaw. "Shall we begin with lies?"

Wilona blushes. "Fine then. She's away, briefly. But where is no business of yours."

He draws a great breath. "All right then. She's her own woman. If she's well enough to travel, then she must be . . ." He trails off. "I needed to know you were unharmed."

"I am as you see me."

Elba comes up to sniff him. Bana scrambles to his feet. For a moment Wilona fears the dog will attack, or that Elba will.

"Bana," Margawn growls. "Still. He won't hurt the pig. He does what I tell him. But I would prefer . . . Do you not think . . ."

"Come, Elba. Come." Wilona plucks a shrivelled turnip from a basket on the table and guides Elba into a corner where there is a pile of straw for her to sleep upon. Margawn throws a log on the fire, and the hound returns to a spot beneath the table. When Elba chews happily on her treat, Wilona ties her with a rope to a post. She's painfully aware of every movement she makes and how Margawn watches her. When she turns back he's removed his cloak and hung it on the hook by the door. He sits on the stool and leans back with his elbows on the table, his long legs stretched out toward the fire. The light makes his beard gleam.

"You make yourself at home."

He sits up straight, his hands on his knees. He reaches in the pouch at his belt and holds out a spoon, intricately carved. "I've brought you a token."

"I don't need gifts."

She sees he's thinking. She feels like a vixen under the gaze of a man considering the best way to tame her. Her colour rises. Does he think he can snare her with pretty gewgaws?

He looks toward three baskets piled on the floor, the ones that had held the anonymously deposited supplies, and suddenly it makes sense to her.

"*You* left the food, didn't you?" Caelin's doorkeeper, packing baskets? The unlikely image of his big scarred hands wrapping bread and chicken legs in cloth and saving the cheese from his own plate to set aside for her is unsettling. Hardened warriors do not behave like that.

"The food?"

"That's been left at our door. It was you! Don't deny it."

He hesitates, long enough for her to think she's mistaken, then shrugs. "Fine, I won't. But it was a gift, not a baited hook. There's no trap and no obligation."

"I meant no insult. I appreciate the kindness."

"Come here. There's no need to be afraid."

Why does she feel this resistance? Why must she bite down on her words? She won't tell him she's unafraid; too strong a denial will reveal that she is a little afraid. She won't blurt out she's no virgin, for surely he must know this. Men talk, worse than women in the weaving house, their tongues and judgment loosened by ale and a love of boasting. She has no doubt what happened between her and Godfred at the spring festival has passed round the hall. She knows, too, that Margawn has knowledge of women, as a travelled and experienced warrior, whereas her own experience of love is woefully limited. It's the one area where, apart from a knowledge of the herbs to prevent pregnancy, Touilt taught her nothing. She won't say that if he wants her he must come to her, for that's a coy game she's no stomach for. He's already come to her. She let him in. Now all there is to do is cross the floor and touch him. Margawn holds out his hand and smiles.

The smile transforms everything. It's a smile wrapped in hope and sorrow and even humility. Yet, it's not the beauty of the smile nor the beauty of the face that finally decides the issue in her heart; it's not the promise of pleasure, even. It is the kindness there in the tawny river-water eyes. This man of war, guardian of Caelin's hall, battle-scarred, hard as old oak, with muscles and gristle and tendon, who has run more than one man through with a sword, a spear, a dagger, who has snapped necks with one quick twist of those enormous hands, is weary, heart-sore from all he has seen and all he has done, and craves as much comfort as he offers. She sees it's not mere flesh he desires, but more, and something no one has ever asked of her, something she never knew she possessed. And she sees that what he offers is a thing that she's not, until this moment, known she also craved. The room fills with the offering.

It's strange, suddenly, in an instant so fierce and quick it surely must be an unearned gift from the gods, to understand a thing for the first time. Had she been asked the day before, she'd have laughed at such a silly question, but she sees now that up until this very night, what she named as *trust* was not trust at all, only a conviction her defences would hold. She smiles back and no longer cares that her hair is unkempt, or her nails ragged, or that the smell of her body may not be as sweet as it might be if she'd known he was coming, and washed and scented herself with rose and lavender. None of that matters. She trusts him.

The room is silent apart from the whispering hush of her bare feet on the reed-covered planks as she moves to him. She places her hand in his and, gently, he closes his fingers over hers. He pulls her onto his knee, puts his palms on either side of her face, and under the mass of his hands, her skull feels as fragile as an eggshell. He brings her mouth to his and kisses her, soft as swan down. A part of her mind watches from outside herself, and wonders at his gentleness, at the restraint in him. His breath and hers mingle, and his hands curl round her, her neck, her back. She is aware of every spot he touches, of the spreading warmth. She expected this to be as it was with Godfred, full of urgency and startled pleasure. But this is different. Her arms go round his neck and she melts into him, flows toward him, surrenders to him, without haste, liquid. He slides his arm under her legs and stands, lifting her as though she weighed no more than a lamb. She nestles on his shoulder as he carries her to her bed. It's much too short for him and his feet dangle, and they laugh as they undress each other and begin the exploration of skin, mapping sensitive spots, charting curves and warm hollows and the boundaries between hair and flesh, tender spots and calloused ones. Their fingers trace scars and freckles and moles. She makes him lie still, first on his stomach and then his back, while she runs her fingers and her hair and her lips over every part of him, separating even his toes, parting his hair, lifting his great muscle-gnarled arms, spreading his legs. She licks salt from beneath his arm and from the concave landscape near his sharp hip, samples the yeasty musk from the root of him. When she is satisfied there is no undiscovered place on his body, he lays her down, kisses her from ear to instep, buries his face between her legs, tastes her, and breathes in her tangy, river-weed scent, and she cannot tell what is lip or tongue or finger. And then the urgency does rise, and need, quick and sweet, is upon them both, and they cling to their passion and each other, and for a moment they are nowhere and nothing matters but that they are skin against skin, and all around the glow of the fire plays on their bodies like ruby honey.

They wake up before the dawn, curled into each other, hardly aware of where one ends and the other begins. When they are sticky and satisfied, he suggests they go together to the river to pull water to warm for washing.

"It'll be quick," she says, shivering, slipping into her tunic. "It's a cold morning." She watches him struggle into his under tunic, his hair standing up every which way. The dog rises and bangs his great head on the underside of the table. He shakes and stretches, and yawns hugely, revealing a great many teeth. Elba barely rolls over.

"Ready?" Margawn says.

"Outside, in the open? It's truly settled with Lord Caelin then."

"It's settled."

She searches his face. Some things are settled, she sees, but perhaps not all. She fears Caelin's mind is more subtle than Margawn's. If the lord wants to destroy her for . . . for what, exactly? From the first moment she arrived, it was clear he didn't trust her, and these years have apparently turned distrust into the need to break, dominate, or cull. She cannot help but wonder if her refusal to convert is merely the excuse Caelin needs to crush her. She wouldn't want Margawn caught in that. "You're not afraid to be seen with me, the woman who will not convert?" she says.

He shrugs. "King Edwin was clear. The people make their own choices. He himself didn't submit to baptism until ten months after he gave his daughter Eanflaed over to the priests. He kept his promise but took his time and considered it. Why shouldn't you do the same?"

"But I'm not considering. And what about you, my bear?"

"What about me?" He works his way into his shoes and ties the lacing on his calf.

"Have you truly lost all respect, all loyalty, to the old gods, or do you wear your new religion like a shield, to be worn when needed in battle, and afterward set aside?"

"I'm a simple man, Wilona. What do I know of gods? I've never seen one or spoken to one, and so whether I don't see this one or that, what I name the god I never see, what gift I bring to his altar, makes little difference. This new god seems good enough, if that's Lord Caelin's will."

"Where's your own mind? Your own opinion? Your own faith?"

"I've vowed to follow my lord, Caelin, and so I do. He believes through this god we'll be stronger, victorious in battle, part of a larger, more powerful tribe. Caelin's been a fine chieftain. It's good enough for me."

"Just like you've pledged loyalty to Caelin, I've pledged loyalty to the gods and goddesses."

"You must do what your honour dictates, and so must I." He stands and puts his arms around her. "When you've seen the things I've seen—the terror in men's eyes as they lie with their guts spilled out in the mud, and never a shadow of the Valkyries come to sweep them to Woden's hall; or babies on the end of spears, and pregnant women with their bellies ripped open; or the heads of good men on spikes, with no more life in them than a squashed beetle—it's hard to believe any of the gods care much for us, new or old. Ricbert says life is like a chieftain's hall. Inside it's light and fire and warmth and feasting, but outside it's cold and dark. A sparrow flies in through a window at one end, flies the length of the hall, and flies out through a window at the other end. That's life. At birth we emerge from the unknown, and for a brief time we're on this earth with a fair amount of comfort and happiness, if we're fortunate to have as generous a chief as King Edwin, but then we fly out the window at the other end, into the cold and dark and unknown future. If the new religion can lighten that darkness, then maybe we should follow it."

Wilona smiles. So, that's what it boils down to—not salvation from suffering here in *Middangeard*, but a promised feasting hall in the afterlife, open to all, not just the warriors taken to Woden's side. But why go to this new heaven-hall if none of one's ancestors are there? It seems selfish, but she doesn't want to spoil what they have right here, right now, with arguing. She pushes him away. "Come, the sun will rise soon and we should get to the river." She unties Elba. "She'll want to follow. Do you mind?"

Bana greets the sow, his tail wagging. "It seems they've made friends. Let her join us if she wants to."

Elba moves off into the nearby stand of trees, looking for mush-rooms. Wilona's glad to see it, for it means the pig feels safe after the assault on the hut. She doesn't relish being followed *everywhere* by a sow. Wilona looks up toward the sacred mountain, a black behemoth, still wreathed in shadow.

"Ah, so that's where Touilt has gone, is it?" says Margawn, following her gaze.

It seems pointless to lie, and she doesn't want mistrust between them. She nods.

"Did she say when to expect her back?"

"When the spirits are done with her."

"Well, if they're not done by this time tomorrow, I'll go up after her."

Tears unexpectedly sting Wilona's eyes. They walk by the well and the yew. Wilona bathes her face in the sacred water, offering up a prayer to the goddess, refraining from gazing on the likeness of Mary. When finished she says, "And what about this life after death? When all is said and done, will you be happy in the Christian heaven, without your ancestors?" She doesn't presume by saying *without me.* Even with the bond between them, it's her nature to doubt the longevity of love.

He looks over the rolling landscape. The dawn chorus trills and a haze of pinkish light tinges the horizon. "Looks like bad weather on the way," he says, and points to the mackerel clouds in the brightening sky. "Let's hope Touilt returns quickly."

"I didn't think you were the sort of man who avoids hard questions."

"What is there to say? The dead are buried, spirits haunt the woods and mounds, and some say they hear their cries on the wind; others see ghosts on the high moors—the dead don't seem like a happy bunch. Maybe the Christian heaven will be better, or maybe it'll be no more than the grey, cold underworld my mother frightened me with, wanting me to grow up and be a warrior, admitted to Woden's hall and his unending battles. I'll tell you the truth, Wilona, since that's what I want between us. And the truth is this: I'll be happy enough, I think, when my time comes, to simply sleep and not dream. But who knows, I may scream and writhe and beg like other men I've known."

"These aren't the great tales of battle told in the hall." Is it possible other warriors feel this way? That they're not the fearless boasters they seem to be around the fire? She knows so little of men.

"I'm not one to give advice, but you should hear this. I've no fear of being seen with you, or of the companions, indeed of the entire village, knowing I claim you as my own."

He stops walking and so she stops as well. *Claimed? She has been claimed?*

He puts his hand over hers. "Everyone will know not to trouble you unless they want to trouble me too. My protection only goes so far, though, Wilona, so be loyal to your gods, if that's what your honour dictates, but make sure you give Caelin no cause to think you chose them, or any god, over loyalty to him." He begins walking again. "Some laws cannot be broken by anyone."

He's right. Touilt and she stand on a rickety bridge. It brings bile to her throat to think she might have to toady to those who failed the gods and misused her and Touilt. But it's wise to be clever as well as faithful. "I'll race you," she says, and runs down the path toward the burbling, sparkling river.

She has been claimed.

Wilona spends the rest of the day working on the herbs and tinctures, making note of what herbs she must gather before the weather turns, and salvaging crockery jars. She must fire more pots; so many have been shattered. Now and then she goes outside to see if she can catch sight of Touilt on the path. Hour after hour passes with no sign either of the seithkona or anyone else. If it weren't for the occasional sound of distant hammers from the village when the wind shifts, she might think she was completely alone on the plateau. Everything seems so quiet now the king and all the strangers have moved on. Her nerves are jangly, as if the skin has been rubbed off her fingertips. Her thoughts keep returning to Touilt and she loses her concentration, finds herself staring at a bunch of dried leaves without understanding why.

And then, at last, as the afternoon sun lengthens, and the sky thickens with bad weather, a speck on the long path slowly becomes larger. Touilt. Wilona runs to her, takes her bundle from her. "Are you all right?"

Touilt's face is serene under the bruises, and it takes Wilona aback. What is there to be calm about? "The spirits came to me, Wilona."

"And what did they tell you?"

"The gods have spoken. We will stay. Kings come and go. The gods of the wood and sky and sea and earth and wind will last as long as there is wood, sky, sea, earth, and wind."

Chapter EIGHTEEN

The snow falls, not thickly, but enough to fur the trees and soften the outline of the rocks. The air is sharp and the sun dazzling, making the snow sparkle and hurt the eyes. Robins and fieldfares land on the juniper, dislodging small clumps of snow into the whisking wind. Late one night, Dunstan sends word to Touilt and Wilona that Roswitha's time is upon her. They prepare their pouches of runes and a basket of herbs with gratitude. Recently, babies have been born without them.

"This should be an easy birth," says Wilona as they walk through the snow-softened, winter-muffled village. "Roswitha's hips are made for babies."

The next day, however, the air inside Dunstan and Roswitha's dwelling is so thick with the smell of blood and excrement, fear and smoke, mugwort and sweat, one could climb it like a ladder. Wilona and Touilt work with determination and many prayers. They've seen the look in each other's eyes, and watched hope fade. Touilt sits at Roswitha's head, whispering in her ear. Wilona feels inside Roswitha's body, her arms and tunic stained with blood. Roswitha closes her eyes in pain, and Wilona makes a sign to Touilt, spreading her fingers next to her throat and ear. Touilt understands and blanches. The cord is wrapped around the baby's neck, in itself not so dangerous—the baby is not yet breathing through its lungs and so there's no fear of strangulation—but Wilona suspects Roswitha's pelvis is pinching the cord. With every contraction it compresses, and the danger to the child increases.

Touilt soothes Roswitha's brow and comes round to Wilona. "If Roswitha dies, we must cut the child from her body and try to save it," she whispers.

"She's not dead yet."

Not dead, but weak. Her face is a pale moon with blue-red smudges under her eyes and white around the mouth. She gasps and cries, and the midwives have long since stopped trying to tell her to be calm.

"Pray!" Touilt says, and no one is surprised to hear Roswitha invoke the name of the goddess. "You must push. With all your might."

"I can't. I'm done."

"You can. You must." Wilona climbs behind the sobbing woman and heaves her up until she's in a squatting position. Roswitha is heavy and her muscled thighs are streaked red. "Think of Dunstan."

It's not the first time things have ended badly at a birth. Mothers died, babies died, and such things were part of the pattern of wyrd. She and Touilt have, over the years, attended other such births, two where the mothers died, one where both mother and child succumbed. But Roswitha is different. Roswitha of the creamy skin and round, laughing eyes is Wilona's friend. She has to live. If she dies, how will Wilona face Dunstan? Roswitha strains and grunts. Drops of thick, dark blood blot the straw. She collapses against Wilona, and it's all Wilona can do to hold her on the birthing-platform. The door opens and a gust of wind scatters embers from the fire. The monk, Egan, stands in the door, and behind him Dunstan paces back and forth in the yard, chewing on his knuckle.

"This is no place for you, priest," Touilt says. "Have you no decency?"

"I've come to help, if I can." His voice is as soft as calfskin.

"You cannot. The goddess claims this place." Wilona holds Roswitha with one arm against her chest. The labouring woman is in so much distress she's oblivious to modesty. Wilona holds her hand up and opens her palm, revealing the painted runes.

If she expected the monk to be struck down by the power of the goddess or frightened by her, she's disappointed. His face merely shows concern.

"It seems the goddess doesn't protest my presence, and the lady might need all the help we can give her."

With that, Roswitha screams and throws her head back so violently Wilona only just manages to move aside and avoid having her nose broken. Roswitha breaks out of her embrace and lurches onto all fours. There is blood but there, yes, the baby is coming. The crown, blue and bloody, streaked with white, appears between her legs. Egan approaches, stumbling on his robe, and kneels by Roswitha's head. He holds out a silver cross. He begins speaking, quickly, breathlessly, his eyes wide and his skin dripping sweat as though he were the one in such agony. *"Ave Maria, gratia plena, Dominus tecum. Benedicta tu in mulieribus—"* Roswitha moans, and it sounds like a dying animal.

"Get away from her! Keep your filthy spells to yourself, priest!" Touilt stands behind him, trembling with rage.

"I pray to the mother of God," he says, his eyes never leaving Roswitha's face. *"Sancta Maria, Mater Dei, ora pro nobis peccatoribus, nunc, et in hora mortis nostrae."*

Wilona's fingers work inside the birth canal, trying to ease the cord loose. In a loud voice she calls, "Frige, wife of Woden, Queen of the gods, friend of women in their time, hear me now, and take this harm from us."

Their voices rise to different gods and mingle with the woman's cries. The air shivers and shakes, and then Roswitha's body goes rigid as bone and in her great effort even her breath stops.

"Push," whispers Wilona.

"Sancta Maria, Mater Dei," whispers Egan.

The baby slips out, blue and silent and still.

"Praise be to God," Egan says.

Touilt pushes Egan aside and lunges for Roswitha, whose eyes roll back in her head. Wilona reaches for the baby an instant before Roswitha collapses onto it, but something is terribly wrong. The baby's shape . . . the head is bulbous, the body . . . *what is that!* She pulls the child away. Roswitha struggles insensibly. Egan reaches for her, and to Wilona's surprise, Touilt lets him, accepting his help to turn Roswitha on her back. Wilona snatches a blanket and wraps the child in it. What should be inside the child is outside, and there are no legs to speak of. Touilt's and Wilona's eyes meet. Touilt bows her head and closes her eyes.

"Why is there no cry?" Roswitha says.

"Be still, be still."

Touilt cuts the cord and ties it, fingers working quickly. She points to the basket, and Egan hands it to her. She pulls out handfuls of soft moss. Roswitha must be packed.

"My child isn't crying!"

Wilona checks. A mercy. It drew no breath. She takes Roswitha's hand. Her friend's face is alabaster. "You must be strong, Roswitha. There will be other babies, lots of other babies."

Tears fall in shining rivulets down Roswitha's plump cheeks. "I want my child."

"No, the child is gone. Let me care for . . ." She hesitates. *What was it, boy or girl?* ". . . her. I'll see she's buried with proper rites."

Egan moves behind her, toward the motionless bundle in its blanket, the reddish-brown stains seeping through. "I'll baptize the child and bury it as a Christian."

She might have guessed. She bites back the words searing her throat. What good has the White Christ done? How has he proved himself more powerful than Frige? Perhaps that was what killed the child. Perhaps it was pulled apart by jealous gods.

"Is that what you wish, Roswitha?" Touilt asks.

She just cries and nods and cries some more. "Dunstan," she says.

Yes, Dunstan must be told. "Come; let's make you pretty for your husband." Wilona brushes matted hair back from Roswitha's clammy brow. She straightens the bedclothes as Egan bends over the tiny corpse and draws back the covering. He gasps, and then angles his body so Roswitha cannot see. *Well, at least he has some compassion, if little sense.* He says some sort of prayer and blesses the child, his hand shaking. When he is finished he looks at Wilona. His sharp-boned face is twisted with emotion, his lips skewed, the startlingly bright eyes blinking with something like astonishment. They beseech Wilona for something, but she doesn't know what.

"Will you call the father, or shall I?" she says.

Under Touilt's ministrations, the afterbirth has passed. She applies the moss. "The bleeding is slowing," she says.

Egan rewraps the baby and recovers himself somewhat, passing a hand before his face. "I will bring Dunstan." Yet he seems frozen, gazing down at the lump beneath the gore-marred cloth.

"Soon?" Touilt dips a cloth in water and wipes Roswitha's face.

"He'll be so disappointed in me," says Roswitha.

As the priest exits, letting in a blast of wind, Wilona kneels by her. "No, he'll be nothing of the sort. He loves you deeply, and you know it. Who knows why the gods take this one and leave that one? It's a hard world and your baby will never know hunger or—"

"Roswitha!" Dunstan bursts through the door to his wife, his cloak flapping, his hair wild, his face mottled. He drops to his knees next to the bed and takes her face in his hands. "I love you. You must not die!"

"She won't die," says Touilt, wiping her bloody hands on a cleanish cloth. "She'll be fine, in time."

"The baby," Roswitha begins, and then dissolves in tears.

Wilona stands in front of the baby's corpse.

Dunstan hangs his head. "So that's what I saw on Brother Egan's face."

"It's for the best," says Wilona, softly. Dunstan flinches. She need say no more.

Egan stands by the door. "The child is with Christ now. Safe in the arms of our heavenly Father. Free from all pain. Surrounded by the saints."

"As you say, Brother." Dunstan's voice is thick.

"We'll baptize the child, then." He comes to Dunstan and puts his hand on his shoulder. They're not that much different in age, Wilona realizes, although the monk looks older. "Will you tell me what you were to name her?"

"We hadn't decided yet," says Dunstan, his eyes never leaving his wife's face.

"The name comes in the days after the birth," says Wilona. "It's a message from the gods, and carries with it the child's responsibilities and gifts."

Egan turns to her and she's surprised to see his expression contains no contempt.

"Perhaps if we pray for a while, the name might come to us now. Shall we try?" he says.

Dunstan nods and kneels next to Roswitha. Egan takes up the child's body, kneels next to Dunstan and turns to Wilona and Touilt. "Will you not pray with us, sisters?"

"We cannot pray to your god." Touilt moves backwards, into the shadows.

"Pray to whom you will, and let love carry your heart's intention to heaven's ears." His glittering eyes hold no sarcasm. He closes them and speaks in a soft murmur.

The wind whistles through the thatch and smoke from the fire dances in the drafts, twirling round the rafters. The hut is dim now that the sun has slipped, in the short days of autumn, over the rounded hump of the mountain. The joking, weary voices of men drift into the hut as they return to their wives and children from their work in the fields, woods, or workshops. Roswitha lies on her back, her eyes closed. Her throat works with suppressed sobs and her fingers entwine with Dunstan's as she clutches his hand to her breast. His head is bowed. His free hand covers his eyes, and his chin trembles. Egan holds the bloody bundle and rocks it while he prays, his face tilted toward the ceiling.

Wilona sees them as though through an open door, beyond a threshold she cannot cross. She feels her spirits around her, smells the wild, open-heath scent of them, feels the flutter of feather and wing, but she cannot deny there's something else in the room. As thick as the air is with blood and afterbirth and grief, filled with the loss of all those things that might have been, there's yet a sweet, strange comfort mantled across the shoulders of those three, encircling them as tangibly as the presence of her own Raedwyn, and bringing solace in the same way. The scene draws inward, becomes both clearer, more precisely visible, and at the same time more distant. She is separated from them by the thinnest but most effective of veils. They are claimed by Christ, surrounded by him. Egan's face shimmers with tears, and he appears as consumed with grief as if the

child were his own. He is completely enveloped in his communication
with his god, as surely as if he were in a trance, and perhaps he is.
An enchantment Wilona cannot name has overtaken this place. She
should use every spell at her command to banish this White Christ
from a place hallowed by the goddess, but oddly she feels neither the
desire nor an urgent need to do so. Instead, she prays to Frige and
to Eostre, and to the spirits who care for small, lost creatures. She
asks that the child be found and guided safely to her ancestors. She
asks for mercy in the midst of grief. For an instant she feels hands
on her head, smoothing her hair, and then they're gone.

Roswitha says, "I am naming her Leofrun."

Whatever glamour surrounds them does not diminish, exactly, but
it parts, as though made of wind and water, and Wilona is once again
included, no longer outside, while around her, above her is the flutter
of feather and wing. Raedwyn remains. But where is Touilt? Wilona
spins round, and there she is, no more than a smudgy blur in the
corner, drawn in, camouflaged by the spirits, cloaked with shadow.
Touilt, too, then, has felt the presence of something other than the
old gods, but protected herself with magic beyond Wilona's ken.

Dunstan smiles at his wife through his tears. "It's a good name,"
he says.

Egan unwraps the blanket slightly and recoils involuntarily. Life's
cruelty seems to come as a shock. A tear trickles from his eye and
falls on the baby's twisted, inside-out form. He holds his charge in
such a way that Roswitha and Dunstan still cannot see, and Wilona
is grateful.

A movement beside her and Touilt speaks. "You have no further
need for me."

Wilona hasn't noticed her gathering her belongings and wrapping
her cloak about her. She sweeps from the room. Quickly, Wilona
grabs for her things, and places a hasty kiss on Roswitha's brow. "Do
you want me to stay?" she says.

Roswitha looks at Egan and then back at Wilona. "You've done
your work," she says. "Brother Egan will care for us now."

When she turns, Touilt is already gone. As she closes the door
behind her, she finds Margawn waiting outside, as she hoped he

would be. He puts his arms around her. "Touilt told me before she stalked off. I thought it best to leave her be. Sad news," he says. "How are you?"

"It was hard on Roswitha. She'll have to wait a while before having another. Luckily, Dunstan's the sort of man who'll give her time to heal." She disentangles herself from his embrace and takes his arm. "I'm weary, Margawn. Take me home."

------ ◆ ------

When at last Roswitha falls asleep and there is no more Egan can do before the burial tomorrow, he creeps out of the hut and stumbles into the deeply shadowed snickets. He needs urgently to get away from people, and the hideous frailty of human life. He wants a high place, and he wants to be alone. His mind is scattered. He'd been praying for mother and child when something picked him up by the scruff of the neck and propelled him into the birthing room. It was against all reason, his invading the place of women's mysteries, and yet he had been compelled. *Why?* There had been power in that room. He felt it like a heat blast when he entered. There would be talk in the village, questions about why the child had been born malformed. Someone would be held accountable. His heart told him the seithkonas were not to blame. And yet that power. It was thick, dark, disturbing. Only his most earnest invocation had brought the light of Christ into the room. If the Adversary found purchase there, he had to consider the women were involved, but surely, as victims, not as witches. Surely. His pace quickens and soon he is running through the village, past the vegetable plots, the thatched workshops, past the pigsties, the silent halls, the byres, and then he forces his legs to slow so he doesn't startle the guard at the village gate.

"Bit late for a stroll," says the grizzled, barrel-chested man, eyeing him.

"A hard night . . ." Egan stammers, unsure of how to say it. "Forgive me, I . . ." He can't recall the man's name.

The man nods. "Dunstan's wife, is it?"

Althred, yes, that's it. "Indeed, bless her."

"Aye," says Althred. "Margawn told me on his way back from escorting the seithkona woman. Might not have been wise, ah, to leave that sort alone with the mother."

"Sort?" Egan looks up to the sacred hill. He'll go there, as soon as this man lets him pass. He'll go up there and let the night winds cleanse his soul. The snow shines, glints, beneath the thick crescent moon.

"Well, I hardly need to tell you. People are none too pleased. Way things ended up. Considerable power those women got. Might shoulder a grudge or two, you catch my meaning."

Egan's head snaps round to face Althred. "No, no. They did all they could . . . everything. No one could have done more."

Althred lays a finger beside his nose. "You say so. You say so. But some of us think it best they move on. Lord Caelin seems to think so. One way or t'other."

For a moment Brother Egan isn't quite sure what the man means, and then he does. "I have no intention of . . . chastisement. They've done nothing to be punished for, Brother Althred. We must be clear on that. We must not gossip." He believes this; he is sure he does. And yet, there's a small wedge of doubt, a niggle of fear.

"Gossip is it? That's an old woman's game." The guard looks insulted and spits on the ground. "You mind telling me where on Woden's earth . . . pardon . . . where are you headed at this hour?"

"I'm going to pray."

"Prayers are best said safe inside the village walls."

"I'll be fine."

"Suit yourself. I've no orders to stop you." Althred mutters something under his breath and turns away.

It's a hard, cold climb up the ice-slippery path to the hillside. The exertion keeps Egan warm, even in his thin robe and cape. His feet are wet, his fingers stiff. There's no sound save for the wind and his laboured breathing. With every step he prays for the soul of the child and for the parents, and for forgiveness for his weakness, for questioning God's will. *How, Lord, how could you let such a thing come to pass? And if it was not God's will, but that of The Enemy?* He prays for Touilt and Wilona too.

At last he stops, too tired to go farther. He's quivering. The moonlight is a steely blue-grey stain on the snow. He fears he may not be able to contain the howl growing inside him. He chews his knuckle, the misshapen child's image branded inside his skull. To think the Blessed Mother suffered so to bring the Son of God into the world. He sobs. He had always pictured the Divine Birth as painless, bloodless, peaceful. Now he sees it as it must have been: child of God, made human in all ways, born to a human woman, on a bed of bloody straw, in writhing pain among the beasts of the barn. The smell of manure and Joseph's fear mingling with the scent of heaven. Memories of misshapen calves, and lambs with two heads, and piglets born so malformed . . . all instantly put to death if they breathed at all, their bodies quickly burned. Whispers among the brothers of demons, speculation about what such horrors meant. Augury and omens.

Was Sister Roswitha prey to elves? To a curse? How can he protect these people in his care? How has he failed them? Every time he closes his eyes he sees the grotesque form of the dead child, more demon than infant. Perhaps it is true that the seithkona . . . No, he cannot think that, for he saw the grief on the women's faces. He mustn't be tempted into evil thoughts about anyone. He must see only the light of Christ in every person.

There are no trees this high. The village is but shadows and flickers far below. The world is silver and cold, full of mystery, the sky impossibly vast, impossibly deep. *Lord, we cannot understand Thy ways. We can only trust Thee. Only love Thee. Only do Thy will.* He longs to disappear, to meld completely into the body of God. He removes his cloak, his tunic, and then his undergarment, standing in only his brodekins, and then he kicks them off and stands barefoot. The wind makes his eyes tear.

Egan prostrates himself on the freezing ground, rubbing snow all over his body. He welcomes the bite of it. Let the wind chew on his skin. He begs the angels to flog him with icy starlight until no trace of his sinful doubts is left. He wills himself to accept everything , even the pain, even the misery. It burns him, the frozen earth. It burns.

He loses track of time, then hears a sound. Low. Animal. Egan raises his head and there, just a few feet away, are two shaggy, grey wolves, their eyes yellow. One sits on its haunches and scratches its ear with a hind leg. One is lying down, head on its paws. It rears up a little and opens its jaws, steamy breath in grey puffs. Egan's heart pounds. Were his limbs not turned to stone with the cold, he might try to flee. As it is, he moves slowly, every muscle screaming. He puts his hands beneath his shoulders and pushes up, expecting the animals to attack. He prays only that they be quick. The sitting wolf, seeing him move, stops scratching and growls low. Egan is on all fours now. He slowly sits back on his heels and faces the beasts. The second wolf stretches backwards, hind quarters in the air, front paws stretched out. It yawns hugely, teeth flashing in the moonlight. Egan wonders how long they watched him, and why they didn't simply tear him to pieces.

He wishes he could put on his cloak. His teeth are chattering. The noise is very loud in his head and the wolves must hear it as well, for they flick their ears and look quizzical. He shivers. His belly shakes, his arms shake, beyond his control. The wolves will strike now, he is sure of it. They stand and nip at each other as though preparing for the feast. He closes his eyes. *Pater noster, qui es in caelis, sanctificetur nomen tuum* . . .

A series of yips and barks and Egan opens his eyes. The wolves run off across the land, kicking up clumps of snow, disappearing into the shadowed side of the hill. It is only then he remembers Touilt and her wolf pelt, remembers she's said to be a *gandrieth,* one who shape-shifts and rides the wolf-spirit.

———— ◆ ————

The next day, Touilt's mood still hasn't softened. She is sitting on a stool by the fire, ripping the skin off a hare, while Wilona puts on her cloak. "Roswitha chose the monk and dismissed us like servants. So be it. If you go, you go alone."

"She's my friend."

Touilt spits into the embers. "A seithkona has no friends."

"I won't be long."

Wilona walks up the slope to the village. She disagrees with

Touilt. She has friends. Dunstan is her friend, and Touilt's, too. So is Roswitha. And even Ricbert cares for them, although he let them down the day the vision-platform was destroyed. Then there's Margawn. What is he, if not a friend? Heart friend. Wilona sighs. Touilt has reason to be hurt, but it's the hurt talking. Roswitha was weary and in shock last night. Today will be different.

She finds Dunstan talking outside his hut with several people. Women, all friends of Roswitha, wrapped in warm cloaks and holding their hoods against the biting wind. Begila carries the baby Wilona and Touilt brought into the world six moons ago, when the meadows had been full of wildflowers and the sky full of swallows and swifts. Wynflaed blows on her chapped hands, and Saewara is thinner than ever, her skin muddy. Wilona fears she won't see the next summer. Two men, also: Dunstan's brother, Deneheard, who unlike Dunstan is a member of Caelin's army and tends his plot and his six children when he's not fighting; and Cynric, who can skin a deer faster than any other man in the village. Wilona notes, as she always does when she sees Deneheard, that he's inordinately fond of strutting, puffing his chest out, and showing off his scars. It's as though he swallowed his brother's measure of swagger. Just then, Cynric elbows Deneheard and the talking comes to an abrupt halt as they turn to her.

Her heart skips. "What's happened? Is Roswitha worse?"

"No, no, she's better this morning," Dunstan tries to smile but fails.

"Thank the goddess." Something, though, is wrong. Not that the death of an infant is not enough to make the gathering a solemn one, but there's more here. Wilona is suddenly as alert as a hare sensing a hawk's passing shadow. "I've brought her a tea that should help."

Dunstan, standing in front of the door, looks absurdly sheepish. "She's sleeping now."

"Is she?"

"She is," says Deneheard, "and when she wakes, the women will care for her."

"I'm glad to hear it," says Wilona. No one but this burly warrior, with the same wild hair as his brother, will meet her eyes, and what she sees in them sends ice down her spine. "Why would you be so unfriendly, Deneheard? I'm sure you don't wish to make me feel unwelcome." She's careful to put no threat behind the words, and to keep an open smile. Let him think her chiding is a joke.

"You may feel what you like."

"I must get my baby out of the wind." Begila turns and fairly jogs away. "You should come too, Saewara," she tosses over her shoulder.

"Aye, excuse me. I'll be back to see Roswitha when she wakes." Saewara follows, more slowly.

"Will you let me in to see my friend?"

Dunstan shuffles his feet and finally raises his eyes. "I don't think it's wise just now."

"He doesn't think it wise now or later," says Deneheard.

"Doesn't he?" Wilona keeps her eyes on Dunstan, who studies his feet again. "Oh, Dunstan, you hurt me."

"I'm sorry for that," he says.

"If you change your mind, you know where I am." As she walks away, tears sting her eyes. She should have listened to Touilt.

Wynflaed, who has in the past sought her out many times, looking for charms to make her drunken husband a kinder man, or to heal a child's croup, or to ease the cramps of her moon-time, hisses, "Sorceress."

It's all Wilona can do not to run from the blade of that spear.

Chapter NINETEEN

And so the talk begins, coming like the first snows, beginning with a certain tinge of pewter in the air, pale grey clouds sitting low, and then a flake or two, falling but not lasting, melting into the ground. *The baby died because the* seithkonas *refuse the Christ.* And then more snow, until it fills the air and obscures vision. *The child was born with a devil's mark.* It's impossible to catch every snowflake, to swat away the coming wall of white. *Who is Wilona, after all? A stranger under a black cloud, with no family. Perhaps the* seithkonas *killed the baby, or cursed it, in their rage against the Christ.*

Wilona and Touilt hear their fear, their murmurs riffling the thatch when the wind blows, their harsh words in the crackle of the hearth-flames. They rise up in Wilona's dreams: Caelin and Elfhild, Begila, Aelfric the potter, Maccus the bone-worker, making the sign of the cross with a dagger in their hands. In the waking world, when they pass her, people clutch their crosses, although this happens rarely now since they avoid the seithkonas, and choose the other path to the river.

Touilt wraps herself in heavy furs and spends more nights riding the spirits on the sacred mountain, while Wilona clings to Margawn when she can, in a way that gives her pleasure but does little for her pride. And no one comes to the seithkonas for help. No one asks for herbs, for dream-interpretation, for prophesy. No one pays them for their services, and were it not for Margawn, their stores of grain and fat and milk would be dangerously low.

Touilt draws away even from Wilona and, moreover, she has

developed a cough. Wilona begs her not to go to the mountain so often, for surely if they burn the sacred herbs and gaze into the smoke and water, the spirits will visit them just as well in the warm hut, but Touilt says that without a drum, she needs the summit, the ruins, the open air. "I'll get you a hide; we'll make a new drum," Wilona says, but Touilt simply shakes her head.

Margawn is rarely able to get away, and Caelin seems to send him on errands at the far ends of the estate more and more often. On the nights Touilt rides the spirits and Wilona is left alone, she sleeps with a dagger beside the bed. It's unnatural to sleep without the sound and comfort of someone else's breathing near. She tells herself the spirits are with her here as much as anywhere, but there are times it doesn't feel that way. When the owl hoots from the yew, it's as soothing as a mother's voice.

As the days turn to weeks, Yule passes with more new rituals in Caelin's hall, and again the women refuse the invitation, this one more tersely worded. *Lord Caelin says you are to come*. Elfhild sends them a goose, though, and Touilt weeps, saying she suspects Caelin has no knowledge of the gift. Touilt, no longer the lean and sizzling force she once was, weeps more often. Her stomach is bloated, her bowels loose, the stool bloody. They try every remedy—wood betony, knotgrass, lousewort, plantain, pennyroyal, comfrey, and sow-thistle. They sing the sacred songs, cast the runes, gaze into the flames, and toss the bones, but the will of wyrd is inscrutable, and Wilona fears her foster-mother is living with one foot inside the other world. Finally, Touilt stops going to the mountain.

Coming back from the river one day, Wilona proudly holds up the pike she's caught, stamping snow from her brodekins.

Touilt doesn't rise from the bed. "I might be able to eat a little. I feel stronger today."

Wilona tries to look cheerful as she stirs the smouldering coals in the hearth. Touilt peeks out from the pile of furs, her skin yellowish and her lips pale. "Did I let the fire go out? I can't be expected to do everything, with you not here for hours."

She must have been deep asleep, Wilona thinks, not to notice how cold it is. "No matter, the embers are still glowing." She adds twigs to the fire and blows until it flares. Whatever elf-shot sickness is eating through Touilt, the pain makes her carnaptious, quick to take offence. It frustrates Wilona that she can do so little to soothe it. As she nurses the fire into life, Touilt, scowling, wraps a shawl around her shoulders.

Late that afternoon, when she's given Touilt poppy tincture for the pain and trusts she's resting as comfortable as is possible, Wilona meets Margawn at the small cave near the river, the one she's long thought of as *her* place. Her place, yes, but she's happy to make it their place. They've made it snug—they've packed earth and moss into the chinks in between the rocks on the natural walls and roof, woven a vented door at the entrance, so they have privacy but won't asphyxiate from the fire's smoke. Margawn has brought piles of only slightly ratty furs from the hall, a pair of stone cressets in which wicks float in oil, and even a pot for cooking. Along a wall, they formed a platform of earth for a bed and covered it with straw and furs. Bana usually claims a place near the hearth by the cave entrance. With the fire blazing and their bodies close, it's warm enough.

As darkness falls they burrow under furs after making love. He holds her in his arms, barely waiting for their breathing to slow before he says, "We can't ignore this, Wilona. It's serious. Lord Caelin won't be pacified much longer."

"I know."

"There's only one thing to do, as I think you realize."

"We have to hold on until spring. Listen to that wind! I fear we've missed our opportunity."

"You don't have to wait until spring; you can take instruction now. The baptism can wait. It's the intention you need to make clear."

She sits up and turns away from him, showing him her knotty spine. "I meant we have to move away from the village."

"Where did you get a crack-pated idea like that? Where would you go? No other village will have you."

Wilona bristles. "We'll go farther into the wood then. Live with the spirits, where we belong." Margawn's sudden, explosive laugh makes her want to slap him. "We'll not bow to the Christian god! Not now, not ever."

He puts his arms around her, and though she's stiff with indignation he draws her close. "Live alone in the wild? Don't be absurd. You wouldn't last a winter."

She pushes at him with her knees and elbows until he releases her. "The gods have guided me through the wilderness before."

"You're too stubborn! There's only so much I can do, Wilona." He pauses and she senses him gathering like a wave before it breaks. "I want to marry you," he says.

"Oh, Margawn. You mustn't harbour dreams of changing me."

"Marry me."

"That's not my wyrd, my bear, and you know it."

He says, "You make me feel like a poor excuse for a man."

"How can you say that to me? When I give myself to you and only you!"

He runs his hand along her back. "I can count your ribs. I've been bringing you what I can, but I'm under Caelin's eye. Dunstan's child's only part of it. He left the door of his hall open to you and Touilt during Yule and you refused to come. It's a serious insult." His hand goes still. "Lord Caelin hasn't abandoned his interest in you."

The hungry, violent expression on Caelin's face that day at the amphitheatre returns to her. "I don't want your charity, Margawn, only your friendship."

"You're too proud by half. It puts us both at risk."

"Would you rather I encouraged Caelin's—how did you put it— *interest* in me?"

"Careful."

Smoke trails along the lines of rock and root above her. He's risked much for her sake. He's right. She's too proud. "Forgive me. It was a stupid thing to say."

Margawn takes her by the shoulders and turns her to meet his eyes. "Seek out Brother Egan, Wilona."

"And what can the monk do for me?"

"He has influence. Caelin listens to him more than Ricbert now. I pray you'll not find yourself without Touilt for many seasons yet, but we must face facts. You must befriend Brother Egan."

She sits with her leg tucked under her, the glow of the fire on her skin. "There's no point approaching him, unless I wish to be saved." She laughs, bitterly. "And in the saving I'm lost."

"You're more clever with words than I am, but it'll bring you only harm. I think you misjudge the man."

"He's a Christian. Enemy of the goddess. What more is there?"

"I've heard him speak on your behalf."

"Nonsense."

"Truth, Wilona."

"Why should he?" This throws an even more sinister cast on the situation. If her enemy has had to defend her to her neighbours, to Lord Caelin, what must they be calling for?

"You know the rumours. Take care Caelin has no reason to call you and Touilt to defend yourselves."

"They've called us witches outright then?" Her stomach roils.

Margawn adjusts himself so he's sitting behind her, her body between his legs. His sex nestles against her buttocks, stirs gently. He draws the furs around them both. "You've heard it," he says softly in her ear.

"Soon they'll say I've set a charm upon you."

"Oh, they already say that. Godfred has some opinion on your charms, it seems."

She blushes and is grateful her face is turned away from him. "And what do you think?"

"I think Godfred will miss that tooth." He chuckles and so does she. He smells of sweat and leather, like the good clean smell of a horse. "But it was Brother Egan who said he sees no evil in you and Touilt. He said your heart's kind, that there's no danger in you, only . . ."

"Only what? Come on. You've come this far."

"Well, I believe the word he used was 'ignorance.' We are to pray for you, that you might see the light of Christ."

"I don't need his milky prayers."

"You're missing the point. He had the opportunity to wield the talk like a sword and cut you out forever, but he didn't. He even said he thought your knowledge of herbs was formidable."

"I'm flattered."

"Think about it. That's all I ask. For both our sakes."

She parts his lips with her tongue to silence him.

Some hours later, she returns to the hut, and Margawn and Bana return to the warriors' hall. Wilona stands with her ear to the door. There's no sound from inside, and when she opens it the reek of sickness assails her. Wilona rushes to her guardian and finds Touilt's skin clammy and her hands trembling. The floor beside the bed is spattered with pink-tinged vomit. Guilt burns Wilona's gut. "What can I do?" she says, for there must be something, there must be.

"What haven't we twice tried?" The voice is weak. "I long for sleep."

She mixes the herbs and roots as Touilt taught her. She makes the signs of the runes over the mixture. She sings the songs. She stokes the fire with juniper. She brings the cup to the sick woman and cradles her as she drinks, as Touilt taught her to hold the sick. She opens Touilt's tunic and there, upon the leaf-thin skin, grey as that of a shelled snail, she paints the sacred signs and moves her hands, as Touilt taught her, over the great, unnatural bulge, full not of life but of the vermin of death. She prays and sings, and sings and prays, and feels Raedwyn, feather and wing, above and all around her, feels the ripples of his strength and warmth run through her shoulders, down her hands, spreading over the body of the woman who is as much a mother as she is ever likely to have, over the soft, fragile, pain-wracked body. She keens softly, breathes in the decay from the old woman's body and the wild-thyme and star-clear-night scent of her fetch, and sings and rocks and prays, and keeps watch with the presence of the great owl behind her and around her. She has kept the shutter cracked a bit, so that as she drives the evil out with prayers and the power of the runes, it will have a path back to where it belongs. When the moon is past its zenith, casting a silver sliver of light across the floor, Touilt stops moaning, her breathing softens, the muscles in her face relax, her hands stop twitching. Finally, she rests.

Chapter TWENTY

Perched on the roof, Egan stuffs bracken into the small holes that Ricbert noticed a few days ago. Under his knee he holds the new straw and, once each hole is plugged, he places a bundle on top. He pulls a hazel spar from the basket on his back and secures it to the underlying thatch with a willow rod tied in a rose knot.

"To your left—that looks like a weak spot," calls Ricbert from his stool below. He points.

Egan reaches for more bracken from the pouch at his waist.

The thatch smells sweet. Even though it's been in the storage shed for months, it still carries the memory of summer. The air is chill, though, even at this time of day, with the sun high above them.

Below, Ricbert rubs his hands and blows on them.

"Brother, why not go in and sit by the fire? This won't take too much longer," says Egan.

"You'll need more straw," says Ricbert. "I see another place that needs patching."

Egan sighs as he watches his living-companion walk to the shed, his feet placed carefully to keep from slipping on the icy patches. He suspects Ricbert simply likes to see him up on the roof and off his knees. The older man has mentioned, more than once, that the villagers will respect him more if he is less inclined to meditation and more inclined to manual labour. And he's right. Egan has been too focused on his own piety. Didn't Father Bresal warn him of this?

He descends the ladder to help fetch the straw. His hands are chafed and cracked from the finicky work in such cold weather.

He meets Ricbert coming out of the shed and takes the straw bundles from him. As he does, the older man grunts and gestures with his chin. Egan turns around and isn't surprised to see two village women—Begila and Wynflaed—rounding the corner of the chapel. Oh, God, he thinks, not the women again. What on earth will it be this time? Charms for the bread, for the hearth, for the cooking pot? He prays over children, over thresholds, over marriage beds, and over sheep. He sees the disappointment in the faces of mothers when he doesn't leave them with a potion or a charm. There's hardly an hour when someone doesn't arrive wanting something, most of which he doesn't know how to give. "Shall I keep working on the thatch and let you see what they want?" he asks.

"Oh, it's not me they want, Brother Egan. Not me at all."

Egan senses bitterness behind the words, but a touch of pleasure at Egan's discomfort as well. "Yes, you're right. It's my duty. They want Christ."

"Of course they do," says Ricbert. With that, he turns and walks back to their sleeping quarters.

"Welcome, sisters," says Egan as he places the straw bundles on the stool.

Begila and Wynflaed, who look alike enough to be sisters, both robust women with round faces, strong arms, and freckles, return his greeting. Begila carries a small basket, which she holds out to him.

"For me? How kind." Inside are a slightly wrinkled cabbage and some white carrots.

"Just something for the pot," says Begila. She nudges Wynflaed.

"It's about my Osric," says Wynflaed.

Egan attempts to keep a slight smile on his lips. Wynflaed's husband is a difficult man, probably of great usefulness on the battlefield, but in times of peace he has no outlet for his violent nature. He drinks too much, and when he drinks he uses his fists on his wife and children, and on the furniture and the animals, and anything else in his way.

"Is he ill?"

Begila snorts, and Wynflaed says, "I've been praying like you said to do, but nothing changes."

"We must have faith."

Wynflaed wipes her dripping nose with her cape. "That's all well and good, but it won't help much if he breaks my boy's arm. Almost wrenched it out of the socket last night."

"Do you wish me to speak with him?"

Begila jumps in. "You talk to him and he's liable to clout you one." She looks him up and down. "Don't think you'd stand up as well as young Randulf. Least he's got the strength to whack his father with a board if he has to and put him to sleep for a bit."

Wynflaed's son, Randulf, is twelve. "We must turn the other cheek, sisters, and pray that Christ's love opens Osric's heart."

Wynflaed says, "Touilt used to prepare a draught for him. I slipped it into his drink when I could see he was going to be ructious."

He can see it in their faces—they suspect they've made a bad choice. And what can he say? That they should go to Touilt for such things when Lord Caelin has expressly forbidden it?

"What have you got for us?" asks Begila, one eyebrow raised and her lips pulled down.

"I might have something," he says. "Can you wait?"

"Got to be getting back," says Wynflaed.

"Just a moment, then. Perhaps you'd like to go into the chapel and pray while you wait?"

Begila and Wynflaed exchange glances, then Wynflaed shrugs. The women walk into the chapel, although Egan is not convinced they will pray.

In the sleeping quarters he finds Ricbert sitting by the open door, wrapped in his cloak, close enough to the fire to be warmed by it. "What did they want?"

"A potion, something to make Osric kind."

Ricbert's laugh is deep. "That one needs to go back to war."

Egan rummages on the shelves over a small table. He finds dried chamomile in a little jar.

He has no knowledge of anything but the most rudimentary herb-lore, nothing more than scraps he remembers from his mother.

Chamomile to dispel nightmares, wood crowfoot for catarrhal afflictions, knit-back for bruises and broken bones. For now, chamomile will have to do. He says a prayer over it, blesses it with the sign of Christ.

He returns to the chapel to find the women outside again. He hands Wynflaed the jar. She opens it and sniffs. "That's chamomile," she says. "Like swatting a bear with a willow branch."

"It's been blessed, sister, made holy with the word of Christ. It carries the power of God's love."

"Made holy?" says Wynflaed. She sniffs again. "You said a charm over it?"

"Yes, the charm of Christ."

"Well, thank you then." She holds her finger up to her nose. "I'm counting on Christ, and on you."

"We all rely on Christ, sister," he says.

The women leave and he turns to find Ricbert leaning up against the chapel wall. "You don't yet understand us," he says. "We're loyal to our chiefs, providing they're good to us, providing they provide, if you catch my meaning."

"The one true God provides for all things," says Egan.

"Yes, without doubt," says Ricbert. "In the next world. But it's this one you have to pay attention to while you're living in it."

Egan is kneeling before the altar, praying through the night. A single candle glows on the stone under the wooden cross. The tiny flame barely holds the surrounding darkness at bay. He focuses on the fragile globe of grace and yet, even as he trusts it, he shudders to think of all the evil slinking in the shadows. His breath forms puffs of mist around his lips and nostrils. His knees send spears of pain up into his thighs and hips. He prays harder. *Consecrate my speech, Christ, Lord of the seven heavens! May the gift of precision be granted me, King of the bright sun.* He prays for the right words, for the gifts of patience, of understanding. He feels he's failing at the task God has set before him. His head droops. He pictures himself as a man made of straw, being pulled apart by the villagers' hands, which want, crave, tear at him. He snaps awake again. He focuses on the wavering flame. There is Christ, even in the darkest corners. He feels Christ with him, but he knows that when the sun rises and once again the people come, wanting this, wanting that, wanting everything, it seems, except what he has to offer, he will lose this feeling. If he doesn't find a way to be alone with God, to have just a little time to commune with the Holy One . . . He fears for his own soul.

Chapter TWENTY-ONE

Wilona sits on a stool near Touilt's bed and mends her under-tunic, her face close to the material. She cannot waste a candle for the sake of her eyes, and the light from the fire is low. It is just past dawn and Touilt has, at last, fallen into poppy-induced sleep. Wilona longs for someone to talk to about Touilt, but Caelin has called Margawn to accompany him to a meeting of the king's army in Bebbanburgh. King Edwin is preparing to invade the Isle of Man and then to do battle with his old rival, King Cadwallon of Gwynedd. Their goodbyes had been hasty and unsatisfying. He left a sack of grain and some dried ham; he stacked wood and held her tight. He pleaded with her, again, to reconsider her stance, and in order to please him, to make their parting less sour, she said she'd think about it.

Wilona works the bone needle in and out of the cloth. She must seek the guidance of her spirits. The power of the holy well seems to have diminished since its rededication to Christ's Mary. Wilona stares into the middle distance. Dried herbs hang from the rafters and a bunch of nettle catches her attention. She puts her sewing down, stands on her stool, quietly, so as not to disturb Touilt, and breaks off a handful of dark leaves. She moves to her small wooden chest and uses the key attached to the chatelaine on her belt to unlock it. The lid opens with a slight grinding. From inside she takes the bag of runes, a small stone bowl, and a cat skin. She takes them to the hearth, where she squats and unrolls the skin. The calico fur is soft and crackles with a subtle energy. She invokes the spirits and concentrates, reaching out to feel Raedwyn. With the wooden ash-scoop, she plucks three bright orange embers and puts them in the stone bowl. Over these she crumbles the dried nettle, and the pungent, slightly acrid scent purifies the air. She closes her eyes and softly sings a song of gratitude to the rune spirits, begging for their guidance. Touilt stirs and moans but doesn't awaken. Wilona reaches into the rune sack and lets her fingers roll and play among the smooth stones until her skin tingles. She curls her fingers around the rune that speaks to her, then rubs it between her palms, telling it she's grateful for its wisdom and guidance. Only then does she place it on the cat skin.

The rune *mann*, face down. Her heart catches. It's the rune of humankind, of responsibilities to others, signifying kindness and the fellowship of the hall, but also a time of solitude and separation. It means both communication and the possibility of deception. The x at the centre of the symbol is the web of wyrd, a reminder that all things perish and fall away, that change will come and all life is transient.

Wilona replaces the runes in their bag. It could mean parting from Touilt, but could it also mean Wilona should go into solitude to find the solace of the gods? It's a message, but unclear. She must go where Touilt has gone, to the sacred mountain. She snared a hare yesterday; it will make a fitting sacrifice.

She builds the fire so it will burn for a few hours and bundles up, with wool packed inside her thin brodekins. She hates the idea of rousing Touilt, but if the old woman wakes and finds Wilona gone, she may panic. Touilt opens her eyes and nods when Wilona tells her of her plan, but then begins to cough again, and it takes more poppy tincture to calm her.

Just after sunrise Wilona sets off, her hood up and an over-cloak of sheepskin around her shoulders. She carries a rucksack filled with the hare, juniper twigs, firewood, flint, and two hard-boiled eggs for the walk home. She slips a flagon of cider tied to a strap over her shoulder and takes up her staff. Over the past few weeks she fashioned it from a fallen yew branch, and carved the small figure of an owl on the top. She begins the walk up the sloping path. Although she could walk along the river's edge, following the upward path from the edge of the village, steering clear of her neighbours, she doesn't want to give the impression she's creeping around. She'll walk alongside the village walls if not through it.

There's no snow today, but the granite sky hangs low, scraping the mountain's top. The ground is frozen and slippery, and the wind plucks at her clothing and hair, nips her cheeks, and causes her eyes to tear. Two squirrels chatter and chase each other, squabbling over some prize. Her mind flashes back to that long-ago day when the red squirrel tried to raid the robin's nest and was killed by the hawk, just as the spirit-illness fell upon her. So much changed that day, when Raedwyn claimed her. Remembering makes her aware of the great owl's reassuring presence. Overhead, a flock of fieldfare thrushes swoops down, showing their white underwings, loudly chuckling, warbling, and whistling, in search of a rowan tree to strip of berries. Their energy lifts Wilona's mood.

She skirts the dyke and follows the path toward the coppice wood. From the village come the high-pitched, excited voices of children. Wilona imagines them throwing snowballs and making snow-faeries. Now she sees Baldred the woodcutter and one of his sons, their backs piled high with hazel rods, approaching along the path. Baldred is a squat, bandy-legged man, with wide shoulders from years of swinging an axe. Since his wife, Oslafa, died in childbirth, it's as though he lives under a storm cloud. He has three children to care for, the oldest this boy now with him, Bardolf, who looks like a spider with the bundled sticks on his back, whereas Baldred looks like a grumpy beetle. Wilona's gait becomes awkward under their gaze. She tries to arrange her features in a pleasant expression. "Good day to you, Baldred."

"And to you."

"It's a harsh day for work in the wood."

"Fences won't wait for mending." He nods as he passes her. "Don't dawdle, boy."

Bardolf ducks his head in a way that might be taken for a nod and Wilona smiles, but when he doesn't return the courtesy, she wishes she had not. She keeps her eyes resolutely forward. A gust of wind makes her pull her chin in and tighten the cloak at her throat. At least they didn't make the sign of the cross to ward off evil.

The path leading to the sacred mountain snakes along the far side of the royal compound. The cold ground beneath her feet makes her bones ache, and every step causes the light snow to fly up and settle in the tops of her brodekins. At this distance she's able to see beyond the fortification walls to the amphitheatre. The gold carvings on King Edwin's hall are so rich they glint, even on this cloudy day.

The path curves around the base of the sacred mountain to the western side, where the climb is easier, and from there leads to the stream running down to the River Glen. Hers are not the only footsteps. Someone has come before her, and not long ago. Someone coming to the stream? Perhaps someone's hunting for partridge or plover, although it's easier to find wintering ducks along the riverbank this time of year.

A gust of wind whips snow in her face. She stops, pulls her scarf over her forehead, and adjusts the ring-brooch at her neck, drawing her hood tighter. She scans the distance to determine where the footprints might turn away. The sun slides from behind a cloud and flashes brilliantly, blindingly, against the snow, as though the field were scattered with crystals. She squints but is loath to close her eyes against such beauty. Overhead a hawk circles, looking for mouse tunnels, and cries, she imagines, in exaltation at being so free, so fast.

The footprints continue, and if she's to follow the urgings of her spirits, she has no choice but to do the same. As she ascends, the royal compound and the village below become smaller, although when the wind swirls, it carries sounds—laughter, the rhythmic crack of an axe, dogs barking. The fields are soft as sun-bleached linen. The oxen and cattle in the winter pens look as small as hounds.

The trees are scrubby, wind-bent and stunted. The way is steeper and her breathing laboured. She relies on her staff. She can't imagine how Touilt managed this climb, ill as she's been. The spirits must have carried her. She comes round the far slope, where the sun shines brightest. Had there been a plateau on that side, no doubt the old kings would have built their compound there to benefit from the longer, warmer days, but perhaps the gods jealously guarded that place for themselves.

Still the footsteps continue on the snow-covered path before her. Here, on the hushed far side of the slope where the commotion of village life cannot reach her, it's easy to imagine they've been sent to guide her. Unless, of course, they were made by darker forces— elves. The thought comes to her with a dropping sensation in her stomach. She halts; her head snaps up and she looks all around. She sets down her bundle and from it takes the juniper bough, rubbing the berries between her palms and over her face for protection. She touches the piece of iron in the pouch between her breasts, intoning the words that call the spirits to her defence.

Touilt's face floats before her—hollow, ashy, distorted by pain, eyes burning with fever. Wilona rewraps her bundle and ties it over her shoulder. One foot in front of the other, onward until the spirits tell her to stop; onward, in the footsteps of ghosts.

How much time goes by is hard to tell. She suspects that, were the sun to come out again, it would already be near its apex. Her stomach grumbles and growls and she's lightheaded, which is as it should be. Her hunger, like the hare, is a sacrifice. She pictures *sowilo* before her, rune of the sun, which looks like Thunor's lightning bolt; rune of safety, health, the achievement of goals. She holds her heart steady and her step confident.

Glancing up, she sees what looks like a giant beehive. No, not a hive, but something made of stones. Badly made at that. It's little more than a pile of rocks. It looks as though it might tumble at any moment. The footprints lead directly to it. What evil spirits, trolls, wights, monsters hide here on the far side of the mountain? She lets the wind buffet her. Her ears sting from the cold and her nose runs. The clouds are so low it seems she could reach up and pull them down over her. Her nostrils flare. She inches to the eastern side of the structure and sees an opening. The wind dies down for a moment and a tendril of smoke curls from the chinks between the topmost stones.

She is reluctant to approach the opening, because whomever or whatever is inside will have the advantage. She will be in light, while they will be hidden by the shadowed interior. She grips her staff, holding it like a club. But wait . . . a huddled shape by the entrance, a man, thin as an icicle and as pale, shirtless, his arms spread wide . . .

Wilona raises her staff, takes a step backwards, nearly tripping over her own feet, and cries out. The figure in the stone hut cries out as well. Wilona crouches, ready to fight or run, as Egan steps into the light, pulling a cloak hastily around his torso. He blinks like a mole, his leaf- coloured eyes cool and otherworldly.

Chapter
TWENTY-TWO

"Sister Wilona? Is that you?" Egan shields his eyes. "I heard a noise."

"I've disturbed you, forgive me." A swath of his skin, mottled and marbled with cold, is visible between the cloak folds, while his hands are reddish, wizened. She averts her eyes from his partial nakedness. "I'll leave you." He's mad, surely, alone here on the hillside, half-naked in the frigid air—bad enough on a sunny day, but to crouch in the darkness?

"Isn't it odd you and I should meet this way? Surely it's the hand of God," he says. "I feel as though you've been sent to me."

His sing-song accent is more pronounced than usual, and she wonders if his lips are frozen. "It's not your god who called me. This mountain is sacred to my gods." She realizes he's wearing nothing on his feet. "Do you mean to die up here? Don't you have brodekins and proper clothing?"

He looks at his feet as though he's forgotten he has such things. "I hardly feel them," he says in a small voice, and then promptly sits down in the snow.

"Are you mad?" Wilona moves to him and hauls him upright. "You can't sit in the snow. Get up. You'll freeze your feet. Where are your shoes? Your shirt? Have you no furs?"

She half pushes, half pulls him into the hut, being careful neither of them falls into the miserly fire. The hut is earth-floored, with a fur on the ground and an unlit torch stuck in a chink in the wall. Here and there, light lances through other small holes, although from inside, the structure seems quite solid. In fact, it's cleverly constructed, each stone balanced so it leans against its neighbour, arcing gently inward. She glances warily above her head, imagining stones raining down, but the ceiling looks as though it will hold.

Wilona sets Egan down as gently as she can, but he lands with a thump and the thin cloak falls from him, revealing his chest. It's pale as the underbelly of a fish, but covered here and there with deep scratches and wounds. A belt cinched round his torso is dotted with barbs that lance his flesh. She slips her pack from her shoulders and reaches to unlace the belt from Egan's middle, but he puts his hand over hers.

"No, sister, you must not remove it. It reminds me of my sins; it purifies me."

"Purifies? Nonsense. These wounds will fester and kill you." She slaps his hand away. She tosses the sinister, bloody belt to the ground. She spies a discarded bundle of clothing near the fire and reaches for it, tossing him the undershirt, woollen overshirt, and shoes. "Put your feet by the fire, else you'll have frostbite. Surely not even your god wants you lame."

He does as he's told, and she averts her eyes while he pulls his arms through his garments. She stokes the fire, adding branches from a small stack of wood nearby.

When he's wrapped more warmly, she asks, "Do you have anything for heating water? A pot?"

His teeth chatter. Wilona takes this as a good sign; his body is relaxing a little and trying to revive itself. He points to a leather pouch, in which she finds a little dried meat, a loaf of bread, and a small iron pot. She pours her cider into the pot and heats it. When it begins to steam she shields her fingers with her sleeves and plucks it from the fire. She waits until the edge of the pot has cooled sufficiently, and hands it to Egan.

"You must drink first, Sister," he says.

"You fear I poison you?"

He smiles shyly. "I wish only to be a good host, even if you're the one offering me nourishment."

Wilona takes a tiny sip. The pale, brownish liquid is foggy and a seed floats on the top. The taste is sweet, clean, invigorating. She holds the pot toward him. "You may consider your courtesies fulfilled. Now drink. All of it."

Egan takes the pot, his sleeves pulled over his palms, cupping the hot iron. He looks up at her and says, "You are an angel come from Christ."

"No need for insults," she says.

For a moment she thinks she's gone too far, but then his eyes crinkle, his shoulders bounce, and he makes small wheezing sounds she realizes must be laughter. "No insult intended," he says. "Would you prefer I name you Angel of the Mountain?"

"I am seithkona, no more, but no less," she says.

He takes another sip and nods. "Agreed. You are all of that."

Wilona looks around her again. Save for the pinpricks of light, and the rain they will let in, it really is a solid building, not so different from her cave by the river. For a moment she imagines Margawn's great calloused hands on her body, her breasts, her buttocks, lifting her . . . she blushes and rubs her hands over the fire, commanding her mind to return to the present. "What is this place? I thought you lived with Lord Ricbert."

"This is where I come to be alone with God."

"How can you be with your god here, the mountain sacred to *my* gods, not yours?" In fact, when she considers it, she's surprised the gods haven't knocked him off the mountain completely. How can they let this invader build on such holy ground?

"God is everywhere."

Stealthily, without his seeing it, Wilona makes the rune-sign of protection against her palms with her thumbs. What does he mean? Is there an army of invisible spirits somewhere? This monk, even in his fragile state, speaks the language of war.

He looks thoughtful, his eyes on the nearly empty pot. "I love the people, but now and then I need solitude. I need to hear the heartbeat of God in the song of the wind, the cry of the birds, the patter of the rain, even the stones."

What does he know of the gods' heartbeat? She scans the space, looking for a drum, but sees none. Does he speak to stones? Does he mean the rune stones? "I hadn't thought Christians respect the spirits of the wild places. Doesn't your master Paulinus say we must reject all such things, that the spirits are evil?"

He nods. Those eyes—on a woman they would be called beautiful. At first she's so distracted by their water-weed tint, she can't understand what's so odd in his expression. Then it comes to her. He's not looking at her as a man looks at a woman. There's neither desire nor condescension in his eyes. He regards her, it seems, as an equal. She holds her head a little higher and wonders if this might be some Christian trick, designed to make her drop her guard. She wills Raedwyn—feather and wing—to come protect her. His presence comes easily enough, which is confusing, for the owl spirit is here with no scent of fear or rage. Can it be this priest is no threat? Or has he laid some charm even on her fetch?

"Paulinus is a great thinker, with large and complicated thoughts. I'm not a great thinker. At best I'm a little boat of faith in a sea of mystery." He pauses. "Do you believe the world is holy, Sister?"

She frowns at his calling her *Sister* again. He's no kin to her, yet to insist he call her Lady Wilona is pompous and self-important. "I do," she says. "And alive with spirits."

"We're not far apart, then. I believe we walk through the body of God—every pebble and stalk, every thicket, stream, and mountain, animated by God's love."

"You speak like one who holds the old ways, but you reject the old gods."

He tilts his head to the side, smiling. "I don't think in terms of rejection, Sister. I only know it was through Christ I saw a glimpse of heaven. I fasted and prayed, and fasted and prayed, and one midnight, on a high place not unlike this one, an angel appeared and showed me what the world will be like when Christ's teachings spread and men turn away from vengeance, pride, and war, and toward forgiveness, humility, and peace. She showed me that even the tiniest speck of sand bursts with the breath of Mystery." He raises his eyes to the stones above his head, as though he expects them to part and the light of heaven to pour down on him. "I wish I could share the beauty and the power of that love with you. Believe me, it's not a case of rejecting one thing; it's simply a matter of longing so much for something more—for God's ineffable love—that I can't rest until I spend myself in its service."

Wilona concludes that if this half-starved, elf-eyed monk thinks the teachings of Christ, or any other god, will turn men away from war and pride and vengeance, he must be mad indeed. She half pities him, and yet his respect for the wild places seems sincere, and when she thinks of the way he treated Dunstan and Roswitha, she cannot deny his gentleness. "You confuse me, priest."

He detaches his gaze from the ceiling. "I don't mean to, and I'm no priest, Sister Wilona, just a monk."

"The king's monk."

"I'm Christ's disciple and I answer to Him, seeking only to celebrate His creation and praise Him. Surely we can agree the world is marvellous, full of wonder, an expression of a grace far beyond our understanding."

"I'm a servant of the goddess, that's all, and I answer to Her before all. But yes, I suppose we can agree on some things."

Egan claps his hands and his face glows. "Oh, sister, you do cheer me!"

Wilona searches his face for mockery but finds only the happiness of a simpleton who thinks wearing a barbed belt and freezing to death will bring about his vapid heaven. He laughs and, sudden as a storm cloud, his face becomes serious.

"But what brings you here today? And how may I help you? I owe you something, a great deal in fact, for the cider, not to mention the future use of my toes." He looks shamefaced. "Surely I was spared by your appearance only because I'm still of some small use. So, tell me what you seek here."

Wilona purses her lips. She doesn't want to reveal the reason for her journey, and at the same time she's aware she must hurry if she's to perform the rites and return to Touilt before mid-winter's early dark. Already the shadow moves along the entrance, slanting further than makes her comfortable.

"I'm seeking guidance, I suppose." Egan looks at her encouragingly, and if the concern in his elf-eyes is false, he's a better liar than she judges him to be. "Lady Touilt's not well," she says, before she's made up her mind she wants to tell him. It's terrible, the relief she feels just to have told someone, even this half-mad Christian.

"Not well!" His brow furrows. "How so?"

Touilt's face, sharp-toothed, wolfish, snarling with fury, flashes before her. Touilt will tear out her throat if she reveals the seithkona's weakness. She's said far too much, and anger bubbles up, bitter and hot. Damn his kindness, damn his talk of compassion and wonder. He's enchanted her into letting down her guard. "It's nothing, I'm sure. Dyspepsia."

She gathers her things, and Egan rises to his feet and then sways, his hand to his eyes. Spots of blood have soaked through his tunic.

She reaches out to steady him. "Are you faint?" *Is there no end to the weakness of this idiot?*

"No, no, I only rose too quickly. It will pass." He takes her hand in both of his. "I'll pray that Sister Touilt's health may be restored."

"As I said, nothing more than a bit of bad pork, no doubt." Wilona shakes her hand free. "If you can't make your way back to the village alone you must wait for me to return and I'll help you, otherwise let us part here."

"You mustn't let me take up any more of your time. I'll return to the village and light a candle for Sister Touilt on Christ's altar, asking for your foster mother's healing."

"She has no need of your intervention; her wyrd is decided by the gods. Can I trust you to keep what I have told you between us? Do you swear it?"

"Upon my vows, sister, but don't you think your friends will want to know? They'll want to care for you both."

"You may not have noticed, but we have few friends in the village these days."

Egan presses his palms together as he touches his index fingers to his lips. "It's a time of adjustment. People are perhaps confused. I'll speak about the virtues of mercy and compassion."

Can that be the kindness foreseen in the rune? The hairs on the back of Wilona's neck lift at the thought of this Christian petitioning her neighbours on their behalf. "Just honour your oath and keep your mouth shut," she says, more severely than she intended. Egan looks as though she's slapped him. She can't bear to be here a moment longer and, without another word, steps out of the hut.

"You're my friend," he calls after her. "I'll not betray you. May God bless you and Sister Touilt."

Wilona grinds her teeth and flinches as a particularly bitter gust of wind strikes her. If Caelin listens to this man, as Margawn said he does, he's not the fierce warrior he once was. She suspects Margawn, for the first time, of deceiving her. The rune again . . . She shifts the bundle on her shoulder and tightens her hood. There's no time to waste. Perhaps the Christian had, by some sorcery, set himself in her path to delay her. She glances over her shoulder. Egan stands in his doorway, watching her. He's so thin and pale that were it not for the stone structure around him, she fancies he'd fly off into the ether. He raises his hand to wave but she turns away and quickens her pace, a spell of protection on her lips.

———◆———

Egan watches Wilona walk determinedly up the hill, slipping a little here and there on the snow. She leans into the slope as though she were pulling a great load, every step stiff-legged with determination. The news her foster mother is ill is distressing for him—how much more so for her. He's tempted to break his vow and inform Lady Elfhild. Surely she would find a way to soften her husband's heart. But he has promised. There is so little he can do for Wilona. He had thought himself quite clever when he'd secretly left baskets of food for the women and, knowing Touilt and Wilona would refuse any gift that came from him, cleverer still when he'd made Margawn promise he would take credit for it should the occasion arise to do so. Now it seems like a paltry gesture. *What loneliness the girl faces.*

Perhaps he and Wilona are more alike than they are different. She seems to have adapted well to her life apart from the village. Although it is a sin, he envies her. What he wouldn't give to be able to stay here in this little hut forever, with the majesty of creation, God's greatest miracle, filling his senses. He never has to strain to see God in the deer and weasel, the stones, the trees, the stars; it's only among humans that sometimes, sometimes, he doubts.

Wilona grows smaller until at last she rounds the hillside's curve and is out of sight. Egan falls to his knees. "Oh, praise and glory be to you, My Lord, for sending her to me. Show me how to reach her, Lord. Show me." He prays for guidance until a niggling sense he has neglected his flock too long creeps in, and he rubs life back into his cramped limbs. It's some minutes before he can stand. When he does, he raises his eyes to the summit. Fog rolling in, and no sign of Wilona. She's in God's hands. He says a blessing for her safety and begins his descent.

Chapter
TWENTY-THREE

Wilona steps into the ring of ancient stones. The wind howls and whistles and clouds sweep in, turning the landscape foggy and grey, softening shapes and allowing her to see no more than a few feet. It would be easy to think she's been transported into the misty world of Niflheim. Quickly, she takes the firewood, the hare she's brought as a sacrifice, and the tinder and flint from her bundle. With her staff, she draws a protective circle around the west-facing stone. She builds a fire, and then bathes herself in the smoke. She holds the hare aloft, the fur soft between her fingers. She calls Raedwyn, until she feels him around her.

The mist rolls away, and sunlight floods the mountaintop. The snow is a glittering dazzle of eye-piercing white. Wilonas heart soars, flying on the wings of the unseen owl. She sings the song honouring and inviting the spirits . . . from the east . . . *Winged One, Spirit of Air, your daughter calls you* . . . from the south . . . *Fierce One, Spirit of Fire, your daughter calls you* . . . from the west . . . *Swift One, Spirit of Water, your daughter calls you* . . . from the north . . . *Hoofed One, Spirit of Earth, your daughter calls you*. She calls the spirits of moon and stars, of the earth creatures, and of air and water, those that burrow or crawl or fly. She asks them to bring her any messages from the gods. She asks Eostre to come, and Freo too, goddesses of healing and protection, of life and strength. She purifies her dagger in the fire and opens the belly of the hare so the entrails spill on the sacred ground. In thanksgiving, she offers the carcass to the spirits. She stands before the flames, closes her eyes, to receive what may come. Burning fur, woodsmoke. Snow. Stillness, flame-crackle, wing-flutter, wind-whisper.

Something murmurs, a high-pitched whine. The spirits come. Her skin flushes warmth, and it's all she can do not to open her eyes and look, but she knows if she does, the spirits will vanish. Two voices hum, one in each ear. She concentrates, but it's impossible to catch every word.

"Into shadow . . ."

". . . all suffering ends . . ."

". . . to barrow and fire . . ."

". . . what tears then mends . . ."

A hot whirlwind swirls round her and then is gone. In her mind's eye she sees an overturned cart, charred black, the wooden wheels slowly spinning, like the flailing legs of a dying beetle. One of the shafts is broken, and the cart rests unevenly on stony ground. She cries out and her eyes fly open. An opaque wall of fog surrounds her. Under its wet mass she can't see beyond the circle, and even the sacrificial fire seems blurred. Bitter smoke stings her nostrils. Her muscles are cramped. The hare's carcass is twisted and black. As always with such ceremonies, more time has passed outside her than inside. With the fog this thick, it is impossible to tell the position of the sun, but the light is dying.

What she saw lingers—the overturned wagon, symbol of the rune *raidho* in the reverse. Disruption, crisis, death. Wilona's heart is like a stone tied to her foot, dragging her down into the river of grief. She tries to find an alternative meaning. The spirits can be obtuse. If all suffering is to end, and what tears will mend, then surely there's the possibility of healing. One voice spoke of shadows, barrows and fire, but the other . . . Can it be Touilt's fate still hangs in the balance, that the Norns have not yet finished weaving their pattern?

She'd hoped for more. She'd hoped the spirits would reveal some healing charm. The damp fog seeps through to her bones and she wraps her cloak tight. She listens, longing to catch some faint whisper, but the fog presses against her mouth and nostrils as the damp wool presses to her skin. She scatters the last of the juniper over the carcass, speaks her prayers of thanks, gathers her possessions, and sets off. She must accept what the gods have offered. They have their ways, their purpose; it's not for her to question. Dizzy with hunger and exertion, she peels the two eggs, stuffing them into her mouth, the yellow yolks dry and crumbly. She eats handfuls of snow to quench her thirst and make swallowing easier. Her head clears, but she has little in the way of reserve. She begins walking.

When she comes upon the monk's hut it is deserted. Once more, she follows in his footsteps and wonders if she'll find him collapsed on the path. The wind has picked up, and the fog has rolled out, but clouds have gathered and a light snow falls. The sun slides below the far line of hills, and as darkness descends, she's grateful for both the early half-moon and the monk's footprints before her.

When Wilona finally stumbles into the hut it's fully dark. The hearth glows, but the flames have died, and clearly Touilt had neither the inclination nor the strength to keep it fed. She has, however, lit a lamp near her bed and now peers at Wilona with fever-bright eyes.

"And what have you learned, my child?" she says, her voice a croak.

"That the gods are with us still." Wilona kneels by the fire, blowing on the embers until they spring to life again. There's no hiding anything from Touilt, but illness may dim her powers of perception. Shadows dance across the walls. The air carries an acrid, cloying smell.

"And did they tell you I'll see my husband soon?"

Touilt's husband died long before Wilona came to Ad Gefrin, and Touilt has rarely spoken of him, having put such things aside when she was claimed by the gods. To have her talk of reuniting with him now is unsettling.

"They said no such thing." Wilona edges a few of the glowing coals to the side of the hearth, tosses a handful of sage onto them, breathing deeply of the sweet smoke.

Touilt makes a sound that starts as laughter but ends in coughing—horrible, hacking, convulsing coughs. Wilona hurries to her and helps her sit up, rubbing her back, holding a cloth to her mouth. When the spasm finally ends, Wilona gasps, for the cloth is stained with dark blood.

"How long have you been coughing blood?"

"I can't keep track of time."

"I'll make a poultice, and you must eat something. What have you eaten today? There are bones for broth and some mutton."

Touilt pushes her away. "I can't eat. My body rejects everything." She clutches at her chest and her face distorts with pain. Her fingers dig deep into Wilona's arm. "I fear I'm being punished."

"No, Touilt, no. You've done nothing to warrant punishment."

Touilt claws at Wilona. "You know nothing. All those nights, all those nights!" Her teeth are stained with blood. "I went to the summit. I sought the spirits, but all I saw was death, rot . . . daggers and spears and axes . . . carrion . . ." She falls back, her breath laboured. "Crows and cattle, fire and clay. Heads hanging from the trees and all the graves open."

Wilona shivers, as much from the darkness she sees in Touilt's eyes as from her words. "You're in pain, Mother, and fevered. I'll give you something to sleep, and you'll feel better when you wake." She reaches for the poppy tincture. The bottle is nearly empty. The poppy is known to cause strange dreams; maybe that's where these horrors come from. There are two more bottles; it won't last forever.

"The gods call for slaughter, Wilona, and I fear it. They call for death."

Wilona holds the trembling woman in her arms and hushes her. When she quiets, Wilona pours some of the poppy tincture into a cup of wine and holds it for Touilt to drink. "Sleep. I'm here; the spirits are with us; the goddess watches over us. Sleep."

But sleep refuses to come. Exhausted as she is, Wilona mixes horehound, barley meal, and honey syrup; she makes poultices of betony, cinquefoil, and sinfull. When coughs wrack Touilt's body, Wilona refreshes the poultice and forces her to sip a little horehound in heated wine. At last, near dawn, Touilt slips into a kind of slumber and Wilona dozes too, her head on Touilt's bed.

Dying is hard work. Touilt worsens quickly, struggling for breath, weaker every day. Day to night and night to day, the seithkona writhes and moans and coughs, her skin nearly translucent, her bones standing out as though they mean to burst through her thinning flesh. The furs and blankets are spattered with the dark blood from Touilt's failing lungs. Wilona doesn't know how many days have passed. Touilt's tongue is cracked and dry. The older woman's limbs have shrunken alarmingly, even as her belly distends. Wilona keeps her as clean as she can, but the hut is fetid. Although ice pellets hit the roof all day yesterday, still she opens the shutters a crack, preferring the cold to the stench. No matter how much mugwort, sage, and juniper she burns on the hearth, the air doesn't clear. Whatever ill spirit has taken possession of Touilt, no prayer, no charm, no amulet, no tincture, decoction or poultice weakens it. Touilt, still alive, is rotting.

Wilona's tear-swollen eyes burn constantly. The pattern the Norns have woven is set. Touilt has, by grace of the gods, already lived longer than many. It's not the worst thing, Wilona tells herself, for at last, when the seithkona's body is placed in the barrow, she will travel to the dark world and be reunited with the husband and sons she loved. Wilona only wishes Touilt weren't so frightened. Where does this fear come from, and why does it come to one who spent her life in the company of the spirits? Surely she can't think they've deserted her now? The air is thick with them.

As evening comes, Touilt is quiet, and Wilona takes advantage of the lull to nibble a piece of oat bannock. She has little appetite but knows she must eat. If she falls ill as well, she'll be of no use to Touilt. The bannock is dry and crumbles in her mouth, sticking in her throat. She reaches for the pitcher of buttermilk.

The chickens outside squawk and then Elba grunts. Someone is coming. Quickly, Wilona puts down the pitcher and opens the door, brushing her hands on her tunic. She peeks through the shutter.

Egan and Ricbert are walking down the path, hooded heads held down against a sleety rain. As they near the hut, Wilona's heart beats erratically. Let them pass by, she prays, let them pass by.

Knock. Knock. Knock.

"Good day," Egan calls. "Hello?"

Chapter
TWENTY-FOUR

"Good day, Sister Wilona." Egan tries to sound cheerful, and yet when Wilona opens the door, looking as though she'd like to gouge out his eyes, he takes a small step backwards. Father Bresal comes to mind, insisting the whole world waits with bated breath for the Good News of Christ's coming. *Gather them gently, as Christ does his sheep, Brother Egan, gently.* What would he make of this pagan priestess?

Wilona's own eyes have sunk deep in her head, and she's lost weight. Her cheekbones stick out and her skin looks pulled tight. Its lustrous pearly light is gone. Her hair is matted, her tunic filthy. *Abba, let me forget myself to serve her.*

Ricbert, looking wet and cold, clears his throat. "We've seen neither you nor Lady Touilt lately. We thought we should pay you a visit."

Wilona searches Egan's face. Ah, he understands: *she's looking for signs I've betrayed her.* Her suspicion pricks him, but why should she trust him? He flicks his eyes to Ricbert and gives his head a tiny shake. "It was Brother Ricbert's idea. Even when he visits Mary's well he sees no sign of you. He inquired round the village and then suggested we visit."

"Your kindness is appreciated but quite unnecessary."

"Oh, well, that is good to know." Egan's hood slips away and the icy rain falls on his head.

Wilona has no cloak and the overhanging thatch gives little protection from the driving, nearly horizontal rain. She shivers and crosses her arms, water trickling from her hairline. She glances down at her soiled tunic and looks surprised. Egan tries to keep his face impassive, but she blushes and he knows he has failed.

"We've brought you a few things," says Ricbert, extending a basket. "Just some cheese and meat."

"Does Lord Caelin know you're here?"

"We're your friends, sister," says Egan.

"He doesn't then." She grabs the basket from Ricbert. "Well, never mind."

Egan's surprised she says no more, but it's obvious she's frantic to get rid of them. Any doubt he had about the urgency of their mission is gone.

Ricbert moves toward her. "Wilona—"

She puts her hand up. "We're in the midst of certain . . . delicate . . ."

She chooses her words carefully, Egan sees, avoiding mention of now-forbidden practices.

". . . women's matters."

Egan almost smiles. It's a good ruse. Men, especially religious men, are queasy about women's mysteries.

"Ah," says Ricbert. "Well, then."

Ricbert looks at Egan and shrugs. Perhaps the man is right. He knows Wilona and Touilt best, and if he thinks they should be left alone, Egan can't deny it. He'd prefer not to intrude. For a moment he thinks they'll leave, and all will be as well as it can be, but then a terrible noise from inside, part moan, part shriek, the sort of noise an animal might make while chewing its leg off to escape a snare.

"Mother of God!" Egan crosses himself.

"Wilona . . . Wilona . . ." Touilt's voice is a thin wail upon the wind.

"I think we'd best go inside, don't you?" Ricbert's face is stern and determined.

Wilona looks as though she might try and bar the way, but then she softens. "She won't want you," she says.

"I've known her since birth, Wilona, long before you arrived!" Ricbert moves her aside and lifts the latch.

Wilona follows him inside. Egan says a brief prayer, makes the sign of the cross, and enters the hut. The hearth fire burns brightly, but the rest of the hut is in shadow. The air is pungent with juniper and sage, yet nothing can mask the terrible stench. He resists the urge to pull his cowl over his mouth and nose.

Ricbert crosses to Touilt's bed and sits on a stool. "Ah, old friend," he says, "I see it's not good with you."

"My husband visited me." Touilt's face is the colour of dry clay.

"Hengest." Ricbert nods. "An honourable man who fought bravely."

"I miss him."

Egan stands with his hands clasped round his wooden cross, praying softly.

"The priest," says Touilt, grimacing.

The dreadful thinness of her face makes it even more wolfish than ever; the length of the jaw is exaggerated, the eyes feral. Her eyes lock onto Egan and he forces himself to return her gaze, not to look away from the agony, horror, and fear.

"You're safe from him, Mother. I'm here." Wilona squats by the side of the bed.

Touilt cries out and presses her hands to the swelling in her belly. Wilona turns to Egan. "There, on the shelf, inside the basket. Yes. There's a vial there, blue glass. Bring it."

Egan scrambles to find the right vial, and Wilona prepares its contents in honey-wine. Touilt sucks it like a hungry baby, then frowns and winces, her hands kneading her stomach. "I want him . . ." She points a skeletal finger at Egan.

Egan's heart leaps like a stag in his chest. *Praise God.*

———◆———

Wilona thinks perhaps Touilt wishes to place a curse upon the monk. She knows it's only fear and pain speaking. Touilt would never use dark arts.

Touilt grabs her sleeve. "Bring him," she says, her eyes glassy, her teeth stained brown from the poppy tincture and the blood. "I want him. I want him to take me to his god."

Bile rises in Wilona's throat. "You don't know what you're saying, Mother." *She's raving.* It breaks Wilona's heart. The tears she's swallowed break forth. Perhaps she should take away the potion. The pain would be even more terrible, but at least Touilt would be lucid.

Touilt struggles to rise and points again at Egan. "His god promises a paradise of light." She coughs and Ricbert is spattered with blood specks. Touilt fights and swallows and chokes and grips the front of Wilona's tunic. "I'm surrounded by shadows! By horrors . . . Wilona, help me . . . demons . . . monsters . . . my visions writhe with them!" She collapses. "Peace, I want peace . . ."

Touilt flails as Wilona makes a sign of protection over her. "Ricbert, calm her if you can."

The old priest, strong yet, holds Touilt's arms so she doesn't harm herself. From the shelf, Wilona plucks a bag of wood-sage, roots and leaves—the cure for insanity—and fastens it about Touilt's neck.

"Will you not leave us, and let that be the peace you promise?" Wilona fairly spits the words at Egan.

The monk's face contorts. "I cannot, sister. I'm bound. Forgive me for increasing your distress. I cannot leave."

Wilona works quickly. In her mind she fashions the *algiz* rune, which connects her to all things. She calls Raedwyn from the wild wood, and feels him flutter above her. *"May Eostre, goddess of rebirth, who brings the plants to life each spring, bring you to new life,"* she intones. *"May Thunor receive you. May Woden own you. May Thunor protect you with the hammer that came from out of the sea, and may the lightning hold all evil away."* She chants the sacred song. Her hands dance about the fretting body of her foster mother, but no matter how she tries, Touilt will not be calm. Near to death as she may be, her will is strong and she'll not be denied. She screams for the priest, and the screaming turns to coughing, and then a horrible combination of the two. It goes on and on until Wilona fears for her own sanity. The entire room darkens, draws into itself. Wilona feels strangled, as if her head is about to burst wide open in a red explosion—red for blood, for rage, for the scald of regret. She pushes her hands over her ears. It doesn't help. She throws herself on Touilt's convulsing, howling body. It doesn't help.

At last, her face swollen and blotchy, Wilona acquiesces. "All right, Christian. Help her if you can. Help her." There's a cold spot behind her, to her left. Raedwyn has gone. She doesn't blame him. If she could she'd follow him.

Egan nods, his face grim, and steps forward to the end of the bed.

Touilt's eyes are wild. Wilona wipes her mouth. She brushes the hair from her forehead as she would a child's. It's cold as stone. Ricbert stays next to Touilt, who gazes up at Egan as though he is an angel from the White Christ's heaven. Wilona steps away. She takes Touilt's key from her belt and opens Touilt's chest. She takes out the wolf pelt, the one Ricbert brought her in secret after Coifi destroyed the original. She buries her face in it, breathing in the scent of the den, the earth, the moonlight, and the memory of magic. She lays the pelt on the bed next to Touilt, and Touilt's hand, more claws than fingers, reaches out and buries itself knuckle-deep in the fur. Then she groans and pulls away. Her stomach seizes, and her chest heaves with such might Wilona fears the woman's ribs might break. She has only enough time to roll Touilt on her side. Blood gushes forth in such a torrent that Wilona's tunic is soaked. Ricbert leaps back and stands next to Egan, who mumbles a prayer. The blood is so dark. Wilona feels no guilt when she hopes Touilt will die, safe in the arms of the gods and the ancestors, before the Christian interloper can work his foul magic.

But it is not to be. Touilt hangs on with the tenacity of an ivy tendril to the trunk of life. Wilona senses the distressed spirits of the house scattering to the rafters and the corners. She can almost hear their angry chatter.

"Let me save her soul, Sister Wilona," says Egan softly.

Wilona does not move from her place beside Touilt. The air is sickly sweet and holds the tang of iron. *A woman who devoted her life to working with the gods and helping others. How dare he say her soul needs saving.* "She's in the grip of death-visions."

He holds a crucifix in one hand, a small glass vial filled with liquid in the other. "And do you deny the power of such a vision?"

Touilt moans, and plucks at her. It feels like a bird's beak.

"Priest," she gasps. "Save me."

"What about your husband, Touilt? What about your sons?"

"They call to me. They point to the priest."

Wilona gasps. Surely a trickster spirit has possessed Touilt. "No!"

Touilt screams again, and Wilona claps her hands over her ears. Ricbert steps forward. The shadows of the two men envelop Wilona and she feels her power leave her.

"Brother Egan means her no harm, Wilona. It will ease her passing. I know you love her."

Wilona swipes at her cheeks. "More than anyone. She's all I have."

Ricbert places a gnarled hand on her arm. "There's nothing to fear, Wilona."

"Let Christ grant her peace. By God's grace, her loved ones, it seems, already rest in paradise; let her join them, as she wishes, Sister Wilona," says Egan.

It's obscene. Touilt is dying and they're a pack of dogs fighting over her bones. She looks at Ricbert, whose eyes are intent, fierce even, in their concern, but she sees no danger there. It would be simpler if she did. Touilt's fingers keep plucking at her. Wilona steps aside. "I won't be stopped from my own prayers."

"All prayers are beloved of God," says Egan.

She sits heavily on a stool by the fire, one hand at the owl feather in the pouch at her breast. With the other she makes the rune signs in the air. Ricbert stands just behind her, and then she feels his hand on her shoulder. Were it not for the anchor of his touch, she fears she might just fly across the room onto Egan's back and wrestle him away from Touilt.

Egan, eyes shadowed beneath the heavy ridge of his brow, bends over Touilt. Her mouth is open, stretched not in a smile, but in a rictus of longing and fear. The priest makes a sign, like a rune, on his brow, his lips, and his heart.

"Do you want to be admitted to the paradise of Christ?" he says. Touilt nods.

"What do you ask of the Church of God?"

Wilona says, "She cannot answer you, fool." Ever so slightly, Ricbert's hand tightens on her shoulder.

Egan glances at her and nods. "Touilt, do you ask for faith?"

Touilt nods and closes her eyes. Wilona thinks perhaps it will be over then, that wyrd has snatched the seithkona from the edge of the abyss. But no, she opens her eyes.

"Do you accept that faith offers life everlasting?"

At these words Touilt's face relaxes; she looks upward. Wilona follows her gaze, longing to see what the broken, dying woman sees, praying it is her wolf come to take her. There's nothing but the rafters, the cobwebs, the thatch.

The sound of Touilt's voice startles them all. "Life everlasting," she says. Her voice is shredded, ragged. Still, the words are clear.

Wilona drops her head and tears fall on her tunic. How can Touilt, who has walked between worlds, be so afraid of dying? What is there to fear? Is death not the end of pain, the beginning of rest, when one is reunited with the ancestors, when all work, save that of blessing the living, is done? Surely she can't believe her beloved dead have become traitors and crossed to the Christian heaven? She curses herself for giving Touilt so much of the dream-inducing tincture. It's the pain. It's the potion. There's no other explanation.

"If then," Egan says, "you desire to enter into life, keep the commandments, thou shalt love the Lord thy God with thy whole heart and with thy whole soul and with thy whole mind, and thy neighbour as thyself." He brings his mouth close to Touilt and breathes over her, three times, forming a cross on her body with his breath each time. "Go forth from her, unclean spirit, and give place to the Holy Ghost."

"There is nothing unclean about Touilt!" Wilona cries.

"Hush," says Ricbert. "The words are the same for everyone. Hush."

"You are calling for ghosts to possess her! Ricbert! Think!"

"Be at peace, Wilona. Only good shall come of this."

Ah. She sees the truth in his eyes. This is a great coup, the deathbed conversion of the seithkona. Power will shift hands as lightly as a drinking horn. *Oh, Touilt, what have you done?* Her stomach churns.

"Receive the sign of the cross both upon your forehead," Egan says, as with his thumb he marks Touilt, "and also upon your heart. Take to you the faith of the heavenly precepts; and so order your life as to be, from henceforth, the temple of God."

Order her life from henceforth? Wilona almost wants to laugh. Touilt will not see the dawn. It's a farce.

"Let us pray," Egan continues.

His strange mumbling language means nothing to Wilona. The monk lays his hands on her head and Ricbert replies, "Amen." Now Egan removes a tiny silver locket from a pocket inside his habit, takes something from it, and puts it in Touilt's mouth. She hardly seems to notice, though her eyes are fixed on his. Touilt can't close her mouth, just moves her tongue a little. He then takes the small glass vial and pours the clear liquid on Touilt's brow three times, saying as he does, *"Ego te baptizo in nomine Patris, et Filii, et Spiritus Sancti."* He rests his hand on her head and says some words, too softly to hear. He turns from the dying woman, his work done. "She is saved. Her soul is saved. May she die in peace and find her eternal rest with Christ."

Touilt's eyes close. Her breathing is so shallow and slow that with each deflation of her chest, Wilona fears it will not rise again. Ricbert, with one final gentle squeeze, removes his hand from her shoulder and bends down in front of her. "I don't think it will be long now. Do you want me to stay?"

She shakes her head, her throat too tight for words to pass through, her entire being a single throb of regret. What made these men come now, this night, and why had she let them in? She feels as though she's plunged a dagger into Touilt's heart. She's failed her foster mother, her teacher, her guardian. She has failed.

"If you need me, send for me. We'll send a boy to wait at the door."

Egan clears his throat. "Wilona, sweet sister, I ask you now, at this sacred, blessed moment when the veils between the worlds are thin. Won't you join your foster mother? Won't you also accept the promise of everlasting life offered you by Christ the Lord?"

"You've a bold nerve, priest." She's on her feet and trembling. She takes Touilt's cold hand in hers. Memory flashes—she's sat this way before, by the bed of another dying mother, in a village long ago, when she was the only one left alive. Touilt's eyes open briefly and try to focus, but close again. "Leave us. Send no boy. I'll not call."

Wilona holds Touilt's hand in both of hers and lets her tears fall. In a moment she hears the latch fall into place as the door closes.

Then she's alone with Touilt, whose chest still moves, though barely. All that was strong and robust about her is gone. The fire in Touilt's eyes has been doused, replaced by a glassy stare.

Wilona tries to feel Raedwyn, tries to call him to her, but there's nothing, just shadow and the thickness of night on the other side of the wall. It presses in. The walls bend and creak. There are no words to say, for Touilt has placed herself outside the pattern of wyrd. There's nothing now but the strange unknown, a hollow shaft leading up into a starless night, a sucking hole through which Touilt's soul is doomed to disappear. "Come back to me, little mother, just for a moment." *Tell me it was all a fevered mistake.* She looks at Touilt and knows it's a vain hope, for the mist of death surrounds her now, the eerie vapour-like matter she's seen around the dead before. Touilt's spirit, her energy, is seeping outward now, leaving, preparing itself for the journey to . . . to where? To where? Wilona groans. *It is too much! Too much!*

Wilona sings the song for the dying, chants the runes *eihwaz* and *raidho,* knowing it's useless; the gods will refuse to come to the aid of someone who has denied them. Wilona prays the gods may forgive Touilt, understand she was seduced by pain and fear and by the White Christ's enchantments. And then Wilona realizes Touilt's chest no longer moves, and the smoky vapour around her head is gone, and the eyes are still, and the jaw is slack, and the hand no longer cares who holds it. Wilona opens her mouth and releases into the uncaring night the scream of a heart broken and alone.

Chapter TWENTY-FIVE

The next day, something scratches at the door. The hair on Wilona's arms stands up.

"Bana, stop that. Wilona, are you there?"

And so, Caelin and his army have returned. Would she have had the strength to keep the Christian out if Margawn had stood beside her? *Too late.*

She longs to crawl inside his arms and sleep there forever, but she can't bring herself to let him in; to do so would mean one thing has ended and another will begin. "Go away."

"I've spoken with Ricbert."

She wants him to stop talking. She can't say goodbye to Touilt yet. Wilona presses her palms to the rough door. "Understand, love, and grant me this little time."

She hears Margawn building a fire outside. He and the hound will wait.

All through that day and night, Wilona watches over the body, singing the sacred songs. She brushes Touilt's hair and washes her, arranging her limbs, wrapping her chin so her mouth will not gape. All tension has left her face, and the lines have softened. Wilona draws runes upon her chest, not caring what the Christians will think. She dresses her in her blue tunic and lays the wolf-tooth necklace at her throat. She weights her eyes with pieces of rowan. She lights a candle and scents the air with amber resin.

She sits with her back against the door, knowing Margawn is sitting on the other side. Shadows flicker on the walls, scratching and tapping in the rafters, shimmering in the corners—spirits, restless and confused, fill the dwelling but Raedwyn is not among them.

Perhaps she dozed, or perhaps time moved on without her, but when the knock comes at the door, morning's light slips through the cracks between the shutters. She lies on the ground beside Touilt's bed. She's as cold as if she were in the grave herself.

"Wilona, you must open the door now. It's time." Margawn's voice, deep and soft.

Every muscle and bone in her body aches, and her eyes feel filled with sand. She looks down. Her hands tremble. Even with the amber and the sage, the room is saturated with the thick, sickly sweet scent of decay. She kisses her foster mother's cheek, already tinged faintly green. Margawn is right. It is time.

She opens the door and blinks, blinded. She shields her eyes. What a sight she must be. She doesn't care. Margawn stands before her, so alive and vibrant, he looks more god than man. Bana stands next to him, his nose quivering. He whimpers and she scratches the dog's ear. He licks her hand.

There, behind Margawn, wrapped in furs, is Lady Elfhild, her golden hair glinting, her eyes the colour of the sky, her expression part distress, part compassion. Brother Egan, too, looking pious and pale, and Ricbert, the old heron. Two slaves shift from foot to foot, ordered to carry the body, no doubt, their eyes wide, clearly unhappy at the prospect of entering the house of a seithkona and touching her discarded husk. Margawn reaches for her, but she holds her hands up, knowing if he touches her she'll dissolve.

"Dear Wilona," says Lady Elfhild, stepping forward. "What a terrible time, and your grief must be agony. Will you let us in? Will you let us offer you assistance and comfort?"

"You've come for her body?"

"She must be buried," says Ricbert. "With all honour."

Wilona nods and steps outside, away from the door. A draft passes her face as the spirits of the house, Touilt's spirits, rush into the ether. Although she sees nothing, she watches their path all the same. Then Margawn's hand is on her shoulder, and her face is in his chest, and his arms are round her. She doesn't see them take the body.

Half a dozen graves, dug in the new graveyard during autumn, before the ground became hard and unyielding, gape like hollow eye sockets. A hurriedly nailed together wooden cross stands at the head of Touilt's earthen bed, held in place with stones, and the Irish monk mutters his Latin incantations, shivering in his thin cloak. The day is bone-chilling, and the sun on the mountain snow so bright it hurts Wilona's eyes. It should be raining, she thinks. There should be a thunderclap of rage, a deluge of tears from the forsaken gods. Wilona finds herself wondering if there's any point to serving the old gods, or the new one, for that matter, if it all comes to this.

Wilona stands with Margawn and Bana at the back of the crowd that has come to see the old seithkona buried as a new Christian. Even Lord Caelin has come. He caught Wilona's eyes just once. Only Margawn's arm round her waist stopped her from rushing to him and slapping the smugness right off his face. She fights not to look at him again, knowing she won't be able to control herself. Dunstan and Roswitha stand near her, their friendship seemingly returned in the face of her grief. They don't know how to comfort her, for she pulls away from every human touch except Margawn's. It's in their eyes: they think she'll join the flock now that Touilt has, now that her mother-ewe is gone.

Everything seems strangely defined, as if some membrane has fallen from her sight. It's terrible, this clarity. Each stalk poking up through the snow trembles in anticipation of a heavy foot; each seam on every garment seems about to split, each thread ready to unravel. The leafless trees seem flayed and shrinking. Six crows walk near the fence as though banished. Now and again one or another stretches its neck and caws indignantly.

"I'll make her a finer marker," says Dunstan. "As soon as I can."

"*Cineres cineribus,*" Egan says. "*Pulverem pulveri . . .*"

"Yes," says Roswitha, her voice low. "One with a circle round the cross, and a wolf carved in the stem." She reaches out as though to touch Wilona, but Bana stands and fixes his eyes on her and she draws back. Roswitha chews her lower lip and shrugs at Dunstan.

The monk holds up a handful of earth and drops it into the pit where Touilt's body lies, wrapped in a plain linen cloth, with only a bronze crucifix, a small bowl, and a comb from Lady Elfhild, in the grave with her. The clod of frozen earth hits the body like a stone. He invites others to do the same, but few take him up on the offer. Wilona thinks they have no wish to look upon a grave so ill-stocked for this supposed afterlife.

The service finishes. People begin to wander off, but elfish Egan comes toward her, Lady Elfhild and Lord Caelin with him. Something like fury slithers up Wilona's throat. She clamps her mouth shut. Lord Caelin has more swagger in his step than ever before, whereas Lady Elfhild retains her calm composure. Wilona's muscles tense. Margawn takes her firmly by the elbow.

Before she can stop him, Egan takes her hand in both of his. "I cannot imagine your grief," he says.

"No, you cannot." His hands are cold as stone.

"Won't you let us come back with you and talk awhile?" says Lady Elfhild. There, too, in the lady's eye, as in Roswitha's and Dunstan's, the hunger, the eagerness, to bring her in, to claim her, the last holdout, as one of Christ's own.

The desire to leap into their embrace, away from her solitude, stabs her. But it's not her they want. They only want another Christian. They only want obedience. She will not look at Caelin. "You are most kind, Lady, but you'll forgive me if I'm not strong enough to talk." She slides her fingers from Egan's grip and, crossing her arms, tucks them inside her sleeves.

"I'll see her home," says Margawn. "With my lord's permission?"

Caelin nods and says something about what a loss Touilt's death is. "But at least in the end she was saved—isn't that so, Brother Egan?"

"We must be joyful she rests with Christ."

"Hopefully she taught you enough of the healing arts to serve us," he says to Wilona. "She was loyal, if occasionally too proud. I trust you'll not make the same mistakes. Perhaps her lack of civility can be traced to her illness. Now that's done with, I trust you'll feel free to show your gratitude for our hospitality."

Margawn's fingers are a vice on her arm. "My foster mother trained me well," she says.

Egan looks up at Margawn. "Take good care of our friend, Margawn. And Sister, if you need anything, anything at all, you must send word. Nothing will be denied you."

Does he mean to drown her in his compassion? "I'm grateful for your concern. We all grieve Lady Touilt's passing."

"Indeed," they mutter. "Such a sad loss." "A life of honour." And so on.

And with that, the groups separate, leaving Wilona and Margawn and the dog on the path away from the village. The sun dips behind the great hill, and within seconds the light changes from gold to silver, and the wind picks up. Wilona imagines it is the spirit-wind carrying the dead to the land of the ancestors, but then remembers Touilt will not be carried there. There's no way to know where, if anywhere, she will be carried. For the first time, Wilona considers the possibility that there is nothing but a great chasm in the world of the dead. If there are no gods, no ancestors to catch the soul, one just keeps falling. She starts at the terror of it.

"Are you faint?" says Margawn.

She pulls away. "I must go back."

With a feeling in her chest like a cloth being wrung tighter and tighter, she returns to the graveside. The earth has been filled in, mounded slightly, raw as a wound, and the plain cross stands like a splinter in the frozen flesh of earth. Part of her wants to fall on the ground, dig with her bare hands until she meets Touilt again, and then cover both their bodies with the same hard earth. The other part of her wants to spit on the grave.

Yes, there it is, the white-hot coal inside Wilona's head, making it pound and burn as she grinds her jaw. *How could you do it? How could you leave me here and put yourself beyond even the reach of our gods?* It's all well and good to say pain and potion swayed a great woman in the midst of her weakness, but Touilt should have chosen pain and clarity over poppy-dreams. The old woman broke faith, and if Wilona failed her, Touilt returned the favour.

She remembers that first night, when she lay in a strange bed, a broken child blistered by grief, come from the-gods-know-where, her memory blasted by whatever had happened. She reached up and took Touilt's hand, then woke in the morning with the seithkona's arms around her. That wild smell of the wolf pelt, thyme, and Touilt's own tangy sweat is in her nostrils even now. She thought then perhaps Touilt had claimed her out of affection, or at least pity, but now it seems she only used her for her own purpose. Used and then discarded. For it appears Wilona has been tossed into a new world where the things Touilt taught her are useless. Touilt apparently gave no thought to what might happen to Wilona if she chose the new god. Even had she survived, been miraculously healed by the White Christ, Wilona would have had to make the same choice she's faced with now, for there's no ambiguity: she must either convert or be cast aside; join the flock or be culled.

Sounds from the village drift on the air: the laughter of children, the bark of dogs, and the rough voices of men. She imagines the slaves turning the roasting spits, stirring the stews, lighting the lamps. If she were a mere slave, a bondswoman with no influence, she would be safer than she is now. She nudges the soft dirt at the grave's edge. Then she kicks it, sending a spray of earth onto the cross.

"Wilona!" Margawn grips her arm and will not be shrugged off. "Stop this now. I can imagine how you feel, but if you value your hide you'll stop."

She sucks in air. He's right, of course. Caelin has cut off the lips of those whose words displeased him, cut off the hands of those whose deeds displeased him, and severed the heads of his enemies in war, impaling them on posts around the hall as signs of his might and his right to wield it. She must control herself.

Margawn turns her to face him. "I don't mean to be cruel, Wilona, but you must remember you're not here by blood tie."

"You think I've forgotten I'm a stranger?" Margawn's hands hurt her, but she won't give him the satisfaction of wincing.

He frowns. "You've been seithkona here because Lord Caelin permitted it, in deference to Touilt. All that's changed." He releases her and runs his hand over his face.

His beard is unbraided and longer than it was. There are new lines in his face. So wrapped up has she been in her grief she hasn't really looked at him. Her heart softens. The life of a warrior is hard.

"You must see the hazard," he says. "You must adapt. You've skill as a healer; put aside your grief and anger, mould your talent to the new form."

"I'm tired, Margawn." She casts one last look at the grave, and turns away. "Will you see me home? I've missed you."

"You'd miss me less if you agreed to be my wife."

She slips her arm through his. Bana nudges her hip and she ruffles his fur to let him know she isn't angry with him, either. "And what sort of marriage would we have, if I did agree, the handfast or the Christian rite?" She puts her hand against Margawn's cold lips. "For this night, can we leave such things outside the door?"

He nods and puts his arm around her as the wind knifes through her woollen cloak. How cold Touilt must be.

Touilt's bed is stained and soiled. Death is such an ugly, undignified thing. Margawn drags the mattress outside for Wilona to burn in the morning. She hasn't eaten since the night before. Her stomach growls. Margawn builds the hearth fire to a roar. They find what there is to eat, a little hard bread, which they dip in apple-wine, some smoked ham, a nub of cheese. And when the hunger of one kind fades, another rises. It's been weeks since their parting and they're ravenous, the tang of death adding urgency to the act. At first it is all a tumble of arms and legs, of tongues and teeth, and Wilona cries out sharply when she comes, tears on her face, as much from grief as pleasure. They are gentler after that. When they are done, a sort of calm descends, veiled in sorrow, but the edges of Wilona's mourning have been rendered less sharp by Margawn's touch.

He pulls her close, her head on his wide chest. "It's difficult to imagine this place without Touilt," he says. "She was good to me.

She cared for my mother in her last days. And . . ." He pauses and under her ear his heartbeat quickens. "I've never said this to anyone. But after my first battle, I had certain . . . terrors. I was haunted by . . . there were things . . . King Cerdic and his queen . . . I didn't expect . . ." His voice trails off.

In a flash, Wilona knows what Margawn means, as surely as if he'd spoken aloud. Shortly after his ascension to the throne, King Edwin called the companions to make war against Elmet, to avenge the assassination of his nephew, Hereric, whose widow, Breguswyth, and two daughters, Hereswith and Hild, were now his wards. He took his vengeance out on Elmet's King Cerdic and his queen by blood-eagle, opening their rib cages near the spine, and placing their still-breathing lungs on their own backs. A hideous death for a man, but to watch a woman die so? It would scar a good man's soul.

"Men do what they must in war. There's no dishonour."

He shakes his head. "It was a dark time, and without her I might have been lost. Touilt had power. There was much of the warrior spirit in her."

"Aye," says Wilona. "There was." Yet, at the end there was little bravery at all, as far as she could see. She keeps her silence, and dozes.

After a time he gently shakes her. "Wilona?"

She's groggy, and with waking, the pain of losing Touilt returns. She burrows under the furs, nuzzling into Margawn's side. "Must you leave?"

"I can't stay long, and we should talk."

She doesn't like the sound of that and shakes her head to clear the dream webs. She raises herself on her elbows.

He takes a deep breath, and she can see by the bluish smudges under his eyes he did not sleep long. "I wish there was more time to mourn with you, but I'll be called away again soon. We're to go to Eoforwic soon, perhaps at the new moon. Penda of Mercia is ambitious and war is coming."

"This is the news from your time in Bebbanburgh?"

He nods. "King Edwin hoped Penda would join with him, but Penda won't. He's taken control of Wessex and the territory of the Hwicce."

"And you think there will be war."

Margawn grunts. "Isn't there always? But we'll prevail."

"But you'll have to go."

"Aye."

He draws her to him, and once more they find comfort in each other, but no act of love can postpone his parting forever, and before the hour is out she is alone again.

Is there no limit to the breaking of a heart?

Wilona picks up Touilt's wolf pelt and holds it to her face. There's little of Touilt's smell left, only something unclean. Perhaps she took her scent with her, or perhaps her wolf has disappeared back to the misty lands.

Raedwyn. Where is the great owl? Gone with the wolf? She's been loyal to him; will he not be loyal to her? She closes her eyes, softly sings the chant to call him. Nothing. Only the rustle of some small creature in the storage corner. She uses her palm on her chest to beat a rhythm that matches that of her heart. She wills the chant and the heart drum to find him. And then, something stirs.

Flutter of wing and feather, above her, around her, that perfume of the moors, wild and clean and sweet. Her song quiets to a whisper. Her face is wet with tears. She feels Raedwyn near her, looming, protective, and yet as fretful as her own heart. He seems to flit and flap, turning his vast wings this way and that, as though looking for escape. It's clear to her then: he's no longer comfortable in Touilt's hut—in her hut. This place has been claimed by the White Christ. Raedwyn moves like a thing wary of a snare, a trap. Is that what he has to tell her? This place, home for all these years, where she'd been claimed, she thought, by Touilt, is now a snare.

If she's to stay, she must do so without Raedwyn. And without him, what is there? The whim of kings? Of lords and priests? She cannot cease to be seithkona. Can she? She glances to where the vision-platform once stood; the outline where the boards were torn away is still faintly visible. Perhaps, since she is the only healer in the village, she wouldn't have to convert, exactly. Perhaps Lord Caelin would permit her, in return for her craft, a certain leeway. She needn't call herself seithkona. She can keep some things secret. She has the herbs, the plant-lore . . . and there's another possibility: she could marry. Her skin tingles; her breath quickens. To live as other women live . . . She cries out and her hands fly to her head, pulling her hair. But she is *not* other women. And the herbs? Without the prayers that accompany them, without the runes to bind them, who knows how much power they retain?

She sighs. She's let her imagination fly too far. Another thought comes to her: It's one thing for the nobility to switch gods with the same ease they switch allegiance to a more generous, stronger leader, but it's another for the people to do so, *truly* do so. Oh, they might be seduced by the pomp, the thrill of something new, but what about six moons from now, or twelve? Kings depend on the people to feed them, but the people depend on the land, the animals of the wood, the elemental beings, and they know how to appease and please; they know what rituals work and how to invoke fertility and plenty. Surely they will not be so quick to destroy their own gods. For a time, certainly, they might be mesmerized by this new religion, but when it fails them, as it must, when famine, illness, and war visit, they'll come back to the old gods. Brother Egan may have the sheep corralled for now, but once the novelty's worn off and the bright new rituals have lost their gleam, the people will be alone again on the land of their ancestors, with the gods of their fathers. They'll need her again.

She feels Raedwyn moving off. She gathers her thoughts as she would a flock of wayward chicks. Calm comes, with a bitter taste of grief, but calm nonetheless. She knows then that Raedwyn speaks to her, for it's unnatural to be calm in such circumstances, but his wing-breath carries sleep and dreams and the sure knowledge that he stands by her still. It's enough, for this night at least.

Wilona curls into a ball and falls into something like sleep, where she dreams of her mother's hands and of Touilt's, and the two sets of hands become like one, smoothing her hair, kneading dough, winding wool, plucking herbs, stirring the porridge, tying the loom weights, untangling a thread, unknotting a knot, unravelling a skein . . .

Chapter
TWENTY-SIX

A.D. 628, *MONTH OF THE GLORY GODDESS*

Egan bends over Ricbert and tries to guide his stylus over the wax-filled tablet, but Ricbert pushes his hand away. "I can do it myself," he says. The door is open to let light in, and a steady rain drips from the thatch. Ricbert rubs his hands together over a brazier and picks up the stylus again. Although the letters are legible, they are hardly graceful. He tosses the stylus onto the table and rubs his knobby, swollen knuckles.

"It's this ache in my joints. At my age I can't be expected to learn this sort of thing. What possible difference could it make? All this chicken-scratching—what does it *mean*? I've managed to live this long without benefit of Latin, or of your precious writing for that matter." He taps his head. "I studied twenty years, man! Twenty years to memorize the wisdom, and now you want me to chuck it aside for scribbles in wax. At my age. Idiotic."

"The wisdom's not lost, Brother, only augmented. It's not a matter of doing away with one in favour of the other, but rather a new opportunity. We value the poet's arts, and no one could honour the traditions more. I know it's difficult, Brother, but the king wants all monks to learn the language of the church."

"I don't see why."

"The monks on Ioua Insula commit to the page all kinds of sacred texts, the Gospels as well as the words of great holy men. That way, long after we're returned to dust, Christ's words and the inspired wisdom of the saints will be ready for the next man."

"Until a fire comes along and then, *poof*, all your precious wisdom disappears in a puff of smoke."

"All the more reason for scriptoriums to make haste. An individual library might indeed burn down, but not all of them. The work as a body is divinely protected."

Ricbert merely raises an eyebrow. Alas, Brother Ricbert is not an eager or quick student. Egan is about to suggest they return to the memorization of the psalms, when they hear approaching footsteps.

"Thank the gods," says Ricbert. He glances at Egan and rolls his eyes. "Right. God. Thank *God*."

It is Fugol, a boy of nine or ten years, a messenger from Caelin's hall. He pokes his head round the open door of the church. "Excuse me, my lords . . ."

"Come in, Fugol, and please, none of this 'my lords.' We are all brothers in Christ here," says Egan, waving the boy in. Brother Ricbert makes some small noise, which Egan decides to ignore.

The boy shrugs. "Well, Lord Caelin sends his greetings and requests your presence."

"Now?"

"If not sooner."

"That's not good," mutters Ricbert.

"Is something wrong, Fugol?" Egan's heartbeat has quickened.

"I don't know, do I?" The boy fusses with his belt. "I'm just told to fetch you."

Caelin waits for them in the small antechamber of his private quarters. He is seated at a high-backed chair in front of a long table, and across from him sits Cena of the black beard, Caelin's battle-scarred commander. Furs are draped invitingly on benches, and hangings adorn the walls. In one, a mighty stag has fallen to the hounds, its throat rent and its head bent back in agony, a group of hunters at the ready. The other depicts one of the many battles of Lord Caelin's career: swords and spears, men writhing, blood spurting. A dozen or more candles are glowing, although it's only mid-afternoon and still quite light. A jug of wine, cups, the remains of a chicken, and some pieces of bread clutter the table. The air smells of meat and the thick aroma of two giant hounds lolling in a corner.

"My lord, you asked for us?" says Ricbert.

Caelin wipes his fingers on his red tunic. "Come in. There's a small matter we need to discuss." He gestures to a servant in the shadows. "Bring that bench over here and pour some wine."

Egan helps the servant by lifting one end of the bench. "No wine for me, thank you. Just a little water."

"I'll have his," says Ricbert.

Caelin laughs. "Good man."

When they are seated, Caelin says, "Bad business about the Lady Touilt. Sad. She died hard, I hear."

"Few deaths are easy, my lord," says Brother Egan. "But we may be comforted she died safely in the arms of Christ."

"Yes, well, we're grateful for that." Cena rakes his fingers through his beard. "Still, didn't persuade her ward, did it?"

"Exactly," says Caelin. "I thought," he continues, "you might use the moment to solve the problem of the girl."

Egan glances at Ricbert, who studies the wine in his cup. Egan feels as he always does when in the presence of powerful men who draw their strength not from the glory of Christ Jesus but from the might of their bulging biceps, their swords and spears: he feels inferior, juvenile, and brittle as a wheat stalk in mid-winter.

"I pray for her—"

Caelin flicks his fingers in the air. "Well and good. But you've been praying for some time now, Brother Egan, and yet still she keeps herself apart. My doorkeeper, Margawn, warms himself at her fire, and yet even that doesn't convince her."

"She's just a woman, Lord," says Ricbert. "She's no trouble to you."

Caelin chuckles. "Ricbert, old friend, you're unmarried and perhaps not accustomed to the wiles of females. You don't know the trouble they can cause. Here's my problem: there's been rumour in the village, ever since that elf-spawn child was born to the woodworker." He turns his gaze on Egan. "You were there; you saw it. Can you deny it was elf-stricken?"

"Whatever afflicted the child, Lord, I saw no evidence of sorcery, only tragedy."

"And what, in your opinion, caused this tragedy, if not evil? Surely you're not saying your Christ had anything to do with it? Did the parents sin? Are they being punished then?"

Egan's rib cage begins to feel too small for his thumping heart. "No, no, of course not. When our Lord Christ healed the blind man he told the people the man's affliction was not a punishment for sin, neither his nor his parents'."

"And to what then did he attribute this suffering?"

It's a bad example. Egan's mind is muddled. He cannot think clearly in this small place. It seems as though Caelin has an argument already laid out, and no matter which way Egan steps, it's exactly where Caelin wishes.

"I'm no scholar, nor a philosopher to answer the question of why suffering exists."

Caelin scowls. "But doesn't your beloved gospel address the issue?"

"Well, yes. In the case of the blind man, but . . ."

"But what? What does it say about why the man was born blind?"

"It says the man was born blind so that God's works might be revealed to him."

Cena picks his front teeth with a silver-plated thorn. "Exactly. Now shouldn't you be revealing God's work to the seithkona?" He spits onto the floor.

"She . . . she doesn't wish instruction, yet, Lord Caelin. If we give her time I'm sure she'll—"

"I don't choose to give her more time, monk. I'm tired of this. The king, whose ring I wear, has seen fit to convert to this new religion. Who does the girl think she is to refuse his gift?" He pounds the table, making the cups jump and one of the dogs bark. "I had some affection for Touilt. Her husband was killed defending us from raiding Picts with my brother when he was lord. She served us well, and she was old and ill. I had patience. I have no patience with this girl, and little, frankly, with you. Neither of you is kin to us, remember. You are here at the request of Bishop Paulinus, although one wonders if you were to go missing how much he'd regret you. If the girl goes missing, no one will regret her at all."

Cena laughs, short and sharp. "Save Margawn, Lord."

"Give him a slave to warm his bed and he'll soon forget her," says Caelin. "Listen to me, monk. Wilona shall accept her place among us, or she can leave. She can marry Margawn—I'll not stand in the way of that if he wants to take on the wildcat—but as long as she keeps to the old ways and sets herself apart, she's a burr under my arse. Who knows what curses she might cast on the herds and the crops. Who knows what mischief, or worse, she might get up to, especially now she's alone. Touilt taught her much. Perhaps too much. I'll not have the little weasel among the hens. I don't care how it's managed—if it ends with her hanging from a tree limb, so be it." He turns to Cena. "I had a mind to strangle her when she first arrived here with the smell of magic all over her, and would have if it hadn't been for Touilt."

Egan coughs and Caelin glares at him. To have the girl's blood on his hands is unthinkable. Why can't he find the right words? He opens his mouth. "Forgive me, Lord Caelin, you mean only to protect your people, but truly, I see no danger. The girl grieves for her foster mother, but anyone can see she's grateful for the home you grant her here. Can't we give her a little time, let her be drawn to the God of all men—"

Caelin's fist slams down on the table again and Egan jumps. "By Woden's one eye, Christian, you make me wonder where the strength of this god is. Get out, both of you. Have your god work his magic on her, and if he fails to do so, I'll work my own! And make it happen before Eostre's moon."

Egan hesitates, scrambling for other, better, words, for he senses he has only made the situation worse. Ricbert grabs the back of Egan's tunic and yanks him out the door. It's all Egan can do to swallow the searing shame in his throat.

Ricbert stomps along the muddy path. "You've got to learn when to shut up."

"I cannot for the life of me understand why Lord Caelin is so troubled by one young woman."

"Indeed, it might just be for your life, if you're not careful. That she's just one young woman and yet still she defies him is precisely the point. Just the sort of thing that might cause tongues to wag and jokes to be made, and believe me, Caelin is *not* a man to be laughed at. The next time he calls for the army to be gathered—a time never far off—and some farmer doesn't wish to fight but would prefer to sit by his warm hearth, Caelin can't have him thinking about the girl who refused his invitation and paid no price for it, now can he?"

"I'll pray for her heart to open," says Egan. He must, he thinks, go up to the hut on the hillside.

"You do that," says Ricbert. "I'll talk with Margawn. If anyone has sway over her, he does."

———————— ◆ ————————

The winter weather breaks. Moisture drips from the hedgerow into the thirsty earth. The streams turn to torrents as the snow melts on the high ground, and waterfalls form. Curlews, otters, and dippers appear in the river. Roe deer fawns step lightly through the woods. Wilona walks along the river path to the cave. She carries a small bundle of cold dock-pudding patties—made from onions, nettles, and oatmeal, fried in bacon fat—to fortify her when her vision work is done. The cave has become the place where she communes with the spirits undisturbed. Evergreen boughs tied with owl feathers cover the entrance. Inside, wrapped in Touilt's wolf hide, she stores her runes and her charcoal-filled iron bowl, her chicken-feather pillow, her blue cloak, her herbs, her cat-skin hood and gloves, and her tinder and flint. Caelin has made it clear such things have no place near the village any longer, and she doesn't dare be caught with them in her hut.

Willow warblers and whinchats call to each other in the trees as she walks through the spring-bright wood. Daffodils, celandine, and stitchwort bejewel the undergrowth. At the spot where the river bends, although there's nothing to see but a slight shimmer in the air, nothing to feel but a slight shift in temperature, she steps through a familiar yet invisible veil. It's an odd sensation, as though she takes two or three steps forward only to have the path remain unchanged; she walks but goes nowhere, and then, another two steps, and the path is just a path again.

Over the past week, an increasing sense of unfocused, but nonetheless prickling, urgency has nagged Wilona. Her dreams are restless wanderings through unfamiliar landscapes, and she's always looking for something lost. She hears Raedwyn cry from the branches of the yew. Margawn's conversation—too often about the merits of the new religion—sets her teeth on edge.

Last night Margawn sat at Wilona's table, his belly full of roast chicken. He rolled a cup of wine between his palms and talked of what Brother Egan had said about the coming Christian holy days, when Christ vanquishes death. "He told us how the Christ appeared to his loyal warriors after he was put to death, how he returned to them and shared a feast."

Wilona picked a bit of meat from a wing bone and shrugged. "Eostre vanquishes death every spring, by bringing life back to the earth. So far, this Christ has told me nothing new." Margawn stared into his cup. "It's confusing. He says the dead saints came from their tombs after his resurrection; but afterwards they returned to their tombs to await the final resurrection of all. One would think if the dead had been raised, they might stay raised."

"A hard god to please." Wilona moved her stool behind him and began braiding his hair.

"Not so strict as all that, though. Brother Egan has decorated the altar with white lilies and eggs and says at the feast afterwards we'll eat stewed hare and crossed buns. It seems he wishes to make the people feel at home, adding the new ways to the old."

Clever beast! "Not quite. Eggs and hare and Eostre's buns, all for the people and the priests, but none for the goddess. In spite of all those words about mercy, he sounds like not only a harsh god but a greedy one."

"You find fault with everything." He grumbled, pulled his hair from her hands, drained his cup, and poured more.

He was not subtle, her golden bear. He's been tasked with her conversion. She didn't wish to argue, especially not when rumours of war are gathering like crows in the trees. So she let him talk.

The shadows are lengthening as she arrives at the cave. She pushes the boughs aside and lights a fire in the entrance. She unwraps her sacred objects, swathes herself in Touilt's wolf hide, and waits for darkness to fall. When it does she lights the charcoal and burns the herbs, washing in the smoke. She sings and she waits, and then, on owl wings . . . she flies . . .

Touilt's face first, as it was when first she knew her. Neither smiling nor weeping, but half-hidden beneath a blue mantle. A great drum sounds, boom, boom, boom. Smoke, the smell of burning. Hands grasping. Shine and glint of axe and blade. Hands outstretched, hands clawing in the dirt. A terrible smell, damp and decay and death. There have been screams, but they are done now and silence settles like carrion crows. Shapes, dark and swift and slinking . . . The vision clarifies . . . The ground is strewn with the dead, bloated, gnawed by wolves, eyes pecked by ravens, hacked like butchered meat; hair matted with dried blood. Faces destroyed, but she knows them all. Neighbours, her one-time friends. The royal compound, a smoking, collapsed shell; the marvellous carvings now charred; the tapestries, the benches, Lord Caelin's ornate chair, nothing but greasy black skeletons beneath the caved-in rafters.

The owl cries, a deep moaning. It perches in the yew, high up, the long ear-tufts making it look fierce and angry. It lifts and sails, higher and higher, circling the field of the dead, and she is the owl, looking down, and all around and everywhere there is nothing but the silent dead, the burned, stench rising like a fog. Wait, something moves, there away by the river, something moves, crawling, alive, a woman. She turns on her back upon a great stone, battered, bloody, her eyes searching . . .

Wilona shudders and gasps, and opens her eyes. The fire has died down to sparking ash, and beyond the cave entrance the night is black, with only slivers of silver slicing through the trees from a thin, setting moon. She feels woozy and her belly cramps. She lurches outside to the river and vomits. When the convulsions are done she lies with her cheek on the rocks and weeps. She feels sure the vision has come from Touilt, which is a consolation, for even in the Christian heaven, if that's where she is, it seems she can reach Wilona still. But, such horror!

There is no doubting it. War is coming. And they will lose. There are no gods to protect the village any longer.

Two days and nights pass, until at last, as the sun sets below heavy rain-bearing clouds, Margawn appears at her door, his face grim. At his side, Bana looks as though he's been caught trying to steal a roast chicken off the table.

"What is it?" Wilona asks.

"I've come from the council."

They sit on furs near the hearth. Wilona ladles mutton stew into bowls. They eat in silence. Judging from the far-off cast of Margawn's eyes, she suspects he tastes the food no more than she does.

Since returning from the cave, she's been in a sort of half-dream, smelling death on every breeze, seeing signs of destruction in every cloud formation, every pebble pattern on the path. Yesterday, she noted seven swallows flying low over the grazing cattle, and a bat swooping three times around the hut. This morning the fire flared in the hearth and then burned hollow. A white weasel crossed her path as she drew water. If she thought she could argue herself out of the terror of her vision, the omens do not permit it.

A branch pops in the fire and Wilona squeals. Margawn laughs at her. "You're jumpy as a flea."

"I have reason, don't I? You and I both know war will come, and soon."

She puts his bowl along with hers in the bucket of washing water. He looks as harried as a treed bear. She comes back and sits on his lap, nestling against him. "I spent the night in the cave."

"And what did your spirits tell you?" His arms tighten around her.

"Things too terrible to believe."

He sucks in his breath. "I doubt that. There's little I haven't seen on the battlefield." He pauses. "And will see again before long."

Wilona looks into his eyes. "You think you're going to war, but war's coming here."

"Here? What do you mean?"

"I saw it. Rivers of blood, the village burned, all dead, the compound in ruins. You must hear me, and you must take the message to Caelin. This war will be lost. Death will overtake Northumbria like a red flood."

He blinks, his eyes wide.

"We'll all be slaughtered. Right here."

"I can't tell Caelin that."

"The king must be warned."

"And where shall I say I heard this prophecy? From the woman forbidden to prophesize?"

"Can you speak to Lady Elfhild?"

"She spends a great deal of time with Brother Egan. She's become devout." He shakes his head. "I don't think she'd approve."

"I'm more frightened than I've ever been and feel no shame saying so." She looks up into Margawn's worried eyes. "If you go off to Edwin's war, I fear I'll never see you again."

He puts his hands on her shoulders and his fingers almost meet in the middle of her back. "Not all of Gwynedd's armies combined would keep me from coming back to you. I swear it, Wilona."

"No man can swear such a thing. Your wyrd is in the weaving of the gods."

"Brother Egan says there's no greater power in the world than love. He says it's the thread that stitches the world together." He shakes her gently and grins at her. "Marry me, Wilona. Become my wife."

She slaps his arm. "I cannot! The goddess has no objection to our love, but the life of the village and children and the weaving house are forbidden for a seithkona. Love is something else, I think, but . . ."

"Touilt married and had children."

"They died and then the gods claimed her. After that she could not marry and could have no more children."

"So am I to understand," he frowns, "that there are to be no children?"

"Surely you knew that."

"And did Touilt teach you how to keep a child from this world?" He untangles himself from her and pours himself wine from the earthen jug.

"Margawn," she says softly, "do you want me to stop being seith-kona? If I could, perhaps I would, but the choice isn't mine. You don't know what you're asking. You have no idea of the price for betraying the gods."

"By your standard, everyone in Ad Gefrin's betrayed the gods, and yet I see no price being paid. If anything they're more content. This new god of redemption suits them."

"And you?"

"I've told you before, one god is as good as another to me. I'm my lord's man."

"Not mine, then." She stands and faces him.

His eyes flash. "And you're not mine, either, it seems. You belong to Eostre, is it? Or is it the horned one?" He drains his cup and pours another.

Oh, he can be clever with words. He insinuates she's put the horns on him with her wild god. He calls her a whore to the gods. Let her silence condemn his cruelty. And he must feel guilty, for after a moment he says, "I have no objection to you living here still, Wilona, after we're married. It can be our home."

"It's our home now."

"It is NOT!" He hammers his hand on the table and the crockery jumps. "I can't properly protect unless you're my wife."

"You won't be here whether I'm your wife or not."

"But you'll be known as my wife."

"What? Your sign will be upon me?"

Margawn glares at her. "Wilona. Think. You must know Lord Caelin will not permit you to remain here unless you convert."

"I'd hoped he'd leave me be, since I'm harming no one and since Touilt trained me as a healer." She sits on the bed, not wanting to ask him to join her, but hoping he will.

"You're a thorn in his shoe. You must convert."

"I will not. You've always known this, Margawn. I don't expect you to incur Caelin's wrath for my sake."

"Don't speak like an idiot."

She chooses to ignore this. "You must do what you think is right."

He sits next to her. "Right or not, I must do what Caelin orders, as long as he's my lord." He hangs his head, his hands over his eyes. When he looks up again his mouth is twisted. "You have until Eostre's moon to accept Christ, maybe a little longer, since Caelin's mind is occupied with war. The army's leaving for Bebbanburgh when the moon begins to wax. I don't know how long we'll be gone. It might be a year."

"So long as that!"

He nods, and presses his lips together as though he doesn't quite trust his voice. There's a bleakness to him she hasn't seen since he spoke of King Cerdic's blood-eagling. While she waits, he'll be at war, in the midst of horror and death. She knows he grows weary of that game all men are supposed to crave. She wants to protest, to beg him to stay, but that's nonsense. Duty and honour bind them both like leg irons. The least cruel thing is to be as brave as he is. "We shouldn't argue then," she says. "We've little time."

"We have less even than that. Tomorrow I'm riding with Cena to the villages across the estates. We're to call all able men to service. After that, I'm to ride directly to Bebbanburgh. We have only tonight, my love." He puts his arms around her. "What will you do?"

She cannot help it. She clings to him, trying to embed his smell in her senses. And so it has come; she has no choice but to surrender or retreat. She had not, until right now, decided whether to tell him, but considering both her vision and his imminent departure . . ."I won't stay here."

He makes an impatient sound. "Really? And where will you go? Don't say you'll live in the wild alone. That would be madness."

She holds his gaze now. "I'll go to our cave."

"Our cave?"

"Don't laugh, Margawn. I'll leave word with Roswitha where I'm to be found. Although she hasn't forgiven me completely for the baby's death, she may already be with child again, and that will go a long way to helping her and Dunstan forget. I suspect there are some in the village who might be more inclined to seek out my services if they can do so in secret."

"Tell me this is a jest." He holds her at arm's length.

"Why? We made it comfortable. I don't recall you complaining. It's spacious enough. I might even move the bed and table. Besides, it's not so unusual. It's not like I live inside the village walls now. It's just a few miles more."

"Things have changed, in case you've forgotten."

She shrugs off his hands and tucks her arm through his, pulling him close. "All the more reason. They've taken the well from me, and they come here now almost daily, making their ablutions and prayers. As long as I refuse to convert, I'm a piece of bark in their eye—a thorn in Caelin's shoe, as you said—but if I go away, I'll trouble those who are troubled less, and those who secretly keep to the old ways can seek me out away from prying eyes."

"You want to live in a cave like an animal, like some mad hermit? Where's the dignity in that?"

"Dignity's not dependent on the grandeur of your hall but on the steadfastness of your heart." She smiles and shakes her head. "There's no point arguing. My mind's made up."

"And what if Caelin's not satisfied? What if he sends his men for you?"

"Then I'll deal with that as I must." She will tie rocks to her belt and throw herself in the river before she'll convert. She doesn't say so, but the look in his eyes tells her she doesn't have to.

They go round and round this way for some time, until she stops his mouth with hers and uses her tongue and lips and fingers and thighs to distract him. Yet even when he enters her and they ride pleasure to the place where they are more one than two, a small part of her stays apart, watching, as though he has wandered far ahead of her and she already aches for his return.

Chapter TWENTY-SEVEN

The next day Wilona rises early, tries not to think of Margawn's departure, and begins packing. She pulls the small wagon from the byre and sets it in front of the door. She'll hitch Elba to it. She's barely begun to sort through her meagre belongings when a familiar bark startles her. Bana. She stumbles in her rush to the door. When she opens it, instead of Margawn, she finds Egan lurching along the path, yanked by Bana at the end of a hide leash. The monk has a pack on his back and resembles a bundle of rag-tied twigs about to come undone. When the dog bolts for her, Egan staggers and must let go the lead or be dragged to the ground.

"Bana! Stop. Sit. *Sit!*" She holds her hands up against the dog's affection. He wriggles and wags his tail, at last collapsing like a rug at her feet. "What are you doing here?" she asks Egan. "What's Margawn's hound doing here? Where's Margawn?"

Egan eyes the dog. "Brother Margawn asked me to bring you the dog."

"Bana's his battle-hound. He must go with him!"

"He was quite clear. He had me lock Bana in the church until he'd left, in fear the dog would follow him. He wanted me to bring the dog to you, for your protection and company while he's away."

So Margawn forced her into the Christian's company after all. "My protection! What nonsense. I need no protection. The gods protect me." Bana's attention moves from her to the far hills, and

Wilona senses the dog may dash off to find his master. She wonders if she should let him.

As though reading her mind, Egan steps forward, gingerly picks up the end of the leash and ties it to the wagon wheel. "Brother Margawn also bid me tell you he'll be at peace if he knows the dog is with you, and that you do him a great favour caring for him in his absence."

"Indeed, since the beast must eat his weight daily."

Egan smiles. "It seems he thought of that as well." He slips the pack from his back and leans it by the door. "There is a cured joint inside, and others will come to you regularly. Brother Margawn has arranged it with young Fugol. It should," he says with a wink, "be more than enough for the dog."

"It seems he thought of everything," she says sourly.

"He cares greatly for you, sister."

The dog sits up, leaning against her leg for reassurance. She cannot help it; she scratches his great, shaggy head. Wilona sees that Margawn has tried to tie her to this place. She can't abandon the dog he loves, cannot refuse the gift he's given her, but she can't tell this monk of her plans, and unless she does, and arranges to have the meat brought to her by the river, how will she feed the beast?

"Send the boy to me and I'll decide what to do once I hear the promise from him."

"You can believe me, sister, I assure you." He sounds more baffled than hurt.

Surprisingly, she finds she doesn't want to insult him. "It's not you I question, monk. It's the memory of servant boys."

"Fugol's a good boy."

"Send him to me or take the dog back."

"As you wish, sister. And know you can rely on me for anything you need. I would be honoured." He looks at her with nearly the same expression as the hound. "You're not alone here."

Wilona bets he would be happy indeed to have the seithkona in his debt.

"We hope you'll join us for the feast on Eostre's moon."

"I'll think about it. Good day."

"Peace be with you, sister."

When Fugol arrives, she threatens him with a curse upon his testicles if he reveals anything.

The skinny, black-eyed boy blanches. "Lord Margawn, he's my friend. I don't need threats to do right by his woman."

"Perhaps, but trust is earned, Fugol, and I'll see you earn it, believe me. I'm a good friend to have, but a terrible enemy."

She tells the boy where he's to find her. "Do you know the place?"

"I can find it." His eyes grow wide. "You're a brave one."

She clears her throat to hide the chuckle. "I want you to take a message back to the woodworker, Dunstan, and his wife."

He nods.

"Tell them to care for my cow, that they can use the milk for the coming baby, and any calf born they may call their own. They're the only ones you may tell of my whereabouts. Yes?" Roswitha will tell others, and likely the boy will as well, but it will take a few days, and by then she'll be settled. "Now, be off with you. And mind yourself, lest you find prunes dangling between your legs."

The boy just shakes his head.

She spends the rest of the morning packing and sorting her few belongings. She can't help but compare this journey to that other one she took so many years ago. As she looks around the small hut, which has been her home for all these years, the child she once was returns, wandering, stumbling over the moors. That hearth, those rafters, the corner over her bed where the spider spun its web, the place where Touilt's bed had been, the spot where the vision-platform stood—so many things to say farewell to. Again she is a cast-out orphan, and although the journey to the cave is not so very great, it feels as long as the road between lives.

She rubs a knuckle across her cheek. No time for tears. Bana pushes his head against her, sensing her distress. "Good boy. It's all right." She bends down and hugs him. She hates to admit it, but having the dog with her is a deep comfort. When she's ready at last, she begins to place Elba between the wagon shafts, but thinks better of it, harnessing Bana instead. He is, after all, the size of a pony, and Elba may well be pregnant. She ties Elba to the back. The cart is laden with her jars and bundles of herbs and roots, tinctures and salves, her small trunk, a stool, loom weights, the dismantled loom, and four chickens in crates. The sheep will fend for themselves, and she'll return in a day or so to bring one or two back with her. It's true that now Bana is with her, there will be less danger of wolves. The black cow with the milk-white horns will calve before long, but she won't fit in the cave for safety at night, so must be left with Dunstan. Tears sting Wilona's eyes and she swipes roughly at them. It is a cow. Just a cow.

She can't linger. She might be able to make a second trip before the sun sets. She has her food stores, roots and herbs, cloth and cooking pot, bowl and cup, broom, distaff and spindle, blankets and furs, lamps and candles, as well as two pretty enamelled bronze and glass brooches, and the carved comb she carried to Ad Gefrin. A woman could live with much less. As she closes the door behind her she rests her forehead against the wood. She reaches up, runs her hand along the wolf head, scarred from Coifi's axe.

She walks along the river, Bana pulling the wagon. When she comes to the hollowed-out, lightning-struck oak and the path narrows, she unhitches the dog and secures the wagon with stones beneath the wheels. She ties some of the goods to Elba's back. The woman, the dog, and the pig continue until they come to the bend in the amber-coloured water and the cave. She'll sleep on the earthen platform tonight, after shaking out the furs, and tomorrow she'll gather fresh grass for a mattress. With spring about to come into full bloom, it is a good time to plant a garden, but in the meantime, food will be scarce. She's carried what she could—honey and smoked ham, some grain, a few onions. She'll have to set traps for game, fish, and eel.

The river dances high, frothing with spring runoff. There, she thinks, is where I will set the eel-buck. There is where I can build a weir. She'll have to plant a vegetable patch on higher ground beyond the leafy canopy of trees growing along the river, but in winter, when the trees are bare, it will be bright enough, and in summer, pleasant in the shade.

By nightfall the animals are fed, a fire burns in the rough hearth, and Wilona rests under her cloak on the sleeping platform, which is made soft with pine boughs and deer hide. She needs more furs and tomorrow must set snares for otters, beaver, wild cats, and hares. Bana lies between hearth and entrance, Elba on a pile of straw at the back of the cave. Wilona's wedged a yew bough above the entrance, and it acts as a boundary between the outside world and her home. She'll find mistletoe and other sacred plants to wind around the limb, further strengthening its powers. She has the end of a loaf Margawn brought. It's hard now, but with a little softness still in the core. She sucks on the dough, coaxing every last drop of flavour. Who knows when she'll taste bread again? She chews and chews until it's only a memory and swallows at last with deep regret.

The night world begins to stir and, burrowed in the earth as she is, it seems a closer, more intimate world than it ever has before. Something snuffles and roots outside, an owl screeches, a fox barks, and some small creature cries out. She'll have to find a way to befriend the spirits of this place. She lifts the owl-feather pouch from its place between her breasts and presses it between her palms, blowing on it between her thumbs. She rocks back and forth, singing the sacred song, now and then tossing wood on the fire. From the entrance, above her, around her, she senses the flutter of wings and feather. Where else would Raedwyn be but here, in this wild place? She'll become more owl than human. Her fetch is constant, ever-abiding, faithful. She sings and rocks until at last her spirit drifts from the cave, out into the vast star-bright night, floating.

She dreams of a dew-damp meadow near ancient mossy oaks. Figures no more substantial than river-mist lead her toward a small mound in the earth. Looking down, she sees a stone set upon a little hole. At the urging of her wispy companions, she places the toes of her right foot upon it, and perhaps she dwindles to the size of a field mouse, or perhaps the earth mound swells around her. Either way, she crosses the threshold, for that is what the stone is, and finds herself in a long tunnel, which should be black as pitch but is not. She makes out the roots of trees—polished to a bronze glow—snaking out of the walls and back in again, creating a complicated design like the veins on the back of an old woman's hands. The ground beneath her feet is smooth and warm, and although she wonders if she ought to be afraid, she cannot rouse fear, just walks on and lets the wraiths lead her.

In the morning, as the entrance of the cave is turning pewter with early light, Wilona wakes up and feels something important has happened. For a moment she thinks she might be trapped in the faery mound where she dream-travelled, but no, that's only the sound of the river laughing, and there is the entrance to the cave, Bana shaking himself, and the pig with her mischievous expression. If the elves took Wilona, they brought her back. If they were curious about her, then whatever they discovered in the sleep-thin night has given them cause to trust. As well they should. She's given up much to remain faithful to the spirits of the wood, the water, and the oak. She smiles as she stretches and scratches Elba's back, thinking perhaps she's not as alone here as she feared. She has a little honey, which she'll leave for the spirits, and perhaps, if she can arrange with Roswitha for some milk now and then, she can offer that as well. If she's to live in harmony with these creatures, they'll expect offerings.

She throws back the fur and looks around, imagining her new home as it might be. She'll gather rushes to freshen the earth floor and absorb the damp. There are places where she can fit branches in the ceiling for hanging herbs and she can hang game to smoke over the fire. She's brought a stool and the smaller of the trunks, and it's enough to have a place to sit by the fire and a place to keep those small things that have meaning—her mother's comb and Touilt's brooches. Although really, what value do such things have here and now? She can't eat her baubles and they won't keep her warm and dry. Still, if on some lonely night it gives her comfort to hold a bit of sparkly metal in her hand and fancy she sees her foster mother's eyes in the glint of firelight, who will blame her?

She stands, stretches, and scratches at a bite. She'll have to pick a big bunch of mint to place in the bedding and keep the nits at bay. The chickens squawk unhappily from their cages. She'll have to build a sturdy coop outside. She releases them and moves aside the woven door. Elba rushes past her, trotting into the dawn to scrounge her breakfast from the forest floor. Bana pads off a little ways to leave his mark against the tree trunks. The hens flap angrily and dash from the cave, pecking at insects. Wilona follows them outside. She'll have to dig a netty downriver, but for now the bushes will do. When she's done she washes quickly in the chill river and then returns to the cave, where she stokes the fire, empties some of the water into a pot, and throws in a handful of oats.

Food first, comfort later. While the oats are cooking, she ties snares. Her hands work automatically, tying knots while her mind wanders ahead, considering where along the animal trails she will place them. She eats her oats while seated at a flat rock near the opening to the cave, listening to the grackles chatter in the trees and the sound of water sluicing over the stones.

———◆———

"Do you think we should look for her?" asks Egan.

"I do not," says Ricbert.

The two men walk up the path from the abandoned hut. When Wilona didn't appear in church at the feast of Christ's resurrection, Caelin had been livid and sent them to find her. But the door of her hut hung open and the hearth was cold. When Egan stepped inside, a mouse skittered across the floor, and for one unsettling moment, he fancied she might have turned herself into the tiny creature. The table was bare. No furs lay on the bed. The cooking utensils were gone, and the iron chain where once the cooking pot had hung was missing. Even stripped, though, the place reeked of magic. It was curled into the thatch like smoke, but he hadn't felt anything evil. The spirits he sensed were outcast ones, thin as marsh gas, despairing as lost lambs. He sprinkled holy water into the corners and prayed for their release and peace.

"We don't really want to find her, do we?" Ricbert now continues.

Egan looks back over his shoulder to the hut, so small and lonely next to the great yew. "I suppose not, but what if she's ill or has met with an accident?" Egan didn't like to think of her alone and frightened somewhere, with a broken leg or worse.

"She took her belongings. An accident seems unlikely."

"She asked to see Fugol the day I brought the hound."

"Ah. Well then, I suspect we'll hear where she's gone before long."

"And Lord Caelin? What will he say?"

"He'll no doubt be glad to be rid of her. It might just appease him. I suspect she's fine."

Ricbert knows something, Egan is sure. The man's too calm. He's fond of the girl and surely, if she truly vanished, he'd be worried. "And I suspect you do more than suspect," says Egan. "Come on now, tell me what you know."

"I know only she isn't here."

"You needn't lie to me, Brother. I wish the girl no harm; you must know that by now."

"And if you were to find out where she is, and Caelin asked you if you knew, would you lie to protect her?"

"I could honestly say she's in God's hands, since no matter where she is I know that much."

They've reached the animal pens and Ricbert stops by the fence, leaning on one of the posts. Some of the sheep run away, others stare disinterestedly. For a few moments Ricbert says nothing, and Egan is content to wait.

"Margawn came to me before he left. Asked me to look out for her, to do what I can for her. She told him of her plans."

"Brother Margawn came to me as well. I thought, well . . . that he might have trusted me."

"I think he hoped you taking the dog to her would make her see sense."

It strikes Egan again what a stranger he is among these people. They make alliances and allegiances, while he stands gawping like the village idiot. Longing creeps in—for the shining island, his little cell, even the uneasy company of his fellow monks, the unity of their chanting voices. Must he live his whole life as an outsider, in the shadows farthest from the hearth? Ah, but it's hard to submit to God's will, if it means such loneliness. *I must not think of myself. Think of the girl.* "Plans? Meaning what?"

"He told me she'd decided to take herself away. She's chosen a place not far. Quite clever, actually, if she can abide it." He looks at Egan, a question in his eyes.

"You wonder if I'm worthy, Brother. I wish you'd learn to trust me. I do long for a friend." He's surprised to hear his own words, and when Ricbert's mouth turns down in contempt, no doubt for his weakness, he would give anything to take them back.

Ricbert clears his throat. "I know you've good intentions. It just seems we're . . . how to put it . . . a fair bit more complicated than the life you've come from. Mistakes can be made without one's realizing it. Costly mistakes. There's a way to handle things here, a certain delicacy . . ."

Egan sees Ricbert doesn't want to offend him, which he supposes might be something like the beginning of friendship. "Tell me only what you're comfortable with, Brother. But rest assured, I'll do nothing concerning Wilona without consulting you first. I'll betray no confidence. My aim is only to bring the love and peace of Christ to those God sees fit to put in my path."

"Yes, a noble aim." Ricbert looks decidedly unconvinced but tells Egan what he's heard about Wilona's plan to live in the cave. "At first I thought it a stupid idea, but frankly, the more I think about it, the smarter I think she is. She can't survive alone, but once people find out she's there, they'll seek her out for . . ." He pauses, casting a sidelong glance at Egan. ". . . for healing charms and so forth. That should provide her with something to live on, and it gives Caelin an excuse not to have to deal with her. Lady Elfhild wouldn't want her to come to harm, and may even convince Caelin to turn a blind eye if nothing happens that can be blamed on Wilona."

Indeed, thinks Egan. An illness among the cattle or the people, a blight on the crops, drought or flood, milk too quickly turned, malformed calves—he shudders. God forbid harm come to any more babies in the village. She's chosen a path even lonelier than his. "Surely she can't stay there forever, though."

The old man looks grim. "Who knows what the future brings? Things change, Brother Egan—you more than most should know that. Caelin may soon have graver matters on his mind than an errant woman."

Chapter
TWENTY-EIGHT

Egan stands over Ulger, the oldest shepherd, who lies on his pallet in the tiny hut. Egan's hand is on the man's forehead. The skin is waxen, tight, and burning. The air reeks of vomit and loose bowels. Ulger reaches for Egan's hand and holds it weakly.

"I don't want to die," he says, through fever-cracked lips.

"Put your faith in Christ, Brother Ulger. Did he not give sight to the blind, heal the sick, and raise the dead?"

"I don't want to die," the man repeats.

Egan turns to the other shepherds, three young boys who huddle round the door. "How long has he been like this?"

One of the boys, the one with the wandering left eye, says, "It come on him quick. We was sitting up the night, watching the sheep in the western pens. And then he just says he don't feel quite right and kind of slipped over. Started puking right after. Thought it was some such as he ate, but I don't think so anymore, do you?"

"I don't know what it is."

One of the other boys, a chubby lad with thin brown hair, sits down in the doorway. "I'm not feeling right myself," he says.

Ulger rolls over on his pallet and retches, a thin, pale, watery stream, slightly flecked with blood.

"Brother Egan." Fugol stands at the door, his face red and his breathing laboured.

"What is it, boy?"

"Lady Elfhild. She been taken ill. You're to come right away, and . . ."

Egan crosses himself. "What? Out with it!"

"Looked for you at the church, didn't I. Brother Ricbert's there. He don't look so good."

"May the Lord God protect us!" Egan is loath to leave the sick, frightened man, but he can't ignore Lady Elfhild. "Are there more?"

"Might be." Fugol backs away from the doorway. "You'd best come."

"Yes, yes." What should he do? He tries to recall his mother's concoctions. Mint for the stomach. Brown apples for loose stools. And what else? Honey? The boy sitting by the door clutches his stomach. "You," he says to the boy with the wandering eye. "Brew some apple tea with honey. Make him drink whatever he can keep down in small sips, yes?" The boy hesitates and glances away. He will not do as he is told. He'll head for the hills the minute Egan leaves. "You put your soul in danger if you leave. He'd care for you if you were ill."

"He bloody wouldn't," mumbles the boy. "Selfish bastard."

"Then you must be better. All right, all right. Bring him to the church. Carry him if you must. I'll care for him myself."

"I don't much care to touch him," says the boy.

"You'll do as you are told, and do it quickly! Don't make me come back here, boy! Should you fall ill, do you want to be left untended?" The boy looks shocked at Egan's tone. Egan is shocked himself. He must be more frightened than he realizes. "You're a good boy," he says, and then rushes past him, hoping the boys will do the right thing.

He is not halfway back to the village when he sees Wynflaed running toward him. He reads it in her face. The sickness is spreading.

At noon the next day, Egan stands before Caelin in the lord's ante-chamber. Caelin has returned to the village to leave final instructions with the men guarding Lady Elfhild. He must leave again in two days to join King Edwin and march on Mercia. Caelin paces, roaring at the servants and kicking the hounds cowering in the corner. The room is hot, and the stench of sickness slips beneath the door from the main hall, which is lined with pallets bearing the ill. Not even the sage thrown on the braziers can clear it.

"Where's your god now?"

"We must trust in Christ, my lord, put our faith in Him."

Caelin crosses the space between them in two steps. "I warn you, Christian, if the lady dies, or if my child does, I'll crucify you like your precious Christ."

Spittle lands on Egan's face, but he doesn't dare wipe it away. "It may be our faith is tested."

"No one tests me! No one!"

Caelin pushes him away so quickly he stumbles and his hip collides painfully against the table edge. "My lord, I've used all my arts, but I'm a monk, not a leech."

"That's clear enough. Then your prayers had better be more effective than your remedies! My patience wears thin, monk."

For a moment Egan fears the Angle will pick him up and snap him like kindling over his thigh. *Dear God,* he prays, *guide me.* And then it comes to him. "Perhaps there's someone who can help us." Caelin eyes him, his face flushed and swollen with anger. He's not used to helplessness. There's a dare in his expression, and the promise of consequence. "There's only one person who knows the healing arts, only one who's been properly trained."

Caelin walks to the far side of the table, picks up a goblet and drains it, then slams the vessel down. He shakes his head, as a horse does when bothered by a fly. "The seithkona."

"Yes, my lord. Sister Wilona."

"She's no longer one of us. She's been gone over a year." He looks directly at Egan and his eyes spark. "How do we know she's not responsible? Who knows what dark arts she practises in that cave of hers? I'd be better off sending my men to burn her out."

Egan's legs go weak. "Give her a chance. I think it is possible that Christ has seized this very opportunity to draw her in. He sees the larger plan, always, and we are but blind mice—"

"I will cut you down like a wheat stalk if you keep talking!"

"Forgive me. I know only this: in prayer her face appeared to me as though Christ himself whispered in my ear. And the truth is the truth . . . she knows leechcraft as no one else." He puts his hands out and shrugs. "I see no other hope. The sickness is spreading, and worsening."

Lord Caelin bows his head. "Do you think so little of your god that you'd seek out the old ones? Are we being punished for our disloyalty?" He holds his own hand up. "Say nothing, Christian. You have my permission. Bring her here. But I warn you: if my lady dies, if my child dies, if Wilona fails, I'll kill you both."

———◆———

Wilona kneels on the fragrant earth, cutting borers out of the squash vine stems. Bana lolls in the shade of a hazel tree. Between Margawn's contributions and the bounty of field and wood, life in the cave the past year has not been so hard. A ham and several grouse hang in the smoke over the hearth. She has honey and dried herbs to flavour the soup, and the vegetables are from her own plot. Although she misses Touilt, the solitude comes easy, and besides, the world is full of life, both seen and unseen. Raedwyn likes it here as much as she does. He sent one of his kind to live in the tree a few feet from the cave's entrance. She's found mouse bones at its base, and droppings. She has a new talon in her pouch.

She stretches her neck. She's been tense and unusually restless all morning. Last night she dreamed of white butterflies and an unfamiliar man whose hair was falling out. These are signs of illness, and yet she feels fine, apart from the twitchiness.

The chickens begin squawking. Bana springs to his feet, hackles raised.

"Bana. Still." The dog obeys but remains focused in the direction of the cave. Wilona cocks her head. Maybe the hens' complaining is merely squabbling over grubs. The racket persists. She dusts her hands off on the rag tied to her tunic belt. She calls Bana to heel, walks to the top of the ridge where she can look down to the river and cave, and sees a young girl with long braids and a scarf tied round her head. From her dress she looks like a servant, perhaps one of Lord Caelin's kitchen maids. Bana growls and Wilona shushes him. The girl, thin as a sparrow, stands shyly at the cave entrance, dips her head to peer inside, and calls hello. Seeing Wilona's not there, she looks worried. She has a flat, wide face, spattered with pimples and slightly tilted eyes. Perhaps she's come looking for a skin remedy. She looks up the river and then down, and at last raises her eyes to the ridge. She lets out a little whoop when she realizes Wilona is watching her, then reveals a gap-toothed smile. Wilona tries to look stern, imagining what tales the girl's been told about the woman who lives in a cave and speaks to the spirits.

"You got hold of that dog?"

"For the moment."

"Sister Wilona," the girl says, and Wilona frowns at the term. "I been told to beg your forgiveness at disturbing you. I've no wish to trouble you and surely wouldn't but for the . . . utmost urgency." She begins, in spite of the dog, to climb up the ridge.

"Stay where you are. I'll come. Wait." Wilona's throat feels raspy and she realizes that, other than a few words here or there to the animals, she hasn't spoken since Fugol came with supplies nearly a full moon ago. She sounds more like a raven than a woman. "Friend," she says to Bana. "Friend." She picks up her sack of onions, beans, and squash, and uses her hoe as a staff on the steep slope.

The girl doesn't wait for her to descend. "Brother Egan sent me. He bids you come."

Wilona steps onto the level ground and sets her basket on the bench. "If Egan wants me, let him come to me. I'm no one's slave to be ordered about."

"No, no, Sister Wilona, it's no order—I was to make that perfectly clear; the fault's all mine if it ain't. He said I'm to tell you it's a request for your wisdom."

The girl puts a tentative hand near the hound and he leans toward it. The girl giggles. "And what," says Wilona, "do I know that your master doesn't? What wisdom have I that the Christian might need?"

"There's sickness in the village. Bad sickness."

Wilona looks up. A single crow roosts in the willow a ways upriver. She makes the sign of Thunor. "What kind?"

"It happened quickly, no more 'n two days, and half the village's sick. Stomach and bowels, some bloody, Brother Egan says." The girl wrinkles her nose. "Smells terrible."

"Are Lady Elfhild and the child sick?"

"Lady Elfhild, but not her child, and the lord's furious."

Lord Caelin is back? Is Margawn with him? Her heart leaps. She dare not ask.

"I'm not sick, but," the girl looks over one shoulder and then the other, "I got this." She pulls a tiny iron piece from her pocket: *Mjölner*, Thunor's hammer. "I don't think Christ knows enough about elves to protect us against 'em, do you?"

"Perhaps not."

"Brother Egan's been praying and brought the sick to the lord's hall. He had 'em at the church, but now there's too many. He prays and gives 'em broth but says you're the only one knows what to do and begs you come." She chews the end of her braid. "Brother Ricbert's ill."

"And Lord Caelin's asking for me?"

"I guess he is. He's worried for the lady."

"What's your name, girl?"

"Gwen."

"Gather the chickens into the coop, Gwen. I've things to prepare." Elba and her six shoats wallow happily in the pen. "And run the pigs into the hut."

The miller's son built her a strong hut against the south side of the cave, in return for tending his father's badly broken wrist, which he'd trapped in the sluice gate. The pigs should be safe enough if she must stay away for the night. She'll leave Bana to guard them. Not even a bear would go up against that dog.

A little while later, having affixed raven feathers and a protection rune to the door so that no one will enter in her absence, Wilona and Gwen follow the path back to the village. Wilona has owl feathers braided in her hair. It is almost an hour's walk. They each carry a basket, and another is strapped to Gwen's back. The baskets contain remedies: bilberry, meadowsweet, bird's tongue, oak bark, walnut leaves, strawberry leaves, chamomile, feverfew. Wilona's mind ticks away, listing the other things she may need but that they will have in the village: apples, charcoal, honey, soured cream.

Gwen hums tunelessly. Wilona shushes her and the girl sulks but is silent. *Who can think with that in their ears?* Whatever's going on in the village, it must be bad indeed if Egan's sent for her. She bites her lip. A plague may be upon them. Perhaps this is the vision of death she saw. She wonders. It is possible she misinterpreted the vision. For the thousandth time, she burns with longing for Margawn. And yet, even now, he might be lying ill, or worse. *No, let him not be at Ad Gefrin.* She longs for Touilt's guidance and wisdom. She slips her hand inside her tunic and, as discreetly as she can, lifts the flask of strawberry wine to her lips. It's sweet and potent, and the warmth travels through her, easing her muscles, easing her mind. She glances over her shoulder, but Gwen pays no attention. Wilona takes another drink. Confidence rolls over her like sun-warmed honey. Elfish Egan has admitted his weakness and is calling for her. As well he should.

When they arrive, the village is eerily quiet. Two dun hounds stand quivering at the side of the tavern wall. When Wilona comes closer they arch their backs and slink away, tails between their legs.

"The sick are in the lord's hall?"

The girl grunts and nods, shifting the basket on her back and sighing as though it were filled with rocks, not dried herbs. They wind through the houses, past the pigpens and herb gardens, past the kitchen plots and hissing geese. In a doorway a child with a wooden horse watches them. Soon they come upon Dunstan and Roswitha's hut. Wilona's relieved to see Dunstan coming from the garden, an infant strapped to his chest. She had not been asked to attend the birth. A pinch in her chest. No time for that now.

"You're well, Dunstan?" She sees the worry in his face. "Is it Roswitha, then?"

He nods. "I heard Brother Egan sent for you. It's good of you to come." He waggles his head back and forth, acknowledging she has reason to refuse. "He said everyone who's ill must go to the hall to be cared for, and that those who are well should stay apart and pray, but is that right? I should be with her." He holds out a bunch of radishes, bright white and purple, the leaves such a hopeful shade of green. "I thought I'd crush them and mix the mash with milk. It's a good remedy, isn't it?"

She touches the baby's head. It's warm but not hot. "Very good. Give the radishes to me; I'll see if it's the right remedy and, if so, I'll prepare it for her myself."

Dunstan sighs and his shoulders drop, as though he is relieved to have someone else take responsibility. "Brother Egan says the healthy should stay apart," he repeats, "in case the evil jumps to us."

Wilona hasn't heard of such an idea before, but she sees the wisdom of it. Let whatever elf-shot darts, whatever flying venoms, be concentrated among those already ill. "Draw a circle round your hut and sprinkle mint all round. Hang onions in the windows and doors, and smoke-vents as well, and change them every morning. Place oak over the doorways, and burn pine needles, rue, and rowan on the hearth." Wilona points to the door. "Paint the lintel red and wrap the baby in a red blanket. You'd do well to wear red yourself, if you have something, or a red piece of yarn around the throat at least. Tell your neighbours to do the same."

He bows his head. "I'm glad you're here. Makes me feel more hopeful."

"You must have hope, Dunstan."

"You might be wondering . . . but Margawn's still away. He and Alfrith have been sent west, to gather the army. Caelin came back with only Cena."

All at once, her heart falls, and then lifts. He's safe, for now. "Tell me, has anyone died?"

"Old Hiroc, but he was ready. Said himself he'd not see another summer. Maccus's grandson, Aylild's child. I heard he died this morning."

As Wilona and Gwen reach the hall the wind carries the stench from inside. A gaggle of women stand at the edge of the yard, half covering their drawn faces with the corners of their mantles. Four crows circle the hall and land on the thatched roof. Two young boys pick up stones from a pile they've gathered at their feet and throw them at the black birds. They miss, but the birds caw and rise into the air again, circling patiently. Soiled blankets and strips of linen lie mounded to one side, flies covering the refuse. The doors and windows are all closed, and a slave, ashen and wild-eyed, stands guard at the door. When Wilona mounts the steps, he holds up his hands.

"No entry. I've orders to stop all from entering."

"Not me, you idiot! I'm sent for."

"This is the seithkona," says Gwen, her sullenness gone now. "Can't you *see* that?" The girl jerks her head in Wilona's direction.

The slave sees the owl feathers and becomes even paler. He crosses himself. "Deepest apologies. Brother Egan's waiting for you."

He opens the door and out rushes the full weight of the reek from within. Wilona reaches in her basket, crushes some lavender flowers between her fingers and rubs them under her nose. Still, she breathes through her mouth as she steps inside. "Come on," she says, but there's no answer. She turns. Gwen has set the baskets down and disappeared. "Bring those," she says to the slave, who looks as though he might faint. "I said bring them!" For a moment the man seems to consider what to fear more, the seithkona or the illness. Wilona draws herself up and shakes her head so the owl feathers dance. He grabs the baskets and scrambles inside.

She follows. "Now, take me to Egan."

Chapter TWENTY-NINE

Two lines of pallets lie before the hearth and on each there is a body. Halfway down the hall a tapestry hung from the ceiling separates the women and children from the old men. Some writhe, some moan, some lie worryingly still. She counts them . . . six, seven, eight, old men, women, children . . . far more women than men, since the able-bodied men are with the army. And more children than women. Some women are sitting by the beds of children. Good, she'll make use of them. Roswitha's here, and when she sees Wilona she raises her hand and tries to smile, a good sign. Aelfric, the potter, whose bad legs kept him from the war, lies on his side and holds his great boulder of a belly. His face is a terrible grimace. Toward the far end of the hall Ricbert is squatting over a bucket, his long legs drawn up under his tunic so he looks like a clothed cricket.

The air is stifling, not only with a disgusting odour, but with heat, for despite the fire blazing on the hearth, the overhead vents in the thatch are open just enough to allow the worst of the smoke to escape. The rest floats down, burning her eyes. A pungent scent rises from three iron braziers, but she can't identify the smell.

Wilona's vision wavers and she sucks in her breath as the air shifts and fills with spirits and ghosts. For a moment she's once again a small girl, in a room not unlike this one, surrounded by the dead and dying. Hands reach and pluck at her. She closes her eyes and sees the pale, freckled hands that have so often haunted her dreams. Her mother's hands, no face, no body, just those clawing, grasping hands . . . She opens her eyes and the room spins. A bell rings and she follows the sound, willing it to bring her back to the hall, to leave the ghosts in the past. A female servant is walking through the room, holding a bronze bell and a small hammer. Wilona lets her eyes cling to the woman.

"Sister, you've come!" Egan's voice reaches her before she can find him in the murk. "We need your wisdom. This is a terrible thing."

His emerald eyes stand out even more than usual above the dark smudges beneath. He looks like a forest-ghost. His smile, though, is wide. He wipes his hands on a rag and his expression is pleading, which gives her satisfaction. A little flake of ice pricks the inside of her gut. She must be careful. He may have called her in order to blame her later if things go badly. Well, if she's to be blamed, let it be because she did all she could, not because she was stingy with her knowledge.

"Lord Caelin knows I'm here?"

"Indeed he does. We have faith in your skills and your good heart."

He's a poor dissembler. Whatever Caelin thinks of her, the quality of her heart does not concern him. She scans the stains and muck on his tunic.

"I'm horrible, am I not? But I can't keep up no matter how I try." He looks around the hall. "It happened so quickly. I don't know what we've done to so displease God."

Although Wilona could easily tell him what he's done, instead she says, "I need water, and lots of it, to boil the herbs. And you must get slaves to clean away the filth. Burn the discarded bedding outside. Squalor darkens the spirit."

"Yes, yes, of course."

It's remarkable the way he defers to her.

"You, girl!" Wilona grabs the sleeve of a slave carrying an armload of soiled cloths. "When you're done with that, get apples and make juice, as much as you can. If there are any browned apples lying about, use them first, and cut the rest and leave them until they brown and add some pulp in the juice. Have the mothers give it to their children. They must drink." The girl skitters away, nodding her head. "Is there a pattern?" Wilona turns back to Egan. "Were they in a group? Was there a feast? Some way for them to be elf-shot at once?"

"Not that I know of. Many of the women were at the river, washing clothes yesterday. The children with them, I suppose. "

"No mind. What's done is done." She points at the braziers. "What are you burning?"

"Angelica mostly, mixed with pine resin and bay laurel."

She raises an eyebrow. It won't do to let him see her surprise that he knows such things. "We've work to do. Tidy yourself, and then come back and help me. And open the windows and doors before I start vomiting myself. We're safe from airborne venoms until the sun goes down. Did they teach you nothing in that monastery?"

She goes from patient to patient with authority, determining who's in most need of help. The children are the worst, and two small boys barely respond when she pinches the back of their hands. The skin tents up like that of a dried-out old woman. "Give them water, until you have juice, and then juice, by the spoonful if you must, but give them a full jug each, right away," she says to their mothers, Begila and Sunild. An old man she recognizes as one of the shepherds lies still as stone, a puddle of bloody feces around his bed. What is his name? Ulfrid? Ulfric? Ulger. "Can you hear me? Can you hear me, Ulger?" He doesn't blink and his mouth hangs open, although he barely breathes, revealing a swollen, woolly tongue. Wilona puts her palm on his forehead and says the charm for the dying.

Lady Elfhild lies two pallets over, just on the other side of the tapestry, her golden hair matted and her skin fish-belly white, stretched across her high cheekbones. Her lips are cracked and bleeding, and she gazes up at Wilona with glazed, sunken eyes. She lifts her small hand and takes hold of Wilona's tunic.

"I'm thirsty," she whispers.

Wilona calls out to a slave carrying water. "Bring that here," she says, taking a cup. "Why are you here, Lady, and not in your quarters?"

"My daughter, my husband," she says softly. "And the people . . ."

Wilona nods. She wants both to protect her child and Lord Caelin and to show the people she's no more important, in this time of peril, than they are. Wilona thinks more of the woman for it. "Are you vomiting?" When Elfhild shakes her head, Wilona holds the cup to her lips and uses her arm to support her head. She drinks with her eyes closed.

When she has drained the cup she grabs Wilona's hand. "There's something else." Her other hand goes to her belly.

"How far along?"

"Three moons." She must notice Wilona's look, for she says, "My lord, Caelin, returned only briefly, and Margawn wasn't with him."

"I'll fashion a special charm for you, if your husband doesn't forbid it."

"You are good." Elfhild holds Wilona's wrist. "I've always said so."

"You've been a friend, Lady." Wilona hands the cup back to the slave and tells her to keep giving fluid to all who can drink, and after the juice, to give clear broth.

"Go to them," says Elfhild.

Wilona nods and makes the signs of protection in the air above the lady.

Roswitha is pale, and her face is damp with sweat, although her teeth are chattering. Next to her pallet is a bucket half-filled with slop. Putrid, to be sure, but there's no sign of blood. "Any bleeding?"

Roswitha shakes her head. "Oh, but the cramps are terrible."

"But you can get up to use the bucket, yes?"

"Yes."

"Good." She holds her hand. "You're not so bad. You'll be back with your husband and child in no time."

"Do you promise?" Roswitha's nails dig into Wilona's arm.

Wilona looks at the woman's innocent, round face. How hurt Wilona had been when she wasn't asked to attend the birth of the new baby. A small, feral, cramped, and slinking part of her would like to inflict a little of that hurt back. Roswitha's eyes widen, her bottom lip trembles slightly, and then she's overtaken with chattering again. Wilona disentangles her hand from Roswitha's. "I promise," she says.

As she passes down the line of pallets, she notes that old Ulger's spirit is no longer among them. She pulls a cloth over his face, and the woman sitting watch over her child next to the body gasps. A male slave hunkers near the fire, trying to stay within the protection of the smoke. "You there!" Wilona snaps her fingers. "Wrap this body." She looks around for Egan and beckons him. "Where did you put the bodies of Hiroc and the child, Aylild's child?"

He looks past her and sees the shepherd's motionless form. He falls to his knees beside the bed, making the sign of the cross. *"In nomine Patris, et Filii, et Spiritus Sancti."*

"Pray later, priest, we've work to do now."

He turns to her, and she draws back from the pain in his eyes. Can he care as much about this low-born shepherd, barely more than a slave, as he did for Dunstan's malformed son?

"A moment, Sister. Evil must stand aside while I pray for this man's soul."

"When it suits you then, have the body placed with the others. It does the sick no good to rest among the dead. Tends to make one lose hope, wouldn't you agree?"

"We are in God's hands, Sister." He closes his eyes and lays his hands on the man's chest. *"Ave Maria, gratia plena, Dominus tecum. Benedicta tu in mulieribus, et benedictus fructus ventris tui, Iesus. Sancta Maria, Mater Dei . . ."*

She leaves him to it, and enlists another servant into organizing the herbs and roots, tinctures, and decoctions. Within the hour, the hall has quieted and the air is less foul. Once the medicines are ready she goes from pallet to pallet, deciding which remedy to use. Even though Egan follows behind her, she makes the sign of the healing, protective rune *uruz* above every head. Each patient drinks the bitter brews of oak bark, bilberry, meadowsweet, and strawberry leaves. She sings the sacred song against elf-arrows:

> *Out, little spear, if you are here!*
> *I stood under the yew, under a shield of moonlight,*

Where the mighty women gather their strength.
Out little spear, if you are here!
If there is anything here shot in the blood,
Or shot in a limb, may your life never be harmed;
If it was the shot of elves,
I will help you now.
This to cure you of elf-shot,
I will help you.
Be you whole, may the Goddess help you.

Egan follows her, intoning his own prayers. *"Pater noster, qui es in caelis, sanctificetur nomen tuum . . ."* He sprinkles them with water from the holy well and makes the sign of the cross. She wishes he would stop, fearing one action will cancel out the other, but she has no authority over him. If he intends to mitigate her power, she will in turn mitigate his.

"Seithkona!"

She knows the booming voice immediately. Lord Caelin is standing by Lady Elfhild's pallet. Wilona places her hands on her hips. He called for her, asked for her help. He needs her; let him treat her with respect. She raises her chin. She's not quite as defiant as she pretends, but she'll not admit that. "My lord, I'm pleased to see you well."

He strides toward her, slaves and servants scattering from his path. When he stands before her, glaring down, it's all she can do to keep her spine straight. She imagines a span of brown wings above her, and there, the soft sweep of feathers . . .

Caelin's voice is like the growl of a cornered badger. "I warn you, girl, it won't go well with you if my wife dies."

Perhaps it is Raedwyn's influence, but for an instant she sees past Caelin's bared teeth and claws to his heart. He loves his wife and is afraid of his powerlessness. She puts her hand on his arm and he glances at it in something very much like shock. "I will do everything, *everything*, I can, use every scrap of my skill and knowledge to serve you and the lady, Lord Caelin. I am, as ever, bound by my honour and my affection." Let him take that any way he wishes. "And now, let me work, my lord. There's much to do."

"Get on with it, then," he mumbles, but the rage has left him.

Wilona cannot help but believe the spirits are softening him. They are mysterious, intervening here but not there, now but not then. "We're in the hands of the gods, in the web of wyrd." She turns away without waiting for a response.

Ricbert is lying down when she reaches him, the last in the line.

"Drink this." She hands him a cup of the medicinal tea, full to the brim. "All of it, and I'll leave more. You must drink until it's all gone."

He grimaces at the taste. "I think I might be ready to die."

"If you can make jokes, I'm quite sure you will not." She looks in the bucket. Yellowish, not red, and with a little solid matter. Good. It takes him several more attempts to drink the brew and he gags. "Oh, be brave, my lord!"

He looks up, his expression tired and wry. "I always said you were a dangerous woman."

"You don't know the half of it," she says. "Wait until you see the bland food I make you eat for the next week."

"I doubt I'll ever eat again." He pats her hand. "We're grateful. And I'll say so to Lord Caelin when I can. He'll be in your debt when Elfhild's well again—"

"The gods willing," interjects Wilona.

"Then perhaps even I will pray," he says, and smiles weakly.

As she ministers to the ill, Wilona feels the room shift and shimmer; she sees small pinpricks of light here and there in the corners, some bright white, some reddish dark. Above her is the flutter of wing and feather, the smell of the heather, the gorse-dappled moors on a star-bright night. She watches the faces of the ill, looking for strange smiles, or oddly tilted eyes, or any expression of pleasure, all of which indicate an evil elf has taken hold. When she passes by Aelfric a chill runs through her, for surely that wide, twisted smile means he's been overtaken by dark elves. He spasms, rounds his back, and a noise like a clap of thunder explodes, releasing a toxic cloud. He sinks back on his pallet, the look on his face an almost humorous mixture of pride and relief.

"I think you'll live, Aelfric, but you may kill the rest of us."

And on and on, as the day slides into evening. The doors and windows are sealed against those evil things that make use of the darkness. She prays and gives medicine, cleans up the filth and gives medicine, prays . . . One by one the ill fall into sleep, some more fitful than others. By daybreak it's clear no one else will die, and the dark elves are banished back to their own land.

In the morning the servants throw the windows and doors open to a new day, and let in the waiting friends and families. Wilona, packing up her now-diminished stores of herbs and roots, watches Dunstan rush in, the baby in his arm, to find Roswitha. Ricbert is resting on his side, sleeping peacefully. Now that the tide has turned, Lady Elfhild has returned to her private chambers.

Egan appears beside Wilona and takes her hands in both of his. "I've no idea what I would have done without you, Sister. Surely God has, once again, sent you to me."

The monk took her hands like this the day they buried Touilt. Whatever makes him think he has the right? She feels as though she's been run through the bramble with a hundred-pound rock tied to her ankles.

"And tell me, had it gone otherwise, had the gods decided many would die, would you still have been grateful for my help?"

He looks as if he's been struck and flushes. "You think I would have blamed you?"

"It occurred to me, and Lord Caelin was quite clear on the matter."

Shockingly, his strange eyes are watering. "Lord Caelin says you will receive reward for what you've done! But, if you felt this way, then why, dear sister, did you come?"

It is a fair enough question. And as she opens her mouth to speak she realizes she's not entirely sure. "I care for these people. They were mine before they were yours. I've known them most of my life. Do I seem so fickle?"

Egan presses his palms together beneath his chin. "I think you're the most loyal person I've ever met. I would not have blamed you. I hope you believe that. Not only do I think you're a good person, but

I have such faith in the Lord Jesus that, had the sickness overcome us, I would know it to be God's will, more mysterious than I can understand, and often painful, but His will nonetheless. I would know we didn't walk in sorrow unaccompanied, and I would take comfort in that, rather than seek to blame the innocent. The power of darkness cannot be denied, but I trust God more than I fear the devil, and I see no evidence of darkness in you, Sister Wilona. I thought you knew that."

"Not all your loving *brethren*," she sneers at the word, "have such visionary powers."

He hangs his head, and she goes back to her packing.

"Sister Wilona, I know a little of your history," he says after a moment. "How you came here haunted by visions of death, how your village was wiped out and you alone, by the grace of God, were spared." He waits, as though expecting her to speak. When she doesn't, he sighs. "I only mean to say, this must have been frightening for you—more for you than most. You have not only my gratitude, but my admiration. *Pax tecum*," he says.

Before she realizes what he is doing, he lets his hand hover over her head. She recoils, landing on the ground. "How have you cursed me, priest?" Faces turn toward them, startled, frightened, eager. Frantically, she makes the sign of Thunor's hammer in the air between them.

"No, no!" Egan says, kneeling beside her. "I only wished you peace, in the Latin tongue—peace be with you."

Her face flaming, she scrambles to her feet and throws the last of her things into her basket. As she stalks away, she turns back to him. "You keep your peace, and I'll keep mine."

Outside, the bright promise of dawn has given way to a fine drizzle under a woolly grey sky. Wilona walks quickly, turning her face up now and then to let the warm rain wash over her, cleansing her of the smell of sickness, the rank fug of fear and feces. The air smells of damp grass and worms and earth. Some people greet her, no doubt wishing once again to be in her good favour. She ignores them, striding through the snickets, past the thatched huts, the gardens, workshops, the pigsties, the sheepfold, the meadow, until at last she comes to the river. She begins to run along the path until she's a safe distance from the village and then stops. She strips off her muddy shoes, her tunic and under-tunic and flings herself into the water.

It strikes her body like cool silk, and she sighs. She floats for a while on her back, luxuriating in the feeling that the drizzly air and the river have become one, that there is no separation between that which is above and that which is below. She lets herself slide under the surface. She opens her eyes. The slippery green weeds ripple and bend; mud clouds puff up where her feet touch the bottom. Her hair slips loose from its braid and sways like the weeds. A school of little silver fish dashes past. It would be so easy, so sweet, to live under the water, where everything is silent and fresh, away from the cry of human pain, away from the stench of human misery. How blissful to let the current pull and push her, free at last of all responsibility, all worry for tomorrow. Above her, at the surface, floats a patch of lily pads, and dangling from one are the long legs of a green frog. Silly, beautiful thing. Her lungs begin to ache and at last she must rise to the surface and breathe air again. Alas, alas . . .

She paddles to the bank and grabs her clothes to rinse them out, since they're wet already. When she's washed away the last traces of illness, she gathers her things and slips the wet tunic over her head. She gathers twigs, hazel, oak, elm, willow, and tucks them in her basket.

Before long she's back at her cave, calming the joyous Bana. Later, with the pigs safe in the hut and the chickens in their coop, a nice fire built in the hearth, and a hare roasting on the spit, Wilona reclines on her bed of furs and reaches for a jug of plum wine. Her lips and tongue yearn for the sweet, warmth-giving nectar more and more often. Yet, with the jug halfway to her lips, something stops her. Egan's hand hovering over her, and the strange words he muttered flash through her mind. She cannot afford to have her senses dulled. She cannot afford to drift into the tempting pool of forgetfulness. She replaces the stopper in the jug and puts it on the shelf.

Wilona takes the twigs she gathered and holds them to the smoke. Seven times she says, *"Turner be turned, burner be burned: let only good come out of this wood."* She spits on each twig, then breaks it, and casts the bits into the flames, where any curse Elfish Egan put on her will die with the fire.

Part THREE

Chapter THIRTY

THE MONTH OF THREE MILKINGS

Wilona walks up the mud-slick path toward her old home, Bana by her side. She rests her hand absent-mindedly on his back. She can no longer recall a time when Bana wasn't with her. She smiles. Margawn was wiser than she gave him credit for, and she'll have to admit that when he returns. She wishes there was some word from him. Longing for him gnaws at her like a hunger pain, and frequently she wakes up thinking he's sleeping beside her, only to have her fingers reach for empty air.

A year has come and gone. Autumn has flung aside her bright skirts, winter wind danced across the striated snow, and now spring flashes her pretty jewels. The otters and the black grouse have returned and the sun is bright, but the early morning air is still sharp. She woke that morning with the familiar sense there's something afoot in the world, something that needs her attention. It's a feeling she can't ignore and so she looks for news, hoping to find someone near the well, or perhaps a shepherd in the pens. It's been more than a moon since anyone sought her out.

Kraaak! Wilona squints against the piercing light to see a raven on a branch. It rocks back and forth on its leathery talons. The bird stretches its neck and emits a low, throaty rattle. *One for sorrow, two for mirth, three for a wedding, four for a birth.* She flaps her cloak and the bird flies off, squawking.

She climbs to the yew tree and, as she reaches level ground, stops. Bana looks at her and then sniffs the air. Smoke comes from the chimney of Touilt's hut. *So, someone's not frightened of living where the seithkona lived.* Resentment sears her chest, but curiosity gets the better of her. Who would dare?

"Come on, boy." She walks to the yew and stands with her back to the rough bark. "Sit," she tells Bana.

She doesn't have to wait long; a few moments later Ricbert, stooped, his thin white hair lifting in the wind, opens the door and steps out, a pail over his arm. He appears at her cave occasionally, insisting each time it's merely by chance, but she knows he's checking on her. Now and then he brings her the meat and cheese Lord Caelin sends her as reward not only for seeing the village through the time of sickness, but for bringing his son safely into the world. It was a difficult pregnancy, with Lady Elfhild weakened from the illness. The child grew in the womb only by the grace of fate and the decoction of guilder rose bark and blackberry leaves that Wilona gave her to stop her bleeding. So Caelin provides her with meat and cheese and sometimes cloth, although he never suggests she come back to her hut.

And now, she sees it's Ricbert's dwelling.

Four hens bustle round the corner, puffed up and clucking. He scatters grain for them. *Well then.* She's not surprised, for she didn't think Ricbert would much like sharing his house with the monk and his penchant for late-night and early-morning prayer. A grey goose waddles from the side of the house and, seeing Wilona and the hound, honks and hisses.

Ricbert turns, sees her, and waves. "Come, come!" he calls. "You're welcome, Wilona, come!"

"It's kind of you to welcome me to your home."

Ricbert looks at the dwelling as though appraising it. "Do you mind very much?"

"You might have told me."

"Aye. I should have." He smiles. "It's a good house, and the better for once being Touilt's, whose house it will always be, in my mind. And yours."

"Well, better you than someone else." Wilona shrugs. "Why should it stand empty? I'll not return and Touilt had great fondness for you." She's grateful he doesn't patronize her by suggesting her return would be welcome.

"Will you come inside and take some broth? This chill digs at my joints."

"You're kind, Lord Ricbert—"

"Ah, *Brother* Ricbert." The old man smiles a little sadly.

"*Friend* Ricbert, then."

He chuckles and pats her shoulder. "You influenced this decision, you know." She raises her eyebrows, questioning. "Brother Egan takes himself off to his stone hut on the mountain when he needs solitude, which is far too uncomfortable for me, and you're in your cave by the river."

He steps inside, and as she enters she tells Bana to sit by the door, but he ignores her and trots in, settling in his old place under the table.

"Let him be," says Ricbert.

Inside is both as she remembers it, and yet completely different. The walls are whitewashed, all trace of the great tree Yggdrasil erased. Tapestries hang on the wall, and the sleeping platform and the single chair are draped with furs. An iron pot dangles from a new chain above the fire. A wooden cross is nailed to the wall. She breathes deeply, trying to catch some lingering scent of Touilt, but it's just an old man's hut now.

"How can I call myself a holy man," says Ricbert, "if I, too, don't find a quiet place for my soul? A place where I may commune with the Lord Most High?"

"I thought you disbelieved all such things? Has Egan opened your heart for Christ?"

Ricbert shrugs, and his neck cracks. He ladles broth from a cooking pot into a bowl and hands it to her. "I wouldn't say that, exactly, but the truth is, living alone—I left my slave with Egan, who promptly freed him, silly man—I can't deny a sort of peace has descended on me. The well, the yew, the sky, the silence and solitude. I do think a lot here. A strange peace." He smiles again. "Or perhaps it's just death calming me before she creeps through the shutter some night."

"Are you ill?" The broth is strong with the taste of mutton and onions, and a bit of fat floats on the surface.

"No. Merely tired."

"I'll bring you a tonic," says Wilona, laying her hand on his arm. Under his tunic the skin hangs looser on his bones that it once did. "I awoke troubled this morning. Is there word from the king, from Lord Caelin, or . . . ?" Her voice trails and she drops her eyes, suddenly shy.

"Nothing of Margawn in particular." His eyes crinkle. "Although I'm sure he's fine, else word would have reached us. Bad news flies while good news walks."

"So will the men come home soon?" She can't help herself.

"Penda and Cadwallon are still problems, but we shall see." He pats her arm.

Wilona nods. "Well, then, my restlessness must be due to the coming solstice."

Ricbert looks at her from beneath his moth-wing brows. "Yes, that's probably it." He doesn't look convinced and she can't think of any way to persuade him.

A few days later, still filled with restlessness, Wilona leaves Bana to guard the animals, and climbs the high slopes of the sacred mountain. She finds a rocky outcrop and watches the village below. Everything looks just as it should. The crops pattern the earth like a soft patchwork blanket. Children run and squeal, chasing dogs and each other. Sheep and cattle dot the fields. Women tend the gardens, weave in the sunlight, or bake bread in the ovens. Men repair thatch, or work the squeaking lathes, or hammer on metal. By the river the wheel on the mill turns slowly, sunlight flashing in the falling water. There's no sign anything is amiss, but, there it is, like a scent of blood on the wind. She sits until the length of the shadows tells her more daylight has passed than remains. It's time to descend, yet on a whim she skirts the slope, toward the monk's stone hut. Just as she's come to the mountain on more than one occasion, so she's come across the monk in his solitary pursuits from time to time.

She's watched him in his stone hut, hidden from his view. He strips himself in all kinds of weather, wearing only a loincloth more often than not, or a thin cloak if the weather is particularly inclement. She's seen him strike himself with a barbed, multi-strand whip. She's watched him stand, nearly naked, in bitter weather, his hands outstretched to the sky. Sometimes he seems to sleep sitting up, cross-legged at the mouth of his hut, and she wonders if he dreams as she does, if he rides the spirits, and what he sees. Hawks circle over his stone shelter. Are his visions as full of death as hers? He's so still, so calm, and although she's sure that on one occasion she saw him weeping, his demeanour is, as a rule, oddly untroubled.

Before long she approaches the slope where he's built his retreat. He's there, sitting cross-legged on a rock, his face turned toward the east, his palms pressed together beneath his chin, and his head bowed. At least he's not shirtless. She chuckles. What would be the point, since it's not inclement? From the corner of her eye she catches movement. Two grey fox cubs tumble along the high meadow. They roll and yelp, nipping and pouncing on each other. The mother is nowhere to be seen, perhaps wisely asleep in her den until night, while her cubs, who know no better, frolic in the open. They stop, raise their snouts, catching Egan's scent, no doubt.

Wilona expects them to scamper back to their den, but they don't. They approach the monk, timidly at first and then more boldly, until finally they crawl over his legs and into his lap, nosing at his chest, licking his chin. Egan opens his eyes as calmly as if such things happened all the time. He smiles at the pups but doesn't start, and doesn't shoo them away, but merely closes his eyes. One of the cubs nips him on the chest, and then, a moment later, both curl up on his legs to nap.

How can it be the wild creatures trust him? When she finally leaves, still not one of the three has moved. She goes home, and when night falls she takes a bowl to the flat stone by the river and gazes into the water, reciting chants for clarity and wisdom, but she sees nothing except a placid, star-bright night.

The season's wheel turns . . . All through the summer, this feeling of something not being right harries her. She puts it down to

Margawn's long absence. All the women in the village must be feeling this way—anxious for news of their men. There's no point in idle worry. She casts the runes on every moon, but the meanings are unclear. Battles, yes, but when aren't there battles? Hardship, but isn't it always so?

On this day, during the Month of the Hunter's Moon, when the leaves are a golden scatter on the forest floor and the coats of the animals grow thick, Wilona ties strips of blue cloth to the limbs of the oak trees and marks her forehead with charcoaled runes. She bows her head and prays.

The wind kicks up and all around her the cloth strips festooning the trees dance like drunken faeries while the treetops tremble. The owl feathers in her matted hair flap before her eyes, and she holds them still as she takes stock of the air's strange tingle. Even the river is fretful and skittish. She listens to the voices on the wind . . . something coming. Bana stirs from his spot near the pigsty, barks, and trots to her. Whatever's coming, he senses it too.

Wilona knows one must pay attention to the language of the weather—the wind, the snow devils, the mists, and the lightning that zigzags across the spring sky. Wilona reads the patterns of gold and red in the autumn leaves. She learns from the animals as well. The delicate, soft-eyed deer that come to drink are full of gentleness and peace. The otter is ever-childlike, joyful, and adventurous. The butterfly—egg to worm to cocoon to wing—is the gods' way of saying all things change, in ways both unexpected and marvellous. The turtle carries his home with him everywhere and moves at his own pace, reminding her to be self-sufficient. The badger is quick tempered and everwilling to fight for what it wants.

The wind goes still again and the world settles. A crow caws twice, and then a third time. Five jackdaws fly from the south. Through the sparse-leafed trees, the curve of the sacred mountain is just visible, covered by a great mass of iron-grey cloud. Wilona draws her shawl around her shoulders, wary as a fox, then hurries into the cave, Bana close on her heels. She tries to light the fire, but it takes a long time to catch, even though the flint and twigs are dry. When at last a flame comes alive she blows on it, charms it to a good blaze.

Outside the sky has turned greenish. She grabs a handful of grain from the store-sack before going out again.

The chickens are hiding under bushes, refusing to return to their coop. Wilona manages to entice some of them with the grain, but then the wind returns with vengeance, the air crackles with strange energy and turns an eerie citrine. The remaining two hens panic and there's nothing Wilona can do but leave. A gust hurls brittle leaves into her face. A flying twig stings her cheek. The trees flail and creak. Her tunic flapping, she herds the pigs and sheep into the hut, retreats to the cave, and pulls the door across the entrance seconds before Thunor brings his hammer down on the holy mountain. The earth shakes.

Snuggled on the sleeping platform, Wilona jumps as the thunder cracks. Bana jumps up next to her, licks her face, and trembles. Outside, the wind moans and howls and the thunder rolls. Wilona's hands look oddly blue. The power of the gods fills her with awe, and she thinks of Elba and how she hated storms. Faithful Elba, who came to the end of her life the year before. She was old and Wilona could tell from the way she walked her joints pained her. It was time. Wilona sang to her and fed her apples and cradled her as she slit her throat. Poor old pig, it was the only thing to do. She cured the meat and hung it above the fire to smoke. She said a respectful prayer with every meal. Wilona misses her solid warmth and grumpy greetings.

Alarmingly close, a great *crack* sucks the air out of her ears. Bana barks. She pulls her cloak over her head.

The tempest lasts a long time, circling around, teasing the land. It flies to the north, and then rushes to the west, and comes round again. When Thunor has at last tired of his play, he meanders away to the north, the deep growl of his laughter slowly fading. Wilona waits until she's sure he won't return before poking her head outside. Bana hesitates, then runs after her, sprinkling his piss on every rock and tree around the cave. The river churns and rushes and a split tree smoulders.

She peeks into the animals' bower. They're safe and only a little skittish, and Wilona says her thanks. The renegade chickens appear from under the bramble, looking muddy and bedraggled. They tear into the coop, spilling nervous droppings as they run.

The sun has nearly set now, and soon the land will be dark. Exhausted from the energy of the storm, Wilona eats a meal of oats, hard-boiled egg, cheese, and greens, and settles into her blankets to sleep. The owl hoots, and she drifts off listening to him . . . She dreams . . . *carrion crows. Shapes . . . dark and swift and slinking. The dead, bloated, gnawed by wolves, eyes pecked by ravens . . . The faces are destroyed, but she knows them all . . . The royal compound, a smoking, collapsed shell, the carvings charred ruin. The tapestries, the benches, Lord Caelin's great ornate chair, nothing but greasy black skeletons beneath the caved-in rafters.*

The owl cries. A deep moaning. It perches high in the yew tree, its large black eyes set in the white and brown feathered disc of its face full of a warning and sorrow. It lifts off and sails, higher and higher, circling, and all around and everywhere is nothing but the dead . . .

The next morning dawns warm and bright and full of birdsong. Wilona rises and takes up her staff.

"Bana, come." She walks through the red and gold woods to her old hut, looking for Ricbert. She finds him with Egan, sitting together on stools by the open door, their heads bowed. She can tell from the way they hold themselves that their conversation is serious.

Ricbert spies her first and taps Egan on the knee. The two exchange glances and then beckon her forward.

"Are you well, Sister?" says Ricbert.

"I'm glad you're together. I must warn you."

Egan stands. "Be seated, Sister. And take rest from your walk." He pats Bana on the head.

"I've no need for coddling. There's no time."

Ricbert pats the stool. "Come, little sister. Nothing's so urgent that you can't sit to tell it. Do an old man the favour of not having to crane his neck."

She sits down and takes a breath to begin, but Egan raises his hand. "I'm sure your news is important, Wilona, but before you begin, there's other news we must tell."

"We haven't told the people yet," says Ricbert. "Do you think . . ."

Wilona looks from one man to the other. Their faces are grave, grim, even. She's been so wrapped in her own worries she didn't register their fear, and somehow, deep in her marrow, she knows it's all related.

Egan holds her gaze. "I think we must." Ricbert shrugs and Egan takes a breath, and then says, "We've received word. There was a battle last moon in a place called Haethfelth. Cadwallon and Penda joined forces, as we feared."

"And the outcome was not in our favour." It all seems so clear now.

Ricbert makes a sort of strangled noise in his throat.

She's surprised to see his chin tremble. "My lord?"

Egan puts a hand on the old man's shoulder. "The war has gone badly. King Edwin is dead. Osfrith, his son too, and his other son, Eadfrith, captured by Penda."

Her hand flies to her mouth. To have a vision is one thing, to hear the news in this world is another. "What about our men? What about Lord Caelin?" She can't bear to say Margawn's name . . .

"Lord Caelin fell with the king."

She grabs Ricbert's hand. "Margawn! Tell me." Bana barks at his master's name.

"We can't know for certain about the rest, but the fact no one's yet returned . . . it doesn't bode well," Ricbert says, in a choked voice. "Our men would fight to the death next to their lord."

Margawn would, he would. Her mind reaches for him . . . stretches out . . . but there's nothing, and surely she would know. She must know—her heart rips with the need to know—but there's no time . . ."I fear I've come to tell you the next part of the tale."

As she recounts her vision, Ricbert's face becomes more drawn, Egan's by turns flushed and ashen. When she's finished, Ricbert hunches his shoulders and gazes far out across the fields. Egan drops to the ground and sits in the mud as though his legs have been cut out from under him.

Ricbert's eyes are glazed with anguish. "Is it possible you dreamed of the war fields, of the battle of Haethfelth and not Ad Gefrin?"

She remembers the smouldering ruin of Caelin's hall. "No. Impossible."

He drops his head.

"We must warn the people." Egan rises and looks at Wilona with something like wonder. "Is there no end to the purposes God has for you, Sister? We didn't know what to do, but now, sure, it's clear. We must warn the people and prepare to leave. We must take the villagers to Bebbanburgh for safety. We must get there before Cadwallon nears Ad Gefrin."

This surprises her, coming from the monk. "And isn't Cadwallon a Christian? Yet you agree he's to be feared?"

Egan looks at his feet. "Yes, that's true," he says. "Surely a Christian king wouldn't harm us . . . but . . . I don't know . . ."

"What choice do we have?" says Ricbert. "Given Wilona's dream, and the fact there are, what, perhaps ten men in the village—Lady Elfhild's housecarls—who are capable of fighting?"

"And so," says Wilona, "after all the blood spilled to combine Deira and Bernicia into Northumbria, Edwin's great vision, everything will go back to the way it was. Kings!" She spits. "What madness their ambition is!" She says nothing of her own plans. Let them think she'll go with them, if they like. She will not. She desires nothing more than to find her spirits, to seek knowledge of Margawn. No army will pay attention to a solitary woman living in a cave, and if they recognize her as seithkona and have any respect for the old gods, they'll not harm her. Even Christians fear the wrath of the forest gods, and the gods will protect her. The dream is evidence they're with her still. A small twinkle of hope flashes in her heart, though. If the people were granted refuge in the great fortress at Bebbanburgh, perhaps the vision could be altered even yet.

———◆———

After consulting with Lady Elfhild, Ricbert and Egan call the people together that night. Rumours have already spread through the village like a blight. Inside the hall, the fires are low and the women, children, and old men huddle in the centre like nervous cattle. When Lady Elfhild appears from her private chambers, the women moan and wail.

"The kingdom is lost!"

"Our men are dead!"

"The gods have abandoned us!"

This is a needle in Egan's heart, but there's no time for that now. He waves his hands and shouts to quiet them. "Your men may be gone to paradise, it's true, for the battle has gone against us. If they're gone to heaven before us, they watch over you, but who knows, some may have escaped—"

"Our men are not cowards to run from the field of battle!" says Sunild, the tanner's wife.

Ricbert takes Egan's arm and says, "Brother Egan only meant they may be regrouping, on their way to save us. But we cannot wait. For the sake of your children, we must go to Bebbanburgh."

At first there is silence. To leave one's home, to be a refugee on the roads, at the mercy of strangers and a burden on kin, is a terrifying prospect.

"We must protect our homes," a young boy says, a threshing fork in his fist.

The women begin to wail anew and clasp their children tighter. The faces of the old men shine with battle-memory and blistering rage.

Lady Elfhild, dressed in her finest indigo robe, with a golden torque at her throat, raises her hand. "You are a brave and noble lad, and you do your family proud. But we must face this. I, too, fear I must now be a widow." She hangs her head until the wave of protest stills. Her eyes glitter with tears, but with a fierce pride as well. "We're an honourable people. We're a loyal people. We do not run from battle. However, as loyal wife to my husband, as mother to his children, my responsibility lies in their protection, as does yours to your children. The messengers tell us the dog Cadwallon is laying waste to the country. If he comes here, and we think he will, we'll not be spared. I want my son to live to avenge his father! As your sons will avenge theirs. We will go to Bebbanburgh and seek sanctuary in the fortress. We will grow strong again and we will live to see Cadwallon torn apart by our vengeance!"

There are cheers at this, and Egan unclenches his jaw. The people will go. He would have used a different argument, but even he sees this is not the time for talk of turning the other cheek.

All through the night and the next day, the village women, children, and old men make preparations, piling wagons, and packing supplies: tools, trunks, clothing, and anything that might be used as a weapon. Daggers are sharpened; clubs are fashioned from knotted branches. The boys will drive the cattle and the sheep and the pigs. The final harvest must be done early, so there are stores to keep them through the winter, but much, unripe, will be left behind. Still, they can't arrive in Bebbanburgh empty-handed. If they appear looking like no more than hungry mouths to be fed over the cold months, they may well be turned away.

They scan the horizon constantly, praying they'll see only earth and sky, and not weapon-glint, not the cloud of dust that signals an approaching army. They pray the rain will stay away, for they'll need a dry road. The village echoes with the sound of clanking pots and crying children and sharp-voiced women.

Brother Egan has little to pack, save for the holy objects—the cross and altar cloth, and the items he uses for communion. He wraps the communion chalice and the silver pyx, inscribed with the words *"Ecce Panis Angelorum."* May the angels protect the innocent, prays Egan. He goes from family to family, helping where he can, stuffing hens into wicker baskets, tying loads onto wagons, and blessing the heads of many children. He goes out with the shepherds, their eyes on the distant roads, and gathers in the sheep from the hills.

At last, the next night, when the village is resting for an hour or two before taking to the road with dawn's first light, he prostrates himself on the church's hard-packed earth floor, and prays, and prays, and prays. His head fills with terrible images, of axes and torn flesh, of babies on the end of swords. *Begone, you devils! I banish you in the name of Christ!* The Adversary seeks to drive him mad with terror, so he'll be of no use to these people. Cadwallon is a Christian.

Surely even if he comes here, he'll not harm defenceless women and children. Surely he'll show mercy. To kill on the field of battle is one thing, but to harm innocents is another. His head spins with the tales of war—monks whose hearts had been cut out, still beating; who had been burned at the stake, boiled in oil— and he cries out, "No! No! *Devil! Do not torment me so! Christ save me! Father save me!*" He sobs, shuddering. He's a child again, wanting to be back on his shining isle. Did not the sea creatures bring him there? It was a mistake for him to leave. He wants his old cell back, the chanted prayers, solitude and peace. He digs his fingers in the ground beneath him, dampened by his weak and pointless tears.

He weeps and prays until he falls into a kind of unconsciousness. He feels the roll and ripple of deep water beneath him, as though the small church were a coracle on a restless sea. He smells salt. Egan's heart slows to match the rhythm of the unseen waves, and a sensation of warmth comes over him. He raises his forehead from the ground, and there before him is a great shimmering light.

He gasps.

She is there.

He tries to rise completely but cannot. It's as though his limbs are sewn to the earth. Still, she is there. All white and gold, with fire round her head and birds hovering above her, beckoning him, a smile on her ruby lips. Her wings are like sails of finest linen, held in a gentle wind. Placid waves lap at her fine-boned feet. He's a boy again, and he will follow her anywhere, even to the gates of death.

Chapter THIRTY-ONE

Wilona works every protection charm she knows. She barely sleeps, and when she does her dreams are full of fire and death, and Margawn, always Margawn. Margawn in the mud. Margawn with a thousand wounds, his blood seeping into the thirsty earth. Margawn's hair stained with gore. Margawn's eyes dull as dry stone, crawling with ants, staring sightless into the unending sky. She pictures it, smells it, tastes it, and yet her very blood rejects the idea. Every time she wakes after drifting off, she calls out his name, the smell of his skin in her nostrils, the taste of him in her mouth. *He cannot be dead. I would feel it.* She weeps and weeps some more and chides herself. There's no time. She must work the charms.

Wilona reads the signs. A swarm of bees settles on a dead log, meaning the hive keeper will not live long. The candlewicks spark, many times, meaning strangers approach. A hen crows, a nightjar settles in a branch near the cave's entrance, and a raven croaks to her left. Whatever's coming is coming quickly. As the second night falls, a large, ragged wolf appears near the river, sending Bana into paroxysms. It takes all Wilona's strength to hold him back. The wolf throws back its head and howls before it disappears in an enveloping fog. Touilt, surely, come to warn her.

This night, Wilona can't sleep, but rather moves from one mist-filled vision to the next, while Bana watches from the hearth. She sits on her hen-feather pillow, the blue cloak around her shoulders, the owl talons at her neck, owl feathers in her hair, yew staff in her hand. The pillow rests on a round, flat rock hauled from the river. Around the rock is a circle of red string, tied with twelve knots, and inside the circle the ground is scattered with cedar boughs and struck with runes. She's pulled bramble bushes, mistletoe, and yew in front of the cave entrance. Only a madman would cross such potent protections, and if he did, he'd find Bana waiting.

Owls gather in the trees—how many, she cannot tell, but there must be four or even five perhaps, judging from their calls. It occurs to her she should run from this place, but run where? How many homes does she have to lose? No. This is her place. *Her* place, and she will keep it. She tells herself to be calm, to trust the gods who have sent such powerful guardians.

It's hard to tell when it occurs to her what she's hearing are not the normal noises of the night. First, she notes the absence of those familiar noises. Silence like a cloak, thick and heavy. The owls have stopped hooting. Bana is on his feet, growling, eyes fixed on the entrance. She fears he'll bark and give them away. She softly calls him, makes him sit next to her, and holds her hand over his muzzle. Then, *Snap!* Something farther off—voices? Is that a shout? A scream? Ghostly, carried on the pre-dawn breeze. Wilona's heart thuds painfully in her chest. It begins. Bana whines and she makes him lie down. The shadows from the solitary candle flicker like reaching fingers. *Come, Raedwyn, come. Come, Eostre, goddess of life, come. Come Tiw, god of war.* She cannot hear the owls. Her mouth is dust-lined. Where have the owls gone?

More noises in the distance now, cries and shouts. Some magic must surely be carrying them to her ears, for it's too far for normal sound to travel from the village. She wonders if she is imagining it. The smell of burning fills the cave, filling her nostrils, thick, pungent, and sticky. She sits cross-legged and the stone digs painfully into her ankle where it rests off the pillow. She's here, in the cave, but the cries are everywhere, flying around the cave like bats. She chants the song of protection, softly, and wills herself to be invisible, no more than a little fox in its den, a mouse in its burrow, an owl in its nest.

A snap. A crack. Men's voices.

She blows the candle out, holds Bana tight, her fingers over his snout. The language the men speak is unknown to her. They laugh, in a careless way.

Pass. Pass by. Pass. A bead of sweat trickles into her eye and her breath catches. She opens her mouth, trying to suck air into her lungs without making a sound. Her feet prickle, the circulation gone. She wiggles her toes and the sensation is intense, burning, like a million hot needles. She moves her legs, putting her feet on the ground but still within the circle. The men are at the river's edge now. Their voices are louder.

In the darkness, she bares her teeth.

The rooster crows. Once, and then again.

In the darkness, her hands are talons. Bana vibrates, needing to bite, to tear, to rend.

Two men. Voices more serious now. The brambles at the door shake.

In the darkness, her throat fills with stifled screams.

The brambles are thrown aside. A large hand breaks through the woven door as though it were stitched from fog. She sees a torch.

She releases Bana.

The dog lunges, silent as a spear, all teeth and fur and fury. Man and beast disappear in an explosion of cursing and flailing arms and legs. Wilona prays they'll think they've stumbled on a monster's den and will run before they're torn to shreds. *Kill, Bana, kill them!* She reaches for her dagger. Her mind spins even as her eyes are pinned to the entrance—only jerking shadows, the flash of steel, of fang. She must fight next to Bana; she must sink in a blade beside his teeth . . . She must stay within the protection of the circle, of the gods. And then, a terrible yelping, silence, and then, it cannot be—*Frige protect us*—a splash as something heavy lands in the water. Only curses after—no bark, no snarl, no growl. In the darkness, she fills her eyes with fire, and hisses. She rattles the owl talons and shakes the yew staff.

A face then, visible in the red glow from the fire's embers. Wide, meaty. Yellow-grey hair and beard. Nose like a turnip. A black cap on his head, a spear in one hand, a shield decorated with white dragons on a red field. The man blinks at her, says something, and another head appears. This one is younger, with a black thrice-braided beard. A helmet with a flat nosepiece, glinting in the torch flame. There is blood on him. Bana's blood.

Black-beard smiles.

Wilona stands, although her feet are dead and her knees weak as water. She shakes the talons, she shakes the staff, she utters words of great power and gnashes her teeth, pressing her arms out like owl's wings.

Black-beard laughs.

Urine runs down the inside of Wilona's leg, staining the ground. The men push aside what's left of the door, step through the hearth ashes, and reach for her. She jumps from the rock, but where will she go? Wilona screams for the goddess and she screams for Raedwyn and she screams for Touilt, and when she is done screaming, still the two men stand before her. She pulls the dagger from her belt.

This time both men laugh, and then hands are upon her and her tunic is torn from her body, and the stench of them is in her nostrils and the taste of them in her mouth, and when her flesh rips she tries hard not to scream, but fails.

Dawn's birdsong breaks through the crow-black night. Wilona pries open an eye. Sprawled on the ground, the two men snore and sputter in drunken sleep. It occurs to her she may be dead, a wraith yet to wander from the place of her murder. With some effort she moves an eye, and the wrenching agony in her head tells her she's still alive. Her hands and feet are bound. It doesn't matter what agony is in her bones, her muscles, her torn flesh—she spies a dagger hilted with silver, stained with the blood, no doubt, of the villagers of Ad Gefrin, lying next to the younger man. Oh, sweet dagger.

She hardly knows she's moving until her fingers wrap round the hilt. How cool it is. How accommodating to her shredded palm, her broken finger. It takes no strength at all. And it's so sharp the ropes on her wrists and ankles are no more than silken string. The black-bearded man's throat is soft as fresh-churned butter, the blood as warm as milk straight from the udder. She sits on his chest. He gurgles but cannot speak. His eyes fill first with fury and then plead for mercy, and she watches as the light dwindles and dies. The older man snores right up until the moment she sinks the dagger between his ribs, and then bucks like a slaughtered sheep and is still.

It takes a long time to drag the bodies to the river. She pulls and pushes and rolls them to the flat rock and then tumbles one in after the other. They land with a splash, as Bana's body did. Brave Bana, gone to be with Margawn again. The bodies float downstream, headfirst, face down, legs and arms spread on the mud-brown water, leaving trails of red. The older one's shoulder snags a drifting branch and it seems he wears it like a thorny crown. She spits in the river after them. They are not the only bodies there. A man and a swollen sheep drift by. And something else, smaller, in a red tunic. She does not look closely. She catches a chicken and wrings its neck; she'll need the meat. The rest of the chickens and the pigs and the sheep she sets free. The animals are wild from the scent of human blood and burning, and run into the forest. Ordinarily she'd send a protection charm after them, but now the idea makes her laugh. She picks up a large stone and hurls it at the tree where the owl nests. It hits the trunk with a dull thud and then falls to the ground, as impotent as Raedwyn, as the gods, any gods. The air's acrid with smoke. Above the trees, it still billows, black as plague.

She knows what she'll find if she climbs the hill to the village. What she doesn't know is whether Cadwallon's army—for surely that's who's come—is still there, or if they've completed their destruction and moved on to the next village. She doesn't know if her attackers were scouts or renegades or stragglers. She only knows she must take herself away. If she's to survive, and she's not entirely sure that's what she wants, she cannot stay here.

She wipes the hair from her eyes, tears the owl feathers from her hair and the pouch from her neck. She squats by the river and washes away all trace of the runes from her hands. The baby finger of her right hand is swollen and hangs at an odd angle. She slips into the cold river with her clothing dangling in scraps from her. She hugs the shore and keeps her gaze upriver, imagining the horror of a body bumping into her . . . *Roswitha. Dunstan. Ricbert.* She lets the current strip her bare, trying not to think of the men's hands on her. It's river current, only river current. She rubs hard between her legs, rinses her mouth again and again.

Her skin is a tapestry detailing her ordeal—scratches, teeth marks, purple and green and red bruises in the shape of fingers and knees, on the inside of her thighs, the inside of her arms, across her breasts, her stomach, a gouge where her left breast seams into her ribs. She'd use the dagger and skin herself to erase every trace if she could.

She doesn't stay in the river long, for the air is cold and she has little reserve strength. Her breath fogs before her face. She finds two stubby twigs and binds them to her broken finger with strips from her under-tunic. She scrambles into the cave. The men have made a mess, breaking jars and scattering herbs under their filthy feet. She dresses in layers and searches for the herbs Touilt taught her will ensure she doesn't carry a child. The jar of smartweed is smashed. So little left. But enough, surely. She scrapes up as much as she can. Pennyroyal, too. She fashions a bundle to sling over her shoulder, stuffed with what food she can carry, including the chicken—enough for a few days. She tucks a dagger and an axe in her belt, throws an otter-pelt cloak around her shoulders and another few pelts in her bundle, tosses her yew-staff into the river, but takes up the warrior's spear.

The day is bright and the leaves a garnet and amber canopy above her head. The light flashes and shadows as she steps through the forest. Every muscle in her body aches, and in the places where her secret flesh is torn and raw, blood seeps. She keeps on moving, and at last finds a good place, far from the stink of death and burning. There's a stream, and two ash trees of similar height and structure, the length of a man apart, and a nearby yew tree. Wilona is no longer interested in holy spaces. She's interested only in the fact this place is good for building shelter, and the stream will give her water and attract game.

She cuts eight poles from the yew, and a number of vines. She works like a madwoman, her mind swirling curses. *May the souls of the men who hurt me wander in the wastelands forever. May their bones drift along the muddy river bottom forever, unburied, unblessed.* With the back of the lean-to facing into the wind, she sets the longest pole in the forks of the two trees. The rest of the poles she sets into the ground, leaning up against this horizontal pole, and lashes them together with vines. She covers the framework with brush, boughs from a pine and a juniper, working her way from bottom to top so that the rain will run off. The scent of the pine needles is so clean she puts a few in her mouth and chews, the sour burst scouring her tongue. She gathers leaves and pine boughs for her bed, covering them with the pelts. When this is done she drives four stakes shoulder-height into the ground and stacks stones and rotting logs on top of one another between them. She fills in the spaces between the logs with twigs, and gathers stones to place in front of this wall for the fire. As night falls the weather turns colder, and this fire-reflector will add to her comfort. She plucks the chicken and roasts it on a spit. While it cooks she heats water in a small pot, brews the smartweed and pennyroyal to ensure the men's seed does not take hold inside her. She brews it strong and drinks it all. She should drink it for four more days, but there's only enough for two. When the bird is ready she tears into the meat with her teeth like a wild thing and tosses the bones into the flames, where they blacken and crackle. As darkness falls she builds the fire, then wraps up in furs, lies down, and curls into a ball.

She watches the fire and grinds her teeth. Every flame is a grasping, reaching hand. Over and over again she closes her eyes, shakes her head to banish the images, until, at last, tears begin to fall. She wipes them away roughly, her broken finger throbbing. The pain in her hand reminds her she's still not dead, but is this a good thing? She longs for Margawn, in this world or the next, but if she dies, how would she find him in the Christian heaven? She remembers what Margawn told her Ricbert had said: *A sparrow flies in through a window at one end, flies the length of the hall, and out through a window at the other end. That is what life is like.* She cannot see now why flying into darkness is a bad thing. What's wrong with that deepest, darkest of slumbers, dreamless, painless, unending? She longs for it.

She begged the gods to save her, to protect her, and instead they gave her visions she could not change, so she is doubly tortured. Wilona considers the possibility the goddess sent those two beasts to punish her for taking Margawn as a lover. Could the goddess be that jealous, that patient, that cunning and cruel? It seems as likely as anything. Some emotion rips through her—intense, scalding. She writhes and cries out. There it is! She hates the gods now, with a fury that burns away the bonds that tied her to them. She *hates* them!

And then, behind the searing fury, comes a wave of clarity, bright as a lightning bolt. Without the gods to answer to, without the gods to please, with only herself to look after and to satisfy, life might become simple. She cannot decide if the gods abandoned her at her hour of greatest need, or if they willed this horror, but either way it's of little matter, for *she* now abandons *them*. There are no owls in the trees, only the sigh of the wind, the sputter of the fire, only the cold and distant silver crescent moon hanging from a ribbon of white cloud. She's just a woman beneath its clear eye. Just a woman. Seithkona no longer. She falls asleep thinking of Ricbert, wondering if he's flown into the darkness beyond life's warm hall. She dreams of fire and screaming and the stench of unwashed men. She wakes and cries for Margawn.

For seven days and nights she lies in the furs, venturing out only for firewood, water, and food. By the third morning she can relieve her bladder without the pain bringing tears to her eyes. The swelling in her hand has gone down, the bruises have begun to fade, and although the nightmares have not diminished, she's confident her sanity will hold.

The weather has turned. The rain is vile, pelting down and extinguishing all but the most roaring blaze. The wood she gathers is wet and nearly impossible to light. She's damp and cold through to her bones, and the food is gone. The woods are dark and dripping and the days short. The metallic scent of oncoming winter is sharp.

She considers hanging herself from the nearby oak. She runs her belt through her hands. The leather's smooth, supple as a snake. She slips it round her neck and pulls it tight. She imagines what it's like to jerk and kick in the air, to claw at her throat as the world speckles and dims. She imagines her tongue swelling in her mouth, and her bowels releasing. Trapped blood throbs in her ears. The flesh of her cheeks and jaw prickles. The hollows below her eyes begin to puff.

She coughs and loosens the belt, her eyes watering. *No.*

Death will come one day, this or another, without her having to run toward it, although were Hel herself to appear right now Wilona would welcome the goddess. However, it seems the only things in the woods are creatures as miserable as she is: a droop-necked deer, several frenzied squirrels, a ragged fox. She considers: Until death appears, she's free from the wishes of the gods. Thus, damned or not damned, there's as much reason to live as not, although the prospect of life would be more attractive if she was somewhere warm and dry. There's only one place she knows.

It's time. She must go back.

Dagger in one side of her belt. Axe in the other. Spear in her hand. Bundle on her back. Her hood over her head, and the fur cloak over her shoulders, she trudges through the haggard wood back to Ad Gefrin.

Chapter THIRTY-TWO

Wilona stops where the path forks. Right leads to the village; straight leads to her cave. Her feet long to keep walking until she arrives back at the cave, profaned though it is, where if she's lucky she'll find nothing more than ghosts and mice. She takes two steps in that direction, then stops. No, she must see the village. She walks a little way and stops again. She cannot. No good awaits her there, she feels it. She turns, walks toward her cave, but something nips at her heels with every step. She stops, turns again.

She pounds her fists against her temples, and snarls through clenched teeth. She considers going back into the woods and letting nature take its course. How strong the lure of oblivion is. If she were a different woman . . . but she's not; she's the one who survives. From the death of her childhood village, to the death of this one, it's her destiny, her fate to be the one who survives.

She must know. She must see with her own eyes. She doesn't know why, for seeing will only replace the monstrous images in her imagination with the monstrous truth. It could be, of course, that the gods lied in the vision they sent her—she wouldn't put even *that* past them now. Perhaps not everyone was slaughtered. She might not be alone. She can't decide if being with others would be a good thing. A kind of numbness has settled into her, as though she's walking on the bottom of the riverbed, moving against a lethargic current, viewing the world through the distortion of water, everything slippery, heavy, and indistinct.

She sets her mud-covered feet on the path toward the village and keeps her eyes on them. She doesn't raise her gaze until she comes to the well. The post has been tossed aside. She peers down into the water. Something's floating, bloated and black. A dog, she thinks.

The hut she once shared with Touilt is a seared, collapsed ruin. A grey sludge, a mix of rain, ash, and charcoal, has formed over and around everything. It smells sour and leaves bitterness on her tongue. Without going closer she knows nothing salvageable remains. In the corner of her eye, something moves, and she swings round, her hand on the dagger.

Ricbert's body hangs from the yew tree, a great wound in his side. His neck is elongated, his head crooked. His blackened and swollen tongue fills his gaping mouth. His eyes sockets are empty. His face is purple and black, faintly green.

Ah, Ricbert. Old friend. Heron. Sparrow.

She drags herself onward, climbing the path. She crosses the defensive ditch and steps over charred logs—all that remains of the stockade walls. Ravens peck and flap and squabble over the dead. They rise and fall like tattered black blankets. It's difficult to tell who is who, for the elements and the animals have not been kind. Surely, that bloated form is Aelfric the potter; even in death his belly is impressive, as is the gash cleaving his skull in two. And there, the miller's son, and the woman's body is that of his mother. Part of a child lies nearby, but its face is gone entirely. Other bodies, farther in, are like coal statues among the shells of the buildings, twisted in the horrible rictus of death by fire, the arms bent, the hands pulled up in front of their faces, the fingers burned away.

She steps over charred bits of stools and chests emptied of anything valuable. Here and there sodden scraps of cloth wave in the wind, remnants of clothing or bedding. In some spots the destroyed huts and halls block the way. She's disoriented, a little dizzy, willing herself not to panic. A leather cup in the path here, a shattered loom there, a piece of crockery, iron hinges . . . the smell of rotting corpses, singed fur, wet ashes . . . Every place looks much as the next, as though she's in a dream, some eerily silent landscape out of time, where everything is stitched together with memory and smoke.

"Get back, demon! Evil spawn!"

The voice is so shocking Wilona steps back, nearly tripping over a broken bench. A dog runs round the corner of what's left of a building. Its jaws are open, tongue dangling, blood flecked. It swerves and disappears behind a pile of rubble.

"Damn you! Damn you!" Egan appears from wherever the dog came from, running, a club in his hand. Seeing Wilona, he halts so quickly he stumbles. Then he becomes very still.

"Egan," she says, more whisper than word.

He draws his lips back, not in a smile. He raises the club over his head, about to hurl it at her. His tonsure is growing in and the hair is as matted as hers. His robe barely hangs on him, revealing scabbed skin, and the fur across his shoulders is bloodied and foul. Healing bruises cover his face, making his leaf-green eyes all the more shocking. Blood stains his hands.

"Demon! Ghost! Be gone in the name of Jesus Christ, Son of God!"

He makes the sign of the cross, spits on the ground, and without another word, turns and jogs back from where he came, leaving Wilona to gaze after him, unblinking. *His eyes! They glitter with madness.* She squats on the ground, trying to gather her wits. If he's alive, there may be others. She stands and wipes her palm on her tunic, leaving a wide black smudge.

Cautiously, she edges around the corner and catches sight of him running between the black-bone ruins. She follows. He makes for the plateau where the king's compound once stood, although she can see even from here it, too, was destroyed. She loses him as she nears what was the amphitheatre, and then she realizes where he's going.

At the graveyard Egan is alone, save for the corpses surrounding him. He's been digging for a long time, Wilona assumes, for line after line of open pits scar the earth, and more mounds beyond that, where bodies must have already been laid to rest. Two are very large. They're like full bellies, the holes like hungry mouths. She shudders. The earth has become a pitiless beast. The great cross, though, has not been burned. It stands bizarrely unscathed at the end of the graveyard.

Before it are a row and a half of old graves, three and a half more of fresh graves, and now, these rows of open pits, waiting. How could he have dragged all those bodies up here? She sees a cart, piled with yet more corpses. There is no oxen, no horse. He must have lashed himself to it. He digs with a ferocity she fears will kill him. Now she understands why his hands have so much blood on them—all that digging with a rough shovel. His palms have split open.

She could walk away. Clearly he's lost his mind. He thinks she's a ghost. He might be right. What more punishing Hel could there be than this? She holds her hands in front of her, looks at the web of dirt-grimed lines criss-crossing her palm, the bluish veins in her wrists, pulsing ever so slightly. She doesn't think she is dead.

Egan steps into the grave he's digging, so his feet are hidden. Wilona steps forward. She doesn't want to come up behind him, fearing what he might do if startled, and she stops, unsure of how to continue. Why not leave him to his ghosts, his god? She looks past him, to the cart. Roswitha lies there, her tunic rucked up, revealing white thighs smeared with blood.

"Brother Egan," Wilona calls, softly, softly. The wind is against her and she tries again, a little more loudly this time. "Brother Egan . . ."

He stiffens, the shovel dripping dirt back into the grave, then turns, holding the shovel as a weapon. He stares at her, his eyes sparking fury and terror.

"It's Wilona. Wilona." She holds her hands out so he can see she has no weapon.

Egan hoists himself from the grave and runs toward her. She steps back, ready to flee if he attacks. She has weapons, but no desire to use them. But he stops. His thin arms and legs stick out from the tatters of his clothing. His feet are bluish-grey, patched red.

"You look cold, Brother Egan. Have you no shoes?"

He lowers the shovel slightly and squints. "Are you a spectre? An apparition come to torment me? In the name of Christ, if you're a spirit, I order you to leave me."

"I'm no ghost, Egan. I'm just Wilona." She shrugs, waves her empty hands. "You see, I'm the woman you know, and I mean you no harm." She slaps the back of her hands lightly. "Flesh, see? Solid as you."

He trembles as though a chill runs through him, and lets the shovel hang. "How can I be sure? I cannot be fooled again."

"Will you let me approach?"

Egan pulls the wooden cross he wears on a thong around his neck from inside his tunic and holds it in front of him. "You cannot approach unless you be flesh and blood."

"Then I'll approach easily." She walks slowly but steadily toward him. As she nears she catches his scent on the breeze and forces herself not to react. It is the smell of decay and rot and death. She wonders if he sleeps among them, to be so saturated with the stench. A battle rages in him—she sees it in his eyes. She's no more than five feet from him when his face crumples and he drops to his knees.

"Thank God. My prayers are answered." Tears cover his face, leaving streaks through the dirt. "Blessed be God, the Merciful."

Wilona squats before him and takes his hands. A wave of unexpected emotion convulses her, and she bursts into tears. They cling to one another, sobbing, their bodies shaking with relief and agony. To feel another's body, breathing, whole.

When at last the tears subside, they sit back and gaze at one another. The blood, the scabs, the bruises tell their tale. Rain begins to pelt down in earnest. The icy rivulets wriggling down her neck make Wilona shiver. Egan's teeth chatter. She waits for him to ask what happened to her. He doesn't ask, only stares. She decides his mind is too blasted for curiosity.

"We must find shelter," she says.

"I cannot leave the dead."

"They'll wait for us."

"They get up and walk the instant I stop working." Egan's face comes close to hers. "I don't want to look. Do it for me." He jerks his head, indicating she should look behind him, at the cart full of corpses. "Are they crawling yet?" He shudders. "They become so angry. They *bite!*"

He has lost his mind.

"They're quiet now," she says. He looks as though he doesn't believe her. The madness that has overtaken him is making him skeptical of her again. "Perhaps with two of us to care for them, they're appeased."

"God sent you," he says.

She looks around. "Is nothing left standing?"

"The beast burned everything." He reaches out and pats her shoulder as though checking to see if she's real. "He locked us in the hall and burned us." His hands pull back into curved little fists. "He laughed. Cadwallon laughed at the screams."

"And did no one escape?"

"No one. No ONE. NO ONE . . ." He is louder with every word.

She takes his hand. "Brother Egan, if your god'ssent me, will you trust me, and do as I say?"

His teeth bang together so forcefully she fears they'll break. "I must bury the dead."

"You can't bury the dead if you're dead yourself, isn't that true? Of course it is. Night is falling. The weather's hard. If we're to help the dead—"

"You will help me, will you not?"

"Yes, I'll help you. But first we must find food and shelter, and sleep awhile and renew our strength. Where have you been sleeping?"

He blinks several times. "I don't know. I think I went to the mountain." He rises and begins to walk in that direction.

"No, Brother Egan. Wait. It's too far from water and too hard a climb." And there's no cover there, nowhere to run to if need be. She takes him by the arm. He comes placidly enough. "Your god sent me to you, yes?"

"He keeps sending you to me. And you're not a Christian. Do you not find that odd?" He looks into her eyes, searching for something. His breath is rancid. A body feeding on itself.

"If he sent me to you, then listen to my counsel. You'll come with me. We'll go to my dwelling. Even if Cadwallon's men looted it, there was little to find, and they can't tear down the walls of a cave."

She prods him away from the graves, away from the dead, and everything is fine until they reach the hut she once shared with Touilt. When he sees Ricbert's body swaying from the tree, he begins to beat his chest and tear at his skin with his nails. She uses all her strength to pull his hands from his face.

"Stop it, Egan! Stop it!"

"He died for me! He died for my sins!" Egan breaks away and runs to Ricbert's body. He pulls at the feet, and for a moment Wilona fears they will come off in his hands, or the head will separate from the body.

"Let go, you can do nothing for him." Something pops, tears. Gagging, she pries his fingers open and drags him away.

He is so weak from exhaustion and hunger that she's able to over-power him without struggle. This gives her some reassurance, for if, in the grip of some delusion, he attacks her, she's confident she can repel him. Still, she doesn't want to hurt him. His eyes are fixed on Ricbert, tears streaming, mouth gasping in spasms. Before she knows she is going to do it, Wilona slaps him across the face. His head snaps back but his hands remain at his sides. He blinks several times. He looks like a small boy. His chin trembles.

"Forgive me," she says, and puts her arm around his shoulders. We'll come back and help Brother Ricbert tomorrow, yes? He'll be safe where he is until then. The animals can't get to him." She doesn't want to think about the bodies in the cart, what condition they'll be in tomorrow with no one to guard them through the long night. Egan rocks back and forth, and she worries he'll collapse again. "Brother Egan, don't you think you should say a prayer for Brother Ricbert? Shouldn't you say the words to bring him to Christ's heaven? That's your responsibility, isn't it?" He gazes at her, locked within whatever maze of horrors his mind has become. "Pray for him, Brother Egan. Pray for him."

The words must reach him, for he gathers himself and his fea-tures rearrange into something like his old self. "You are right again, Sister."

Egan kneels in the wet earth just in front of the swaying corpse and makes the sign of the cross. She cannot tell what words he intones, for although his lips move he speaks softly. Wilona finds herself wanting to kneel down with him. Not to pray to the Christian god, but to honour her old friend. She sits back on her heels, tilts her face and looks up, into the mist-grey sky and the raindrops, pearls tumbling from the fingers of an unbearably distant god. It makes her dizzy and she closes her eyes. The cold water runs into her hair.

Be at peace, Ricbert. Find a home somewhere and rest there. Know you will be remembered. Her insignificance strikes her; she's nothing but an ant under the absurdly remote sky, a speck of dust on the monstrous body of the earth.

When she opens her eyes, Egan stands before her with a blank, hopeless expression on his face. She pushes herself up with her hands and wipes the mud on her skirt. She suspects she'll never be clean again. "Come, Egan. I'm too weary to fight with you."

He says nothing but follows behind like a lamb. As they walk along the rain-pocked river, Wilona notices debris caught at the banks, bits of wood and leaves and cloth, but other than an unsettling hank of blond hair wrapped around a floating branch, there's no sign of human death. The river is healing itself, dragging all the ugly things to the bottom, where they'll be eaten by turtles and fish; or casting them out, where the beasts of land and air will make whatever use of them they can. In another moon everything will be as it was on the river, as though Cadwallon's horror never happened.

When they arrive at the cave, she's as delighted as her fatigue and grief will allow to see that the brambles she threw over the entrance are undisturbed. She laughs, startling Egan, when two chickens run from the underbrush and eye her accusingly, reprimanding her for leaving them alone. Egan gazes down at the river from the flat rock, and Wilona pulls him back from the edge, fearing he might cast himself in. If he does, she won't jump in after him. Enough is enough.

"Pull those brambles away, Egan. Make yourself useful."

He grasps the thorny branches with his bare hands. Spots of bright red blood appear on his stained flesh.

"For the love of Thunor! Wake up, man. Use your tunic round your hands. Must I treat you like a simpleton?"

She realizes she's using the same tone Touilt used with her in her first weeks in the village, when she was as blasted with shock as Egan is now. Touilt tolerated no silliness, as she called it, no mooning. Wilona later nursed a sort of resentment of the seithkona's crusty manner, especially when she'd so craved a mother's comfort, but now, looking at how easy it would be for Egan to crumble into nothingness, she gains a new respect for Touilt's wisdom. He nods, and twists the cloth of his ragged tunic round his hands.

When the entrance is clear and she swings back the woven door, her heart pounds. It may just be her imagination, but she smells her attackers' rancid, salty, ale-infused stench. It wraps around her head, over her mouth and nose like the fat fingers of the turnip-nosed one.

"There's wood drying under the animal shed's overhang, Egan. Bring some in."

Something in the hawthorn bushes on the far side of the sty snaps her to attention. She jerks her dagger from her belt. Egan will be no help in a fight, or will he? His eyes are focused on the spot, his teeth bared. He draws his cross and opens his mouth.

"No!" She points her finger at him, silencing him as she would a child. "Stay."

She picks up a rock and hurls it into the bushes. It thuds to the ground, and she swears she hears a whine, a whimper. Whatever it is, it's hurt. One of the shoats? A sheep crawled off to die? She picks up her spear and inches toward the bush. Egan mutters behind her—prayers, she supposes—and she knows she cannot stop him. She rattles the edge of the hawthorn. Something stirs. She sees a leg, animal, grey fur, wolfish, edible. She raises the spear, is about to lunge, when the shape moves again: an enormous anvil of a head, bloody, matted fur.

"Bana!"

The great tail thumps weakly on the ground.

"Bana, Bana!" She hacks at the branches with the spear, careless of the scratches or the pain in her hand. "Come on, boy. Good dog, wonderful dog!"

Her throat closes, and her face contorts as the tears come again. The dog is in terrible shape. There's a large wound on his neck, another on his back leg, one eye closed and seeping putrid matter. And yet still the big tongue, woolly with dehydration, tries to lick her hand.

"Egan, come here, right now! Help me."

As gently as possible, they half carry, half drag the dog back to the cave. "Find a bowl inside. Get me water from the river, now!"

Egan does as he's told, and when he brings it back she drips water into the dog's mouth, and then, to her delight, his tongue begins to lap from the bowl.

"Christ has protected your dog, Sister. It's a sign of His compassion." Egan caresses the dog's head.

He's an idiot. Where was Christ's compassion for his new followers? But she's not inclined to argue. She covers the dog's head with kisses and examines his wounds. They're slashes more than punctures, except for the eye, which she fears he'll lose. She bathes his wounds, and packs them with betony, honey, and moss. The eye she cleanses as best she can, and she's amazed that he lets her.

When she's done all she can, she and Egan move the dog inside and get to the work of fire and food. She cuts some juniper and rowan boughs from nearby, knowing their smoke will sweeten the air. While Egan gathers wood and builds a fire, she roots through the cave. Mice have been at the oats but have only opened one corner of the sack. It doesn't look as though they've nested inside. The baskets of root vegetables, kept at the coldest end of the cave, are intact as well.

Soon a simple stew of barley and vegetables bubbles over the fire, and they are sitting in steaming clothes, as close to the flames as they safely can. She mashes stew with her fingers, feeding it to Bana. It's pitch black outside now, a silent, moonless night. Wilona spoons the food into bowls and fills two leather cups with hot barley-water and honey.

"Drink. It'll battle the chill." She wishes she'd not used the word *battle.*

Egan seems to swallow his food without chewing. A little colour returns to his face, and even the skin on his feet and legs appears less like the flesh of a corpse. He scratches his armpit. He must be covered in vermin. Her own scalp itches. Now that her appetite is appeased for the moment and she feels warm for the first time in days, exhaustion rolls over her like a rock. It's all she can do to crawl to her pallet. It's damp and she throws a fur over it. "Egan, use whatever you like for a bed. There are furs there." She points to her bundle.

In his right mind he would not try to violate her, not with those vows of his, but he's not in his right mind. She watches him from under half-closed lids but sees only tremors and twitches in his stick-like limbs. Still, best to be cautious. She tucks her dagger under her hip, the hilt at her fingertips. Even mad as he is, though, she can't deny the strange comfort of his presence. He sits near the fire, wrapped in a deer hide, next to the dog. Now and then he twitches a shoulder, an arm, his neck, as though tendrils of guilt encircle him like mistletoe. He'd be useless in a fight, would probably run away. Running away like a hare into some warren at the first sign of trouble is doubtless how he survived Cadwallon's massacre.

"They came upon us while we slept," he says, as though reading her mind. "We were ready. Would have left that very morning. I woke up and there was screaming. They were like ants, swarming, everywhere at once. The men ran out waving daggers and spears and swords, if they had them, but they are not . . . were not . . . fighting men. Perhaps it would have made no difference if we had left the village. They'd have caught us on the road. Although maybe then some of the women might have escaped, fled into the woods with the children. But the road is over so much open ground."

He's rambling, talking more to himself than to Wilona. She puts her knuckle in her mouth. She wishes he'd stop. She wishes he'd keep going. She can't bear to know. She needs to know.

"I cannot pick up a weapon. It's against all I believe in. But I ran out anyway and hoped death would be quick at least. Cadwallon was on a great grey horse, a pale horse, and I knew it was him. A terrible man, with black hair and great white teeth and the fierce blue eyes of a wolf. I held my cross out to him and asked him to stop this madness in the name of Christ." Egan wipes his eyes with the heel of his hands. "He asked me if I was a Christian and I told him I was, that all these people were Christians. He said he, too, was a Christian and my heart rejoiced. And then he laughed. 'And are you the priest here?' he said. I told him I was no priest, just a monk ministering to these souls. He looked down from his horse and made the sign of the cross over me. He said I should be spared then, so I might pray for his soul and show Christian forgiveness. I asked him what he needed to be forgiven for, and he said, 'You shall see.' And he made sure I saw. Made me watch the women raped, the children speared, the men cut down. He made me watch him herd children into the houses and barricade the doors. He made me watch his men set the torches to the thatch while the mothers were kept from saving their babies at sword point. Three women, Roswitha among them, impaled themselves rather than listen to their children's screams as they burned alive." Egan makes a gagging noise and then sobs. "I begged them to kill me. I pleaded with them, but they refused. They laughed. They said Cadwallon needed my prayers." His voice is garbled, strangled. "I don't know why God won't let me die."

"And where was your Christ then, Brother Egan? Where was he then?"

The question seems to startle him, to bring him back to himself a little. He sighs. "My Lord Christ stood beside me, Sister, weeping, as he stands with me now."

"Had he no power to stop it, then?" In the end, Ricbert was right. One god was as good as another, since they were all useless.

"God's time is not our own. Christ will change the hearts of men, and then we will have the kingdom of heaven on earth. He will change the hearts of men."

What would the point be of telling Egan he's an idiot? "Go to sleep. There's work to be done tomorrow." She closes her eyes and within moments the velvet luxury of sleep folds round her. It was strange how comforting another breathing body could be, strange how the ghosts kept their distance from the weak, fractured, dim-witted monk.

"I cannot pick up a weapon," he says softly.

For a moment she thinks she's dreaming, reliving his story, but no.

"It is against everything I believe." His eyes are wide in the firelight, and his hands clutch his cross.

"Egan, hush. You have told me. Sleep."

And for a few moments he is quiet, but only a few.

"I cannot pick up a weapon . . ."

She shushes him again, this time more harshly, for a chill runs along her spine. She rolls to the cave wall and pulls the fur over her ears. He whispers now but cannot seem to stop talking. His voice is like a bee in the cave, buzzing, buzzing. She falls asleep with her fingers in her ears, and when she drifts into wakefulness during the night, she finds him rocking slightly, his lips still moving, his eyes fixed on the fire. When at last dawn comes, she's surprised to find him snoring softly, curled on his side, wrapped in his furs, one hand on Bana's back, the long end of the cross in his mouth like a child's thumb.

Chapter THIRTY-THREE

Egan walks beside Wilona through the dead village, past the dead houses. The unforgiving wind whispers the names of the dead, and the shadows recall their features. He jumps at every movement, every skulking dog, every flapping bit of cloth, every crow. Phantoms linger along the hedgerows, peek out from the ditches, crouch on burned beams, not quite in focus but unmistakable. Wilona has wrapped a cloth over her mouth and nose, and only when Egan sees this does he notice the smell—pungent, sweet, thick, rancid—rising up from the ground. He's numb, and knows this and doesn't mind. There's safety in numbness. But he's distressed to be a burden on Wilona. She must tell him to put on a cloak, to eat the ducks she caught in a net and roasted over the fire, to drink the hot broth. He tries to do as he is told.

They return to the cave every night to find Bana still alive, healing, his tail wagging with increasing enthusiasm. Egan tells Wilona it's a holy miracle. As she cleans the dog's eye, which is now nothing but a sunken socket, and smears honey on the wounds, she says nothing. One night the dog lies down next to Wilona's pallet, and Egan watches as she kisses the top of his head. "Silly dog. Best of dogs," she says.

It is a holy moment, and he hides his tears from her, for he knows she already thinks he's too soft. But he's not soft, he's emptied, a shell surrounding nothing. Every time he closes his eyes the horrors return, all the more agonizing for being caused by Cadwallon, a Christian. So what does that word mean, then? *Christian*. What does anything mean?

His thoughts swirl. He longs for understanding. Every night he dreams, but only of horrors, never of his angel, never of peace. He tosses and turns on the hard bed of earth, clawing the dirt for signs of God.

And every day he and Wilona bury the dead. On Lady Elfhild's grave they place a wreath of mistletoe on a wooden cross.

When the last body, one of the young swineherds, is in the ground, and the earth mounded above him, Egan and Wilona stand on either side of the grave. It's a weird, unhinged moment. Tears roll down his face.

"I don't know what to do now," he says. "I hadn't thought I'd be alive." He smiles a little, crooked smile. "You've denied me death, Sister."

"It will come for us sooner or later."

He leans on his shovel. "But what are we to do now? Should we try to walk to Bebbanburgh?"

"And find Cadwallon waiting for us?"

Egan shudders. "No, you're right. It's just . . . I have no purpose . . . I don't know what God wants of me."

"Apparently he wants you to live." She makes what sounds a little like a chuckle. "You seem so disappointed. Well, Egan, if that's what your God's decided, then I think you'd best get on with it and indulge him. And that means, now that we've organized the dead, we must organize the living—ourselves. There's no way of knowing what's going on in the royal courts, or who'll win the right to rule this land."

He squints and looks across the plain. Heavy, woollen-rough clouds tower across the sky, casting patchwork shadows across the land. The purple-grey mountain still stands, the sun still plays coyly behind the clouds. If he casts his gaze away from the slaughtered village, it's possible to still see something marvellous, some clean and eternal thing. For the first time since the horror, a small wedge of peace works its way into his heart. The worst may not be over, but this storm at least is done. The dead are the dead. They are a clan of empty spaces in the world that will never again be filled, but surely they are in heaven. He slaps lightly at the sides of his face, as though waking himself up. "You're the wisest of women." He rubs his eyes and turns his attention to the burned-out buildings. "We have to see what can be salvaged. Everything matters."

"Exactly," says Wilona. "Winter's coming swiftly now. If we're to see the spring, we must make use of every little thing."

They're not surprised there's not much to salvage from the village, and a sad task it is, picking through these scraps of lives—a child's wooden boat, a woman's broken comb, a shattered charred loom. But they retrieve two cooking pots, several axe heads, six deer hides, and two sacks of only slightly singed grain miraculously spared from fire by a sturdy bin. The gardens yield overlooked turnips, parsnips, and a few late cabbages.

Egan refuses to go into Caelin's rooms. He stands at what remains of the steps and shakes his head, remembering the special death Cadwallon designed for the lady and her children. "Lady Elfhild. The children . . . ," he says. "I cannot. I cannot."

Wilona doesn't push the matter. She goes in alone and finds wine and ale, somehow missed by the looters, under a pile of ruined furs at one end of Caelin's private chambers.

Over the next week, three sheep wander back into the village and now graze near the cave. Bana is almost back to what he was, except for his partial vision. Egan still has strange fits during which he repeats the tale of the slaughter until he falls into a sort of stupor.

But over the next weeks, he tells the tale less. Wilona is as firm with him as Touilt had been with her, and she forbids his self-punishing regimes, his desire to stand in the icy river and pray all night, and his refusal of food, which he says purifies his body. She bullies him, pushes and prods him into the cave, under the furs; she forces a spoon into his hand and makes him eat. Under her ungentle ministrations, he begins to put on a little weight.

Wilona, on the other hand, finds her appetite less and less hardy. In fact, she fears she might have eaten or drunk something that is upsetting her stomach and draining her strength, for she is increasingly exhausted. Waves of nausea beset her and she vomits frequently. Nothing helps, not wild ginger or mint infusions. She is irritable and short with Egan, even more than usual.

One afternoon, the rain outside is mixing with sleet, and the hens have retreated to their coop. Bana lies near the fire, across Egan's feet, and Egan hones their axes and knives against a whetstone. The soft hiss of the iron against the stone is the only noise except for the whistle of the wind and the patter of the rain. Wilona bends low toward the light, mending a pair of leather boots.

"They are more mend than boot," she says.

Egan chuckles. "You're a miracle worker. Your needle must be blessed."

She tries to think of something sharp to say, for Egan's constant talk of blessings and miracles grates on her nerves. She opens her mouth to tell him so, but before she can, the smell of the plovers roasting over the low fire reaches her nostrils and she gags. She hurls herself out of the cave.

She barely makes it to the river's edge before her stomach convulses. She doubles over, her back rounding, her neck straining. Very little comes up. She's been sick, it seems, for weeks. She rinses her mouth out, trying not to give in to the waves of nausea.

Egan stands behind her. "Can I do something?"

"Leave me."

"There are some things a man can hardly understand, let alone make better."

For an instant she's not sure what he means, and cannot care less, given the state of her insides. And then it hits her. She reels, grasping at the rocks to keep from tumbling into the water. Let it not be! She counts. Two moons. It cannot be. She counts again.

What an idiot she is. Why had this possibility not occurred to her? But she took the herbs. They should have worked. She touches her breasts and realizes how tender they are, and swollen. Clearly, herbs or no herbs, the gods have decided. How they must be laughing. What are they playing at now? Her hands are fists. She gave up everything for them—Margawn, Margawn's sons and daughters! What might have been if she had been less concerned about the gods and more concerned with her own heart? And now they play this perverse joke on her. They took away everything. And now *this*?

And now this.

The gods have given me this. A sacred gift.

"Come back inside, Sister. It's cold and you must take care of yourself, as you so often say to me."

In a sort of trance—all she can see is her own stupidity and the cruelty of the gods—she allows him to lead her inside and to wrap a fur around her shoulders.

"There now. Feeling better?"

She counts again, forward this time. The child will be here when? First Travelling Month? Second Travelling Month, perhaps. "What month do you think it is, Egan?"

"We're near to Yule, Sister." He looks stricken. "Perhaps we're past Mother's Night. God forgive me! Can it be I missed the birth of our Lord?" He closes his eyes and moves his lips in prayer.

She places her hands on her belly. She knows certain herbs and roots that even now would be effective. It would be more dangerous now than taking them sooner. And does she even have any in her stores? How could she not have considered this possibility? She has been as addled as Egan. She gives her head a shake. *Focus!*

"What do you think has happened in the wide world, Wilona? Why do you think we've seen no one?"

"I think everyone's dead."

"I wish someone would come." Egan stops sharpening the axe head and picks at a scab on his knuckle. "I would like to live by the sea once more. Perhaps we should go to Ioua Insula. I don't think God wants me here any longer."

Wilona wishes he would stop talking. His mind is still fractured, and in truth she wonders if he will ever be what he once was. Perhaps he was always a little mad; she remembers the barbed belt he wore about his middle. Still, mad or not, how can he be so cavalier about this? Can he not imagine the horror she endured? By Thunor. He's never asked. Not once.

She realizes she's making slow circles on her stomach with her palm. She imagines a baby nestled deep inside the dark, warm cave of her body. She wonders if it can read her thoughts, if it knows she contemplates killing it. What difference would it make, though? Babies die all the time. She has no gods to answer to now, no code to live by save that of her own survival. What difference would it make?

Chapter THIRTY-FOUR

Some moons later, when the length of day and night are once again in balance, when a hint of warmth has returned, and when the otters' footprints once more mark the riverbank, late one night, when Egan has fallen asleep, Wilona rises from her pallet. Bana raises his great head and makes a low inquiring growl.

She creeps from the cave. The dog stands and stretches, pressing back on his forelegs and yawning hugely. He wags his tail and pads over to her, butting her thigh with his head. She scratches behind his ears. "Oh, fine, come on then. I don't imagine I could stop you."

She climbs the hill behind the cave, up onto clear land, the dog beside her. She stands facing the moon, a full moon, shining as brightly as a polished shield. The ground all around is silver with frost, cold and pure. Her breath is a cloud around her face.

Wilona rests her hands on her stomach. She feels the child inside flutter now from time to time. She has not, in the end, been able to put an end to the pregnancy. The child is hers and, having so very little, to reject it is impossible. "What a strange family we will make, Bana. A mad monk, a faithless orphaned woman, a child conceived in violence, born into a dead village, and you." The dog licks her hand and leans against her leg.

Before her the limitless land swells and rolls, lit by the moon, so full of life, yet so bare. She and Egan might be the only humans left alive for miles and miles and miles, in all of Northumbria.

It feels that way. He talks more and more of returning to Ioua Insula, his holy, shining island, and she's beginning to wonder if it might not be the best thing. If she can stand one Christian, it's not impossible she could stand an island full of them, for the sake of this child.

Suddenly she is a little girl again, standing on the moors, with nothing but the dead behind her, and only the icy, mysterious, vacant future before her. Such a star-bright night. Then as now.

All things turn and spiral back like this, it seems. From this horror-time a peace-time will follow, if only briefly. Crops will be sowed and harvested. Another king, another court, and what is broken will be built, as the seasons turn, as day turns into night and night into day again. She closes her eyes and sees before her the loom weight Touilt once wore, on which was carved a spiral. Death and birth. The gods who die and are born again. And what, when all is said and done, is the point? There is life in her. Sacred and mysterious.

It's odd how the gods, even the Christian god, seem benevolent and majestic when they're left alone in the earth and sky, without the interference of people. What was it Egan said about his god? *My Lord Christ stood beside me, Sister, weeping, as he stands with me now.* What might it mean to have the gods stand weeping with you? Not to be alone?

But she's not alone. Wilona's hands spread across her swollen belly and her heart cramps and writhes. The child will be an almost-orphan with no clan . . . only Wilona to stand between him or her and all the wanton violence of the world. She would not wish such loneliness on anyone.

Bana's ears prick and his head whips round. He trots a few paces in front of Wilona, in the direction of the village, and whines. The hackles on his back rise and he stretches out his neck. He growls, low, and his hind legs tremble. Wilona puts her hand on his back to quiet him, but his gaze is pinned to some point out of her sight. He is rigid. She looks where the dog looks, straining to see.

Figures. Just visible in the thick moonlight. Two? Three? Near what used to be the animal pens at the eastern side of the village. Wilona's skin shrinks and her fingertips prickle. The child inside her kicks out. Ghosts? Risen on the full moon? Or Cadwallon's scouts? The figures look stationary, but after a moment she realizes this is just a trick of the light. They're moving, and moving this way. She thinks there are two, not three. One much larger than the other. The large one carries something, a staff or a spear.

"Bana! Come!" She calls the dog, grabbing a handful of his fur. He wriggles and squirms, and it's all she can do to hold him. He wants to protect her this time, she's sure, the way he tried and failed to do before. She forces him back to the cave, her feet slip-sliding on the still-frozen paths. She must slow down. If she falls and breaks a leg she and the child are both doomed. She must wake Egan; they must arm themselves and go into hiding until they know who's coming. The noise must have woken Egan, for he's already on his feet, swatting sleep from his eyes.

"Someone's coming!"

"Who?"

"How should I know? It might be a friend, but it might not. Douse the fire. Grab that axe; until we know for sure, we must hide."

"Cadwallon?" He steps back into the cave's recesses as though to hide there.

"Egan! Don't be an idiot. If it's Cadwallon's men and they find you here, they'll kill you."

He sits down. "Then I think I'll stay."

Bana barks and she shushes him, then grabs the front of Egan's tunic and puts her face close to his. "I will kill you myself if you don't get up, you idiot. I need all the help I can get right now, and if you die I'm likely to die as well. Do you understand?"

Egan smiles, and Wilona sees he would be happy to die, at last, and be free of the terrible guilt of living. It is all she can do not to strangle him. There is little time and she sees the addled monk won't come unless she drags him. It surprises her, the stab in her heart she feels at the idea of losing him. "Suit yourself, Christian. Hide yourself as best you can." She ties a piece of rope around Bana's neck, picks up the axe and tucks her dagger in her belt. "May your god have mercy on your soul," she says.

As she glances back she sees Egan sitting calmly, throwing wood on the fire. *Idiot! Idiot!* Her heart is a wild thing flapping in her chest and she puts the stinging in her eyes down to fear.

She runs with the dog upriver to the lightning-struck, hollow oak. The river might be forded safely there if she needs to run. Whoever is coming will have to pass her before they reach the cave, if they're on the river path. She will be able to see them without them seeing her. If they're foe, she'll wait until they pass, cross the river, and hide in the wood. She hunkers down in the tree's deep, dark, mushroom-scented cleft, her back against the soft wood, and pulls Bana in with her. The ground beneath her yields, crackling with ancient acorn shells. She puts her arms round the dog's neck and buries her head in his rough, wiry fur.

It's hard to say how long she sits there, for time has its own rules and the folk of the wild wood will play tricks when it amuses them. Then Bana begins barking and she can't silence him. He twists and bucks and convulses so violently she fears her wrist will break. Then, in a mighty leap, he breaks free and bounds down the path, baying like a mad thing. Damn him! He'll lead them to her! She must run. But how can she let him fight for her alone again? She rises, stands in the path, frozen . . . and then the dog goes silent. Her heart seizes. The barking starts again, wildly, hysterically.

"Bana! Stop. All right! Stop. *Stop*, I said, by Thunor!"

It cannot be.

"Wilona? Wilona!"

The gods are tricking her. But hasn't some part of her always known? She always said she'd know if his heart no longer beat.

"Wilona! Wilona, are you there? It's Margawn. It's Margawn!"

She cannot seem to make her body work, her voice . . . Her hands fly to her mouth.

"Wilona? Can you hear me? It's Margawn!"

It is.

Whatever spell had held her breaks and she runs, tripping once over a tree root, then catching her balance. She cannot speak; there is no breath left for words, only for running. A shape in the path before her. Large. Like a bear. Margawn, her golden bear. But not. Something wrong, not the same. *But him, yes him, yes him, yes him, him . . .*

She's in his arms before she can think, and then she knows it's him, by smell and touch and taste, by him calling out her name and she calling out his. It's no ghost, but him, alive, impossibly alive, against all odds, ripped from the very web of wyrd, alive and hers and whole . . . wait—no, not whole.

She pulls back and looks at him and cries out. His face is freshly scarred, a puckered line twisting his cheek from mouth to ear. And his body, his poor body, is not the size he once was. Of the arms she clings to, one is not an arm at all, just a stump, a hen's wing.

"Oh, my love," she says. He tilts his head away from her, but she turns it back. "No, no, it was just shock. You can't think I care!" She kisses him. Bana runs in ecstatic circles around them, whining and wriggling like a pup.

"I would have returned to you sooner, if I could." He buries his face in her hair, and in a hot rush she realizes he is crying. "It was a long time before I came to myself. I said I'd come back to you."

"You did. You said you would. You have." And yet she knows, even as she holds him, clings to his heaving, shuddering shoulders, that he is not the man he was, that whoever he is, whatever he is, he is no longer a warrior. It is more than his body; he carries weariness like a weight now deep in his flesh, his bones, his soul. "You're here. Here with me. You'll rest," she finds herself saying, her voice drowning in tears. "You'll rest now."

"A mute woodcutter, only that, imagine."

She doesn't understand, and doesn't care. "It's all right, my bear. We'll get you food and sleep."

But he keeps talking. "When the battle was done, a woodcutter found me still alive. There might be others. I don't know. If there are, they've fled south."

He sits on a nearby fallen log, as though his legs have finally failed him. Bana tries to lick his face. Wilona makes him sit, which he does, heavily, on Margawn's feet, and he won't be budged.

Margawn puts his good right arm around Wilona. "I don't know why Cuthberht didn't leave me there. Others would have, or finished me off. But he didn't. He dragged me to his hut and kept me alive somehow." He turns his face to her and it is more beautiful than any sun-filled morning. "I'm no soldier now. No threat to any king." He squeezes her. "I feared I wouldn't find you . . . and when I saw the village . . ." His face crumples and it's some moments before he's quiet. When he regains himself he says, "I was so sure I'd lost you."

Her eyes are pinned to his face, and her heart beats like the wings of a trapped falcon. "I survived, but . . . the gods didn't protect me. Bana tried his best and paid for it, as you see." She wants to wait, to give him time to rest, but only the shock of the moment has stopped him noticing. In another minute they will stand, and he will see her properly. "I fought them, but in the end . . ." She brings Margawn's hand to rest on the swell of her belly.

He stiffens and utters a choked cry.

What a homecoming welcome is this. She refused his children, and now, in her belly, the enemy's spawn. "I avenged my honour while they slept."

His face contorts again. He pulls his hand from hers and covers his eyes. "By the gods, I'm sick of honour."

"You and I survived. That's all that matters."

He takes his hand from his eyes. "A child?"

She searches his face. "I thought I'd prevented . . . this. I was wrong, and then, well, I couldn't. Margawn, I want the child."

"Even though?"

"Even though."

Something struggles within him, she sees it as his features tighten, and he closes his eyes. She holds her breath and all that might be seems to teeter on the tip of that moment. When he opens his eyes what she sees is not disgust, as she feared it might be, but hope, or at least the hope of hope.

"Yes," he says. Such a tiny word, and yet in it such enormity.

The world steadies itself. She breaths again.

He says, "I only thought of getting back to you. No further." He pulls her to him. "It's all that mattered then, or now."

And now it is she who weeps, stopping only when Bana insists on licking her face, and then Margawn's, and as they push him away they discover, to their surprise, that they're laughing, just a little, but laughing, still.

It occurs to her then. "And the man I saw you with, the woodcutter? Where's the man to whom I owe so much?"

Margawn whistles. A moment later an old man comes along the path. His face is wrinkled as a dried apple, and as sweet. Wilona kisses him on both cheeks, making him blush so brightly his skin shines pink even in the moonlight.

"I call him Cuthberht," says Margawn. "Since he couldn't tell me his name. He seems to like it well enough."

The old man nods and smiles, revealing the blackened remains of several teeth.

Later, they will talk of many things, but for now there is nothing left to say. She wraps her arms around Margawn and will not let go as the three of them walk toward the cave.

Egan and Cuthberht, it seems, have much in common. The woodcutter pulls a finely carved cross from beneath his tunic when he sees Egan's. The monk's face shines.

"God is good," he says, and the two men embrace and sit quietly by the fire together, the lack of words no loss between them.

Later, Wilona and Margawn stand by the river in the silvery-shiver, holding tight to each other. Bana noses about in the stones and then sits by Margawn. The dog stares at the black outline of a nearby oak and growls. Wilona puts her hand on the dog's head. He vibrates; every muscle tense.

"What is it, boy?" she says. "What do you see?"

Something moves in a nearby oak. An owl, unnaturally large, takes shape and rises into the sky. Wilona's heart skips a beat and she tracks its flight. It soars high in the star-filled sky and then, for a moment as oddly long as the owl is oddly large, it's silhouetted in front of the moon, the enormous wings seeming to envelop the radiant and all-encompassing disc so that the two things are made one. And then the bird breaks free and blends into the black night beyond the moon, while the flutter of wings and feather and the scent of the moors remain.

Wilona holds Margawn's hand as they watch the sky, then he

moves his hand to her belly, stretching his fingers wide. Warmth spreads through her like honey. She covers his hand with both of hers and presses, tightly, so tightly nothing will ever pry her fingers from his.

Acknowledgements

Writing any book is an adventure. The writer sets out in a little boat on a vast sea of ignorance, hoping to find land. Writing a novel like this one, set so far in the past, is like launching a paper airplane out the window of a spaceship in the hopes of hitting some sort of habitable planet. Were it not for the help of an army of navigators, I'd still be floating around out there.

Beyond the research, though, this book is a work of imagination. Anyone looking for mistakes in historical accuracy will no doubt find them. I haven't tried to write a historical text, rather I've scooped up the broad facts of seventh-century Northumbria, put them into a pot with gleanings about what life may have been like during the time, seasoned it with observations, fancies, and fears, hung the pot over the fire of my obsessions, and hopefully produced an entertaining and thought-provoking fictional story. My friend, Sister Rita, says she thinks this book is an allegory for the journey of my own soul. Perhaps it is.

I am, as always, grateful to David Forrer and Kim Witherspoon at Inkwell Management. They always saw the flares I shot when lost and panicked, and sent help.

Thanks, too, to everyone Sandra Kasturi and Brett Savory at ChiZine. What a pleasure it is working with you.

Thanks to Michael Rowe, a kindred spirit who makes wonderful introductions.

Thanks to Maria diBattista and Holly Johnson, who give me so much perspective and encouragement, and to Allyson Latta and Stacey Cameron for keen insights and keen eyes.

I greatly appreciate the generosity of people who gave so freely of their time and knowledge during my research trip to England (what My Best Beloved calls the Anglo-Saxon Forced March Northwards) back in 2008. They are: Lynn Nick, Van Nick, and Jackie Wright, who guided me through the great burial mounds of Sutton Hoo; Canon Kate Tristam in Lindisfarne, who shared stories of St. Hild; Reverend Jonathan Goode and archaeologist Robin Daniels in Hartlepool; Katherine Bearcock at the York Museum; Lance Alexander at West Stow; archaeologist Graeme Young at Bamburgh Castle; Professor James Fraser in the Scottish History Department of the University of Edinburgh; Alice Blackwell at the National Museum of Scotland; archaeologist Paul Frodsham in Yeavering (Ad Gefrin); guide extraordinaire at York Minster, John Rushton; Professor Christopher Norton in the University of York's Centre for Medieval Studies, King's Manor; Roy and Eileen Thomas (for wonderful hospitality!); Jenny James for her information on birds of the River Deben; as well as Aidan O'Neill and Douglas Edington for delicious food and delightful friendship.

I have a long bibliography posted on my website, as well as a graph showing the Anglo-Saxon calendar.

– www.LaurenBDavis.com –

About the Author

Born in Montreal, Quebec, on September 5, 1955, Davis lived in France for over a decade (1994–2004), and now resides in Princeton, New Jersey, where she runs the Sharpening The Quill Writers Workshops and is past Writer-in-Residence at Trinity Episcopalian Church.

She studied creative writing at Indiana University. Early in her career, Davis was mentored by Timothy Findley, at the Humber College School for Writers, where went on to be mentor herself (2007–2009). She was past European Editor for the *Literary Review of Canada* from 1999 to 2002.

Davis has taught fiction writing at the Wice (Paris); The American University of Paris; The Geneva Writers' Conference; and Seattle University's Writers' Conference in Allihies, Ireland. Davis has also lectured on writing at Trent University, Rider University, Humber College and The Paris Writers' Workshop, and has done numerous readings.

Her novel *Our Daily Bread* was long-listed for the Scotiabank Giller Prize, and named as one of the "Very Best Book of 2011" by *The Globe & Mail*, and "Best of 2011" by *The Boston Globe*; *The Radiant City* (2005) was a finalist for the Rogers Writers Trust Fiction Prize. *The Stubborn Season* (2002), was chosen for the Robert Adams Lecture Series. Adams's lecture was televised on TVOntario's program *Imprint*. *An Unrehearsed Desire* (2008) was longlisted for the Relit Awards. Her short fiction has also been shortlisted for the CBC Literary Awards and she is the recipient of two Mid-Career Writer Sustaining grants from the Canada Council for the Arts, in 2000 and 2006.

EMB
RACE
THE
ODD

THE ACOLYTE
NICK CUTTER

Jonah Murtag is an Acolyte on the New Bethlehem police force. His job: eradicate all heretical religious faiths, their practitioners, and artefacts. Murtag's got problems—one of his partners is a zealot, and he's in love with the other one. Trouble at work, trouble at home. Murtag realizes that you can rob a citizenry of almost anything, but you can't take away its faith. When a string of bombings paralyzes the city, religious fanatics are initially suspected, but startling clues point to a far more ominous perpetrator. If Murtag doesn't get things sorted out, the Divine Council will dispatch The Quints, aka: Heaven's Own Bagmen. The clock is ticking towards doomsday for the Chosen of New Bethlehem. And Jonah Murtag's got another problem. The biggest and most worrisome . . . Jonah isn't a believer anymore.

AVAILABLE NOW
ISBN 978-1-77148-328-5

ALSO AVAILABLE FROM CHIZINE PUBLICATIONS

THE HOUSE OF WAR AND WITNESS
MIKE CAREY, LINDA CAREY, AND LOUISE CAREY

1740. With the whole of Europe balanced on the brink of war, an Austrian regiment is sent to the furthest frontier of the empire to hold the border against the might of Prussia. Their garrison, the ancient house called Pokoj.

But Pokoj is already inhabited by a company of ghosts from every age of the house's history. Only DROZDE, the quartermaster's mistress, can see them, and terrifyingly they welcome her as a friend. As these ageless phantoms tell their stories Drozde gets chilling glimpses not just of Pokoj's past but of a looming menace in its future.

AVAILABLE NOW
ISBN 978-1-77148-312-4

CHIZINEPUB.COM

INFINITUM
GMB CHOMICHUK

With enough time, you can fix anything.

Special Investigator Nine works in The Paradox Bureau, an agency that polices the temporal diaspora and prevents crimes before they happen. Sent on assignment to the 1940s (to the very place and time he was originally recruited), he must avoid altering his own past while investigating a seemingly unpreventable murder.

Why would an organization dedicated to preventing murder before it happens cover up a series of grisly killings? Nine must rely on his memory of the past rather than receive help from the future to solve a series of murders that can't be prevented.

AVAILABLE NOW
ISBN 978-1-77148-324-7

ALSO AVAILABLE FROM CHIZINE PUBLICATIONS

THE FLAME IN THE MAZE
CAITLIN SWEET

The Flame in the Maze picks up the thread of the tale begun in *The Door in the Mountain*. The Princess Ariadne is scheming to bring her hated half-brother Asterion to ultimate ruin; Asterion himself, part human, part bull, is grappling with madness and pain in the labyrinth that lies within a sacred mountain; Chara, his childhood friend, is trying desperately to find him. In a different prison, Icarus, the bird-boy who cannot fly, plans his escape with his father, Daedalus—and plots revenge upon the princess he once loved. All of their paths come together at last, drawn by fire, hatred, love and hope—and all of them are changed.

AVAILABLE NOW
ISBN 978-1-77148-326-1

CHIZINEPUB.COM

COLD HILLSIDE
NANCY BAKER

"With *them*, there are no happy endings." Generations ago, the last remnants of a dying empire bargained with the Faerie Queen for a place of safety in the mountains and each year the ruler of Lushan must travel to the high plateau to pay the city's tribute. When an unexpected misfortune means that the traditional price is not met, Teresine, once a refugee slave and now advisor to the Sidiana, must navigate the treacherous politics of the Faerie Court, where the Queen's will determines reality and mortals are merely pawns in an eternal struggle for power.

AVAILABLE NOW
ISBN 978-1-77148-310-0

THE YELLOW WOOD
MELANIE TEM

For Alexandra Kove, the path of her life took her far from the claustrophobic forest where her father raised her. She believed that she had to escape, that her only road was away from the family and circumstances of her birth. Now, her road has turned back, converged with the paths of the family she thought was safely in her past.

AVAILABLE NOW
ISBN 978-1-77148-314-8

ALSO AVAILABLE FROM CHIZINE PUBLICATIONS